Romance readers around the world were sad to note the passing of **Betty Neels** in June 2001. Her career spanned thirty years, and she continued to write into her ninetieth year. To her millions of fans, Betty epitomized the romance writer, and yet she began writing almost by accident. She had retired from nursing, but her inquiring mind still sought stimulation. Her new career was born when she heard a lady in her local library bemoaning the lack of good romance novels. Betty's first book, *Sister Peters in Amsterdam*, was published in 1969, and she eventually completed 134 books. Her novels offer a reassuring warmth that was very much a part of her own personality. She was a wonderful writer, and she is greatly missed. Her spirit and genuine talent live on in all her stories.

BETTY NEELS

The Mistletoe Kiss
& The Vicar's Daughter

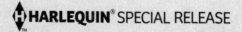

HARLEQUIN® SPECIAL RELEASE

ISBN-13: 978-1-335-00792-6

The Mistletoe Kiss & The Vicar's Daughter

Copyright © 2019 by Harlequin Books S.A.

The Mistletoe Kiss
First published in 1997. This edition published in 2019.
Copyright © 1997 by Betty Neels

The Vicar's Daughter
First published in 1996. This edition published in 2019.
Copyright © 1996 by Betty Neels

Recycling programs for this product may not exist in your area.

Printed in U.S.A.

CONTENTS

THE MISTLETOE KISS

Chapter 1

It was a blustery October evening, and the mean little wind was blowing old newspapers, tin cans and empty wrapping papers to and fro along the narrow, shabby streets of London's East End. It had blown these through the wide entrance to the massive old hospital towering over the rows of houses and shops around it, but its doors were shut against them, and inside the building it was quiet, very clean and tidy. In place of the wind there was warm air, carrying with it a whiff of disinfectant tinged with floor polish and the patients' suppers, something not experienced by those attending the splendid new hospitals now replacing the old ones. There they were welcomed by flowers, a café, signposts even the most foolish could read and follow...

St Luke's had none of these—two hundred years old and condemned to be closed, there was no point in wasting money. Besides, the people who frequented its dim corridors weren't there to look at flowers, they followed the painted pointed finger on its walls telling them to go to Casualty, X-Ray, the wards or Out Patients, and, when they got there, settled onto the wooden benches in the waiting rooms and had a good gossip with whoever was next to them. It was their hospital, they felt at home in it; its lengthy corridors held no worries for them, nor did the elderly lifts and endless staircases.

They held no worries for Ermentrude Foster, skimming up to the top floor of the hospital, intent on delivering the message which had been entrusted to her as quickly as possible before joining the throng of people queuing for buses on their way home. The message had nothing to do with her, actually; Professor ter Mennolt's secretary had come out of her office as Ermentrude had been getting into her outdoor things, her hours of duty at the hospital telephone switchboard finished for the day, and had asked her to run up to his office with some papers he needed.

'I'm late,' said the secretary urgently. 'And my boyfriend's waiting for me. We're going to see that new film...'

Ermentrude, with no prospect of a boyfriend or a film, obliged.

Professor ter Mennolt, spectacles perched on his magnificent nose, was immersed in the papers before him on his desk. A neurologist of some renown, he was at St Luke's by invitation, reading a paper on muscular dystrophies, lecturing students, lending his knowledge on the treatment of those patients suffering from diseases of the nervous system. Deep in the study of a case of myasthenia gravis, his, 'Come,' was absent-minded in answer to a knock on the door, and he didn't look up for a few moments.

Ermentrude, uncertain whether to go in or not, had poked her head round the door, and he studied it for a moment. A pleasant enough face, not pretty, but the nose was slightly tip-tilted, the eyes large and the wide mouth was smiling.

Ermentrude bore his scrutiny with composure, opened the door and crossed the room to his desk.

'Miss Crowther asked me to bring you this,' she told him cheerfully. 'She had a date and wanted to get home…'

The professor eyed her small, slightly plump person and looked again at her face, wondering what colour her hair was; a scarf covered the whole of it, and since she was wearing a plastic mac he deduced that it was raining.

'And you, Miss…?' He paused, his eyebrows raised.

'Foster, Ermentrude Foster.' She smiled at him. 'Almost as bad as yours, isn't it?' Undeterred by the cold blue eyes staring at her, she explained, 'Our names,' just in case he hadn't understood. 'Awkward, aren't they?'

He had put down his pen. 'You work here in the hospital?'

'Me? Yes, I'm a telephonist. Are you going to be here for a long time?'

'I can hardly see why the length of my stay should interest you, Miss Foster.'

'Well, no, it doesn't, really.' She gave him a kind smile. 'I thought you might be a bit lonely up here all by yourself. Besides I rather wanted to see you—I'd heard about you, of course.'

'Should I feel gratified at your interest?' he asked coldly.

'No, no, of course not. But they all said how handsome you were, and not a bit like a Dutchman.' She paused then, because his eyes weren't cold any more, they were like blue ice.

He said levelly, 'Miss Foster, I think it might be a good idea if you were to leave this room. I have work to do, and interruptions, especially such as yours, can be annoying. Be good enough to tell Miss Crowther on no account to send you here again.'

He bent over his work and didn't watch her go.

Ermentrude went slowly back through the hospital and out into the wet October evening to join the queue at the nearest bus stop, thinking about the professor. A handsome man, she conceded; fair hair going grey, a splendid nose, heavy-lidded eyes and a firm mouth—which was a bit thin, perhaps. Even sitting at his desk it was easy to see that he was a very large man. Still quite young, too. The hospital grapevine knew very little about him, though.

She glanced back over her shoulder; there were still lighted windows on the top floor of the hospital; one of them would be his. She sighed. He hadn't liked her and, of course, that was to be understood. She had been ticked off on several occasions for not being respectful enough with those senior to her—and they were many—but that hadn't cured her from wanting to be friends with everyone.

Born and brought up in a rural part of Somerset, where everyone knew everyone else, she had never quite got used to the Londoners' disregard for those around them. Oblivious of the impatient prod from the woman behind her, she thought of the professor sitting up there, so far from anyone… And he was a foreigner, too.

Professor ter Mennolt, unaware of her concern, adjusted his spectacles on his nose and addressed himself to the pile of work on his desk, perfectly content with his lot, careless of the fact that he was alone and a foreigner. He had quite forgotten Ermentrude.

The bus, by the time Ermentrude got onto it, was packed, and, since it was raining, the smell of wet raincoats was overpowering. She twitched her small nose and wondered what was for supper, and, after a ten-minute ride squashed between two stout women, got off with relief.

Five minutes' walk brought her to her home, midway down a terrace of small, neat houses in a vaguely shabby street, their front doors opening onto the pavement. She unlocked the door, calling, 'It's me,' as she did so, and opened a door in the narrow hallway. Her mother was there, sitting at a small table, knitting. Still knitting, she looked up and smiled.

'Emmy—hello, love. Supper's in the oven, but would you like a cup of tea first?'

'I'll make it, Mother. Was there a letter from Father?'

'Yes, dear, it's on the mantelpiece. Have you had a busy day?'

'So-so. I'll get the tea.'

Emmy took off her raincoat and scarf, hung them on a peg in the hall and went into the kitchen, a small, old-fashioned place with cheerful, cheap curtains and some rather nice china on the dresser shelves. About all there was left of her old home, thought Emmy, gathering cups and saucers and opening the cake tin.

Her father had taught at a large school in Somerset, and they had lived in a nearby village in a nice old house with a large garden and heavenly views. But he had been made redundant and been unable to find another post! Since an elderly aunt had recently died and left him this small house, and a colleague had told him of a post in London, they had come here to live. The post wasn't as well paid, and Mrs Foster found that living in London was quite a different matter from living in a small village with a garden which supplied her with vegetables all the year round and hens who laid fresh eggs each day.

Emmy, watching her mother coping with household bills, had given up her hopes of doing something artistic. She drew and painted and embroidered exquisitely, and had set her sights on attending a school of needlework and then starting up on her own—she wasn't sure as what. There had been an advertisement in the paper for a switchboard operator at St Luke's, and she had gone along and got the job.

She had no experience of course, but she had a pleasant voice, a nice manner and she'd been keen to have work. She'd been given a week's training, a month's trial and then had been taken on permanently. It wasn't what she wanted to do, but the money was a great help, and one day her father would find a better post. Indeed, he was already well thought of and there was a chance of promotion.

She made the tea, offered a saucer of milk to Snoodles the cat, handed a biscuit to George the elderly dachshund, and carried the tray into the sitting room.

Over tea she read her father's letter. He had been standing in for a school inspector, and had been away from home for a week. He would be coming home for the weekend, he wrote, but he had been asked to continue covering for his colleague for the next month or so. If he accepted, then it would be possible for Mrs Foster to be with him when it was necessary for him to go further afield.

'Mother, that's wonderful—Father hates being away from home, but if you're with him he won't mind as much, and if they're pleased with him he'll get a better job.'

'I can't leave you here on your own.'

'Of course you can, Mother. I've Snoodles and George for company, and we know the neighbours well enough if I should need anything. I can come home for my lunch hour and take George for a quick walk. I'm sure Father will agree to that. Besides, Father gets moved from one school to the other, doesn't he? When he is nearer home you can be here.'

'I'm sure I don't know, love. The idea of you being on your own…'

Emmy refilled their cups. 'If I had a job in another town, I'd be on my own in some bedsitter, wouldn't I? But I'm at home. And I'm twenty-three…'

'Well, I know your father would like me to be with him. We'll talk about it at the weekend.'

By breakfast time the next morning Mrs Foster was ready to concede that there was really no reason why she shouldn't join her husband, at least for short periods. 'For you're home by six o'clock most evenings, when it's still quite light, and I dare say we'll be home most weekends.'

Emmy agreed cheerfully. She was due to go on night duty in a week's time, but there was no need to remind her mother of that. She went off to catch a bus to the hospital, glad that the rain had ceased and it was a nice autumn day.

The switchboard was busy; it always was on Fridays. Last-minute plans for the weekend, she supposed, on the part of the hospital medical staff—people phoning home, making appointments to play golf, arranging to meet to discuss some case or other—and all these over and above the outside calls, anxious family wanting news of a patient, doctors' wives with urgent messages, other hospitals wanting to contact one or other of the consulting staff. It was almost time for her midday dinner when a woman's voice, speaking English with a strong accent, asked to speak to Professor ter Mennolt.

'Hold the line while I get him for you,' said Emmy. His wife, she supposed, and decided that she didn't much like the voice—very haughty. The voice became a person in her mind's eye, tall and slim and beautiful—because the professor wouldn't look at anything less—and well used to having her own way.

He wasn't in his room, and he wasn't on any of the wards she rang. She paused in her search to reassure the voice that she was still trying, and was rewarded by being told to be quick. He wasn't in Theatre, but he was in the Pathology Lab.

'There you are,' said Emmy, quite forgetting to add 'sir'. 'I've a call for you; will you take it there?'

'Only if it's urgent; I'm occupied at the moment.'

'It's a lady,' Emmy told him. 'She told me to hurry. She speaks English with an accent.'

'Put the call through here.' He sounded impatient.

It wouldn't hurt him to say thank you, reflected Emmy as she assured his caller that she was being put through at once. She got no thanks from her either. 'They must suit each other admirably,' said Emmy under her breath, aware that the bossy woman who went around with a clipboard was coming towards her. As usual she was full of questions—had there been delayed calls? Had Ermentrude connected callers immediately? Had she noted the times?

Emmy said yes to everything. She was a conscientious worker, and although it wasn't a job she would have chosen she realised that she was lucky to have it, and it wasn't boring. She was relieved for her dinner hour presently, and went along to the canteen to eat it in the company of the ward clerks and typists. She got on well with them, and they for their part liked her, though considering her hopelessly out of date, and pitying her in a friendly way because she had been born and brought up in the country and had lacked the pleasures of London. She lacked boyfriends, too, despite their efforts to get her to join them for a visit to a cinema or a pub.

They didn't hold it against her; she was always good-natured, ready to help, willing to cover a relief telephonist if she had a date, listening to emotional outbursts about boyfriends with a sympathetic ear. They agreed among themselves that she was all right—never mind the posh voice; she couldn't help that, could she, with a father who was a schoolmaster? Besides, it sounded OK on the phone, and that was what her job was all about, wasn't it?

Home for the weekend, Mr Foster agreed with Emmy that there was no reason why she shouldn't be at home on her own for a while.

'I'll be at Coventry for a week or ten days, and then several schools in and around London. You don't mind, Emmy?'

She saw her mother and father off on Sunday evening, took George for a walk and went to bed. She wasn't a nervous girl and there were reassuringly familiar noises all around her: Mr Grant next door practising the flute, the teenager across the street playing his stereo, old Mrs Grimes, her other neighbour, shouting at her husband who was deaf. She slept soundly.

She was to go on night duty the next day, which meant that she would be relieved at dinner time and go back to work at eight o'clock that evening. Which gave her time in the afternoon to do some shopping at the row of small shops at the end of the street, take George for a good walk and sit down to a leisurely meal.

There was no phone in the house, so she didn't have to worry about her mother ringing up later in the evening. She cut sandwiches, put *Sense and Sensibility* and a much thumbed *Anthology of English Verse* in her shoulder bag with the sandwiches, and presently went back through the dark evening to catch her bus.

When she reached the hospital the noise and bustle of the day had subsided into subdued footsteps, the distant clang of the lifts and the occasional squeak of a trolley's wheels. The relief telephonist was waiting for her, an elderly woman who manned the switchboard between night and day duties.

'Nice and quiet so far,' she told Emmy. 'Hope you have a quiet night.'

Emmy settled herself in her chair, made sure that everything was as it should be and got out the knitting she had pushed in with the books at the last minute.

She would knit until one of the night porters brought her coffee.

There were a number of calls: enquiries about patients, anxious voices asking advice as to whether they should bring a sick child to the hospital, calls to the medical staff on duty.

Later, when she had drunk her cooling coffee and picked up her neglected knitting once again, Professor ter Mennolt, on his way home, presumably, paused by her.

He eyed the knitting. 'A pleasant change from the daytime rush,' he remarked. 'And an opportunity to indulge your womanly skills.'

'Well, I don't know about that,' said Emmy sensibly. 'It keeps me awake in between calls! It's very late; oughtn't you to be in your bed?'

'My dear young lady, surely that is no concern of yours?'

'Oh, I'm not being nosey,' she assured him. 'But everyone needs a good night's sleep, especially people like you—people who use their brains a lot.'

'That is your opinion, Ermentrude? It is Ermentrude, isn't it?'

'Yes, and yes. At least, it's my father's opinion.'

'Your father is a medical man, perhaps?' he asked smoothly.

'No, a schoolmaster.'

'Indeed? Then why are you not following in his footsteps?'

'I'm not clever. Besides, I like sewing and embroidery.'

'And you are a switchboard operator.' His tone was dry.

'It's a nice, steady job,' said Emmy, and picked up her knitting. 'Goodnight, Professor ter Mennolt.'

'Goodnight, Ermentrude.' He had gone several paces when he turned on his heel. 'You have an old-fashioned name. I am put in mind of a demure young lady with ringlets and a crinoline, downcast eyes and a soft and gentle voice.'

She looked at him, her mouth half-open.

'You have a charming voice, but I do not consider you demure, nor do you cast down your eyes—indeed their gaze is excessively lively.'

He went away then, leaving her wondering what on earth he had been talking about.

'Of course, he's foreign,' reflected Emmy out loud. 'And besides that he's one of those clever people whose feet aren't quite on the ground, always bothering about people's insides.'

A muddled statement which nonetheless satisfied her.

Audrey, relieving her at eight o'clock the next morning, yawned widely and offered the information that she hated day duty, hated the hospital, hated having to work. 'Lucky you,' she observed. 'All day to do nothing...'

'I shall go to bed,' said Emmy mildly, and took herself off home.

It was a slow business, with the buses crammed with people going to work, and then she had to stop at the shops at the end of the street and buy bread, eggs, bacon, food for Snoodles and more food for George. Once home, with the door firmly shut behind her, she put on the kettle, fed the animals and let George into the garden. Snoodles tailed him, warned not to go far.

She had her breakfast, tidied up, undressed and had a shower and, with George and Snoodles safely indoors, went to her bed. The teenager across the street hadn't made a sound so far; hopefully he had a job or had gone off with his pals. If Mr Grant and Mrs Grimes kept quiet, she would have a good sleep… She had barely had time to form the thought before her eyes shut.

It was two o'clock when she was woken by a hideous mixture of sound: Mr Grant's flute—played, from the sound of it, at an open window—Mrs Grimes bellowing at her husband in the background and, almost drowning these, the teenager enjoying a musical session.

Emmy turned over and buried her head in the pillow, but it was no use; she was wide awake now and likely to stay so. She got up and showered and dressed, had a cup of tea and a sandwich, made sure that Snoodles was asleep, put a lead on George's collar and left the house.

She had several hours of leisure still; she boarded an almost empty bus and sat with George on her lap as it bore them away from Stepney, along Holborn and into the Marylebone Road. She got off here and crossed the street to Regent's Park.

It was pleasant here, green and open with the strong scent of autumn in the air. Emmy walked briskly, with George trotting beside her.

'We'll come out each day,' she promised him. 'A pity the parks are all so far away, but a bus ride's nice enough, isn't it? And you shall have a good tea when we get home.'

The afternoon was sliding into dusk as they went back home. George gobbled his tea and curled up on his chair in the kitchen while Snoodles went out. Mrs Grimes had stopped shouting, but Mr Grant was still playing the flute, rivalling the din from across the street. Emmy ate her tea, stuffed things into her bag and went to work.

* * *

Audrey had had a busy day and was peevish. 'I spent the whole of my two hours off looking for some decent tights—the shops around here are useless.'

'There's that shop in Commercial Road…' began Emmy.

'There?' Audrey was scornful. 'I wouldn't be seen dead in anything from there.' She took a last look at her face, added more lipstick and patted her blonde head. 'I'm going out this evening. So long.'

Until almost midnight Emmy was kept busy. From time to time someone passing through from the entrance hall stopped for a word, and one of the porters brought her coffee around eleven o'clock with the news that there had been a pile-up down at the docks and the accident room was up to its eyes.

'They phoned,' said Emmy, 'but didn't say how bad it was—not to me, that is. I switched them straight through. I hope they're not too bad.'

'Couple of boys, an old lady, the drivers—one of them's had a stroke.'

Soon she was busy again, with families phoning with anxious enquiries. She was eating her sandwiches in the early hours of the morning when Professor ter Mennolt's voice, close to her ear, made her jump.

'I am relieved to see that you are awake and alert, Ermentrude.'

She said, round the sandwich. 'Well, of course I am. That's not a nice thing to say, sir.'

'What were you doing in a bus on the Marylebone Road when you should have been in bed asleep, recruiting strength for the night's work?'

'I was going to Regent's Park with George. He had a good walk.' She added crossly, 'And *you* should try to sleep with someone playing the flute on one side of the house, Mrs Grimes shouting on the other and that wretched boy with his stereo across the street.'

The professor was leaning against the wall, his hands in the pockets of his beautifully tailored jacket. 'I have misjudged you, Ermentrude. I am sorry. Ear plugs, perhaps?' And, when she shook her head, 'Could you not beg a bed from a friend? Or your mother have a word with the neighbours?'

'Mother's with Father,' said Emmy, and took a bite of sandwich. 'I can't leave the house because of George and Snoodles.'

'George?'

'Our dog, and Snoodles is the cat.'

'So you are alone in the house?' He stared down at her. 'You are not nervous?'

'No, sir.'

'You live close by?'

What a man for asking questions, thought Emmy, and wished he didn't stare so. She stared back and said 'Yes,' and wished that he would go away; she found him unsettling. She remembered something. 'I didn't see you on the bus…'

He smiled. 'I was in the car, waiting for the traffic lights.'

She turned to the switchboard, then, and put through two calls, and he watched her. She had pretty hands, nicely well-cared for, and though her hair was mousebrown there seemed to be a great deal of it, piled neatly in a coil at the back of her head. Not in the least pretty, but with eyes like hers that didn't matter.

He bade her goodnight, and went out to his car and forgot her, driving to his charming little house in Chelsea where Beaker, who ran it for him, would have left coffee and sandwiches for him in his study, his desk light on and a discreet lamp burning in the hall.

Although it was almost two o'clock he sat down to go through his letters and messages while he drank the coffee, hot and fragrant in the Thermos. There was a note, too, written in Beaker's spidery hand: Juffrouw Anneliese van Moule had phoned at eight o'clock and again at ten. The professor frowned and glanced over to the answering machine. It showed the red light, and he went and switched it on.

In a moment a petulant voice, speaking in Dutch, wanted to know where he was. 'Surely you should be home by ten o'clock in the evening. I asked you specially to be home, did I not? Well, I suppose I must forgive you and give you good news. I am coming to London in three days' time—Friday. I shall stay at Brown's Hotel, since you are unlikely to be home for most of the day, but I expect to be taken out in the evenings—and there will be time for us to discuss the future.

'I wish to see your house; I think it will not do for us when we are married, for I shall live with you in London when you are working there, but I hope you will give up your work in England and live at Huis ter Mennolt—'

The professor switched off. Anneliese's voice had sounded loud as well as peevish, and she was reiterating an argument they had had on several occasions. He had no intention of leaving his house; it was large enough. He had some friends to dine, but his entertaining was for those whom he knew well. Anneliese would wish to entertain on a grand scale, fill the house with acquaintances; he would return home each evening to a drawing room full of people he neither knew nor wished to know.

He reminded himself that she would be a most suitable wife; in Holland they had a similar circle of friends and acquaintances, and they liked the same things— the theatre, concerts, art exhibitions—and she was ambitious.

At first he had been amused and rather touched by that, until he had realised that her ambition wasn't for his success in his profession but for a place in London society. She already had that in Holland, and she had been careful never to admit to him that that was her goal... He reminded himself that she was the woman he had chosen to marry and once she had understood that he had no intention of altering his way of life when they were married she would understand how he felt.

After all, when they were in Holland she could have all the social life she wanted; Huis ter Mennolt was vast, and there were servants enough and lovely gardens. While he was working she could entertain as many of her friends as she liked—give dinner parties if she wished, since the house was large enough to do that with ease. Here at the Chelsea house, though, with only Beaker and a daily woman to run the place, entertaining on such a scale would be out of the question. The house, roomy though it was, was too small.

He went to bed then, and, since he had a list the following day, he had no time to think about anything but his work.

He left the hospital soon after ten o'clock the next evening. Ermentrude was at her switchboard, her back towards him. He gave her a brief glance as he passed.

Anneliese had phoned again, Beaker informed him,

but would leave no message. 'And, since I needed some groceries, I switched on the answering machine, sir,' he said, 'since Mrs Thrupp, splendid cleaner though she is, is hardly up to answering the telephone.'

The professor went to his study and switched on the machine, and stood listening to Anneliese. Her voice was no longer petulant, but it was still loud. 'My plane gets in at half past ten on Friday—Heathrow,' she told him. 'I'll look out for you. Don't keep me waiting, will you, Ruerd? Shall we dine at Brown's? I shall be too tired to talk much, and I'll stay for several days, anyway.'

He went to look at his appointments book on his desk. He would be free to meet her, although he would have to go back to his consulting rooms for a couple of hours before joining her at Brown's Hotel.

He sat down at his desk, took his glasses from his breast pocket, put them on and picked up the pile of letters before him. He was aware that there was a lack of lover-like anticipation at the thought of seeing Anneliese. Probably because he hadn't seen her for some weeks. Moreover, he had been absorbed in his patients. In about a month's time he would be going back to Holland for a month or more; he would make a point of seeing as much of Anneliese as possible.

He ate his solitary dinner, and went back to his study to write a paper on spina bifida, an exercise which kept him engrossed until well after midnight.

Past the middle of the week already, thought Emmy with satisfaction, getting ready for bed the next morning—three more nights and she would have two days off. Her mother would be home too, until she rejoined her father later in the week, and then he would be working in and around London. Emmy heaved a tired, satisfied sigh and went to sleep until, inevitably, the strains of the flute woke her. It was no use lying there and hoping they would stop; she got up, had a cup of tea and took George for a walk.

It was raining when she went to work that evening, and she had to wait for a long time for a bus. The elderly relief telephonist was off sick, and Audrey was waiting for her when she got there, already dressed to leave, tapping her feet with impatience.

'I thought you'd never get here…'

'It's still only two minutes to eight,' said Emmy mildly. 'Is there anything I should know?'

She was taking off her mac and headscarf as she spoke, and when Audrey said no, there wasn't, Emmy sat down before the switchboard, suddenly hating the sight of it. The night stretched ahead of her, endless hours of staying alert. The thought of the countless days and nights ahead in the years to come wasn't to be borne.

She adjusted her headpiece and arranged everything just so, promising herself that she would find another job, something where she could be out of doors for at least part of the day. And meet people…a man who would fall in love with her and want to marry her. A house in the country, mused Emmy, dogs and cats and chickens and children, of course…

She was roused from this pleasant dream by an outside call, followed by more of them; it was always at this time of the evening that people phoned to make enquiries.

She was kept busy throughout the night. By six o'clock

she was tired, thankful that in another couple of hours she would be free. Only three more nights; she thought sleepily of what she would do. Window shopping with her mother? And if the weather was good enough they could take a bus to Hampstead Heath...

A great blast of sound sent her upright in her chair, followed almost at once by a call from the police—there had been a bomb close to Fenchurch Street Station. Too soon to know how many were injured, but they would be coming to St Luke's!

Emmy, very wide awake now, began notifying everyone—the accident room, the house doctors' rooms, the wards, X-Ray, the path lab. And within minutes she was kept busy, ringing the consultants on call, theatre staff, technicians, ward sisters on day duty. She had called the professor, but hadn't spared him a thought, nor had she seen him as he came to the hospital, for there was a great deal of orderly coming and going as the ambulances began to arrive.

She had been busy; now she was even more so. Anxious relatives were making frantic calls, wanting to know where the injured were and how they were doing. But it was too soon to know anything. The accident room was crowded; names were sent to her as they were given, but beyond letting callers know that they had that particular person in the hospital there was no more information to pass on.

Emmy went on answering yet more calls, putting through outside calls too—to other hospitals, the police, someone from a foreign embassy who had heard that one of the staff had been injured. She answered them all in her quiet voice, trying to ignore a threatening headache.

It seemed a very long time before order emerged from the controlled chaos. There were no more ambulances now, and patients who needed admission were being taken to the wards. The accident room, still busy, was dealing with the lesser injured; the hospital was returning to its normal day's work.

It was now ten o'clock. Emmy, looking at her watch for the first time in hours, blinked. Where was Audrey? Most of the receptionists had come in, for they had rung to tell her so, but not Audrey. Emmy was aware that she was hungry, thirsty and very tired, and wondered what to do about it. She would have to let someone know...

Audrey tapped on her shoulder. She said airily, 'Sorry I'm late. I didn't fancy coming sooner; I bet the place was a shambles. I knew you wouldn't mind...'

'I do mind, though,' said Emmy. 'I mind very much. I've had a busy time, and I should have been off duty two hours ago.'

'Well, you were here, weren't you? Did you expect me to come tearing in in the middle of all the fuss just so's you could go off duty? Besides, you're not doing anything; you only go to bed...'

The professor, on his way home, paused to listen to this with interest. Ermentrude, he could see, was looking very much the worse for wear; she had undoubtedly had a busy time of it, and she had been up all night, whereas the rest of them had merely got out of their beds earlier than usual.

He said now pleasantly, 'Put on your coat, Ermentrude; I'll drive you home. We can take up the matter of the extra hours you have worked later on. Leave it to me.'

Emmy goggled at him, but he gave her no chance

to speak. He said, still pleasantly, to Audrey, 'I'm sure you have a good reason for not coming on duty at the usual time.' He smiled thinly. 'It will have to be a good one, will it not?'

He swept Emmy along, away from a pale Audrey, out of the doors and into his Bentley. 'Tell me where you live,' he commanded.

'There is no need to take me home, I'm quite able—'

'Don't waste my time. We're both tired, and I for one am feeling short-tempered.'

'So am I,' snapped Emmy. 'I want a cup of tea, and I'm hungry.'

'That makes two of us. Now, where do you live, Ermentrude?'

Chapter 2

Emmy told him her address in a cross voice, sitting silently until he stopped before her home. She said gruffly, 'Thank you, Professor. Good morning,' and made to open her door. He shook her hand and released it, and she put it in her lap. Then he got out, opened the door, crossed the pavement with her, took the key from her and opened the house door. George rushed to meet them while Snoodles, a cat not to be easily disturbed, sat on the bottom step of the stairs, watching.

Emmy stood awkwardly in the doorway with George, who was making much of her. She said again, 'Thank you, Professor,' and peered up at his face.

'The least you can do is offer me a cup of tea,' he told her, and came into the hall, taking her with him and closing the door. 'You get that coat off and do whatever you usually do while I put on the kettle.'

He studied her face. Really, the girl was very plain; for a moment he regretted the impulse which had urged him to bring her home. She had been quite capable of getting herself there; he had formed the opinion after their first meeting that she was more than capable of dealing with any situation—and with a sharp tongue, too. She looked at him then, though, and he saw how tired she was. He said in a placid voice, 'I make a very good cup of tea.'

She smiled. 'Thank you. The kitchen's here.'

She opened a door and ushered him into the small room at the back of the house, which was, he saw, neat and very clean, with old-fashioned shelves and a small dresser. There was a gas stove against one wall—an elderly model, almost a museum piece, but still functioning, he was relieved to find.

Emmy went away and he found tea, milk and sugar while the kettle boiled, took mugs and a brown teapot from the dresser and set them on the table while Emmy fed Snoodles and George.

They drank their tea presently, sitting opposite each other saying little, and when the professor got to his feet Emmy made no effort to detain him. She thanked him again, saw him to the door and shut it the moment he had driven away, intent on getting to her bed as quickly as possible. She took a slice of bread and butter and a slab of cheese with her, and George and Snoodles, who had sidled upstairs with her, got onto the bed too— which was a comfort for she was feeling hard done by and put upon.

'It's all very well,' she told them peevishly. 'He'll go home to a doting wife—slippers in one hand and bacon and eggs in the other.'

She swallowed the last of the cheese and went to sleep, and not even the flute or Mrs Grimes' loud voice could wake her.

The professor got into his car, and as he drove away his bleep sounded. He was wanted back at St Luke's; one of the injured had developed signs of a blood clot on the brain. So instead of going home he went back and spent the next few hours doing everything in his power to keep his patient alive—something which proved successful, so that in the early afternoon he was at last able to go home.

He let himself into his house, put his bag down and trod into the sitting room, to come to a halt just inside the door.

'Anneliese—I forgot...'

She was a beautiful girl with thick fair hair cut short by an expert hand, perfect features and big blue eyes, and she was exquisitely made-up. She was dressed in the height of fashion and very expensively, too. She made a charming picture, marred by the ill-temper on her face.

She spoke in Dutch, not attempting to hide her bad temper.

'Really, Ruerd, what am I to suppose you mean by that? That man of yours, Beaker—who, by the way, I shall discharge as soon as we are married—refused to phone the hospital—said you would be too busy to answer. Since when has a consultant not been free to answer the telephone when he wishes?'

He examined several answers to that and discarded them. 'I am sorry, my dear. There was a bomb; it exploded close to St Luke's early this morning. It was necessary for me to be there—there were casualties. Beaker was quite right; I shouldn't have answered the phone.'

He crossed the room and bent to kiss her cheek. 'He is an excellent servant; I have no intention of discharging him.' He spoke lightly, but she gave him a questioning look. They had been engaged for some months now, and she was still not sure that she knew him. She wasn't sure if she loved him either, but he could offer her everything she wanted in life; they knew the same people and came from similar backgrounds. Their marriage would be entirely suitable.

She decided to change her tactics. 'I'm sorry for being cross. But I was disappointed. Are you free for the rest of the day?'

'I shall have to go back to the hospital late this evening. Shall we dine somewhere? You're quite comfortable at Brown's?'

'Very comfortable. Could we dine at Claridge's? I've a dress I bought specially for you...'

'I'll see if I can get a table.' He turned round as Beaker came in.

'You had lunch, sir?' Beaker didn't look at Anneliese. When the professor said that, yes, he'd had something, Beaker went on, 'Then I shall bring tea here, sir. A little early, but you may be glad of it.'

'Splendid, Beaker. As soon as you like.' And, when Beaker had gone, the professor said, 'I'll go and phone now...'

He took his bag to his study and pressed the button on the answering machine. There were several calls from when Beaker had been out of the house; the rest he had noted down and put with the letters. The professor leafed through them, listened to the answering machine and booked a table for dinner. He would have liked to dine quietly at home.

They talked trivialities over tea—news from home and friends, places Anneliese had visited. She had no interest in his work save in his successes; his social advancement was all-important to her, although she was careful not to let him see that.

He drove her to Brown's presently, and went back to work at his desk until it was time to dress. Immaculate in black tie, he went to the garage at the end of the mews to get his car, and drove himself to the hotel.

Anneliese wasn't ready. He cooled his heels for fifteen minutes or so before she joined him.

'I've kept you waiting, Ruerd,' she said laughingly. 'But I hope you think it is worth it.'

He assured her that it was, and indeed she made a magnificent picture in a slim sheath of cerise silk, her hair piled high, sandals with four-inch heels and an arm loaded with gold bangles. His ring, a large diamond, glittered on her finger. A ring which she had chosen and which he disliked.

Certainly she was a woman any man would be proud to escort, he told himself. He supposed that he was tired; a good night's sleep was all that was needed. Anneliese looked lovely, and dinner at Claridge's was the very least he could offer her. Tomorrow, he reflected, he would somehow find time to take her out again— dancing, perhaps, at one of the nightclubs. And there was that exhibition of paintings at a gallery in Bond Street if he could manage to find time to take her.

He listened to her chatter as they drove to Claridge's and gave her his full attention. Dinner was entirely satisfactory: admiring looks followed Anneliese as they went to their table, the food was delicious and the surroundings luxurious. As he drove her back she put a hand on his arm.

'A lovely dinner, darling, thank you. I shall do some shopping tomorrow; can you meet me for lunch? And could we go dancing in the evening? We must talk; I've so many plans...'

At the hotel she offered a cheek for his kiss. 'I shall go straight to bed. See you tomorrow.'

The professor got back into his car and drove to the hospital. He wasn't entirely satisfied with the condition of the patient he had seen that afternoon, and he wanted to be sure...

Emmy, sitting before her switchboard, knitting, knew that the professor was there, standing behind her, although he had made no sound. Why is that? she wondered; why should I know that?

His, 'Good evening, Ermentrude,' was uttered quietly. 'You slept well?' he added.

He came to stand beside her now, strikingly handsome in black tie and quite unconscious of it.

'Good evening, sir. Yes, thank you. I hope you had time to rest.'

His mouth twitched. 'I have been dining out. Making conversation, talking of things which don't interest me. If I sound a bad-tempered man who doesn't know when he is lucky, then that is exactly what I am.'

'No, you're not,' said Emmy reasonably. 'You've had a busy day, much busier than anyone else because you've had to make important decisions about your patients. All that's the matter with you is that you are tired. You must go home and have a good night's sleep.'

She had quite forgotten to whom she was speaking. 'I suppose you've come to see that man with the blood clot on the brain?'

He asked with interest, 'Do you know about him?'

'Well, of course I do. I hear things, don't I? And I'm interested.'

She took an incoming telephone call and, when she had dealt with it the professor had gone.

He didn't stop on his way out, nor did he speak, but she was conscious of his passing. She found that disconcerting.

Audrey was punctual and in a peevish mood. 'I had a ticking off,' she told Emmy sourly. 'I don't know why they had to make such a fuss—after all, you were here. No one would have known if it hadn't been for that Professor ter Mennolt being here. Who does he think he is, anyway?'

'He's rather nice,' said Emmy mildly. 'He gave me a lift home.'

'In that great car of his? Filthy rich, so I've heard. Going to marry some Dutch beauty—I was talking to his secretary...'

'I hope they'll be very happy,' said Emmy. A flicker of unhappiness made her frown. She knew very little about the professor and she found him disturbing; a difficult man, a man who went his own way. All the same, she would like him to live happily ever after...

If he came into the hospital during the last nights of her duty, she didn't see him. It wasn't until Sunday morning, when the relief had come to take over and she was free at last to enjoy her two days off, that she met him again as she stood for a moment outside the hospital entrance, taking blissful breaths of morning air, her eyes closed. She was imagining that she was back in the country, despite the petrol fumes.

She opened her eyes, feeling foolish, when the professor observed, 'I am surprised that you should linger, Ermentrude. Surely you must be hellbent on getting away from the hospital as quickly as possible?'

'Good morning, sir,' said Ermentrude politely. 'It's just nice to be outside.' She saw his sweater and casual trousers. 'Have you been here all night?'

'No, no—only for an hour or so.' He smiled down at her. She looked pale with tiredness. Her small nose shone, her hair had been ruthlessly pinned into a bun, very neat and totally without charm. She reminded him of a kitten who had been out all night in the rain. 'I'll drop you off on my way.'

'You're going past my home? Really? Thank you.'

He didn't find it necessary to answer her, but popped her into the car and drove through the almost empty streets. At her door, he said, 'No, don't get out. Give me your key.'

He went and opened the door, and then opened the car door, took her bag from her and followed her inside. George was delighted to see them, weaving round their feet, pushing Snoodles away, giving small, excited barks.

The professor went to open the kitchen door to let both animals out into the garden, and he put the kettle on. For all the world as though he lived here, thought Emmy, and if she hadn't been so tired she would have said so. Instead she stood in the kitchen and yawned.

The professor glanced at her. 'Breakfast,' he said

briskly and unbuttoned his coat and threw it over a chair. 'If you'll feed the animals, I'll boil a couple of eggs.'

She did as she was told without demur; she couldn't be bothered to argue with him. She didn't remember asking him to stay for breakfast, but perhaps he was very hungry. She fed the animals and by then he had laid the table after a fashion, made toast and dished up the eggs.

They sat at the table eating their breakfast for all the world like an old married couple. The professor kept up a gentle meandering conversation which required little or no reply, and Emmy, gobbling toast, made very little effort to do so. She was still tired, but the tea and the food had revived her so that presently she said, 'It was very kind of you to get breakfast. I'm very grateful. I was a bit tired.'

'You had a busy week. Will your mother and father return soon?'

'Tomorrow morning.' She gave him an owl-like look. 'I expect you want to go home, sir…'

'Presently. Go upstairs, Ermentrude, take a shower and get into bed. I will tidy up here. When you are in bed I will go home.'

'You can't do the washing up.'

'Indeed I can.' Not quite a lie; he had very occasionally needed to rinse a cup or glass if Beaker hadn't been there.

He made a good job of it, attended to the animals, locked the kitchen door and hung the tea towel to dry, taking his time about it. It was quiet in the house, and presently he went upstairs. He got no answer from his quiet, 'Ermentrude?' but one of the doors on the landing was half-open.

The room was small, nicely furnished and very tidy. Emmy was asleep in her bed, her mouth slightly open, her hair all over the pillow. He thought that nothing short of a brass band giving a concert by her bedside would waken her. He went downstairs again and out of the house, shutting the door behind him.

Driving to Chelsea, he looked at his watch. It would be eleven o'clock before he was home. He was taking Anneliese to lunch with friends, and he suspected that when they returned she would want to make plans for their future. There had been no time so far, and he would be at the hospital for a great deal of the days ahead. He was tired now; Anneliese wasn't content to dine quietly and spend the evening at home and yesterday his day had been full. A day in the country would be delightful...

Beaker came to meet him as he opened his front door. His, 'Good morning, sir,' held faint reproach. 'You were detained at the hospital? I prepared breakfast at the usual time. I can have it on the table in ten minutes.'

'No need, Beaker, thanks. I've had breakfast. I'll have a shower and change, and then perhaps a cup of coffee before Juffrouw van Moule gets here.'

'You breakfasted at the hospital, sir?'

'No, no. I boiled an egg and made some toast and had a pot of strong tea. I took someone home. We were both hungry—it seemed a sensible thing to do.'

Beaker inclined his head gravely. A boiled egg, he reflected—no bacon, mushrooms, scrambled eggs, as only he, Beaker, could cook them—and strong tea... He suppressed a shudder. A small plate of his home-made savoury biscuits, he decided, and perhaps a sandwich with Gentlemen's Relish on the coffee tray.

It was gratifying to see the professor eating the lot when he came downstairs again. He looked as though he could do with a quiet day, reflected his faithful servant, instead of gallivanting off with that Juffrouw van Moule. Beaker hadn't taken to her—a haughty piece, and critical of him. He wished his master a pleasant day in a voice which hinted otherwise. He was informed that Juffrouw van Moule would be returning for tea, and would probably stay for dinner.

Beaker took himself to the kitchen where he unburdened himself to his cat, Humphrey, while he set about making the little queen cakes usually appreciated by the professor's lady visitors.

Anneliese looked ravishing, exquisitely made-up, not a hair of her head out of place and wearing a stone-coloured crêpe de chine outfit of deceptive simplicity which screamed money from every seam.

She greeted the professor with a charming smile, offered a cheek with the warning not to disarrange her hair and settled herself in the car.

'At last we have a day together,' she observed. 'I'll come back with you after lunch. That man of yours will give us a decent tea, I suppose. I might even stay for dinner.'

She glanced at his profile. 'We must discuss the future, Ruerd. Where we are to live—we shall have to engage more servants in a larger house, of course, and I suppose you can arrange to give up some of your consultant posts, concentrate on private patients. You have plenty of friends, haven't you? Influential people?'

He didn't look at her. 'I have a great many friends and even more acquaintances,' he told her. 'I have no intention of using them. Indeed, I have no need. Do not expect me to give up my hospital work, though, Anneliese.'

She put a hand on his knee. 'Of course not, Ruerd. I promise I won't say any more about that. But please let us at least discuss finding a larger house where we can entertain. I shall have friends, I hope, and I shall need to return their hospitality.'

She was wise enough to stop then. 'These people we are lunching with—they are old friends?'

'Yes. I knew Guy Bowers-Bentinck before he married. We still see a good deal of each other; he has a charming little wife, Suzannah, and twins—five years old—and a baby on the way.'

'Does she live here, in this village—Great Chisbourne? Does she not find it full? I mean, does she not miss theatres and evenings out and meeting people?'

He said evenly, 'No. She has a husband who loves her, two beautiful children, a delightful home and countless friends. She is content.'

Something in his voice made Anneliese say quickly, 'She sounds delightful; I'm sure I shall like her.'

Which was unfortunately not true. Beneath their socially pleasant manner, they disliked each other heartily—Anneliese because she considered Suzannah to be not worth bothering about, Suzannah because she saw at once that Anneliese wouldn't do for Ruerd at all. She would make him unhappy; surely he could see that for himself?

Lunch was pleasant, Suzannah saw to that—making small talk while the two men discussed some knotty problem about their work. Anneliese showed signs of boredom after a time; she was used to being the centre of attention and she wasn't getting it. When the men did join in the talk it was about the children eating their meal with them, behaving beautifully.

'Do you have a nursery?' asked Anneliese.

'Oh, yes, and a marvellous old nanny. But the children eat with us unless we're entertaining in the evening. We enjoy their company, and they see more of their father.'

Suzannah smiled across the table at her husband, and Anneliese, looking at him, wondered how such a plain girl could inspire the devoted look he gave her.

She remarked upon it as they drove back to Chelsea. 'Quite charming,' she commented in a voice which lacked sincerity. 'Guy seems devoted to her.'

'Surely that is to be expected of a husband?' the professor observed quietly.

Anneliese gave a little trill of laughter. 'Oh, I suppose so. Not quite my idea of marriage, though. Children should be in the nursery until they go to school, don't you agree?'

He didn't answer that. 'They are delightful, aren't they? And so well behaved.' He sounded remote.

He was going fast on the motorway as the October day faded into dusk. In a few days it would be November, and at the end of that month he would go back to Holland for several weeks, where already a formidable list of consultations awaited him. He would see Anneliese again, of course; she would want to plan their wedding.

When they had first become engaged he had expressed a wish for a quiet wedding and she had agreed.

But over the months she had hinted more and more strongly that a big wedding was absolutely necessary: so many friends and family, and she wanted bridesmaids. Besides, a quiet wedding would mean she couldn't wear the gorgeous wedding dress she fully intended to have.

Anneliese began to talk then; she could be very amusing and she was intelligent. Ruerd wasn't giving her his full attention, but she was confident that she could alter that. She embarked on a series of anecdotes about mutual friends in Holland, taking care not to be critical or spiteful, only amusing. She knew how to be a charming companion, and felt smug satisfaction when he responded, unaware that it was only good manners which prompted his replies.

He was tired, he told himself, and Anneliese's chatter jarred on his thoughts. To talk to her about his work would have been a relief, to tell her of his busy week at the hospital, the patients he had seen. But the cursory interest she had shown when they'd become engaged had evaporated. Not her fault, of course, but his. He had thought that her interest in his work was a wish to understand it, but it hadn't been that—her interest was a social one. To be married to a well-known medical man with boundless possibilities for advancement.

He slowed the car's speed as they were engulfed in London's suburbs. She would be a suitable wife—good looks, a charming manner, clever and always beautifully turned out.

On aiming back he said, 'We'll have tea round the fire, shall we? Beaker will have it ready.' He glanced at his watch. 'Rather on the late side, but there's no hurry, is there?'

The sitting room looked warm and welcoming as

they went indoors. Humphrey was sitting before the fire, a small furry statue, staring at the flames. Anneliese paused halfway across the room. 'Oh, Ruerd, please get that cat out of the room. I dislike them, you know—I'm sure they're not clean, and they shed hairs everywhere.'

The professor scooped Humphrey into his arms. 'He's a well-loved member of my household, Anneliese. He keeps himself cleaner than many humans, and he is brushed so regularly that I doubt if there is a single loose hair.'

He took the cat to the kitchen and sat him down in front of the Aga.

'Juffrouw van Moule doesn't like cats,' he told Beaker in an expressionless voice. 'He'd better stay here until she goes back to the hotel. Could you give us supper about half past eight? Something light; if we're going to have tea now we shan't have much appetite.'

When he went back to the sitting room Anneliese was sitting by the fire. She made a lovely picture in its light, and he paused to look at her as he went in. Any man would be proud to have her as his wife, he reflected, so why was it that he felt no quickening of his pulse at the sight of her?

He brushed the thought aside and sat down opposite her, and watched her pour their tea. She had beautiful hands, exquisitely cared for, and they showed to great advantage as she presided over the tea tray. She looked at him and smiled, aware of the charming picture she made, and presently, confident that she had his attention once more, she began to talk about their future.

'I know we shall see a good deal of each other when you come back to Holland in December,' she began.

'But at least we can make tentative plans.' She didn't wait for his comment but went on, 'I think a summer wedding, don't you? That gives you plenty of time to arrange a long holiday. We might go somewhere for a month or so before settling down.

'Can you arrange it so that you're working in Holland for a few months? You can always fly over here if you're wanted, and surely you can give up your consultancies here after awhile? Private patients, by all means, and, of course, we mustn't lose sight of your friends and colleagues.' She gave him a brilliant smile. 'You're famous here, are you not? It is so important to know all the right people...'

When he didn't reply, she added, 'I am going to be very unselfish and agree to using this house as a London base. Later on perhaps we can find something larger.'

He asked quietly, 'What kind of place had you in mind, Anneliese?'

'I looked in at an estate agent—somewhere near Harrods; I can't remember the name. There were some most suitable flats. Large enough for entertaining. We would need at least five bedrooms—guests, you know—and good servants' quarters.'

Her head on one side, she gave him another brilliant smile. 'Say yes, Ruerd.'

'I have commitments for the next four months here,' he told her, 'and they will be added to in the meantime. In March I've been asked to lecture at a seminar in Leiden, examine students at Groningen and read a paper in Vienna. I cannot give you a definite answer at the moment.'

She pouted. 'Oh, Ruerd, why must you work so hard?

At least I shall see something of you when you come back to Holland. Shall you give a party at Christmas?'

'Yes, I believe so. We can talk about that later. Have your family any plans?'

She was still telling him about them when Beaker came to tell them that supper was ready.

Later that evening, as she prepared to go, Anneliese asked, 'Tomorrow, Ruerd? You will be free? We might go to an art exhibition…?'

He shook his head. 'I'm working all day. I doubt if I shall be free before the evening. I'll phone the hotel and leave a message. It will probably be too late for dinner, but we might have a drink.'

She had to be content with that. She would shop, she decided, and dine at the hotel. She was careful not to let him see how vexed she was.

The next morning as the professor made his way through the hospital he looked, as had become his habit, to where Ermentrude sat. She wasn't there, of course.

She was up and dressed, getting the house just so, ready for her mother and father. She had slept long and soundly, and had gone downstairs to find that the professor had left everything clean and tidy in the kitchen. He had left a tea tray ready, too; all she'd needed to do was put on the kettle and make toast.

'Very thoughtful of him,' said Emmy now, to George, who was hovering hopefully for a biscuit. 'You wouldn't think to look at him that he'd know one end of a tea towel from the other. He must have a helpless fiancée…'

She frowned. Even if his fiancée was helpless he could obviously afford to have a housekeeper or at least a daily woman. She fell to wondering about him. When would he be married, have children? Where did he live while he was working in London? And where was his home in Holland? Since neither George nor Snoodles could answer, she put these questions to the back of her mind and turned her thoughts to the shopping she must do before her parents came home.

They knew about the bomb, of course; it had been on TV and in the papers. But when Emmy had phoned her parents she had told them very little about it, and had remained guiltily silent when her mother had expressed her relief that Emmy had been on day duty and hadn't been there. Now that they were home, exchanging news over coffee and biscuits, the talk turned naturally enough to the bomb outrage. 'So fortunate that you weren't there,' said Mrs Foster.

'Well, as a matter of fact, I was,' said Emmy. 'But I was quite all right...' She found herself explaining about Professor ter Mennolt bringing her home and him making tea.

'We are in his debt,' observed her father. 'Although he did only what any decent-thinking person would have done.'

Her mother said artlessly, 'He sounds a very nice man. Is he elderly? I suppose so if he's a professor.'

'Not elderly—not even middle-aged,' said Emmy. 'They say at the hospital that he's going to marry soon. No one knows much about him, and one wouldn't dare ask him.'

She thought privately that one day, if the opportunity occurred, she might do just that. For some reason it was important to her that he should settle down and be happy. He didn't strike her as being happy enough. He ought to be; he was top of his profession, with a girl waiting for him, and presumably enough to live on in comfort.

Her two days went much too quickly. Never mind if it rained for almost all of the time. Her father was away in the day, and she and her mother spent a morning window shopping in Oxford Street, and long hours sitting by the fire—her mother knitting, Emmy busy with the delicate embroidery which she loved to do.

They talked—the chances of her father getting a teaching post near their old home were remote; all the same they discussed it unendingly. 'We don't need a big house,' said her mother. 'And you could come with us, of course, Emmy—there's bound to be some job for you. Or you might meet someone and marry.' She peered at her daughter. 'There isn't anyone here, is there, love?'

'No, Mother, and not likely to be. It would be lovely if Father could get a teaching post and we could sell this house.'

Her mother smiled. 'No neighbours, darling. Wouldn't it be heaven? No rows of little houses all exactly alike. Who knows what is round the corner?'

It was still raining when Emmy set off to work the following morning. The buses were packed and tempers were short. She got off before the hospital stop was reached, tired of being squeezed between wet raincoats and having her feet poked at with umbrellas. A few minutes' walk even on a London street was preferable to strap-hanging.

She was taking a short cut through a narrow lane where most of the houses were boarded up or just plain derelict, when she saw the kitten. It was very small and very wet, sitting by a boarded-up door, and when she went nearer she saw that it had been tied by a piece of string to the door handle. It looked at her and shivered, opened its tiny mouth and mewed almost without sound.

Emmy knelt down, picked it up carefully, held it close and rooted around in her shoulder bag for the scissors she always carried. It was the work of a moment to cut the string, tuck the kitten into her jacket and be on her way once more. She had no idea what she was going to do with the small creature, but to leave it there was unthinkable.

She was early at the hospital; there was time to beg a cardboard box from one of the porters, line it with yesterday's newspaper and her scarf and beg some milk from the head porter.

'You won't 'arf cop it,' he told her, offering a mugful. 'I wouldn't do it for anyone else, Emmy, and mum's the word.' He nodded and winked. She was a nice young lady, he considered, always willing to listen to him telling her about his wife's diabetes.

Emmy tucked the box away at her feet, dried the small creature with her handkerchief, offered it milk and saw with satisfaction that it fell instantly into a refreshing sleep. It woke briefly from time to time, scoffed more milk and dropped off again. Very much to her relief, Emmy got to the end of her shift with the kitten undetected.

She was waiting for her relief when the supervisor bore down upon her, intent on checking and finding fault if she could. It was just bad luck that the kitten should wake at that moment, and, since it was feeling better, it mewed quite loudly.

Meeting the lady's outraged gaze, Emmy said, 'I found him tied to a doorway. In the rain. I'm going to take him home...'

'He has been here all day?' The supervisor's bosom swelled to alarming proportions. 'No animal is allowed inside the hospital. You are aware of that, are you not, Miss Foster? I shall report this, and in the meantime the animal can be taken away by one of the porters.'

'Don't you dare,' said Emmy fiercely. 'I'll not allow it. You are—'

It was unfortunate that she was interrupted before she could finish.

'Ah,' said Professor ter Mennolt, looming behind the supervisor. 'My kitten. Good of you to look after it for me, Ermentrude.' He gave the supervisor a bland smile. 'I am breaking the rules, am I not? But this seemed the best place for it to be until I could come and collect it.'

'Miss Foster has just told me...' began the woman.

'Out of the kindness of her heart,' said the professor outrageously. 'She had no wish to get me into trouble. Isn't that correct, Ermentrude?'

She nodded, and watched while he soothed the supervisor's feelings with a bedside manner which she couldn't have faulted.

'I will overlook your rudeness, Miss Foster,' she said finally, and sailed away.

'Where on earth did you find it?' asked the professor with interest.

She told him, then went on, 'I'll take him home. He'll be nice company for Snoodles and George.'

'An excellent idea. Here is your relief. I shall be outside when you are ready.'

'Why?' asked Emmy.

'You sometimes ask silly questions, Ermentrude. To take you both home.'

Emmy made short work of handing over, got into her mac, picked up the box and went to the entrance. The Bentley was outside, and the professor bundled her and her box into it and drove away in the streaming rain.

The kitten sat up on wobbly legs and mewed. It was bedraggled and thin, and Emmy said anxiously, 'I do hope he'll be all right.'

'Probably a she. I'll look the beast over.'

'Would you? Thank you. Then if it's necessary I'll take him—her—to the vet.' She added uncertainly, 'That's if it's not interfering with whatever you're doing?'

'I can spare half an hour.' He sounded impatient.

She unlocked the door and ushered him into the hall, where he took up so much room she had to sidle past him to open the sitting-room door.

'You're so large,' she told him, and ushered him into the room.

Mrs Foster was sitting reading with Snoodles on her lap. She looked up as they went in and got to her feet.

'I'm sure you're the professor who was so kind to Emmy,' she said, and offered a hand. 'I'm her mother. Emmy, take off that wet mac and put the kettle on, please. What's in the box?'

'A kitten.'

Mrs Foster offered a chair. 'Just like Emmy—always finding birds with broken wings and stray animals.' She smiled from a plain face very like her daughter's, and he thought what a charming woman she was.

'I offered to look at the little beast,' he explained. 'It was tied to a door handle…'

'People are so cruel. But how kind of you. I'll get a clean towel so that we can put the little creature on it while you look. Have a cup of tea first, won't you?'

Emmy came in then, with the tea tray, and they drank their tea while the kitten, still in its box, was put before the fire to warm up. George sat beside it, prepared to be friendly. Snoodles had gone to sit on top of the bookcase, looking suspicious.

Presently, when the kitten had been carefully examined by the professor and pronounced as well as could be expected, he thanked Mrs Foster for his tea with charming good manners, smiled at Emmy and drove himself away.

'I like him,' observed Mrs Foster, shutting the front door.

Emmy, feeding the kitten bread and milk, didn't say anything.

Chapter 3

Anneliese found Ruerd absent-minded when they met on the following day—something which secretly annoyed her. No man, she considered, should be that while he was in her company. He was taking her out to dinner, and she had gone to great pains to look her best. Indeed, heads turned as they entered the restaurant; they made a striking couple, and she was aware of that.

She realised very soon that he had no intention of talking about their future. She had a splendid conceit of herself—it never entered her head that the lack of interest could be anything else but a temporary worry about his work—but she had the sense to say no more about her plans for the future, and laid herself out to be an amusing companion.

She considered that she had succeeded too, for as he drove her back to the hotel she suggested that she might stay for several more days, adding prettily, 'I miss you, Ruerd.'

All he said was, 'Why not stay? Perhaps I can get tickets for that show you want to see. I'll do my best to keep my evenings free.'

He drew up before the hotel and turned to look at her. She looked lovely in the semi-shadows, and he bent to kiss her.

She put up a protesting hand. 'Oh, darling, not now. You always disarrange my hair.'

He got out, opened her door, went with her into the foyer, bade her goodnight with his beautiful manners and drove himself back home, reminding himself that Anneliese was the ideal wife for him. Her coolness was something he would overcome in time. She was beautiful, he told himself, and she knew how to dress, how to manage his large household in Holland, how to be an amusing and charming companion...

He let himself into his house and Beaker and Humphrey came into the hall.

'A pleasant evening, I trust, sir?' asked Beaker smoothly.

The professor nodded absently. Humphrey had reminded him about the kitten and Ermentrude. He frowned; the girl had a habit of popping into his thoughts for no reason. He must remember to ask about the kitten if he saw her in the morning.

Emmy, still refreshed by her days off, was a little early. She settled down before the switchboard, arranged everything just as she liked it and took out her knitting. She was halfway through the first row when she became aware that the professor was there. She

turned to look at him and, since it was a crisp autumn
morning and the sun was shining and she was pleased
to see him, she smiled widely and wished him good
morning.

His reply was cool. He took his spectacles out of his
pocket, polished them and put them on his commanding nose in order to read the variety of notes left for
him at the desk.

Emmy's smile dwindled. She turned back and picked
up her knitting and wished that she were busy. Perhaps she shouldn't have spoken to him. She was only
being civil.

'It's Friday morning,' she said in a reasonable voice,
'and the sun's shining.'

He took his specs off, the better to stare down at her.

'The kitten—is it thriving?'

'Yes. Oh, yes, and Snoodles and George are so kind
to it. Snoodles washes it and it goes to sleep with them.
It's a bit of a squash in their basket.' She beamed at him.
'How nice of you to ask, sir.'

He said testily, 'Nice, nice…a useless word. You
would do well to enlarge your knowledge of the English language, Ermentrude.'

'That is very rude, Professor,' said Emmy coldly,
and was glad that there was a call which kept her busy
for a few moments. Presently she turned her head cautiously. The professor had gone.

I shall probably get the sack, she reflected. The idea
hung like a shadow over her for the rest of the day. By
the time she was relieved, Authority hadn't said anything, but probably in the morning there would be a letter waiting for her, giving her a month's notice.

She went slowly to the entrance, wondering if a written apology to the professor would be a good idea. She began to compose it in her head, pausing on her way to get the words right so that the professor had plenty of time to overtake her as she crossed the entrance hall. He came to a halt in front of her so that she bounced against his waistcoat. Emmy, being Emmy, said at once, 'I'm composing a letter of apology to you, sir, although I really don't see why I should.'

'I don't see why you should either,' he told her. 'What were you going to put in it?'

'Well—"Dear sir", of course, to start with, and then something about being sorry for my impertinence.'

'You consider that you were impertinent?' he wanted to know.

'Good heavens, no, but if I don't apologise I dare say I'll get the sack for being rude or familiar or something.'

She received an icy stare. 'You have a poor opinion of me, Ermentrude.'

She made haste to put things right. 'No, no, I think you are very nice...' She paused. 'Oh, dear, I'll have to think of another word, won't I?' She smiled at him, ignoring the cold eyes. 'But you are nice! I suppose I could call you handsome or sexy...'

He held up a large hand. 'Spare my blushes, Ermentrude. Let us agree, if possible, on nice. I can assure you, though, that you are in no danger of being dismissed.'

'Oh, good. The money's useful at home, you know.'

Which presumably was why she was dressed in less than eye-catching fashion.

'The matter being cleared up, I'll drive you home. It's on my way.'

'No, it's not. Thank you very much, though; I can catch a bus...'

The professor, not in the habit of being thwarted, took her arm and walked her through the door.

In the car he asked, 'What are you doing with your evening? Meeting the boyfriend, going to a cinema, having a meal?'

She glanced at him. He was looking ahead, not smiling.

'Me? Well, I haven't got a boyfriend, so I won't be going to the cinema or out for a meal. Mother and Father are home, so we'll have supper and take George for a walk and see to Snoodles and the kitten. And we'll talk...' She added, 'We like talking.'

When he didn't answer she asked, 'Are you going to have a pleasant evening, Professor?'

'I am taking my finacée to Covent Garden to the ballet, and afterwards we shall have supper somewhere. I do not care for the ballet.'

'Well, no, I dare say men don't. But supper will be fun—especially as it's with your fiancée. Somewhere nice—I mean, fashionable...'

'Indeed, yes.'

Something in his voice made her ask, 'Don't you like going out to supper, either?' She wanted to ask about his fiancée but she didn't dare—besides, the thought of him getting married made her feel vaguely unhappy.

'It depends where it is eaten and with whom. I would enjoy taking a dog for a long walk in one of the parks and eating my supper...' He paused. 'Afterwards.' Which hadn't been what he had wanted to say.

'That's easy. Get a dog. You could both take it for a walk in the evenings and then go home and have a cosy supper together.'

The professor envisaged Anneliese tramping round

Hyde Park and then returning to eat her supper in his company. No dressing up, no waiters, no other diners to admire her—his mind boggled.

He said slowly, 'I will get a dog. From Battersea Dogs Home. Will you come with me and help me choose him, Ermentrude?'

'Me? I'd love to, but what about your fiancée?'

'She returns to Holland in a few days.'

'Oh, well, all right. It'll be a lovely surprise for her when she comes back to see you again.'

'It will certainly be a surprise,' said the professor.

He dropped her off at her house with a casual nod and a goodnight, and began to drive to his own home. I must be out of my mind, he reflected. Anneliese will never agree to a dog, and certainly not to long walks with it. What is it about Ermentrude which makes me behave with such a lack of good sense? And why do I enjoy being with her when I have Anneliese?

Later that evening, after the ballet, while they were having supper, he deliberately talked about Ermentrude, telling Anneliese something of the bomb scare, mentioning the kitten.

Anneliese listened smilingly. 'Darling, how like you to bother about some little girl just because she got scared with that bomb. She sounds very dull. Is she pretty?'

'No.'

'I can just imagine her—plain and mousy and badly dressed. Am I right?'

'Yes. She has a pretty voice, though. A useful attribute in her particular job.'

'I hope she's grateful to you. I mean, for a girl like that it must be a great uplift to be spoken to by you.'

The professor said nothing to that. He thought it unlikely that Ermentrude had experienced any such feeling. Her conversation had been invariably matter-of-fact and full of advice. As far as she was concerned he was just another man.

He smiled at the thought, and Anneliese said, 'Shall we talk about something else? I find this girl a bit boring.'

Never that, thought the professor. Though unable to hold a candle to Anneliese's beauty. If circumstances had not thrown them together briefly, he would never have noticed her.

All the same he smiled a little, and Anneliese, despite feeling quite confident of Ruerd's regard for her, decided there and then to do something about it.

Emmy told her mother and father about going to Battersea Dogs Home with the professor.

'When does the professor intend to marry?' asked her mother.

'I've no idea. He doesn't talk about it, and I couldn't ask him. We only talk about things which don't matter.' She sighed. 'I expect he'll tell me when he's got the time to choose a dog.'

But although he wished her good morning and good evening each day, that was all. He didn't ask after the kitten either.

It was towards the end of the next week when Emmy came back from her dinner break and found someone waiting for her. After one look she knew who it was: the professor's fiancée; she had to be. He would, she thought, decide for nothing less than this beautiful creature with the perfect hairdo and the kind of clothes any woman could see at a glance had cost a small fortune.

She said, 'Can I help? Do you want the professor?'

'You know who I am?'

Emmy said diffidently, 'Well, not exactly, but Professor ter Mennolt mentioned that his fiancée was staying in London and—and you're exactly how I imagined you would be.'

'And what was that?' Anneliese sounded amused.

'Quite beautiful and splendidly dressed.' Emmy smiled. 'I'll show you where you can wait while I try and get him for you.'

'Oh, I don't wish to see him. He was telling me about the bomb scare here and what an unpleasant experience it was for everyone. He told me about you, too.' She gave a little laugh. 'I would have known you anywhere from his description—plain and mousy and badly dressed. Oh, dear, I shouldn't have said that. Forgive me—my silly tongue.'

Emmy said quietly, 'Yes, that's a very good description of me, isn't it? Are you enjoying your visit? London in the autumn is rather special.'

'The shopping is good, and we enjoy going out in the evenings. Do you go out much?'

Her voice, too loud and with a strong accent, grated on Emmy's ears.

'Not very much. It's quite a long day here. When I do go home I walk our dog...'

'You have a dog? I do not like them, and certainly not in the house. I dislike cats also—their hairs...'

Emmy's relief telephonist was showing signs of impatience, which made it easy for her to say that she had to return to her switchboard.

'It's been nice meeting you,' said Emmy mendaciously. For once she agreed with the professor that 'nice' was a useless word and quite inappropriate. She hoped that she would never see the girl again.

'I won't keep you from your work. It was most satisfying to find that Ruerd's description of you was so accurate.'

Anneliese didn't offer a hand, nor did she say goodbye. Emmy and the relief watched her go.

'Who's she?'

'Professor ter Mennolt's fiancée.'

'The poor man. She'll lead him a dance; you see if she doesn't.'

'She's very beautiful,' said Emmy, in a voice which conveyed nothing of her feelings. Though her goodnight in reply to the professor's passing greeting was austere in the extreme.

The following evening, after a wakeful night, and a different day, it held all the hauteur of royalty in a rage.

Not that the professor appeared to notice. 'I'm free on Sunday. Will you help me choose a dog—some time in the morning—or afternoon if you prefer?'

He didn't sound friendly; he sounded like someone performing an obligation with reluctance. 'My fiancée has gone back to Holland this morning,' he added inconsequentially.

'No,' said Emmy coldly. 'I'm afraid I can't.'

He eyed her narrowly. 'Ah, of course—you consider it very incorrect of me to spend a few hours with someone other than Anneliese. The moment she sets foot in the plane, too.'

'No. At least partly.' She frowned. 'It was the bomb which...' she sought for the right words '...was the reason for you speaking to me. In such circumstances that was natural. There is no need—'

He said silkily, 'My dear Emmy, you do not for one moment imagine that you are a serious rival to Anneliese? For God's sake, all I have asked of you is to help me choose a dog.'

'What a silly thing to say,' said Emmy roundly. 'It is the last thing I would think. I am, as you so clearly described me, plain and mousy and badly dressed. Certainly no companion for you, even at a dogs' home!'

He said slowly, 'When did you meet Anneliese?'

'She came here to see me. She wanted to see if you had described me accurately.' Emmy added stonily, 'You had.'

The professor stood looking at her for a long minute. He said, 'I'm sorry, Ermentrude, it was unpardonable of me to discuss you with Anneliese and I had no idea that she had come here to see you.'

'Well,' said Emmy matter-of-factly, 'it's what any woman would do—you could have been lying about me.' She gave a rueful smile. 'I might have been a gorgeous blonde.'

'I do not lie, Ermentrude. I will not lie to you now and tell you that you are neither mousy nor plain nor badly dressed. You are a very nice—and I use the word in its correct sense—person, and I apologise for hurting you. One day someone—a man—will look at you and love you. He won't notice the clothes; he will see only your lovely eyes and the kindness in your face. He will find you beautiful and tell you so.'

Emmy said, 'Pigs might fly, but it's kind of you to say so. It doesn't matter, you know. I've known since I was a little girl that I had no looks to speak of. It's not as though I'm surprised.' She gave a very small sigh. 'Your Anneliese is very beautiful, and I hope you'll be very happy with her.'

The professor remained silent and she put through an outside call. He was still there when she had done it.

He was not a man in the habit of asking a favour twice, but he did so now.

'Will you help me choose a dog, Ermentrude?'

She turned to look at him. 'Very well, Professor. In the afternoon, if you don't mind. About two o'clock?'

'Thank you. I'll call for you then.'

He went away, and just for a while she was too busy to reflect over their conversation. Which was a good thing, she decided, for her bottled up feelings might spill over. She would go with him on Sunday, but after that good morning and good evening would be sufficient.

Later, when she considered she had cooled down enough to think about it, she thought that it wasn't that he had discussed her with Anneliese so much as the fact that he hadn't denied calling her plain which had made her angry. On the other hand, supposing he had denied it—and she'd known that he was lying? Would she have been just as angry? In all fairness to him she thought that she would. She liked him even if there was no reason to do so.

Her mother and father, when she told them on Sunday answered exactly as she had known they would. Her mother said, 'Wear a warm coat, dear, it gets chilly in the afternoons.'

Her father said, 'Good idea—enjoy yourself, Emmy!'

Her parents were going to Coventry on the following day—the last week away from home, her mother assured her, for her father would be round and about London after that. 'You're sure you don't mind?' she asked anxiously. 'I know you're busy all day, but it's lonely for you, especially in the evenings.'

'Mother, I've heaps to do, honestly, and I'll get the garden tidied up for the winter.' Though the garden was a miserably small patch of grass surrounded by narrow flowerbeds which Emmy would hopefully plant.

The professor arrived punctually, exchanged suitable and civil remarks with her mother and father and ushered Emmy into the car. She had gone to great pains to improve her appearance. True, her jacket and skirt were off the peg, bought to last, and therefore a useful brown—a colour which didn't suit her. But the cream blouse under the jacket was crisp, and her gloves and shoulder bag were leather, elderly but well cared for. Since her brown shoes were well-worn loafers, she had borrowed a pair of her mother's. Court shoes with quite high heels. They pinched a bit, but they looked all right.

The professor, eyeing her unobtrusively, was surprised to find himself wishing that some fairy godmother would wave a wand over Emmy and transform the brown outfit into something pretty. He was surprised, too, that she wore her clothes with an air—when he had thought about it, and that hadn't been often, he had supposed that she had little interest in clothes. He saw now that he was wrong.

He made casual conversation as he drove, and Emmy replied cautiously, not at all at her ease, wishing she hadn't come. Once they had reached the dogs' home she forgot all about that. She had never seen so many dogs, nor heard such a concert of barking.

They went to and fro looking at doggy faces, some

pressed up to the front of their shelters, eager for attention, others sitting indifferently at the back. 'They're pretending that they don't mind if no one wants them,' said Emmy. 'I wish we could have them all.'

The professor smiled down at her. Her face was alight with interest and compassion and, rather to his surprise, didn't look in the least plain.

'I'm afraid one is the best I can do. Have you seen a dog which you think might suit me? There are so many, I have no preference at the moment.'

They had stopped in front of a shelter to watch the antics of an overgrown puppy, chosen by a family of children and expressing his delight. There were a lot of dogs; Emmy looked at them all and caught the eye of a large woolly dog with the kindly face of a labrador and a tremendous sweeping tail. He was sitting in the corner, and it was obvious to her that he was too proud to attract attention. Only his eyes begged her...

'That one,' said Emmy. 'There.'

The professor studied the dog. 'Yes,' he said. 'That's the one.'

The dog couldn't have heard them, but he came slowly to the front of the shelter and wagged his tail, staring up at them. When, after the necessary formalities had been gone through, the professor fastened a new collar round the dog's powerful neck, he gave a small, happy bark.

'You see?' said Emmy. 'He knew you'd have him. He's so lovely. Did they say what breed he was?'

'Well, no. There is some uncertainty. He was left to fend for himself until some kind soul brought him here. He's been here for some time. He's rather on the large side for the average household.'

They got into the car, and the dog settled warily on a blanket on the back seat.

'You do like him?' Emmy asked anxiously.

'Yes. An instant rapport. I can only hope that Beaker will feel the same way.'

'Beaker?'

'Yes, my man. He runs the house for me. Did I mention him when I told you about Humphrey? He's a splendid fellow.'

He drew up in front of his house and Emmy said, 'Oh, is this where you live? It's not like London at all, is it? Is there a garden?'

'Yes—come and see it?'

'I'd like to, but you'll have a lot to do with the dog, and you have a day off today, too, haven't you?'

He said gravely that, yes, he had, but he was doing nothing else with it. 'So please come in and meet Beaker and Humphrey and help me to get this beast settled in.'

Beaker, opening the door, did no more than lift a dignified eyebrow at the sight of the dog. He bowed gravely to Emmy and shook the hand she offered. 'A handsome beast,' he pronounced. 'Straight into the garden, sir?'

'Yes, Beaker. He's been at the home for a long time so he's a bit uncertain about everything. Ten minutes in the garden may help. Then tea, if you please.'

Beaker slid away and the professor led Emmy across the hall, into the sitting room and out of the French window into the garden. For London it was quite large, with a high brick wall and one or two trees—a mountain ash, a small silver birch, bare of leaves now, and a very old apple tree.

The dog needed no urging to explore, and Emmy

said, 'Oh, how delightful. It must look lovely in the spring—lots of bulbs?'

When he nodded, watching her face, she added, 'And an apple tree. We used to have several...'

'You had a large garden?' he asked gently.

'Yes. A bit rambling, but everything grew. It was heaven to go out in the morning. And the air—there isn't much air here, is there? Well, not around St Luke's.' She turned away, annoyed with herself for saying so much, as though she had asked to be pitied. 'What will you call him?'

'I was hoping you would think of a name.'

'Something dignified and a bit regal to make up for his unhappy life.' She thought about it. 'No, it should be a name that sounds as though he's one of the family. Charlie—when I was a little girl I wanted a brother called Charlie.'

'Charlie it shall be.' The professor called the dog, and he came at once, lolloping across the lawn, his tongue hanging out, his preposterous tail waving.

'You see?' said Emmy happily. 'He knows.'

The professor put a gentle hand on Charlie's woolly head. 'I think he has earned his tea, don't you? Let us go indoors; we've earned ours, too.'

'Oh, well,' said Emmy. 'I didn't mean to stay, only to see your garden.'

'Charlie and I will be deeply offended if you don't stay for tea. What is more, Beaker will think his efforts aren't sufficiently tempting.'

Not meaning to, she smiled at him. 'Tea would be very nice.'

They had it in the sitting room, sitting by the fire with Beaker's efforts on a low table between them. Tiny

sandwiches, fairy cakes, a chocolate cake and minia-
ture macaroons, flanked by a silver teapot and paper-
thin china cups and saucers.

Charlie, mindful of his manners, sat himself carefully down before the fire, hopeful eyes on the cake.
Presently Beaker opened the door and Humphrey came
in, circled the room slowly and finally sat down beside Charlie. He ignored the dog and stared into the
flames, and Emmy said anxiously, 'Will they get on,
do you think?'

'Yes. Humphrey has no intention of losing face,
though. Charlie will have to play second fiddle.'

'Oh, well, I don't suppose he'll mind now he has a
family of his own. Will your fiancée like him?'

The professor bit into some cake. 'No. I'm afraid not.'

When Emmy looked concerned he added, 'I spend a
good deal of the year in Holland and, of course, Charlie
will stay here with Beaker.'

She poured second cups. 'Do you have a dog in Holland?'

'Two. A Jack Russell and an Irish wolfhound.'

She wanted to ask him about his home in Holland, but
although he was friendly he was also aloof. Emmy, willing
and eager to be friends with everyone, found that daunting. Besides, she wasn't sure what to make of him. In his
company she was happy even when they weren't on the
best of terms, but away from him, looking at him from a
distance as it were, she told herself that there was no point
in continuing their friendship—if it could be called that.

Tea finished, she said a little shyly, 'I think I had
better go home, Professor. Mother and Father are going
to Coventry in the morning. It will be Father's last job
away from home.'

'He enjoys his work?' the professor asked idly.

'He'd rather be a schoolmaster, and not in London.'

'If he were to get a post in the country, you would go with your parents?'

'Yes, oh, yes. I expect I'd have to look for another kind of job. I like needlework and sewing. I expect I could find work in a shop or helping a dressmaker.' She added defiantly, 'I like clothes...'

He prudently kept silent about that. He had a brief memory of Anneliese, exquisitely turned out in clothes which must have cost what to Emmy would have been a small fortune. Emmy, he reflected, would look almost pretty if she were to dress in the same way as Anneliese dressed.

He didn't ask her to stay, but waited while she said goodbye to Charlie and Humphrey and thanked Beaker for her tea, and then went with her to the car.

The streets were almost empty on a late Sunday afternoon and the journey didn't take long. At the house he declined her hesitant offer to go in. He opened her door, thanked her for her help, still standing on the pavement in the dull little street, and waited while she opened the house door and went inside.

Driving back home, he reflected that he had enjoyed his afternoon with Emmy. She was a good companion; she didn't chat and she was a good listener, and when she did have something to say it was worth listening to. He must remember to let her know from time to time how Charlie progressed.

A pleasant afternoon, Emmy told her parents, and the dog, Charlie, was just what she would have chosen for herself. 'And I had a lovely tea,' she told them.

'The professor has a man who runs his home for him and makes the most delicious cakes.'

'A nice house?' asked her mother.

Emmy described it—what she had seen of it—and the garden as well.

'It's not like London,' she told them. 'In the garden you might be miles away in the country.'

'You miss our old home, don't you, Emmy?' her father asked.

'Yes, I do, but we're quite cosy here.' Empty words which neither of them believed.

'I dare say the professor will tell you how the dog settles down,' observed her mother.

'Perhaps.' Emmy sounded doubtful.

She didn't see him for several days, and when he at length stopped to speak to her on his way home one evening, it was only to tell her that Charlie was nicely settled in.

'A very biddable animal,' he told her. 'Goes everywhere with me.'

He bade her good evening in a frosty voice and went away, leaving her wondering why he was so aloof.

He's had a busy day, reflected Emmy, he'll be more friendly in the morning.

Only in the morning he wasn't there. Audrey, who always knew the latest gossip, told her as she took over that he had gone to Birmingham.

'Gets around, doesn't he? Going back to Holland for Christmas too. Shan't see much of him—not that he's exactly friendly. Well, what do you expect? He's a senior consultant and no end of a big noise.'

Which was, Emmy conceded, quite true. And a good

reason for remembering that next time he might pause for a chat. He was beginning to loom rather large on the edge of her dull, humdrum life, which wouldn't do at all. Sitting there at her switchboard, she reminded herself that they had nothing in common— Well, Charlie perhaps, and being in the hospital when the bomb went off.

Besides, she reminded herself bitterly, he considered her plain and dowdy. If I could spend half as much on myself as that Anneliese of his, reflected Emmy waspishly, I'd show him that I'm not in the least dowdy, and a visit to a beauty salon would work wonders even with a face like mine.

Since neither of their wishes were likely to be fulfilled, she told herself to forget the professor; there were plenty of other things to think about.

It was a pity that she couldn't think of a single one of them—within minutes he was back in her thoughts, making havoc of her good resolutions.

She was in the professor's thoughts too, much to his annoyance. The tiresome girl, he reflected, and why do I have this urge to do something to improve her life? For all I know she is perfectly content with the way she lives. She is young; she could get a job wherever she wishes, buy herself some decent clothes, meet people, find a boyfriend. All of which was nonsense, and he knew it. She deserved better, he considered, a home and work away from London and that pokey little house.

But even if she had the chance to change he knew that she wouldn't leave her home. He had liked her parents; they had fallen on bad times through no fault of her father. Of course, if he could get a post as a schoolmaster again away from London that would solve the problem. Ermentrude could leave St Luke's and shake the dust of London from her well-polished but well-worn shoes.

The professor put down the notes he was studying, took off his spectacles, polished them and put them back onto his nose. He would miss her.

'This is ridiculous,' he said to himself. 'I don't even know the girl.'

He forebore from adding that he knew Ermentrude as if she were himself, had done since he had first seen her. He was going to marry Anneliese, he reminded himself, and Ermentrude had demonstrated often enough that she had no interest in him. He was too old for her, and she regarded him in a guarded manner which made it plain that in her eyes he was no more than someone she met occasionally at work…

The professor was an honourable man; he had asked Anneliese to marry him—not loving her but knowing that she would make a suitable wife—and there was no possible reason to break his word. Even if Ermentrude loved him, something which was so unlikely that it was laughable.

He gave his lectures, dealt with patients he had been asked to see, arranged appointments for the future and always at the back of his mind was Ermentrude. She would never be his wife but there was a good deal he could do to make her life happier, and, when he got back once more to Chelsea, he set about doing it.

Chapter 4

Despite her resolutions, Emmy missed the professor. She had looked forward to seeing him going to and fro at St Luke's, even if he took no notice of her. He was there, as it were, and she felt content just to know that he was. Of course, she thought about him. She thought about Anneliese too, doubtless getting ready for a grand wedding, spending money like water, secure in the knowledge that she was going to marry a man who could give her everything she could want.

'I only hope she deserves it,' said Emmy, talking to herself and surprising the porter who had brought her coffee.

'If it's women you're talking about, love, you can take it from me they don't deserve nothing. Take my word for it; I'm a married man.'

'Go on with you!' said Emmy. 'I've seen your wife, she's pretty, and you've got that darling baby.'

'I could have done worse.' He grinned at her. 'There's always an exception to every rule, so they say.'

'No sign of our handsome professor,' said Audrey when she came on duty. 'Having fun in Birmingham, I shouldn't wonder. Won't be able to do that once he's a married man, will he? Perhaps he's going straight over to Holland and not coming back here until after Christmas.'

'Christmas is still six weeks away.'

'Don't tell me that he can't do what he chooses when he wants to.'

'I think that if he has patients and work here he'll stay until he's no longer needed. I know you don't like him, but everyone else does.'

'Including you,' said Audrey with a snigger.

'Including me,' said Emmy soberly.

Emmy was on night duty again. Her mother was home and so was her father, now inspecting various schools in outer London and coming home tired each evening. He didn't complain, but the days were long and often unsatisfactory. He had been told that the man he had replaced would be returning to work within a week or ten days, which meant that he would be returning to his badly paid teaching post. Thank heaven, he thought, that Emmy had her job too. Somehow they would manage.

Emmy had dealt with the usual early enquiries, and except for internal calls the evening was quiet. She took out her knitting—a pullover for her father's Christmas present—and began the complicated business of picking up stitches around the neck. She was halfway round it when she became aware of the professor standing behind her. Her hand jerked and she dropped a clutch of stitches.

'There, look what you've made me do!' she said, and turned round to look at him.

'You knew that I was here?' He sounded amused. 'But I hadn't spoken…'

'No, well—I knew there was someone.' She was mumbling, not looking at him now, remembering all at once that what was fast becoming friendship must be nipped in the bud.

She began to pick up the dropped stitches, and wished that the silent switchboard would come alive. Since he just stood there, apparently content with the silence, she asked in a polite voice, 'I hope that Charlie is well, sir?'

The professor, equally polite, assured her that his dog was in excellent health, and registered the 'sir' with a rueful lift of the eyebrows.

'Your kitten?' he asked in his turn.

'Oh, he's splendid, and George and Snoodles take such care of him.'

The professor persevered. 'Has he a name?'

'Enoch. Mother had a cat when she was a little girl called Enoch, and now he's clean and brushed he's the same colour. Ginger with a white waistcoat.' She added, 'Sir.'

The professor saw that he was making no headway; Ermentrude was making it plain that she was being polite for politeness' sake. Apparently she had decided that their friendship, such as it was, was to go no further. Just as well, he reflected, I'm getting far too interested in the girl. He bade her a cool goodnight and went away, and Emmy picked up her knitting once more.

A most unsatisfactory meeting, she reflected. On the other hand it had been satisfactory, hadn't it? She had let him see that their casual camaraderie had been just that—casual, engendered by circumstances. He was shortly going to be married, she reminded herself; he would become immersed in plans for his wedding with Anneliese.

She was mistaken in this. The professor was immersed in plans, but not to do with his future. The wish to transform Emmy's dull life into one with which she would be happy had driven him to do something about it.

He had friends everywhere; it wasn't too difficult to meet a man he had known at Cambridge and who was now headmaster of a boys' prep school in Dorset. The professor was lucky: a schoolmaster had been forced to leave owing to ill health and there was, he was told cautiously, a vacancy. 'But for the right man. I've only your word for it that this Foster's OK.'

The headmaster wrote in his notebook and tore out the page. 'He can give me a ring…'

The professor shook his head. 'That wouldn't do. If he or his daughter discovered that I was behind it, he'd refuse at once.'

'Got a daughter, has he? Thought you were getting married.'

The professor smiled. 'You can rule out any romantic thoughts, but I would like to help her get out of a life she isn't enjoying; away from London. To do that her father must get a post somewhere in the country, for that's where she belongs.'

His friend sighed. 'Tell you what I'll do. I'll concoct a tale, you know the kind of thing—I'd met someone who knew someone who knew this Foster, and as there was a vacancy et cetera… Will that do? But remember, Ruerd, if I contract any one of these horrible conditions you're so famous for treating, I shall expect the very best treatment—free!'

'A promise I hope I shall never need to keep.' They shook hands, and his friend went home and told his wife that Ruerd ter Mennolt seemed to be putting himself to a great deal of trouble for some girl or other at St Luke's.

'I thought he was marrying that Anneliese of his?'

'And still is, it seems. He was always a man to help lame dogs over stiles.'

'Anneliese doesn't like dogs,' said his wife.

It was the very next day when the letter arrived, inviting Mr Foster to present himself for an interview. And it couldn't have come at a better time, for with the same post came a notice making him redundant from his teaching post on the first of December. They sat over their supper, discussing this marvellous stroke of luck.

'Though we mustn't count our chickens before they are hatched,' said Mr Foster. 'How fortunate that I have Thursday free; I'll have to go by train.'

Emmy went into the kitchen and took the biscuit tin down from the dresser-shelf and counted the money inside. It was money kept for emergencies, and this was an emergency of the best kind.

'Will there be a house with the job?' she asked. 'Littleton Mangate—that's a small village, isn't it? Somewhere in the Blackmore Vale.' She smiled widely. 'Oh, Father, it's almost too good to be true…'

'So we mustn't bank on it until I've had my interview, Emmy. Once that's over and I've been appointed we can make plans.'

The next day, replying sedately to the professor's grave greeting, Emmy almost choked in her efforts not to tell him about the good news. Time enough, she told herself, when her father had got the job. Only then, too, if he asked her.

'Which he won't,' she told George as she brushed him before taking him on his evening trot.

The professor, it seemed, was reluctant as she was to resume their brief conversations. He never failed to greet her if he should pass the switchboard, but that was all. She felt bereft and vaguely resentful, which, seeing that she had wanted it that way, seemed rather hard on him. But at least it boosted her resolve to forget him. Something not easily done since she saw him willy-nilly on most days.

Her father, in his best suit, a neatly typed CV in his coat pocket, left on Thursday morning on an early train, leaving Emmy to fidget through her day's work, alternately positive that her father would get the post and then plunged into despair because he had been made redundant, and finding a job would be difficult, perhaps impossible. In a moment of rare self-pity she saw herself sitting in front of the switchboard for the rest of her working life.

The professor, catching sight of her dejected back view, was tempted to stop and speak to her, but he didn't. A helping hand was one thing, getting involved with her spelt danger. It was a good thing, he reflected, that he would be going over to Holland shortly. He must see as much of Anneliese as possible.

The bus ride home that evening took twice as long as usual, or so it seemed to Emmy. She burst into the house at length and rushed into the kitchen.

Her mother and father were there, turning to look at her with happy faces. 'You've got it,' said Emmy. 'I knew you would, Father. I can't believe it.'

She flung her coat onto a chair, poured herself a cup of tea from the pot and said, 'Tell me all about it. Is there a house? When do you start? Did you like the headmaster?'

'I've been accepted,' said Mr Foster. 'But my references still have to be checked. There's a house, a very nice one, a converted lodge in the school grounds. I am to take over as soon as possible as they are short of a form master. There are still three weeks or so of the term.'

'So you'll be going in a day or two? And Mother? Is the house furnished?'

'No. Curtains and carpets…'

Mr Foster added slowly, 'Your Mother and I have been talking it over. You will have to give a month's notice, will you not? Supposing we have as much furniture as possible sent to Dorset, would you stay on for the last month, Emmy? Could you bear to do that? We'll take George and Snoodles and Enoch with us. The house can be put up for sale at once. There's little chance of it selling quickly, but one never knows. Could you do that? In the meantime your mother will get the house at Littleton Mangate habitable. We can spend Christmas together...'

Emmy agreed at once. She didn't much like the idea of living alone in a half-empty house, but it would be for a few weeks, no more. The idea of leaving St Luke's gave her a lovely feeling of freedom.

'Money?' she asked.

'The bank will give me a loan against this house.' Her father frowned. 'This isn't an ideal arrangement, Emmy, but we really haven't much choice. If you give a month's notice you'll be free by Christmas, and in the meantime there is always the chance that the house will sell.'

'I think that's a splendid idea, Father. When do you start? Almost at once? Mother and I can start packing up and she can join you in a few days. I'll only need a bed and a table and chairs. There's that man—Mr Stokes—at the end of the street. He does removals.'

'I'm not sure that we should leave you,' said her mother worriedly. 'You're sure you don't mind? We can't think what else to do. There's so little time.'

'I'll be quite all right, Mother. It's for such a short time anyway. It's all so exciting...'

They spent the rest of the evening making lists, deciding what to take and what to leave. Tired and excited by the time she got to her bed, Emmy's last waking thought was that once she had left St Luke's she would never see the professor again.

Going to work the next morning, she thought that perhaps she would tell him of the unexpected change in her life.

However, he didn't give her the chance. Beyond an

austere good morning he had nothing to say to her, and later, when he left the hospital, he had a colleague with him.

Oh, well, said Emmy to herself, I can always tell him tomorrow.'

Only he wasn't there in the morning; it wasn't until the day was half-done that she heard that he had gone to Holland.

She told herself that it didn't matter at all, that there was no reason to expect him to be interested in her future. She had already given in her notice and would not tell anyone about it.

Back home that evening, she found her mother already busy, turning out drawers and cupboards. 'Your father's arranged for Mr Stokes to collect the furniture in three days' time.' She beamed at Emmy. 'Oh, darling, it's all so wonderful. I don't believe it. Your father is so happy; so am I. It is a great pity that you can't come with us. I hate the idea of you being here on your own.'

Emmy, wrapping up the best china in newspaper and stowing it carefully in a tea chest, paused to say, 'Don't worry Mother. I'll be working all day, and by the time I get back here and have a meal it'll be time to go to bed—the days will fly by. Won't it be lovely having Christmas away from here?'

Her mother paused in stacking books. 'You've hated it here, haven't you, darling? So have I—so has your father. But we can forget all this once we're at Littleton Mangate. Just think, too, when we've sold this house there'll be some money to spend. Enough for you to go to a school of embroidery or whatever else you want to do. You'll meet people of your own age, too.'

Emmy nodded and smiled and, much against her will, thought about the professor.

He, too, was thinking about her, not wishing to but unable to prevent his thoughts going their own way. It was easier to put her to the back of his head while he was at the various hospitals—Leiden, the Hague, Amsterdam, Rotterdam. There were patients for him in all of these, and he was able to dismiss any thoughts other than those to do with his work while he was in the hospitals consulting, examining, deciding on treatment, seeing, in some cases, anxious relations and reassuring patients.

His days were long and busy but when he drove himself home each evening he had time to think. Anneliese was in France, but she would be back soon and he would spend his leisure with her. But in the meantime his time was his own.

Each evening he turned into the drive leading to his house and sighed with content at the sight of it. It was on the edge of a village, a stately old house behind the dunes, the North Sea stretching away to the horizon, magnificent stretch of sand sweeping into the distance, north and south. The house had been built by his great-great-grandfather, and was a solid edifice, secure against the bitter winter winds, its rooms large, the windows tall and narrow, and the front door solid enough to withstand a seige.

Ruerd had been born there, and between schools, universities and hospital appointments went back to it as often as he could. His two sisters and younger brother—the former married, the latter still at medical school—were free to come and go as they wished, but the house was his now that his father, a retired surgeon, and his mother, lived in den Haag.

He had had a tiring day in Rotterdam, and the lighted windows welcomed him as he got out of the car. They were not the only welcome either—the door was opened and the dogs dashed out to greet him, the wolfhound and the Jack Russell pushing and jostling to get near their master. They all went into the house together, into the large square hall with its black and white marble floor, its plain plastered walls hung with paintings in ornate gilded frames.

They were halfway across it when they were joined by an elderly man, small and rotund, who trotted ahead of them to open double doors to one side of the hall.

The room the professor entered was large and high-ceilinged, with a great hooded fireplace on either side of which were vast sofas with a Regency mahogany centre table between them. There were two tub wing armchairs with a walnut card table between them, and a couple of Dutch mahogany and marquetry armchairs on either side of a Georgian breakfast table set between two of the long windows overlooking the grounds at the back of the house.

Against the walls there were walnut display cabinets, their shelves filled with silver and porcelain, reflecting the light from the cut-glass chandelier and the ormolu wall lights. It was a beautiful room, and magnificent; it was also lived in. There were bowls of flowers here and there, a pile of newspapers and magazines on one of the tables, a dog basket to the side of the fireplace.

The professor settled his vast frame in one of the armchairs, allowed the Jack Russell to scramble onto his knee and the wolfhound to drape himself over his feet, and poured himself a drink from the tray on the table beside him. A quiet evening, he thought with satisfaction, and, since he wasn't due anywhere until the following afternoon, a long walk with the dogs in the morning.

He was disturbed by his manservant, who came bearing letters on a salver, looking apologetic.

The professor picked them up idly. 'No phone calls, Cokker?'

'Juffrouw van Moule telephoned, to remind you that you will be dining with her family tomorrow evening.'

'Oh, Lord, I had forgotten…thank you, Cokker.'

'Anna wishes to know if half an hour is sufficient for you before dinner, *mijnheer.*'

'As soon as she likes, Cokker. It's good to be home…'

'And good to have you here,' said Cokker. They smiled at each other, for Cokker had been with the family when the professor had been born and now, a sprightly sixty-year-old, had become part and parcel of it.

The professor took the dogs for a walk after dinner, across several acres of his own grounds and into the country lane beyond. It was a chilly night, but there was a moon and stars and later there would be a frost.

He strolled along, thinking about Ermentrude. By now her father would know if he had the post he had collocated. No doubt Ermentrude would tell him all about it when he got back to St Luke's. She would give in her notice, of course, and go to Dorset with her parents and he wouldn't see her again. Which was just as well. It was, he told himself, merely a passing attraction—not even that. All he had done was to take the opportunity to improve her life.

'She will be quite happy in the country again,' he told Solly, the wolfhound. He stooped to pick up Tip, who was getting tired, and tucked the little dog under one arm. He turned for home, dismissed Ermentrude from his mind and steered his thoughts to his future bride.

Later, lying in his great four-poster bed, Ermentrude was there again, buried beneath his thoughts and contriving to upset them.

'The girl's a nuisance,' said the professor to the empty room. 'I hope that by the time I get back to St Luke's she will be gone.'

His well-ordered life, he reflected, was being torn in shreds by a plain-faced girl who made no bones about letting him see that she had no interest in him. He slept badly and awoke in an ill humour which he had difficulty in shaking off during the day.

It was only that evening, sitting beside Anneliese at her parents' dining table, joining in the talk with the other guests, aware that Anneliese was looking particularly beautiful, that he managed to dismiss Ermentrude from his mind.

Anneliese was at her best. She knew that she looked delightful, and she exerted all her charm. She was intelligent, asking him all the right questions about his work at the hospitals he was visiting, talking knowledgeably about the health service in Holland, listening with apparent interest when he outlined the same service in England.

'Such a pity you have to go back there before Christmas. But of course you'll be back here then, won't you? Mother and I will come and stay for a while; we can discuss the wedding.'

She was clever enough not to say more than that, but

went on lightly, 'Do you see any more of that funny little thing you befriended at St Luke's?'

Before he could answer, she said, 'Ruerd got involved in a bomb explosion in London.' She addressed the table at large. 'It must have been very exciting, and there was this girl who works there whom he took home—I suppose she was in shock. I saw her when I was staying in London. So plain, my dears, and all the wrong clothes. Not at all his type. Was she, Ruerd?' She turned to smile at him.

The professor had his anger nicely in check. 'Miss Foster is a brave young lady. I think perhaps none of us know enough of her to discuss her. It is quite difficult to keep calm and do whatever it is you have to do when there's an emergency, and to keep on doing it until you're fit to drop. In such circumstances, it hardly matters whether one is plain or pretty, old or young.'

Anneliese gave a little laugh. 'Oh, Ruerd, I didn't mean to be unkind. The poor girl. And we, all sitting here in comfort talking about something we know very little about.' She touched his arm. 'Forgive me and tell us what you think of the new hospital. You were there yesterday, weren't you?'

The rest of the evening passed off pleasantly enough, but, driving himself home, the professor reflected that he hadn't enjoyed it. He had never liked Anneliese's family and friends overmuch, supposing vaguely that once they were married she would welcome his more serious friends, live the quiet life he enjoyed. He tried to imagine them married and found it impossible.

She had seemed so suitable when he'd asked her to marry him—interested in his work, anxious to meet his friends, telling him how she loved to live in the country. 'With children, of course, and dogs and horses,' she had added, and he had believed her.

Yet that very evening he had stood by, while she talked to some of her friends, and listened to her complaining sharply about the nuisance of having to visit a cousin with young children. 'They're such a bore,' she had said.

Her mother, a formidable matron who enjoyed dictating to everyone around her, had chimed in, saying, 'Children should stay in the nursery until they're fit to mix with their elders. I have always advised young girls of my acquaintance that that is the best for them. Besides, they can hamper one's life so. A good nanny is the answer.' She had smiled around at her listeners, saying, 'And I have given Anneliese the same advice, have I not, my dear?'

Her words, echoing in his head, filled him with disquiet.

Emmy meanwhile was busy. She was happy too. At least she told herself that she was several times a day. To live in the country again would be heaven—only would it be quite heaven if she was never to see the professor again? It wouldn't, but there was nothing to be done about that, and it was, after all, something she had wanted badly. Besides that, her mother and father were over the moon. She applied herself to the packing up with a cheerful energy which wasn't quite genuine, buoyed up by her mother's obvious delight.

Mr Stokes, with his rather decrepit van, and an old man and a young boy to help him, stowed the furniture tidily, leaving Emmy's bedroom intact, and a table and two chairs in the kitchen, as well as the bare necessities for living.

'It won't be for long,' said Emmy cheerfully. 'There are two lots of people coming to view the house tomorrow; I'm sure it will be sold by the time I leave.'

Her mother said anxiously, 'You will get a hot meal at the hospital, Emmy? And do keep the electric fire on while you are in the house. Empty houses are so cold.' She frowned. 'I do wonder if there might have been some other way…'

'Stop worrying, Mother. I only need a bed and somewhere to have breakfast.' She didn't mention the long evenings alone and the solitary suppers. After all, it was for such a short time.

She was on night duty again, so she was there to see her mother, sitting beside Mr Stokes, leave for their new home. After they had gone she went into the kitchen and made herself some coffee. The house looked shabbier than ever now that it was almost empty, and without the animals it was so quiet. She put everything ready for an evening meal and went to bed. She was already some days into her notice. It was a satisfying thought as she dropped off. Everything was going according to plan, she thought with satisfaction.

Only she was wrong. Audrey hardly gave her time to get her coat off the following evening before bursting into furious speech.

'The nerve,' she cried. 'And there's nothing to be done about it—or so I'm told. Reorganisation, indeed, necessary amalgamation to cut expenses…'

Emmy took the envelope Audrey was offering her. 'What's the matter? What are you talking about?'

'Read it for yourself. I'm going home—and don't expect to see me tomorrow.'

She stomped away and Emmy sat down and read the letter in the envelope.

There were to be changes, she read, and regretfully her services would no longer be required. With the opening of the new hospital across the river, St Luke's and Bennett's hospitals would amalgamate and the clerical staff from Bennett's would take over various functions, of which the switchboard was one. The letter pointed out that she would be given a reference, and the likelihood of her getting a new job was high. It ended with a mealy-mouthed paragraph thanking her for her loyal services which as she had already given notice, would terminate on Friday next.

She read it through again, carefully, in case she had missed something. But it was clear enough—in two days' time she would be jobless.

She could, of course, join her mother and father. On the other hand there was far more chance of the house being sold if there was someone there to keep the estate agents on their toes and show people around. By the end of the night she had decided to say nothing to her parents. She would be able to manage on her own and she would have a week's salary, and surely an extra month's money, since she had been given barely two days' notice.

It would have been nice to have had someone to have talked things over with. The professor would have been ideal...

As it was, when the porter brought her coffee she forgot her own troubles when he told her that he was to go too. 'They've offered me a job in that new place across the river—less money, and takes me much longer to get to work. Haven't got much choice, though, have I? With a wife and baby to look after?' He glanced at her. 'What'll you do, Emmy?'

'Me? Oh, I'll be all right. Audrey was very angry...'

'You bet she was. Proper blew her top, she did. Didn't do no good. Wrongful dismissal, she said, but it seems it isn't. It's like when a firm goes bankrupt and everyone just goes home. If there's no money, see? What else is there to do?'

'Well, good luck with your job, anyway, and thanks for the coffee.'

Emmy hadn't believed Audrey when she had said that she wouldn't be there in the morning, but she had meant it. Emmy, going off duty late because a relief telephonist had had to be called in, was too tired to notice the icy rain and the leaden sky. Home, she thought, even if it is only my bedroom and a table and chairs.

Only they didn't look very welcoming when she let herself into the empty house. She boiled an egg, made toast and a pot of tea and took herself off to bed. When she had had a sleep she would mull over the turn of events and see how best to deal with it. One thing was certain: there was no way of changing it. And, being a sensible girl, she put her head on the pillow and slept.

She had time enough to think when she got up in the late afternoon. It was still raining and almost dark, and she was glad they had left the curtains hanging and some of the carpets. She showered, made tea and sat down in the kitchen to think. She would call into the estate agents on her way home in the morning and spur them on a bit. The market was slow, they had told her father, but the house was small, in fairly good order and soundly built, like all the other houses in the row. Its selling price was modest, well within the reach of anyone prudent enough to have saved a little capital and who could get a mortgage.

She allowed herself to dream a bit. There would be a little money—not much, but perhaps enough for all of them to have new clothes, perhaps have a holiday— although being in Dorset would be like a holiday itself. She would get a chance to go to a needlework school— night classes, perhaps? Start a small arts and crafts shop on her own? The possibilities were endless. She got her supper presently, and went to work for the last time.

It was a busy night, and when it was over she bade goodbye to those she had worked with and left the hospital for the last time. She had her pay packet in her purse, and an extra month in lieu of notice, and she handed over to her older colleague, who told her that she had been working for the NHS for more than twenty years.

'I don't know what I would have done if I had been made redundant,' she said. 'I've an elderly mother and father who live with me. We make ends meet, but only just—to be out of work would have been a catastrophe.'

It was heartening to find on her way home that there had been several enquiries about the house. The agent, a weasel-faced young man she didn't much like, had arranged for them to inspect the house at any time they wished.

'You'll be there,' he told her airily. 'So it really doesn't matter when they call, if they do.'

'I can't be there all day,' Emmy told him, and was silenced by him.

'You're not on the phone—stands to reason, doesn't it? Someone will have to be there.'

'Will you ask anyone who wants to look round the house to come after one o'clock? I will stay at home for the rest of the day.'

'Suit yourself, Miss Foster. The two parties interested said they'd call in some time today.'

To go to bed was impossible; one never knew, whoever was coming might decide to buy the house. Emmy had her breakfast, tidied away the dishes and sat down on the one comfortable chair in the kitchen. Of course she went to sleep almost at once, and woke to the sound of someone thumping the door knocker and ringing the bell.

The middle-aged couple she admitted looked sour.

'Took your time, didn't you?' observed the man grumpily, and pushed past her into the hall. He and his meek-looking wife spent the next ten minutes looking round and returned to Emmy, who was waiting in the kitchen after taking them on their first survey.

'Pokey, that's what it is,' declared the man. 'You'll be lucky to sell the place at half the asking price.'

He went away, taking his wife, who hadn't said a word, with him. Emmy hadn't said anything either. There seemed to be no point in annoying the man more than necessary. There would be several more like him, she guessed.

The second couple came late in the afternoon. They made a leisurely tour and Emmy began to feel hopeful, until the woman remarked, 'It's a lot better than some we've seen. Not that we can buy a house, but it gives us some idea of what we could get if we had the money.' She smiled at Emmy. 'Nice meeting you.'

Not a very promising start, decided Emmy, locking the door behind them. Better luck tomorrow. Though perhaps people didn't come on a Saturday.

She felt more hopeful after a good night's sleep. After all, it was early days; houses didn't sell all that fast. Only it would be splendid if someone decided to buy the place before she joined her parents.

No one came. Not the next day. She had gone for a walk in the morning and then spent the rest of the day in the kitchen, listening to her small radio and knitting. Monday, she felt sure, would bring more possible buyers.

No one came, nor did they come on Tuesday, Wednesday or Thursday. She wrote a cheerful letter to her parents on Friday, did her morning's shopping and spent the rest of the day waiting for the doorbell to ring. Only it didn't.

The professor, back in London, striding into St Luke's ready for a day's work, paused on his way. While not admitting it, he was looking forward to seeing Emmy again. He hoped that all had gone according to his plan and that her father had got the job the professor's friend had found for him. Emmy would have given her notice by now. He would miss her. And a good thing that she was going, he reminded himself.

He was brought up short by the sight of the older woman sitting in Emmy's chair. He wished her a civil good morning, and asked, 'Miss Foster? Is she ill?'

'Ill? No, sir. Left. Made redundant with several others. There's been a cutting down of staff.'

He thanked her and went on his way, not unduly worried. Ermentrude would have gone to Dorset with her father and mother. He must find time to phone his friend and make sure that all had gone according to plan. She would be happy there, he reflected. And she would forget him. Only he wouldn't forget her...

He left the hospital rather earlier than usual, and on a sudden impulse, instead of going home, drove through the crowded streets and turned into the street where Emmy lived. Outside the house he stopped the car. There was a FOR SALE board fastened to the wall by the door, and the downstairs curtains were drawn across. There was a glimmer of light showing, so he got out of the car and knocked on the door.

Emmy put down the can of beans she was opening. At last here was someone come to see the house. She turned on the light in the hall and went to open the door, and, being a prudent girl, left the safety chain on. Peering round it, recognising the vast expanse of waistcoat visible, her heart did a happy little somersault.

'It is I,' said the professor impatiently, and, when she had slid back the chain, came into the narrow hall, squashing her against a wall.

Emmy wormed her way into a more dignified stance. 'Hello, sir,' she said. 'Are you back in England?' She caught his eye. 'What I mean is, I'm surprised to see you. I didn't expect to...'

He had seen the empty room and the almost bare kitchen beyond. He took her arm and bustled her into the kitchen, sat her in a chair and said, 'Tell me why you are here alone in an empty house. Your parents?'

'Well, it's a long story...'

'I have plenty of time,' he told her. 'And I am listening.'

Chapter 5

Emmy told him without embellishments. 'So you see it's all turned out marvellously. We just have to sell this house—that's why I'm here. We thought I'd have to give a month's notice, and it seemed a splendid idea for me to stay on until I could leave and try and sell the house at the same time. Only being made redundant was a surprise. I've not told Father, of course.'

'You are here alone, with no furniture, no comforts?'

'Oh, I've got my bed upstairs, and a cupboard, and I don't need much. Of course, we thought I'd be at the hospital all day or all night. Actually,' she told him, wanting to put a good light on things, 'It's worked out very well, for I stay at home each day from one o'clock so that I can show people round…'

'You get many prospective buyers?'

'Well, not many, not every day. It isn't a very attractive house.'

The professor agreed silently to this. 'You will join your parents for Christmas? Have you a job in mind to go to?'

'Yes. Well, I've hardly had time, have I?' she asked reasonably. Then added, 'Perhaps I'll be able to take a course in embroidery and needlework…'

She didn't go on; he didn't want to know her plans. She asked instead, 'Did you have a pleasant time in Holland?'

'Yes. I'll wait here while you put a few things into a bag, Ermentrude. You will come back with me.'

'Indeed, I won't. Whatever next? I'm quite all right here, thank you. Besides, I must be here to show people round.' She added on a sudden thought, 'Whatever would your fiancée think? I mean, she's not to know that we don't like each other.' Emmy went bright pink. 'I haven't put that very well…'

'No, you haven't. You have, however, made it quite plain that you do not need my help.'

The professor got to his feet. He said coldly, 'Goodbye, Ermentrude.' And, while she was still searching for the right reply, let himself out of the house.

Emmy listened to the car going away down the street; she made almost no sound. She sat where she was for quite some time, doing her best not to cry.

Presently she got up and got her supper, and since there was nothing to do she went to bed.

She wasn't sure what woke her up. She sat up in bed, listening; the walls were thin, it could have been Mr Grant or Mrs Grimes dropping something or banging a door. She lay down again and then shot up once more. The noise, a stealthy shuffling, was downstairs.

She didn't give herself time to feel frightened. She got out of bed quietly, put on her dressing gown and slippers and, seizing the only weapon handy—her father's umbrella which had somehow got left behind—she opened her door and peered out onto the landing. Someone was there, someone with a torch, and they had left the front door open too.

The nerve, reflected Emmy, in a rage, and swept downstairs, switching on the landing light as she did so. The man was in the empty sitting room, but he came out fast and reached the hall. He was young, his face half hidden by a scarf, a cap pulled down over his eyes and, after his first shock, he gave a nasty little laugh.

'Cor, lummy— An empty 'ouse an' a girl. Alone, are you? Well, let's 'ave yer purse, and make it quick.'

Emmy poked him with the umbrella. 'You get out of this house and you make it quick,' she told him. She gave him another prod. 'Go on...'

He made to take the umbrella from her, but this time she whacked him smartly over the head so that he howled with pain.

'Out,' said Emmy in a loud voice which she hoped hid her fright. She switched on the hall light now, hoping that someone, even at two o'clock in the morning, would see it. But the man, she was glad to see, had retreated to the door. She followed him, umbrella at the ready, and he walked backwards into the street.

Rather puffed up with her success at getting rid of him, she followed him, unaware that the man's mate was standing beside the door, out of sight. She heard him call out before something hard hit her on the head and she keeled over.

She didn't hear them running away since for the moment she had been knocked out. But Mr Grant, trotting to the window to see why there was a light shining into the street, saw them. Old though he was, he made his way downstairs and out of his house to where Emmy lay. Emmy didn't answer when he spoke to her, and she was very pale. He crossed the road and rang the bell of the house opposite. It sounded very loud at that time of the night. He rang again, and presently a window was opened and the teenager hung his head out.

'Come down, oh, do come down—Ermentrude has been hurt.'

The head disappeared and a moment later the boy, in his coat and boots, came out. 'Thieves? Take anything, did they? Not that there's anything to take.' He bent over Emmy. 'I'll get her inside and the door shut.'

He was a big lad, and strong; he picked Emmy up and carried her into the kitchen and set her in a chair. 'Put the kettle on,' he suggested. 'I'll be back in a tick; I'll get my phone.'

As he came back into the kitchen Emmy opened her eyes. She said crossly, 'I've got the most awful headache. Someone hit me.'

'You're right there. Who shall I ring? You'd better have a doctor—and the police.' He stood looking at her for a moment, and was joined by Mr Grant. 'You can't stay here, that's for certain. Got any friends? Someone to look after you?'

Mr Grant had brought her a wet towel, and she was holding it to her head. She felt sick and frightened and there was no one... Yes, there was. He might not like her, but he would help and she remembered his number; she had rung it time and again from the hospital.

She said muzzily, 'Yes, there's someone, if you'd tell

him. Ask him if he would come.' She gave the boy the number and closed her eyes.

'He'll be along in fifteen minutes,' said the boy. 'Lucky the streets are empty at this time of night. Did they take anything?'

Emmy shook her head, and then wished she hadn't. 'No. There's nothing to take; my purse and bag are upstairs and they didn't get that far.' She said tiredly, 'Thank you both for coming to help me; I'm very grateful.'

As far as she was concerned, she thought, they can make all the noise they like and I'll never even think of complaining.

Mr Grant gave her a cup of tea and she tried to drink it, holding it with both shaky hands while the boy phoned the police. Then there was nothing to do but wait. The boy and Mr Grant stood drinking tea, looking rather helplessly at her.

'I'm going to be sick,' said Emmy suddenly, and lurched to the sink.

Which was how the professor found her a couple of minutes later.

The boy had let him in. 'You the bloke she told me to phone?' he asked suspiciously.

'Yes. I'm a doctor. Have you called the police?'

'Yes. She's in the kitchen being sick.'

Emmy was past caring about anyone or anything. When she felt the professor's large, cool hand on her wrist, she mumbled, 'I knew you'd come. I feel sick, and I've got a headache.'

He opened his bag. 'I'm not surprised; you have a bump the size of a hen's egg on your head.' His hands were very gentle. 'Keep still, Ermentrude, while I take a look.'

She hardly felt his hands after that, and while he dealt with the lump and the faint bleeding he asked what had happened.

Mr Grant and the boy both told him at once, talking together.

'The police?'

'They said they were on their way.'

The professor said gravely, 'It is largely due to the quick thinking and courage of both of you that Ermentrude isn't more severely injured. I'll get her to hospital just as soon as the police get here.'

They came a few minutes later, took statements from Mr Grant and the boy, agreed with the professor that Ermentrude wasn't in a fit state to say anything at the moment and agreed to interview her later. 'We will lock the door and keep the key at the station.' The officer swept his gaze round the bare room. 'No one lives here?'

'Yes, me,' said Ermentrude. 'Just for a few weeks—until someone wants to buy it. Do you want me to explain?' She opened her eyes and closed them again.

'Wait until you know what you're talking about,' advised the professor bracingly. He spoke to one of the officers. 'Miss Foster is staying here for a short time; her parents have moved and she has stayed behind to settle things up.' He added, 'You will want to see her, of course. She will be staying at my house.' He gave the address, heedless of Emmy's mutterings.

'Now, if I might have a blanket in which to wrap her, I'll take her straight to St Luke's. I'm a consultant there. She needs to be X-rayed.'

Emmy heard this in a muzzy fashion. It wouldn't do

at all; she must say something. She lifted her head too quickly, and then bent it over the sink just in time. The professor held her head in a matter-of-fact way while the others averted their gaze.

'The blanket?' asked the professor again, and the boy went upstairs and came back with her handbag and the quilt from Emmy's bed. The professor cleaned her up in a businesslike manner, wrapped her in the quilt and picked her up.

'If I'm not at my home I'll be at the hospital.' He thanked Mr Grant and the boy, bade the officers a civil goodnight, propped Emmy in the back of the car and, when she began to mumble a protest, told her to be quiet.

He said it in a very gentle voice, though. She closed her eyes, lying back in the comfortable seat, and tried to forget her raging headache.

At the hospital she was whisked straight to X-Ray. She was vaguely aware of the radiographer complaining good-naturedly to the professor and of lying on a trolley for what seemed hours.

'No harm done,' said the professor quietly in her ear. 'I'm going to see to that lump, and then you can be put to bed and sleep.'

She was wheeled to Casualty then, and lay quietly while he bent over her, peering into her eyes, putting a dressing on her head. She was drowsy now, but his quiet voice mingling with Sister's brisk tone was soothing. She really didn't care what happened next.

When he lifted her into the car once more, she said, 'Not here…' But since the professor took no notice of her she closed her eyes again. She had been given a pill to swallow in Casualty; her headache was almost bearable and she felt nicely sleepy.

Beaker was waiting when the professor reached his house, carried Emmy indoors and asked, 'You got Mrs Burge to come round? I had no time to give you details. If I carry Miss Foster upstairs perhaps she will help her to bed.'

'She's upstairs waiting, sir. What a to-do. The poor young lady—knocked out, was she?'

'Yes. I'll tell you presently, Beaker. I could do with a drink, and I expect you could, too. Did Mrs Burge make any objections?'

'Not her! I fetched her like you told me to, and she'll stay as long as she's wanted.'

The professor was going upstairs with Emmy, fast asleep now, in his arms. 'Splendid.'

Mrs Burge met him on the small landing. 'In the small guest room, sir. Just you lay her down on the bed and I'll make her comfortable.'

She was a tall, bony woman with hair screwed into an old-fashioned bun and a sharp nose. A widow, she had been coming each day to help Beaker for some time now, having let it be known from the outset that through no fault of her own she had fallen on hard times and needed to earn her living.

Beaker got on well with her, and she had developed an admiration for the professor, so that being routed out of her bed in the early hours of the morning was something she bore with equanimity. She said now, 'Just you leave the young lady to me, sir, and go and have a nap—you'll be dead on your feet and a day's work ahead of you.'

The professor said, 'Yes, Mrs Burge,' in a meek

voice, merely adding that he would be up presently just to make sure that Emmy's pulse was steady and that she slept still. 'I know I leave her in good hands,' he told Mrs Burge, and she bridled with pleasure.

For all her somewhat forbidding appearance she was a kind-hearted woman. She tucked Emmy, still sleeping, into bed, dimmed the bedside light and sat down in the comfortable armchair, keeping faithful watch.

'She's not moved,' she told the professor presently. 'Sleeping like a baby.'

He bent over the bed, took Emmy's pulse and felt her head.

'I'll leave these pills for her to take, Mrs Burge. See that she has plenty to drink, and if she wants to eat, so much the better. A couple of days in bed and she'll be quite herself. There's only the mildest of concussions, and the cut will heal quickly.

'I'm going to the hospital in an hour or so and shall be there all day. Ring me if you're worried. Beaker will give you all the assistance you require, and once Ermentrude is awake there is no reason why you shouldn't leave her from time to time. I'll be back presently when I've had breakfast so that you can have yours with Beaker.'

He went away to shower and dress and eat his breakfast and then returned, and Mrs Burge went downstairs to where Beaker was waiting with eggs and bacon.

Emmy hadn't stirred; the professor sat down in a chair, watching her. She suited the room, he decided—quite a small room, but charming with its white furniture, its walls covered with a delicate paper of pale pink roses and soft green leaves. The curtains were white, and the bedspread matched the wallpaper exactly. It was a room he had planned with the help of his younger sister, whose small daughter slept in it when they visited him.

'Though once you're married, Ruerd,' she had told him laughingly, 'you'll need it for your own daughter.'

Emmy, with her hair all over the pillow, looked very young and not at all plain, he decided. When Mrs Burge came back he said a word or two to her, bent over the bed once more and stopped himself just in time from kissing Emmy.

It was late in the morning when Emmy woke, to stare up into Mrs Burge's face. She was on the point of asking 'Where am I?' and remembered that only heroines in books said that. Instead she said, 'I feel perfectly all right; I should like to get up.'

'Not just yet, love. I'm going to bring you a nice little pot of tea and something tasty to eat. You're to sit up a bit if you feel like it. I'll put another pillow behind you. There...'

'I don't remember very clearly,' began Emmy. 'I was taken to the hospital and I went to sleep.'

'Why, you're snug and safe here in Professor ter Mennolt's house, dearie, and me and Beaker are keeping an eye on you. He's gone to the hospital, but he'll be home this evening.'

Emmy sat up too suddenly and winced. 'I can't stay here. There's no one at the house—the estate agent won't know—someone might want to buy it...'

'Leave everything to the professor, ducks. You may be sure he'll have thought of what's to be done.'

Mrs Burge went away and came back presently with a tray daintily laid with fine china—a teapot, cup and saucer, milk and sugar. 'Drink this, there's a good girl,' she said. 'Beaker's getting you a nice little lunch and then you must have another nap.'

'I'm quite able to get up,' said Emmy, to Mrs Burge's departing back.

'You'll stay just where you are until I say you may get out of bed,' said the professor from the door. 'Feeling better?'

'Yes, thank you. I'm sorry I've given you all so much trouble. Couldn't I have stayed in hospital and then gone home?'

'No,' said the professor. 'You will stay here today and tomorrow, and then we will decide what is to be done. I have phoned the estate agent. He has a set of keys for your house and will deal with anyone who wishes to view it. The police will come some time this afternoon to ask you a few questions if you feel up to it.'

'You're very kind, sir, and I'm grateful. I'll be quite well by tomorrow, I can go…'

'Where?' He was leaning over the foot of the bed, watching her.

She took a sip of tea. 'I'm sure Mrs Grimes would put me up.'

'Mrs Grimes—the lady with the powerful voice? Don't talk nonsense, Ermentrude.' He glanced up as Mrs Burge came in with a tray. 'Here is your lunch; eat all of it and drink all the lemonade in that jug. I'll be back this evening.'

He went away and presently out of the house, for he had a clinic that early afternoon. He had missed lunch in order to see Ermentrude, and had only time to swallow a cup of coffee before his first patient arrived.

Emmy ate her lunch under Mrs Burge's watchful eye

and, rather to her surprise, went to sleep again to wake and find another tray of tea, and Mrs Burge shaking out a gossamer-fine nightie.

'If you feel up to it, I'm to help you have a bath, love. You're to borrow one of the professor's sister's nighties. You'll feel a whole lot better.'

'Would someone be able to fetch my clothes so that I can go home tomorrow?' asked Emmy.

'Beaker will run me over this evening. You just tell me what you want and I'll pack it up for you. Professor ter Mennolt's got the keys.'

'Oh, thank you. You're very kind. Were you here when I came last night?'

'Yes—Beaker fetched me—three o'clock in the morning…'

'You must be so tired. I'm quite all right, Mrs Burge. Can't you go home and have a good sleep?'

'Bless you, ducks, I'm as right as a trivet; don't you worry your head about me. Now, how about a bath?'

Getting carefully out of bed, Emmy discovered that she still had a headache and for the moment wished very much to crawl back between the sheets. But the thought of being seen in her present neglected state got her onto her feet and into the adjoining bathroom, and once in the warm, scented water with Mrs Burge sponging her gently she began to feel better.

'I suppose I can't wash my hair?'

'Lawks, no, love. I'll give it a bit of a comb, but I daren't go messing about with it until the professor says so.'

'It's only a small cut,' said Emmy, anxious to look her best.

'And a lump the size of an egg—that'll take a day or

two. A proper crack on the head and no mistake. Lucky that neighbour saw the light and the men running away. It could have been a lot worse,' said Mrs Burge with a gloomy relish.

Emmy, dried, powdered and in the kind of night-gown she had often dreamed of possessing, sat carefully in a chair while Mrs Burge made her bed and shook up her pillows. Once more settled against them, Emmy sighed with relief. It was absurd that a bang on the head should make her feel so tired. She closed her eyes and went to sleep.

Which was how the professor found her when he got home. He stood looking down at her for a long minute, and in turn was watched by Mrs Burge.

They went out of the room together. 'Go home, Mrs Burge,' he told her. 'You've been more than kind. If you could come in tomorrow, I would be most grateful. I must contrive to get Ermentrude down to her parents—they are in Dorset and know nothing of this. They are moving house, and I don't wish to make things more difficult for them than I must. Another day of quiet rest here and I think I might drive her down on the following day...'

Mrs Burge crossed her arms across her thin chest. 'Begging your pardon, sir, but I'll be back here to sleep tonight.'

He didn't smile, but said gravely, 'That would be good of you, Mrs Burge, as long as you find that convenient.'

'It's convenient.' She nodded. 'And I'll make sure the young lady's all right tomorrow.'

'I'm in your debt, Mrs Burge. Come back when you like this evening. Is there a room ready for you?'

'Yes, sir, I saw to that myself.' She hesitated. 'Miss Ermentrude did ask if someone could fetch her clothes. I said I'd go this evening...'

'Tell me when you want to go; I'll drive you over. Perhaps you had better ask her if she needs anything else. Money or papers of any sort.'

Emmy woke presently and, feeling much better, made a list of what she needed and gave it to Mrs Burge.

'I'm off home for a bit,' said that lady. 'But I'll be back this evening. Beaker will bring you up some supper presently. You just lie there like a good girl.'

So Emmy lay back and, despite a slight headache, tried to make plans. Once she had been pronounced fit, she decided, she would go back to the house. She didn't much fancy being there alone, but reassured herself with the thought that lightning never struck twice in the same place... She would go to the estate agents again, too, and there was only another week or so until Christmas now.

Her thoughts were interrupted by the professor and her supper tray.

He greeted her with an impersonal hello. 'Beaker has done his best, so be sure and eat everything.'

He put the tray down, set the bed table across her knees and plumped up her pillows. 'I think you might get up tomorrow—potter round the house, go into the garden—well wrapped-up. I'll take you home the day after.'

'You're very kind, but I must go back to the house, just in case someone wants to buy it. I mean, I can't afford to miss a chance. It'll have to be left empty when I go home at Christmas, and you know how awful houses look when they're empty. So if you don't mind…'

'I do mind, Ermentrude, and you'll do as I say. I'll phone the estate agent if it will set your mind at rest and rearrange things. Do you want me to tell your parents what has happened?'

'Oh, no—they're getting the house straight, and Father's at the school all day so it's taking a bit of time. They've enough to worry about. They don't need to know anyway.'

'Just as you wish. Does Mrs Burge know what to fetch for you?'

'Yes, thank you. I gave her a list. I've only a few clothes there; Mother took the rest with her.'

'Then I'll say goodnight, Ermentrude. Sleep well.'

She was left to eat her supper, a delicious meal Beaker had devised with a good deal of thought. It was he who came to get the tray later, bringing with him fresh lemonade and a fragile china plate with mouth-watering biscuits.

'I make them myself, miss,' he told her, beaming at her praise of the supper. 'Mrs Burge will look in on you when she gets back, with a nice drop of hot milk.'

'Thank you, Beaker, you have been so kind and I'm giving you a lot of extra work.'

'A pleasure, miss.'

'I heard Charlie barking…'

'A spirited dog, miss, and a pleasure to have in the house. Humphrey and he are quite partial to each other. When you come downstairs tomorrow he will be delighted to see you.'

Emmy, left alone, ate some of the biscuits, drank some of the lemonade and thought about the professor.

His household ran on oiled wheels, that was obvious. His Anneliese, when she married him, would have very little to do—a little tasteful flower-arranging perhaps, occasional shopping, although she thought that Beaker might not like that. And of course later there would be the children to look after.

Emmy frowned. She tried to imagine Anneliese nursing a baby, changing nappies or coping with a toddler and failed. She gave up thinking about it and thought about the professor instead, wishing he would come home again and come and see her. She liked him, she decided, even though he was difficult to get to know. Then, why should he wish her to know too much about him? She had no place in his life.

Much later she heard the front door close, and Charlie barking. He and Mrs Burge went home. She lay, watching the door. When it opened Mrs Burge came in, a suitcase in one hand, a glass of milk in the other.

'Still awake? I've brought everything you asked for, and Professor ter Mennolt went to see the estate agent at his home and fixed things up. No one's been to look at the house.' Mrs Burge's sniff implied that she wasn't surprised at that. 'We looked everywhere to make sure that things were just so. And there's some post. Would you like to read it now?'

She put the milk on the bedside table. 'Drink your milk first. It's time you were sleeping.'

Emmy asked hesitantly, 'Are you going home now, Mrs Burge?'

'No, ducks. I'll be here, just across the landing, if you want me. Now I'll just hang up your things...'

Emmy stifled disappointment. There was no reason

why the professor should wish to see her. He must, in fact, be heartily sick of her by now, disrupting his life.

The professor was talking on the phone. Presently he got his coat, ushered Charlie into the back of the car and, with a word to Beaker, drove himself to St Luke's where one of his patients was giving rise to anxiety.

He got home an hour later, ate the dinner which Beaker served him with the air of someone who had long learned not to mind when his carefully prepared meals were eaten hours after they should have been, and went to his study to work at his desk with the faithful Charlie sprawled over his feet.

Waking the following morning, Emmy decided that she felt perfectly well again. She ate her breakfast in bed, since Mrs Burge told her sternly not to get up till later.

'Professor ter Mennolt went off an hour ago,' she told Emmy. 'What a life that man leads, never an hour to call his own.'

Which wasn't quite true, but Emmy knew what she meant. 'I suppose all doctors are at everyone's beck and call, but it must be a rewarding life.'

'Well, let's hope he gets his reward; he deserves it,' said Mrs Burge. 'Time that fiancée of his made up her mind to marry him.' She sniffed. 'Wants too much, if you ask me. Doesn't like this house—too small, she says…'

'Too small?' Emmy put down her cup. 'But it's a big house—I mean, big enough for a family.'

'Huh,' said Mrs Burge forcefully. 'Never mind a family, she likes to entertain—dinner parties and friends visiting. She doesn't much like Beaker, either.'

Emmy, aware that she shouldn't be gossiping, nonetheless asked, 'But why not? He's the nicest person...'

'True enough, love. Looks after the professor a treat.'

'So do you, Mrs Burge.'

'Me? I come in each day to give a hand, like. Been doing it for years, ever since the professor bought the house. A very nice home he's made of it, too. I have heard that he's got a tip-top place in Holland, too. Well, it stands to reason, doesn't it? He's over there for the best part of the year—only comes here for a month or two, though he pops over if he's needed. Much in demand, he is.'

She picked up Emmy's tray. 'Now, you have a nice bath and get dressed and come downstairs when you're ready. I'll be around and just you call if you want me. We'd better pack your things later on; the professor's driving you home in the morning.'

So Emmy got herself out of bed, first taking a look at her lump before going to the bathroom. The swelling had almost gone and the cut was healing nicely. She stared at her reflection for several moments; she looked a fright, and she was going to wash her hair before anyone told her not to.

Bathed, and with her hair in a damp plait, she went downstairs to find Beaker hovering in the hall.

His, 'Good morning, miss,' was affable. 'There's a cup of coffee in the small sitting room; it's nice and cosy there.'

He led the way and opened a door onto a quite small room at the back of the house. It was furnished very comfortably, and there was a fire burning in the elegant fireplace. A small armchair had been drawn up to it, flanked by a table on which were newspapers and a magazine or two. Sitting in front of the fire, waving his tail, asking to be noticed, was Charlie.

Emmy, sitting down, could think of nothing more delightful than to be the owner of such a room and such a dog, with a faithful old friend like Beaker smoothing out life's wrinkles. She said on a happy sigh, 'This is such a lovely house, Beaker, and everything is so beautifully polished and cared for.'

Beaker allowed himself to smile. 'The master and I, we're happy here, or so I hope, miss.' He went, soft-footed, to the door. 'I'll leave you to drink your coffee; lunch will be at one o'clock.'

He opened the door and she could hear Mrs Burge Hoovering somewhere.

'I suppose the professor won't be home for lunch?'

'No, miss. Late afternoon. He has an evening engagement.'

She put on her coat and went into the garden with Charlie after lunch. For one belonging to a town house the garden was surprisingly large, and cleverly planned to make the most of its space. She wandered up and down while Charlie pottered, and presently when they went indoors she sought out Beaker.

'Do you suppose I might take Charlie for a walk?' she asked him.

Beaker looked disapproving. 'I don't think the professor would care for that, miss. Charlie has had a long walk, early this morning with his master. He will go out again when the professor comes home. There's a nice fire burning in the drawing room. Mrs Burge asked me to let you know that she'll be back this evening if you should need any help with your packing. I understand that you are to make an early start.'

So Emmy retreated to the drawing room and curled up by the fire with Charlie beside her and Humphrey on her lap. She leafed through the newspapers and magazines on the table beside her, not reading them, her mind busy with her future. Christmas was too close for her to look for work; she would stay at home and help to get their new house to rights. There would be curtains to sew and hang, possessions to be stowed away in cupboards.

She wondered what the house was like. Her mother had written to tell her that it was delightful, but had had no time to describe it. There had been a slight hitch, she had written; the previous occupant's furniture was for the most part still in the house owing to some delay in its transport. 'But,' her mother had written, 'we shall be quite settled in by the time you come.'

Beaker brought tea presently; tiny sandwiches, fairy cakes and a chocolate cake which he assured her he had baked especially for her. 'Most young ladies enjoy them,' he told her.

Emmy was swallowing the last morsel when Charlie bounded to his feet, barking, and a moment later the professor came into the room.

His 'Hello,' was friendly and casual. He sat down, then enquired how she felt and cut himself a slice of cake.

'I'll run you home in the morning,' he told her. 'The day after tomorrow I shall be going to Holland.'

'There's no need,' said Emmy.

'Don't be silly,' said the professor at his most bracing. 'You can't go back to an empty house, and in a very short time you would be going home anyway. There seems little chance of selling the house at the moment; I phoned the agent this morning. There's nothing of value left there, is there?'

She shook her head. 'No, only my bed and the bed-clothes and a few bits of furniture.'

'There you are, then. We'll leave at eight o'clock.' He got up. 'Charlie and I are going for our walk—I shall be out tonight. Beaker's looking after you?'

'Oh, yes, thank you.'

'Mrs Burge will come again this evening. Ask for anything you want.'

His smile was remote as he went away.

She was still sitting there when he returned an hour later with Charlie, but he didn't come into the drawing room, and later still she heard him leave the house once more. Beaker, opening the door for Charlie to come in, said that Mrs Burge was in the kitchen if she needed her for anything. 'I'll be serving dinner in half an hour, Miss. May I pour you a glass of sherry?'

It might lift her unexpected gloom, thought Emmy, accepting. Why she should feel so downcast she had no idea; she should have been on the top of the world— leaving London and that pokey house and going to live miles away in Dorset. She wouldn't miss anything or anyone, she told herself, and the professor, for one, would be glad to see her go; she had caused enough disruption in his life.

Beaker had taken great pains with dinner— mushroom soup, sole *à la femme*, creamed potatoes and baby sprouts, and an apricot pavlova to follow these.

He poured her a glass of wine too, murmuring that the professor had told him to do so.

She drank her coffee in Humphrey's company and then, since she was heartily sick of her own company, went in search of Mrs Burge. There was still some packing to do, and that lady came willingly enough to give her help, even though it wasn't necessary. It passed an hour or so in comfortable chat and presently Emmy said that she would go to bed.

'We're to go early in the morning, so I'll say goodbye, Mrs Burge, and thank you for being so kind and helpful.'

'Bless you, ducks, it's been a pleasure, and I'll be up to see you off. Beaker will have breakfast on the table sharp at half past seven—I'll give you a call at seven, shall I?'

She turned on her way out. 'I must say you look a sight better than when you got here.'

Emmy, alone, went to the triple looking-glass on the dressing table and took a good look. If she was looking better now she must have looked a perfect fright before. No wonder the professor showed little interest in her company. Anyway, she reminded herself, his mind would be on Anneliese.

She woke in the morning to find her bedside lamp on and Mrs Burge standing there with a tray of tea.

'It's a nasty old day,' said Mrs Burge. 'Still dark, too. You've got half an hour. The professor's already up and out with Charlie.'

The thought of keeping him waiting spurred Emmy on to dress with speed. She was downstairs with only moments to spare as he and Charlie came into the house.

His good morning was spoken warmly. He's glad I'm going, thought Emmy as she answered cheerfully.

'There's still time to put me on a train,' she told him as they sat down to breakfast. 'It would save you a miserable drive.'

He didn't bother to answer. 'The roads will be pretty empty for another hour or so,' he observed, just as though she hadn't spoken. 'We should get to Littleton Mangate by mid-morning. Ready to leave, are you?'

Emmy went to thank Beaker and Mrs Burge, and got into her coat while Beaker fetched her case down to the car. It was bitterly cold, and she took a few quick breaths before she got into the car, glad to see Charlie already sprawling on the back seat. It was almost like having a third person in the car, even though he obviously intended to go to sleep.

It was striking eight o'clock as they drove away, starting the tedious first part of their journey through London's streets and presently the suburbs.

Chapter 6

It was still quite dark, and the rain was turning to sleet. The professor didn't speak and Emmy made no attempt to talk. In any case she couldn't think of anything to say. The weather, that useful topic of conversation, was hardly conducive to small talk, and he had never struck her as a man who enjoyed talking for the sake of it. She stared out of the window and watched the city streets gradually give way to rows of semi-detached houses with neat front gardens, and these in turn recede to be replaced by larger houses set in their own gardens and then, at last, open country and the motorway.

Beyond asking her if she was warm enough and comfortable, the professor remained silent. Emmy sat back in her comfortable seat and thought about her future. She had thought about it rather a lot in the last few days, largely because she didn't want to think too much about the past few weeks.

She was going to miss the professor, she admitted to herself. She wouldn't see him again after today, but she hoped that he would be happy with Anneliese. He had annoyed her on several occasions, but he was a good man and kind—the sort of kindness which was practical, and if he sometimes spoke his mind rather too frankly she supposed he was entitled to do so.

As the motorway merged into the A303 he turned the car into the service station. 'Coffee? We've made good time. You go on in; I'll take Charlie for a quick trot. I'll see you in the café.'

The place was full, which made their lack of conversation easier to bear. Emmy, painstakingly making small talk and receiving nothing but brief, polite replies, presently gave up. On a wave of ill humour she said, 'Well, if you don't want to talk, we won't.' She added hastily, going red in the face, 'I'm sorry, that was rude. I expect you have a lot to think about.'

He looked at her thoughtfully. 'Yes, Ermentrude, I have. And, strangely, in your company I do not feel compelled to keep up a flow of chat.'

'That's all right, then.' She smiled at him, for it seemed to her that he had paid her a compliment.

They drove on presently through worsening weather. All the same her heart lifted at the sight of open fields and small villages. Nearing their journey's end, the professor turned off the A303 and took a narrow cross-country road, and Emmy said, 'You know the way? You've been here before?'

'No.' He turned to smile at her. 'I looked at the map. We're almost there.'

Shortly after that they went through a village and turned off into a lane overhung with bare winter trees.

Round a corner, within their view, was Emmy's new house.

The professor brought the car to a halt, and after a moment's silence Emmy said, 'Oh, this can't be it,' although she knew that it was. The lodge itself was charming, even on a winter's day, but its charm was completely obliterated by the conglomeration of things around it, leaving it half-buried. Her father's car stood at the open gate, for the garage was overflowing with furniture. There was more furniture stacked and covered by tarpaulins in heaps in front of the house, a van parked on the small lawn to one side of the lodge and a stack of pipes under a hedge.

'Oh, whatever has happened?' asked Emmy. 'Surely Father hasn't…'

The professor put a large hand on hers. 'Supposing we go and have a look?'

He got out of the car and went to open her door and then let Charlie out, and together they went up the narrow path to the house.

It wasn't locked. Emmy opened it and called, 'Mother?'

They heard Mrs Foster's surprised voice from somewhere in the house and a moment later she came into the tiny hall.

'Darling—Emmy, how lovely to see you. We didn't expect you…' She looked at the professor. 'Is everything all right?'

He shook hands. 'I think it is we who should be asking you that, Mrs Foster.'

Mrs Foster had an arm round Emmy. 'Come into the kitchen; it's the only room that's comfortable. We hoped to be settled in by the time you came, Emmy. There's been a hitch…'

She led them to the kitchen with Charlie at their heels. 'Sit down; I'll make us some coffee.'

The kitchen wasn't quite warm enough, but it was furnished with a table and chairs, and there were two easy chairs at each side of the small Aga. China and crockery, knives and forks, spoons and mugs and glasses were arranged on a built-in dresser and there was a pretty latticed window over the sink.

Mrs Foster waved a hand. 'Of course all this is temporary; in a week or two we shall be settled in.'

'Mother, what has happened?' Emmy sat down at the table. Enoch and Snoodles had jumped onto her lap while George investigated Charlie.

The professor was still standing, leaning against the wall, silent. Only when Mrs Foster handed round the coffee mugs and sat down did he take a chair.

'So unfortunate,' said Mrs Foster. 'Mr Bennett, whom your father replaced, died suddenly the very day I moved down here. His furniture was to have been taken to his sister's house where he intended to live, but, of course, she didn't want it, and anyway he had willed it to a nephew who lives somewhere in the north of England. He intends to come and decide what to do with it, but he's put it off twice already and says there's no need for it to be put in store as he'll deal with it when he comes. Only he doesn't come and here we are, half in and half out as it were.'

She drank from her mug. 'Your father is extremely happy here, and since he's away for most of the day we manage very well. School breaks up tomorrow, so he will be free after that. We didn't tell you, Emmy, because we hoped—still do hope—that Mr Bennett's nephew will do something about the furniture.'

'Whose van is that outside?' asked Emmy.

'The plumber, dear. There's something wrong with the boiler—he says he'll have it right in a day or two.' Mrs Foster looked worried. 'I'm so sorry we weren't ready for you, but we'll manage. You may have to sleep on the sofa; it's in the sitting room.' She looked doubtful. 'There's furniture all over the place, I'm afraid, but we can clear a space...'

She looked at Emmy. 'I don't suppose the house is sold, Emmy?'

'No, Mother, but there have been several people to look at it. The agent's got the keys...'

'We didn't expect you just yet.' Her mother looked enquiring. 'Has something gone wrong?'

'I'll tell you later,' said Emmy. She turned to the professor, who still hadn't uttered a word. 'It was very kind of you to bring me here,' she said. 'I hope it hasn't upset your day too much.'

'Should I be told something?' asked her mother.

'Later, Mother,' said Emmy quickly. 'I'm sure Professor ter Mennolt wants to get back to London as quickly as possible.'

The professor allowed himself a small smile. He said quietly, 'There is a great deal you should be told, Mrs Foster, and if I may I'll tell it, for I can see that Ermentrude won't say a word until I'm out of the way.'

'Emmy's been ill,' said Mrs Foster in a motherly panic.

'Allow me to explain.' And, when Emmy opened her mouth to speak, he said, 'No, Ermentrude, do not interrupt me.'

He explained. His account of Emmy's misfortunes was succinct, even dry. He sounded, thought Emmy, listening to his calm voice, as if he were dictating a diagnosis, explaining something to a sister on a ward round.

When he had finished, Mrs Foster said, 'We are deeply grateful to you—my husband and I. I don't know how we can thank you enough for taking such care of Emmy.'

'A pleasure,' said the professor in a noncommittal voice which made Emmy frown. Of course it hadn't been a pleasure; she had been a nuisance. She hoped that he would go now so that she need never see him again. The thought gave her such a pang of unhappiness that she went quite pale.

He had no intention of going. He accepted Mrs Foster's invitation to share the snack lunch she was preparing, and remarked that he would like to have a talk with Mr Foster.

'He comes home for lunch?' he enquired blandly.

'Well, no. He has it at school, but he's got a free hour at two o'clock; he told me this morning.'

'Splendid. If I may, I'll walk up to the school and have a chat.'

Emmy was on the point of asking what about when he caught her eye.

'No, Ermentrude, don't ask!' The animals had settled before the stove. The professor got up. 'I'll bring in your things, Ermentrude.'

He sounded impersonal and nonchalant, but something stopped her from asking the questions hovering on her tongue. Why should he want to talk to her father? she wondered.

They had their lunch presently—tinned soup and toasted cheese—sitting round the kitchen table, and Mrs Foster and the professor were never at a loss for conversation. Emmy thought of the silent journey they had just made and wondered what it was that kept him silent in her company. It was a relief when he got into his coat again and started on the five-minute walk to the school.

Mr Foster, if he was surprised to see the professor, didn't say so. He led the way to a small room near the classrooms, remarking that they would be undisturbed there.

'You want to see me, Professor?' He gave him a sharp glance. 'Is this to do with Emmy? She isn't ill? You say she is with her mother...'

'No, no. She has had a mild concussion and a nasty cut on the head, but, if you will allow me, I will explain...'

Which he did in the same dry manner which he had employed at the lodge. Only this time he added rather more detail.

'I am deeply indebted to you,' said Mr Foster. 'Emmy didn't say a word—if she had done so my wife would have returned to London immediately.

'Of course. Ermentrude was determined that you should know nothing about it. It was unfortunate that she should have been made redundant with such short notice, although I believe she wasn't unduly put out about that. I had no idea that she was alone in the house until I returned to London.'

Mr Foster gave him a thoughtful look and wondered why the professor should sound concerned, but he said nothing. 'Well, once we have got this business of the furniture and the plumbing settled, we shall be able to settle down nicely. I'm sure that Emmy will find a job, and in the meantime there's plenty for her to do at home.'

'Unfortunate that Christmas is so close,' observed the professor. 'Is it likely that you will be settled in by then?'

Mr Foster frowned. 'Unfortunately, no. I had a phone message this morning—this nephew is unable to deal with the removal of Mr Bennett's furniture until after Christmas. He suggests that it stays where it is for the moment. I suppose we shall be able to manage...'

'Well, now, as to that, may I offer a suggestion? Bearing in mind that Ermentrude is still not completely recovered, and the discomforts you are living in, would you consider...?'

Emmy and her mother, left on their own, rummaged around, finding blankets and pillows. 'There's a mattress in the little bedroom upstairs, if you could manage on that for a few nights,' suggested Mrs Foster worriedly. 'If only they would take all this furniture away...'

Emmy, making up some sort of a bed, declared that she would be quite all right. 'It won't be for long,' she said cheerfully. 'I'll be more comfortable here than I was in London. And Father's got his job—that's what matters.'

She went downstairs to feed the animals. 'The professor and Charlie are a long time,' she observed. 'I hope Charlie hasn't got lost. It's almost tea time, too, and I'm sure he wants to get back to London.'

The professor wasn't lost, nor was Charlie. Having concluded his talk with Mr Foster, the professor had whistled to his dog and set off for a walk, having agreed to return to the school when Mr Foster should be free to return home.

The unpleasant weather hadn't improved at all. Sleet

and wet snow fell from time to time from a grey sky rapidly darkening, and the lanes he walked along were half-frozen mud. He was unaware of the weather, his thoughts miles away.

'I am, of course, mad,' he told Charlie. 'No man in his right senses would have conceived such a plan without due regard to the pitfalls and disadvantages. And what is Anneliese going to think?'

Upon reflection he thought that he didn't much mind what she felt. She had been sufficiently well brought up to treat his guests civilly, and if she and Ermentrude were to cross swords he felt reasonably sure that Ermentrude would give as good as she got. Besides, Anneliese wouldn't be staying at his home, although he expected to see a good deal of her.

He waited patiently while Charlie investigated a tree. Surely Anneliese would understand that he couldn't leave Ermentrude and her parents to spend Christmas in a house brim-full of someone else's furniture and inadequate plumbing, especially as he had been the means of their move there in the first place. Perhaps he had rather over-emphasised Ermentrude's need to recuperate after concussion, but it had successfully decided her father to accept his offer.

He strode back to the school to meet Mr Foster and accompany him back to the lodge.

Emmy was making tea when they got there.

'You're wet,' she said unnecessarily. 'And you'll be very late back home. I've made toast, and there's a bowl of food for Charlie when you've dried him off. There's an old towel hanging on the back of the kitchen door. Give me that coat; I'll hang it on a chair by the Aga or you'll catch your death of cold.'

The professor, meekly doing as he was told, reflected that Ermentrude sounded just like a wife. He tried to imagine Anneliese talking like that and failed, but then she would never allow herself to be in a situation such as Emmy was now. She would have demanded to be taken to the nearest hotel. He laughed at the thought, and Emmy looked round at him in surprise. The professor didn't laugh often.

He helped her father out of his wet jacket, poured the tea and called her mother, who was hanging curtains in the small bedroom.

'They'll have to do,' she said, coming into the kitchen. 'I've pinned them up for the moment, and it does make the room look cosier.'

She smiled at the professor. 'Did you have a nice walk? Do sit down. Let Charlie lie by the stove; he must be tired. It's a wretched evening for you to travel.'

Emmy handed round toast and a pot of jam. The tea, in an assortment of cups and saucers, was hot and strong. She watched the professor spread jam on his toast and take a bite, and thought of Beaker's dainty teas with the fine china and little cakes. He looked up and caught her eye and smiled.

Mr Foster drank his tea and put down his cup. 'Professor ter Mennolt has made us a most generous offer. He considers that Emmy needs rest after her accident, and that as a medical man he cannot like the idea of her remaining here while the house is in such a state of confusion. He has most kindly offered to take us over to Holland for the Christmas period to stay in his house there. He will be going the day after tomorrow—'

'You said tomorrow...' interrupted Emmy.

'I find that I am unable to get away until the fol-

lowing day,' said the professor smoothly. 'But I shall
be delighted to have you as my guests for a few days.
Hopefully by the time you return the problems in this
house will be resolved.' He added blandly, 'As a doctor,
I would feel it very wrong of me to allow Ermentrude
to stay here until she is quite fit.'

Emmy drew a deep breath. She didn't think he meant
a word of it; he might look and sound like the learned
man he undoubtedly was but his suggestion was preposterous. Besides, there was nothing wrong with her. She
opened her mouth to say so and closed it again, swallowing her protest. She didn't stand a chance against
that weighty professional manner.

She listened to her mother receiving his offer with
delighted relief.

'Surely we shall upset your plans for Christmas?
Your family and guests? How will you let them know?
And all the extra work...'

The professor sounded reassuring. 'I'm sure you
don't need to worry, Mrs Foster. If you can face the
idea of Christmas in Holland, I can assure you that
you will all be most welcome. Rather short notice, I'm
afraid, but if you could manage to be ready by midday
on the day after tomorrow?'

Mr and Mrs Foster exchanged glances. It was an
offer they could hardly refuse. On their way they would
have scrambled through the festive season somehow or
other, always hopeful that Mr Bennett's furniture would
have been moved by the time Emmy arrived. But now
that seemed unlikely, and with Christmas in such a
muddle, and Emmy not quite herself...

Mrs Foster said simply, 'Thank you for a most generous offer; we accept with pleasure. Only don't let

us interfere with any of your family arrangements. I mean, we are happy just to have a bed and a roof over our heads…'

The professor smiled. 'It will be a pleasure to have you—I always think the more the merrier at Christmas, don't you?'

'Your family will be there?'

'I have two sisters with children and a younger brother. I'm sure they will be delighted to meet you.'

He got up. 'You will forgive me if I leave you now?'

He shook hands with Mr and Mrs Foster, but Ermentrude he patted on the shoulder in a casual manner and told her to take care.

When he had gone, Mrs Foster said, 'What a delightful man, and how kind he is. You know, Emmy, your father and I were at our wits' end wondering what to do about Christmas, and along comes Professor ter Mennolt and settles it all for us—just like that.'

Mr Foster was watching Emmy's face. 'A good man, and very well thought of in his profession, I believe. He tells me that he is engaged to be married. I dare say we shall meet his fiancée.'

Emmy said in a bright voice, 'Oh, I have met her—she came to St Luke's one day to see him—she'd been staying over here. She's beautiful, you know. Fair and slender, and has the most gorgeous clothes.'

'Did you like her?' asked her mother.

'No,' said Emmy. 'But I expect that was because she was the kind of person I would like to be and aren't.'

'Well,' said her mother briskly, 'let's get tidied up here and then think about what clothes to take with us. I've that long black skirt and that rather nice crêpe de

Chine blouse; that'll do for the evening. What about you, Emmy?'

'Well, there's the brown velvet; that'll do.' It would have to; she had no other suitable dress for the evening. She thought for a moment. 'I could go in the jacket and skirt, and wear my coat over them. A blouse or two, and a sweater... I don't suppose we'll be there for more than a few days.'

'If we sell the house, you shall have some new clothes, and now your father's got this splendid post...'

'Oh, I've plenty of clothes,' said Emmy airily. 'And they don't matter. It's marvellous that Father's here, and this is a dear little house.'

She looked round her at the muddle—chairs stacked in corners, a wardrobe in the hall, Mr Bennett's piano still in the sitting room. They looked at each other and burst out laughing. 'When you're able to settle in,' said Emmy.

The professor, with Charlie beside him, drove back to Chelsea. 'I do not know what possessed me,' he told his companion. 'Anneliese is not going to like my un-expected guests, and yet what else could I do? Would you like to spend Christmas in such cold chaos? No, of course you wouldn't. Common humanity dictated that I should do something about it... Let me think...'

By the time he had reached his home his plans were made. Over the dinner which Beaker set before him he went through them carefully, and presently went to his study and picked up the phone.

Beaker, bringing his coffee later, coughed gently. 'Mrs Burge and I, sir, we miss Miss Foster.'

The professor looked at him over his spectacles. 'So

do I, Beaker. By the way, she and her parents are going
to Holland with me for Christmas. Due to unavoidable
circumstances, the house they have moved to is unfit
to live in for the moment and they have nowhere to go.'

Beaker's face remained impassive. 'A good idea, if I
may say so, sir. The young lady isn't quite herself after
that nasty attack.'

'Just so, Beaker. I shan't be leaving until the day
after tomorrow—pack a few things for me, will you?
Enough for a week.'

Beaker gone, the professor buried his commanding
nose in a weighty tome and forgot everything else. It
was only as he was going to bed that he remembered
that he should have phoned Anneliese. It would be better to tell her when he got to Holland, perhaps. He felt
sure that she would be as warmly welcoming to his
unexpected guests as his sisters had promised to be.

Emmy slept badly; a mattress on the floor, surrounded by odds and ends of furniture which creaked
and sighed during the night, was hardly conducive to
a restful night. Nor were her thoughts—largely of the
professor—none of which were of a sensible nature.

She got up heavy-eyed and her mother said, 'The professor is quite right, Emmy, you don't look at all yourself.' She eyed her much loved daughter worriedly. 'Was
it very uncomfortable on the mattress? There's no room
to put up a bed, and anyway we haven't got one until we
can get yours from the house in London. Your father
can sleep there tonight and you can come in with me...'

'I was very comfortable,' said Emmy. 'But there was
such a lot to think about that I didn't sleep very well. I
expect I'm excited.'

Mrs Foster put the eggs for breakfast on to boil. 'So am I. We'll pack presently—your father's going up to the school to find out where the nearest kennels are, then he can take these three later this evening.'

'I hope they'll be all right, but it's only for a few days. Wouldn't it be marvellous if we came back and found all Mr Bennett's furniture gone and the plumbing repaired?'

'We mustn't expect too much, but it would be nice. Directly after Christmas your father will go up to London and see the estate agent and arrange for your bed to be brought down here. You need never go back there unless you want to, Emmy.' Her mother turned round to smile at her. 'Oh, Emmy, isn't it all too good to be true?'

There was a good deal to do—cases to pack, hair to wash, hands to be attended to.

'I do hope the professor won't feel ashamed of us,' said Mrs Foster.

Emmy said quite passionately, 'No, Mother, he's not like that. He's kind and, and—' She paused. 'Well, he's nice.' And, when her mother gave her a surprised look, she added, 'He's quite tiresome at times too.'

Mrs Foster wisely said nothing.

They all went to bed early in a house strangely silent now that George and Snoodles and Enoch had been taken, protesting fiercely, to the kennels near Shaftesbury. Emmy had another wakeful night, worrying about her clothes and whether the professor might be regretting his generosity—and what would Anneliese think when she knew? She dropped off finally and had a nightmare, wherein his family, grotesquely hideous, shouted abuse at her. She was only too glad when it was time to get up.

They made the house as secure as they could, piling the furniture tidily under the tarpaulins and tying them down, parking her father's car as near the house as possible and covering it with more tarpaulins. There was just time to have a cup of coffee before the professor was due to arrive.

He came punctually, relaxed and pleasant, drank the coffee he was offered, stowed the luggage in the boot and invited everyone to get into the car.

Mr Foster was told to sit in front, for, as the professor pointed out, he might need directions. 'We're going from Dover—the hovercraft. It's quick, and there is quite a long journey on the other side.'

He got in and turned to look at Mrs Foster. 'Passports?' he asked. 'Keys and so forth? So easily forgotten at the last minute, and I have rushed you.'

'I think we've got everything, Professor...'

'Would you call me Ruerd?' His glance slid over Emmy's rather pale face, but he didn't say anything to her.

It was another cold day but it wasn't raining, although the sky was dark. The professor drove steadily, going across country to pick up the motorway outside Southampton and turning inland at Chichester to pick up the A27 and then the A259. He stopped in Hawkshurst at a pub in the little town where they had soup and sandwiches.

'Are we in good time for the hovercraft,' asked Mrs Foster anxiously.

'Plenty of time,' he assured her. 'It takes longer this

way, I believe, but the motorway up to London and down to Dover would have been packed with traffic.'

'You've been this way before?' asked Emmy's father.

'No, but it seemed a good route. On a fine day it must be very pleasant. I dislike motorways, but I have to use them frequently.'

They drove on presently, joining the A20 as they neared Dover. From the warmth of the car Emmy surveyed the wintry scene outside. How awful if she was to be seasick…

She forgot about it in the excitement of going on board, and, once there, since it was rather like sitting in a superior bus, she forgot about feeling sick and settled down beside her mother, sharing the tea they had been brought and eating the biscuits. Her father had gone to sleep and the professor, with a word of apology, had taken out some papers from a pocket, put on his spectacles and was absorbing their contents.

It was rough but not unbearably so. All the same it was nice to get back into the car.

'Not too tired?' asked the professor, and, once clear of the traffic around Calais, sent the car surging forward, out of France and into Belgium, where he took the road to Ghent and then on into Holland.

Emmy looked out of the window and thought the country looked rather flat and uninteresting. Instead she studied the back of the professor's head, and wished that she were sitting beside him. She caught the thought up short before it could go any further. All this excitement was going to her head, and any silly ideas must be squashed at once. Circumstances had thrown them together; circumstances would very shortly part them. That was an end of that.

She sighed, and then choked on a breath when the professor asked, 'What's the matter, Ermentrude?'

She had forgotten that he could see her in his mirror above the dashboard. 'Nothing, nothing,' she repeated. 'I'm fine. It's all very interesting.'

Which, considering it was now almost dark and the view held no interest whatsoever, was a silly answer.

It was completely dark by the time he turned in at his own gates and she saw the lights streaming from the house ahead of them. She hadn't expected anything like this. A substantial villa, perhaps, or a roomy townhouse, but not this large, square house, with its big windows and imposing front door.

As they got out of the car the door opened and Solly and Tip dashed out, barking a welcome—a welcome offered in a more sedate fashion by Cokker, who greeted the guests as though three people arriving for Christmas without more than a few hours' warning was an everyday occurrence.

The hall was warm and splendidly lighted and there was a Christmas tree in one corner, not yet decorated. Cokker took coats and scarves, and the whole party crossed the hall and went into the drawing room.

'Oh, what a beautiful room!' said Mrs Foster.

'I'm glad you like it. Shall we have a drink before you go to your rooms? Would dinner in half an hour suit you?'

'Yes, please.' Mrs Foster beamed at him. 'I don't know about anyone else, but I'm famished.' She sat down by the fire and looked around her, frankly admiring. 'Ruerd, this is so beautiful and yet you choose to live a good part of your life in England?'

'I go where my work is,' he told her, smiling. 'I'm very happy in Chelsea, but this is my home.'

He crossed to the drinks table and went to sit by Mr Foster, talking about their journey, leaving Emmy to sit with her mother. Presently Cokker came, and with him a tall, stout woman, no longer young but very upright.

'Ah, Tiele,' said the professor. 'My housekeeper and Cokker's wife. She doesn't speak English but I'm sure you will manage very well.'

He said something to her in what Emmy supposed was Dutch.

'Tiele is from Friesland, so we speak Friese together...'

'You're not Dutch? You're Frisian?' asked Emmy.

'I had a Friesian grandmother,' he told her. 'Tiele will take you upstairs, and when you are ready will you come back here again? Don't hurry; you must be tired.'

On their way to the door Emmy stopped by him. 'Aren't you tired?' she asked him.

He smiled down at her. 'No. When I'm with people I like or doing something I enjoy I'm never tired.'

He smiled slowly and she turned away and followed her mother, father and Tiele up the wide, curving staircase. It was inevitable, I suppose, she thought, that sooner or later I should fall in love with him. Only it's a pity I couldn't have waited until we were back home and there would be no chance of seeing him again. I must, decided Emmy firmly, be very circumspect in my manner towards him.

There were a number of rooms leading from the gallery which encircled the stairs. Emmy watched her parents disappear into one at the front of the house before she was led by Tiele to a room on the opposite side. It was not a very large room, but it was furnished beautifully with a canopied bed, a William the Fourth dressing table in tulip wood, two Georgian *bergères* upholstered in the same pale pink of the curtains and bedspread, and a mahogany bedside table—an elegant Georgian trifle.

The one long window opened onto a small wrought-iron balcony; she peeped out onto the dark outside and turned back thankfully to the cheerful light of the rose-shaded lamps. There was a clothes cupboard too, built into one wall, and a small, quite perfect bathroom.

Emmy prowled around, picking things up and putting them down again. 'I wonder,' she said out loud, 'if Anneliese knows how lucky she is?'

She tidied herself then, brushed her hair, powdered her nose and went to fetch her parents.

'Darling,' said her mother worriedly. 'Should we have come? I mean, just look at everything...'

Her father said sensibly, 'This is Ruerd's home, my dear, and he has made us welcome. Never mind if it is a mansion or a cottage. I fancy that it is immaterial to him, and it should be to us.'

They went down to the drawing room and found the professor standing before his hearth, the dogs pressed up against him.

'You have all you want?' he asked Mrs Foster. 'Do say if you need anything, won't you? I rushed you here with very little time to decide what to pack.'

When Cokker came the professor said, 'I believe dinner is on the table. And if you aren't too tired later, sir, I'd like to show you some first editions I have. I recently found Robert Herrick's *Hesperides*—seventeenth century, but perhaps you would advise me as to the exact date?'

The dining room was as magnificent as the drawing

room, with a pedestal table in mahogany ringed around by twelve chairs, those at the head and foot of the table being carvers upholstered in red leather. It was a large room, with plenty of space for the massive side table along one wall and the small serving table facing it.

There were a number of paintings on the walls. Emmy, anxious not to appear nosy, determined to have a good look at them when there was no one about. At the moment she was delighted to keep her attention on the delicious food she was being offered. Smoked salmon with wafer-thin brown bread and butter, roast pheasant with game chips and an assortment of vegetables, and following these a *crème brûlée*.

They had coffee in the drawing room and presently the professor took Mr Foster away to his library, first of all wishing Mrs Foster and Emmy a good night. 'Breakfast is at half past eight, but if you would like to have it in bed you have only to say so. Sleep well.' His gaze dwelt on Emmy's face for a moment and she looked away quickly.

She was going to stay awake, she thought, lying in a scented bath. There were a great many problems to mull over—and the most important one was how to forget the professor as quickly as possible. If it's only infatuation, she thought, I can get over it once I've stopped seeing him.

She got into bed and lay admiring her surroundings before putting out the bedside light, prepared to lie awake and worry. She had reckoned without the comfort of the bed and the long day behind her. With a last dreamy thought of the professor, she slept.

Chapter 7

Emmy was wakened in the morning by a sturdy young girl in a coloured pinafore, bearing a tray of tea. She beamed at Emmy, drew the curtains back, giggled cheerfully and went away.

Emmy drank her tea and hopped out of bed intent on looking out of the window. She opened it and stepped cautiously onto the balcony. The tiles were icy and her toes curled under with the cold, but the air was fresh and smelled of the sea.

She took great gulping breaths and peered down to the garden below. It was more than a garden; it stretched away towards what looked like rough grass, and beyond that she could glimpse the sea. She took her fill of the view and then looked down again. Directly under the balcony the professor was standing, looking up at her, the dogs beside him.

He wished her good morning. 'And go and put some clothes on, Ermentrude, and come outside.' He laughed then.

She said haughtily, 'Good morning, Professor. I think not, thank you. I'm cold.'

'Well, of course you are with only a nightie on. Get dressed and come on down. You need the exercise.'

Emmy felt light-headed at the sight of him, standing there, laughing at her.

She said, 'All right, ten minutes,' and whisked herself back into her room, leaving the professor wondering why the sight of her in a sensible nightdress with her hair hanging untidily in a cloud around her shoulders should so disturb him in a way which Anneliese, even in the most exquisite gown, never had. He reminded himself that Anneliese would be coming to dinner that evening, and regretted the impulse to invite Emmy to join him.

She came through the side door to meet him, wrapped in her coat, a scarf over her hair, sensible shoes on her feet. Tip and Solly made much of her, and she said, 'Oh, what a pity that Charlie isn't here, too.'

'I think that Beaker might not like that. Charlie is his darling, as much loved as Humphrey.'

They had begun to walk down the length of the garden, and at its end he opened a wicket gate and led the way over rough grass until they reached the edge of the dunes with the sea beyond. There was a strong wind blowing, whipping the waves high, turning the water to a tumultuous steel-grey.

The professor put an arm round Emmy's shoulders to steady her. 'Like it?'

'Oh, yes, it's heavenly! And so quiet—I mean, no people, no cars…'

'Just us,' said the professor.

It wasn't full daylight, but she could see the wide sand stretching away on either side of them, disappearing into the early-morning gloom.

'You could walk for miles,' said Emmy. 'How far?'

'All the way to den Helder in the north and to the Hoek in the south.'

'You must think of this when you are in London…'

'Yes. I suppose that one day I'll come to live here permanently.'

'I expect you will want to do that when you're married and have a family,' said Emmy, and felt the pain which the words were giving her. Would Anneliese stand here with him, watching the stormy sea and blown by the wind? And his children? She pictured a whole clutch of them and dismissed the thought. Anneliese would have one child—two, perhaps—but no more than that.

She felt tears well under her eyelids. Ruerd would be a splendid father and his home was large enough to accommodate a whole bunch of children, but that would never happen.

'You're crying,' said the professor. 'Why?'

'It's the wind; it makes my eyes water. The air is like sucking ice cubes from the fridge, isn't it?'

He smiled then. 'An apt description. Let us go back and have breakfast before we decorate the tree—a morning's work. We will come again—whatever the weather, it is always a splendid view.

Breakfast was a cheerful meal; her parents had slept well and the talk was wholly of Christmas and the forthcoming gaiety.

'My sisters will come later today, my brother tomorrow. Anneliese—my fiancée—will be coming this evening to dinner.'

'We look forward to meeting her,' said Mrs Foster, politely untruthful. Maternal instinct warned her that Anneliese wasn't going to like finding them at Ruerd's house. Although from all accounts she had nothing to fear from Emmy, thought Mrs Foster sadly. A darling girl, but with no looks. A man as handsome as Ruerd would surely choose a beautiful woman for his wife.

They decorated the tree after breakfast, hanging it with glass baubles, tinsel, little china angels and a great many fairy lights. On top, of course, there was a fairy doll—given after Christmas to the youngest of his nieces, the professor told them.

'You have several nieces?' asked Mrs Foster.

'Three so far, and four nephews. I do hope you like children...'

'Indeed I do. Ruerd, we feel terrible at not having any presents to give.'

'Please don't worry about that. They have so many gifts that they lose count as to whom they are from.'

Emmy, making paper chains for the nursery, found him beside her.

'After lunch we'll go over the house, if you would like that, but, in the meantime, will you bring those upstairs and we'll hang them before the children get here?'

The nursery was at the back of the house behind a baize door. There was a night nursery, too, and a bedroom for nanny, a small kitchenette and a splendidly equipped bathroom.

'The children sleep here, but they go where they like in the house. Children should be with their parents as much as possible, don't you agree?'

'Well, of course. Otherwise they're not a family, are they?' She stood there, handing him the chains as he fastened them in festoons between the walls. 'Did you sleep here, too?'

'Oh, yes. Until I was eight years old. On our eighth birthdays we were given our own bedrooms.'

He hung the chains, and turned to stare at her. 'You like my home, Ermentrude?'

'Yes, indeed I do. I think you must be very happy here.'

She walked to the door, uneasy under his look. 'At what time do your sisters arrive?'

His voice was reassuringly casual again. 'Very shortly after lunch. It will be chaos for the rest of the afternoon, I expect. Several friends will be coming to dinner.'

She paused as they reached the stairs. 'You have been so kind to us, Professor, but that doesn't mean you have to include us in your family gatherings.' She saw his quick frown. 'I've put that badly, but you know quite well what I mean, don't you? Mother and Father and I would be quite happy if you would like us to dine alone. I mean, you weren't expecting us…'

She had made him angry. She started down the staircase and wished that she had held her tongue, but she had had to say it. Perhaps if she hadn't fallen in love with him she wouldn't have felt the urge to make it clear to him that they were on sufferance, even if it was a kindly sufferance.

He put out a hand and stopped her, turned her round to face him, and when he spoke it was in a rigidly controlled voice which masked his anger.

'Never say such a thing to me again, Ermentrude.

You and your parents are my guests, and welcome in my house. Be good enough to remember that.'

She stood quietly under his hand. 'All right, I won't,' she told him. 'Don't be so annoyed, there's no need.'

He smiled then. 'Should I beg your pardon? Did I startle you?'

'Oh, no. I think I've always known that you conceal your feelings.' She met his look and went pink. 'Now it's me who should say sorry. Goodness me, I wouldn't have dared talk to you like that at St Luke's. It must be because we're here.'

He studied her face, nodded and went on down the stairs, his hand still on her arm.

Lunch was a cheerful meal. The professor and Mr Foster seemed to have a great deal in common; neither was at a loss for a subject although they were careful to include Mrs Foster and Emmy.

Shortly afterwards the first of the guests arrived. The house seemed suddenly to be full of children, racing around, shouting and laughing, hugging the dogs, hanging onto their uncle, absorbing Emmy and her parents into their lives as though they had always been there.

There were only four of them but it seemed more—three boys and a girl, the eldest six years and the youngest two. A rather fierce Scottish nanny came with them, but she took one look at Emmy's unassuming person and allowed her to be taken over by her charges. So Emmy was coaxed to go to the nursery with the children and their mother, a tall young woman with the professor's good looks. She had shaken Emmy by the hand, and liked her.

'Joke,' she said with a smile. 'It sounds like part of an

egg but it's spelt like a joke. I do hope you like children.
Mine run wild at Christmas, and Ruerd spoils them.
My sister Alemke will be here shortly; she's got a boy
and two girls, and a baby on the way.' She grinned at
Emmy. 'Are we all a bit overpowering?'

'No, no. I like children. Only, you see, the professor
is so—well, remote at the hospital. It's hard to think of
him with a family.'

'I know just what you mean.' Joke made a face. 'He
loves children, but I don't think Anneliese, his fiancée,
likes them very much. I sound critical, don't I? Well, I
am. Why he has to marry someone like her I'll never
know. Suitable, I suppose.'

She took Emmy's arm. 'I'm so glad you're here. Only
I hope the children aren't going to plague you.'

'I shan't mind a bit. How old are your sister's children?'

'The boy is five, and the girls—twins—almost three.
Let's go down and have tea.'

Her sister had arrived when they got down to the
drawing room and there were more children, who, undeterred by language problems, took possession of Emmy.

Alemke was very like her sister, only younger. 'Isn't
this fun?' she said in English as good as Emmy's own.
'I love a crowd. Our husbands will come later, and I
suppose Aunt Beatrix will be here and Uncle Cor and
Grandmother ter Mennolt. She's a bit fierce, but don't
mind her. There'll be Ruerd's friends, too; it should be
great fun. And Anneliese, of course.'

The sisters exchanged looks. 'We don't like her,
though we try very hard to do so,' said Joke.

'She's very beautiful,' said Emmy, anxious to be fair.

'You've met her?'

'She came to St Luke's when I was working there, to see the professor.'

'Do you always call Ruerd "professor"?' asked Joke.

'Well, yes. He's—he's... Well, it's difficult to explain, but the hospital— He's a senior consultant and I was on the telephone exchange.'

Alemke took her arm. 'Come over here and sit with us while we have tea, and tell us about the hospital—wasn't there a bomb or something? Ruerd mentioned it vaguely. Anneliese was over there, wasn't she?'

Emmy accepted a delicate china cup of tea and a tiny biscuit.

'Yes, it must have been very difficult for the professor because, of course, he was busier than usual.'

Joke and Alemke exchanged a quick look. Here was the answer to their prayers. This small girl with the plain face and the beautiful eyes was exactly what they had in mind for their brother. They had seen with satisfaction that, beyond a few civil remarks, he had avoided Emmy and she had gone out of her way to stay at the other end of the room. A good sign, but it was unfortunate that Ruerd had given his promise to Anneliese. Who would be coming that evening, no doubt looking more beautiful than ever.

The children, excited but sleepy, were led away after tea to be bathed and given supper and be put to bed, and everyone else went away to dress for the evening. Emmy had seen with pleasure that her parents were enjoying themselves and were perfectly at ease in their grand surroundings. She reminded herself that before her father had been made redundant he and her mother had had a pleasant social life. It was only when they had gone to London and he had been out of work that they had had to change their ways.

Emmy took a long time dressing. The result looked very much as usual to her anxious eyes as she studied her person in the pier-glass. The brown dress was best described as useful, its colour mouse-like, guaranteed to turn the wearer into a nonentity, its modest style such that it could be worn year after year without even being noticed.

Emmy had bought it at a sale, searching for a dress to wear to the annual hospital ball at St Luke's two years previously, knowing that it would have to last for a number of years even if its outings were scanty. It hardly added to her looks, although it couldn't disguise her pretty figure.

She went slowly down the staircase, hoping that no one would notice her.

The professor noticed—and knew then why Emmy hadn't wanted to join his other guests. He crossed the hall to meet her at the foot of the staircase, and took her hand with a smile and a nod at her person. He said in exactly the right tone of casual approval, 'Very nice, Ermentrude. Come and meet the rest of my guests.'

His brothers-in-law were there now, but he took her first to an old lady sitting by the console table.

'Aunt Beatrix, this is Ermentrude Foster who is staying here over Christmas with her parents—you have already met them.'

The old lady looked her up and down and held out a hand. 'Ah, yes. You have an unusual name. Perhaps you are an unusual girl?'

Emmy shook the old hand. 'No, no. I'm very ordinary.'

Aunt Beatrix patted the stool at her feet. 'Sit down

and tell me what you do.' She shot a glance at Emmy. 'You do do something?'

'Well, yes.' Emmy told her of the job at St. Luke's. 'But, now Father has a post in Dorset, I can live there and find something to do while I train.'

'What for?'

'I want to embroider—really complicated embroidery, you know? Tapestry work and smocking on babies' dresses and drawn thread work. And when I know enough I'd like to open a small shop.'

'Not get married?'

'I expect if someone asked me, and I loved him, I'd like to get married,' said Emmy.

The professor had wandered back. 'Come and meet Rik and Hugo and the others.' He put a hand on her shoulder and led her from one to the other, and then paused by Anneliese, who was superb in red chiffon, delicately made-up, her hair an artless mass of loose curls.

'Remember Ermentrude?' asked the professor cheerfully.

'Of course I do.' Anneliese studied the brown dress slowly and smiled a nasty little smile. 'What a rush for you, coming here at a moment's notice. Ruerd told me all about it, of course. You must feel very grateful to him. Such a bore for you, having no time to buy some decent clothes. Still, I suppose you're only here for a couple of days.'

'Yes, I expect we are,' said Emmy in a carefully controlled voice. Just then the professor was called away. Anneliese turned round and spoke to a tall, stout woman chatting nearby. 'Mother, come and meet this girl Ruerd is helping yet again.'

Mevrouw van Moule ignored the hand Emmy put out. She had cold eyes and a mean mouth, and Emmy thought, In twenty years' time Anneliese will look like that.

'I dare say you find all this rather awkward, do you not? You worked in a hospital, I understand.'

'Yes,' said Emmy pleasantly. 'An honest day's work, like the professor. He does an honest day's work, too.' She smiled sweetly at Anneliese. 'What kind of work do you do, Anneliese?'

'Anneliese is far too delicate and sensitive to work,' declared her mother. 'In any case she has no need to do so. She will marry Professor ter Mennolt very shortly.'

'Yes, I did know.' Emmy smiled at them both. It was a difficult thing to do; she wanted to slap them, and shake Anneliese until her teeth rattled in her head. 'So nice to see you again,' she told Anneliese, and crossed the room to join her mother and father, who were talking to an elderly couple, cousins of the professor.

The professor's two sisters, watching her from the other end of the room, saw her pink cheeks and lifted chin and wondered what Anneliese had said to her. When the professor joined them for a moment, Joke said, 'Ruerd, why did you leave Emmy with Anneliese and her mother? They've upset her. You know how nasty Anneliese can be.' She caught her brother's eye. 'All right, I shouldn't have said that. But her mother's there, too…'

She wandered away and presently fetched up beside Emmy.

'You crossed swords,' she said into Emmy's ear. 'Were they absolutely awful?'

'Yes.'

'I hope you gave them as good as you got,' said Joke.

'Well, no. I wanted to very badly, but I couldn't, could I? I'm a guest here, aren't I? And I couldn't answer back.'

'Why not?'

'Anneliese is going to marry Ruerd. He—he must love her, and it would hurt him if she were upset.'

Joke tucked her hand in her arm. 'Emmy, dear, would you mind if Ruerd was upset?'

'Yes, of course. He's—he's kind and patient and very generous, and he deserves to be happy.' Emmy looked at Joke, unaware of the feelings showing so plainly in her face.

'Yes, he does,' said Joke gravely. 'Come and meet some more of the family. We're endless, aren't we? Have you met my grandmother?'

Twenty people sat down to dinner presently. The table had been extended and more chairs arranged round it, but there was still plenty of room. Emmy, sitting between one of the brothers-in-law and a jovial man—an old friend of the family—could see her parents on the other side of the table, obviously enjoying themselves.

The professor sat at the head of the table, of course, with Anneliese beside him and his grandmother on his other hand. Emmy looked away and concentrated on something else. There was plenty to concentrate upon. The table for a start, with the lace table mats, sparkling glass and polished silver. There was an epergne at its centre, filled with holly, Christmas roses and trailing ivy, and candles in silver candelabra.

Dinner lived up to the splendour of the table: sorrel soup, mustard-grilled sole, raised game pie with braised celery, brussel sprouts with chestnuts, spinach purée and creamed potatoes, and to follow a selection of desserts.

Emmy, finding it difficult to choose between a mouth-watering trifle and a milanaise soufflé, remembered the bread and jam they had once eaten and blushed. She blushed again when the professor caught her eye and smiled. Perhaps he had remembered, too, although how he had thought of anything else but his beautiful Anneliese sitting beside him...

Emmy, savouring the trifle, saw that Anneliese was toying with a water ice. No wonder she was so slim. Not slim, thought Emmy—bony. And, however gorgeous her dress was, it didn't disguise Anneliese's lack of bosom. Listening politely to the old friend of the family talking about his garden, Emmy was thankfully aware that her own bosom left nothing to be desired. A pity about the brown dress, of course, but, since the professor had barely glanced at her, it hardly mattered—a potato sack would have done just as well.

Dinner over, the party repaired to the drawing room and Emmy went to sit by her mother.

Mrs Foster was enjoying herself. 'This is delightful, Emmy. When I think that we might still be at the lodge, surrounded by someone else's furniture... I do wish we had brought a present for Ruerd.'

'Well, there wasn't time, Mother. Perhaps we can send him something when we get back home. Has he said how long we're staying here?'

'No, but he told your father that he has to return to England on Boxing Day, so I expect we shall go back with him then.' Mrs Foster added, 'I don't like his fiancée; she'll not make him a good wife.'

They were joined by other guests then, and the rest of the evening passed pleasantly enough. Around midnight Anneliese and her mother went home. She went from one group to the other, laughing and talking, her hand on the professor's sleeve, barely pausing to wish Emmy and her mother goodnight.

'I'll be back tomorrow,' she told them. 'Ruerd has excellent servants but they need supervision. So fortunate that Ruerd offered you a roof over your heads for Christmas. Of course, it was the least anyone could do.'

She gave them a brittle smile and left them.

'I don't like her,' said Mrs Foster softly.

'She's beautiful,' said Emmy. 'She will be a most suitable wife for Ruerd.'

Alemke joined them then and they chattered together, presently joined by several other guests, until people began to drift home. All this while the professor had contrived to be at the other end of the room, going from one group to the other, pausing briefly to say something to Mrs Foster, hoping that Emmy was enjoying herself. The perfect host.

The next day was Christmas Eve, and Anneliese arrived for lunch wrapped in cashmere and a quilted silk jacket. At least she came alone this time, playing her part as the future mistress of Ruerd's house with a charm which set Emmy's teeth on edge.

Somehow she managed to make Emmy feel that she was receiving charity, even while she smiled and talked and ordered Cokker about as though she were already his mistress. He was called away to the phone, and she took the opportunity to alter the arrangements for lunch, reprimand Cokker for some trivial fault and point out to Emmy in a sugary voice that there would be guests for lunch and had she nothing more suitable to wear?

'No, I haven't,' said Emmy coldly. 'And if you don't wish to sit down to the table with me, please say so. I'm sure the professor won't mind if I and my mother and father have something on a tray in another room.' She added, 'I'll go and find him and tell him so...'

Anneliese said urgently, 'No, no, I didn't mean... It was only a suggestion. I'm sure you look quite nice, and everyone knows—'

'What does everyone know?' asked the professor from the door.

He looked from one to the other of them, and Emmy said in a wooden voice, 'Oh, you must ask Anneliese that,' and went past him out of the room.

The professor said quietly, 'The Fosters are my guests, Anneliese. I hope that you remember that— and that you are in my house!'

She leaned up to kiss his cheek. 'Dear Ruerd, of course I remember. But Emmy isn't happy, you know; this isn't her kind of life. She told me just now that she and her parents would be much happier having lunch by themselves. I told her that she looked quite nice—she's so sensitive about her clothes—and that everyone knew they had no time to pack sufficient clothes.'

She shrugged her shoulders. 'I've done my best, Ruerd.' She flashed him a smile. 'I'm going to talk to your sisters; I've hardly had time to speak to them.'

The professor stood for a moment after she had left him, deep in thought. Then he wandered off, away from the drawing room where everyone was having a drink before lunch, opening and closing doors quietly until he found Emmy in the garden room, standing by the great stone sink, doing nothing.

He closed the door behind him and stood leaning against it. 'You know, Emmy, it doesn't really matter in the least what clothes you are wearing. Anneliese tells me that you feel inadequately dressed and are shy of joining my guests. I do know that clothes matter to a woman, but the woman wearing them matters much more.

'Everyone likes you, Emmy, and you know me well enough by now to know that I don't say anything I don't mean. Indeed, they like you so much that Joke wants you to stay a few weeks and help her with the children while Nanny goes on holiday. Would you consider that? I shall be in England, Rik has to go to Switzerland for ten days on business, and she would love to have your company and help.'

Emmy had had her back to him, but she turned round now. 'I wouldn't believe a word of that if it was someone else, but you wouldn't lie to me, would you?'

'No, Emmy.'

'Joke would really like me to stay and help with the children? I'd like that very much. But what about Mother and Father?'

'I'll take them back when I go in two days' time. Probably by then the problem of the furniture will have been settled.' He smiled. 'They will have everything as they want it by the time you get back.'

'I'll stay if Joke would like that,' said Emmy.

'She'll be delighted. Now come and eat your lunch— we will talk to your mother and father presently.'

She sat next to him at lunch, with Rik on her other side and Hugo across the table, and between them they had her laughing and talking, all thoughts of her clothes forgotten. That afternoon she went for a walk with Joke and Alemke and the children, down to the village and back again, walking fast in a cold wind and under a grey sky.

'There'll be snow later,' said Joke. 'Will you come to church tomorrow, Emmy? The family goes, and anyone else who'd like to. We have midday lunch and a gigantic feast in the evening. The children stay up for it and it's bedlam.'

There was tea round the fire when they got back, with Anneliese acting as hostess, although, when Joke and Alemke joined the others, she said with a titter, 'Oh, dear, I shouldn't be doing this—Joke, do forgive me. I am so used to being here that sometimes I feel that I am already married.'

Several people gave her a surprised look, but no one said anything until Alemke started to talk about their walk.

The professor wasn't there and neither, Emmy saw, were her mother and father. She wondered if Anneliese knew that she had been asked to stay on after Christmas and decided that she didn't—for Anneliese was being gracious, talking to her in her rather loud voice, saying how glad she would be to be back in her own house, and did she know what kind of job she hoped to get?

Emmy ate Christmas cake and said placidly that she had no idea. Her heart ached with love for Ruerd but nothing of that showed in her serene face, nicely flushed by her walk.

She didn't have to suffer Anneliese's condescending conversation for long; she was called over to a group reminiscing about earlier Christmases, and presently

Aunt Beatrix joined them, with Cokker close behind, bringing fresh tea. Everyone clustered around her, and Anneliese said bossily, 'I'll ring for sandwiches; Cokker should have brought them.'

Aunt Beatrix paused in her talk to say loudly, 'You'll do nothing of the kind. If I want sandwiches, Cokker will bring them. I dare say you mean well,' went on Aunt Beatrix tartly, 'but please remember that I am a member of the family and familiar with the household.' She added sharply, 'Why aren't you with Ruerd? You see little enough of each other.'

'He's doing something—he said he would have his tea in the study.' Anneliese added self-righteously, 'I never interfere with his work, *mevrouw*.'

Aunt Beatrix gave a well-bred snort. She said something in Dutch which, of course, Emmy didn't understand and which made Anneliese look uncomfortable.

Cokker returned then, set a covered dish before Aunt Beatrix, removed the lid to reveal hot buttered toast and then slid behind Emmy's chair. 'If you will come with me, miss, your mother requires you.'

Emmy got up. 'There's nothing wrong?' she asked him quietly, and he shook his head and smiled. 'You will excuse me, *mevrouw*,' said Emmy quietly. 'My mother is asking for me.'

She went unhurriedly from the room, following Cokker into the hall as Aunt Beatrix, reverting to her own tongue, said, 'There goes a girl with pretty manners. I approve of her.'

A remark tantamount, in the eyes of her family, to receiving a medal.

Cokker led the way across the hall and opened the study door, ushered Emmy into the room and closed the door gently behind her. The professor was there, sitting at his desk, and her mother and father were sitting comfortably in the two leather chairs on either side of the small fireplace, in which a brisk fire burned.

There was a tea tray beside her mother's chair and the professor, who had stood up as Emmy went in, asked, 'You have had your tea, Ermentrude? Would you like another cup, perhaps?'

Emmy sat down composedly, her insides in a turmoil. I must learn to control my feelings, she reflected, and said briskly, 'Cokker said that Mother wanted to see me.'

'Well, yes, dear—we all do. Ruerd was telling us that his sister would like you to stay for a while and help with her children. We think it's a splendid idea but, of course, you must do what you like. Though, as Ruerd says, you really need a holiday and a change of scene, and we can get the lodge put to rights before you come back home.'

Emmy could hear the relief in her mother's voice. The prospect of getting the lodge in order while cherishing her daughter—who, according to the professor, needed a quiet and comfortable life for a few weeks—was daunting. The lodge would be cold and damp, and there were tea-chests of things to be unpacked, not to mention getting meals and household chores. Having a semi-invalid around the place would be no help at all. Much as she loved her child, Mrs Foster could be forgiven for welcoming the solving of an awkward problem.

Wasn't too much concern being expressed about her health? wondered Emmy. After all, it had only been a bang on the head, and she felt perfectly all right.

'I'll be glad to stay for a little while and help Joke with the children,' she said composedly.

'Splendid,' said the professor. 'Ermentrude will be in good hands, Mrs Foster. Cokker and Tiele will look after my sister and the children and Ermentrude. Alemke will go home directly after Christmas, and so will Aunt Beatrix and the cousins. It will be nice for Cokker to have someone in the house. Joke will be here for a couple of weeks, I believe, and I'll see that Ermentrude will have a comfortable journey home.'

He's talking just as though I wasn't here, reflected Emmy. For two pins I'd say... He smiled at her then and she found herself smiling back, quite forgetting his high-handedness.

Dinner that evening was festive. Emmy wished that she had a dress to do justice to the occasion, but the brown velvet had to pass muster once again. Anneliese, in the splendour of gold tissue and chiffon, gave her a slight smile as she entered the drawing room—much more eloquent than words.

Despite that, Emmy enjoyed herself. Tonight it was mushrooms in garlic, roast pheasant and red cabbage and a mouth-watering selection of desserts. And a delicious red wine which Emmy found very uplifting to the spirits.

Anneliese's father came to drive her home later, and Emmy felt everyone relax. It was an hour or two later before the party broke up, everyone going to their beds, in a very convivial mood. She had hardly spoken to the professor, and his goodnight was friendly and casual.

'A delightful evening,' said Mrs Foster, bidding Emmy goodnight at her bedroom door. 'Ruerd is a de-

lightful man and a splendid host. Although I cannot
see how he could possibly be in love with Anneliese.
A nasty, conceited woman, if you ask me.'

'She's beautiful,' said Emmy, and kissed her mother
goodnight.

Christmas Day proved to be everything it should
be. After breakfast everyone, children included, loaded
themselves into cars and drove to the village church,
where Emmy was delighted to hear carols just as she
would have expected to hear in England—only they
were sung in Dutch, of course. The tunes were the same;
she sang the English words and the professor, standing
beside her, smiled to himself.

Lunch was a buffet, with the children on their best
behaviour because once lunch was over they would all
go into the hall and the presents would be handed out
from under the tree, now splendidly lighted. Everyone
was there—Cokker and Tiele and the housemaids and
the gardener—but no Anneliese.

'She'll come this evening,' whispered Joke. She
added waspishly, 'When the children are all in bed and
there is no danger of sticky fingers.'

Handing out the presents took a long time; there was
a great deal of unwrapping of parcels and exclamations
of delight at their contents, and the children went from
one to the other, showing off their gifts. There was a
present for Mrs Foster, too—an evening handbag of
great elegance—and for Mr Foster a box of cigars. For
Emmy there was a blue cashmere scarf, the colour of
a pale winter sky. It was soft and fine, and she stroked
it gently. Every time she wore it, she promised herself,
she would remember the professor.

Tea was noisy and cheerful but, very soon afterwards, the children—now tired and cross—were swept away to their beds. Nanny came to fetch them, looking harassed, and Emmy asked Joke if she might go with her. 'Just to help a bit,' she said diffidently.

'Oh, would you like to?' Joke beamed at her. 'Alemke has a headache, but I'll be up presently to say goodnight. You'd truly like to? I mean, don't feel that you must.'

Emmy smiled. 'I'd like to.'

She slipped away and spent the next hour under Nanny's stern eye, getting damp from splashed bathwater and warm from coaxing small, wriggling bodies into nightclothes. They were all settled at last and, with a nod of thanks from Nanny, Emmy went back downstairs. Everyone was dressing for dinner, she realised as she reached the hall.

Not quite everyone; she found the professor beside her.

She turned to go back upstairs again. 'I ought to be changing,' she said quickly. 'Thank you for my scarf. I've never had anything cashmere before.'

He didn't say anything, but wrapped his great arms round her and kissed her.

She was so taken by surprise that she didn't do anything for a moment. She had no breath anyway. The kiss hadn't been a social peck; it had lingered far too long. And besides, she had the odd feeling that something was alight inside her, giving her the pleasant feeling that she could float in the air if she wished. If that was what a kiss did to one, she thought hazily, then one must avoid being kissed again.

She disentangled herself. 'You shouldn't…' she began.

'What I mean is, you mustn't kiss me. Anneliese wouldn't like it...'

He was staring down at her, an odd look on his face. 'But you did, Ermentrude?'

She nodded. 'It's not fair to her,' she said, and then, unable to help herself, asked, 'Why did you do it?'

He smiled. 'My dear Ermentrude, look up above our heads. Mistletoe—see? A mistletoe kiss, permissible even between the truest strangers. And really we aren't much more than that, are we?'

He gave her an avuncular pat on the shoulder. 'Run along and dress or you will be late for drinks.'

Emmy didn't say anything; her throat was crowded with tears and she could feel the hot colour creeping into her face. She flew up the staircase without a sound. Somewhere to hide, she thought unhappily. He was laughing at me.

But the professor wasn't laughing.

Chapter 8

There was very little time left for Emmy to dress. Which was perhaps just as well. She lay too long in the bath and had to tear into her clothes, zipping up the brown dress with furious fingers, brushing her hair until her eyes watered.

She had made a fool of herself; the professor must have been amused, he must have seen how his kiss had affected her—like a silly schoolgirl, she told her reflection. If only she didn't love him she would hate him. She would be very cool for the entire evening, let him see that she considered his kiss—his mistletoe kiss, she reminded herself—was no consequence at all.

Her mother and father had already gone downstairs; she hurried after them just in time to see Anneliese making an entrance. Vivid peacock-blue taffeta this evening. In a style slightly too girlish for the wearer, decided Emmy waspishly, before going to greet Grand-mother ter Mennolt—who had spent most of the day in her room but had now joined the family party, wearing purple velvet and a cashmere shawl fastened with the largest diamond brooch Emmy had ever set eyes on.

Emmy wished her good evening and would have moved away, but the old lady caught her arm. 'Stay, child. I have seen very little of you. I enjoyed a talk with your parents. They return tomorrow?'

'Yes, *mevrouw*. I'm staying for a little while to help Joke while her nanny goes on holiday.'

'You will be here for the New Year? It is an important occasion to us in Holland.'

'I don't know; I shouldn't think so. Will it be a family gathering again?'

'Yes, but just for the evening. You are enjoying yourself?'

'Yes, thank you. Very much.'

'Excellent. Now run along and join the others.' The old lady smiled. 'I must confess that I prefer the quiet of my room, but it is Christmas and one must make merry!'

Which described the evening very well—drinks before dinner sent everyone into the dining room full of *bonhomie*, to sit down to a traditional Christmas dinner—turkey, Christmas pudding, mince pies, crackers, port and walnuts...

The cousin sitting next to Emmy, whose name she had forgotten, accepted a second mince pie. 'Of course, not all Dutch families celebrate as we do here. This is typically English, is it not? But you see we have married into English families from time to time, and this is one of the delightful customs we have adopted. Will you be here for the New Year?'

'I don't know. I don't expect so. I'm only staying for a few days while Nanny has a holiday.'

'We return home tomorrow—all of us. But we shall be here again for New Year. But only for one night. We are that rare thing—a happy family. We enjoy meeting each other quite frequently. You have brothers and sisters?'

'No, there is just me. But I have always been happy at home.'

'The children like you…'

'Well, I like them.' She smiled at him and turned to the elderly man on her other side. She wasn't sure who he was, and his English was heavily accented, but he was, like everyone else—except Anneliese and her parents—friendly towards her.

After dinner everyone went back to the drawing room, to talk and gossip, going from group to group, and Emmy found herself swept up by Joke, listening to the lively chatter, enjoying herself and quite forgetting the brown dress and the way in which the professor avoided her.

It was while Joke, her arm linked in Emmy's, was talking to friends of the professor's—a youngish couple and something, she gathered, to do with one of the hospitals—that Anneliese joined them.

She tapped Emmy on the arm. 'Ruerd tells me you are to stay here for a few weeks as nanny to Joke's children. How fortunate you are, Emmy, to find work so easily after your lovely holiday.' She gave a titter. 'Let us hope that it hasn't given you ideas above your station.'

Emmy reminded herself that this was the professor's fiancée and that after this evening she need not, with any luck, ever see her again. Which was just as well, for the temptation to slap her was very strong.

She said in a gentle voice, aware that her companions were bating their breath, 'I'm sure you will agree with me that work at any level is preferable to idling away one's life, wasting money on unsuitable clothes—' she cast an eloquent eye at Anneliese's flat chest '—and wasting one's days doing nothing.'

If I sound like a prig, that's too bad, thought Emmy, and smiled her sweetest smile.

Now what would happen?

Joke said instantly, 'You're quite right, Emmy—I'm sure I agree, Anneliese.' And she was backed up by murmurs from her companions.

Anneliese, red in the face, said sharply, 'Well, of course I do. Excuse me, I must speak to Aunt Beatrix...'

'You mean *our* aunt Beatrix,' said Joke in a voice of kindly reproval. Anneliese shot her a look of pure dislike and went away without another word.

'I simply must learn to hold my tongue,' said Joke, and giggled. 'I'm afraid I shall be a very nasty sister-in-law. Alemke is much more civil, although it plays havoc with her temper.'

She caught Emmy's sleeve. 'Come and talk to Grandmother. She will be going back to den Haag in the morning. Well, everyone will be going, won't they? Ruerd last of all, after lunch, and that leaves you and the children and me, Emmy.'

'I shall like that,' said Emmy. She was still shaking with rage. Anneliese would go to Ruerd and tell him how rude she had been, and he would never speak to her again...

She was talking to her mother when Anneliese went home with her parents. She gave them no more than a cool nod as she swept past them. The professor, as a good host should, saw them into their car and when he came back went to talk to his grandmother. It wasn't until everyone was dispersing much later to their beds that he came to wish the Fosters a good night and to hope that they had enjoyed their evening.

'I trust that you enjoyed yourself, too, Ermentrude,' he observed, looking down his splendid nose at her.

How nice if one could voice one's true thoughts and feelings, thought Emmy, assuring him in a polite voice that she had had a splendid evening.

He said, 'Good, good. I have to go to Leiden in the morning, but I shall see you before we go after lunch.'

For the last time, thought Emmy, and kissed her mother and father goodnight and went up the staircase to her bed.

Once breakfast was over in the morning people began to leave—stopping for a last-minute gossip, going back to find something they'd forgotten to pack, exchanging last-minute messages. They went at last, and within minutes the professor had got into his car and driven away too, leaving Emmy and her parents with Joke and the children.

Mrs Foster went away to finish her packing and Mr Foster retired to the library to read the *Daily Telegraph*, which Cokker had conjured up from somewhere. Since Joke wanted to talk to Tiele about the running of the house once the professor had gone, Emmy dressed the

children in their outdoor things, wrapped herself in her
coat, tied a scarf over her head and took them off to the
village, with Solly and Tip for company.

They bought sweets in the small village shop and
the dogs crunched the biscuits old Mevrouw Kamp offered them while she took a good look at Emmy, nodding and smiling while the children talked. Emmy had
no doubt that it was about her, but the old lady looked
friendly enough and, when she offered the children a
sweetie from the jar on the counter, she offered Emmy
one too. It tasted horrid, but she chewed it with apparent pleasure and wondered what it was.

'*Zoute* drop,' she was told. 'And weren't they delicious?'

For anyone partial to a sweet made of salt probably
they were, thought Emmy, and swallowed the last morsel thankfully.

They lunched early as the professor wanted to leave
by one o'clock. He joined in the talk—teasing the children, making last-minute arrangements with his sister,
discussing the latest news with Mr Foster. But, although
he was careful to see that Emmy had all that she wanted
and was included in the talk, he had little to say to her.

I shan't see him again, thought Emmy, and I can't
bear it. She brightened, though, when she remembered
that she would be going back to England later and there
was a chance that he might take her if he was on one
of his flying visits to one or other of the hospitals. The
thought cheered her so much that she was able to bid
him goodbye with brisk friendliness and thank him
suitably for her visit. 'It was a lovely Christmas,' she
told him, and offered a hand, to have it engulfed in his.

His brief, too cheerful, 'Yes, it was, wasn't it?' made

it only too plain that behind his good manners he didn't care tuppence...

She bade her mother and father goodbye, pleased to see what a lot of good these few days had done them. A little luxury never harmed anyone, she reflected, and hoped that the lodge would be quickly restored to normal.

'When you get home everything will be sorted out,' her mother assured her. 'Your father and I feel so rested we can tackle anything. Take care of yourself, love, won't you? Ruerd says you could do with a few more days before you go job-hunting.'

If it hadn't been for the children the house would have seemed very quiet once its master had driven away, but the rest of the day was taken up with the pleasurable task of re-examining the presents which they had had at Christmas, and a visit to the village shop once more to buy paper and envelopes for the less pleasurable task of writing the thank-you letters.

On the following day they all got into Joke's car and drove along the coast as far as Alkmaar. The cheese museum was closed for the winter, but there was the clock, with its mechanical figures circling round it on each hour, and the lovely cathedral church, as well as the picturesque old houses and shops. They lunched in a small café, off *erwtensoep*—a pea soup so thick that a spoon could stand upright in it—and *roggebrood*. The children made Emmy repeat the names after them, rolling around with laughter at her efforts.

It was a surprisingly happy day, and Emmy was kept too busy to think about the professor. Only that night as she got into bed did she spare him a thought. He would be back in Chelsea by now, with Beaker looking after him. He would have phoned Anneliese, of course. He would miss her, thought Emmy sleepily, although how a man could miss anyone as disagreeable as she was a bit of a puzzle.

There was a phone call from her mother in the morning. They had had a splendid trip back; Ruerd had taken them right to their door, and there had been a letter waiting for them, telling them that the furniture would be removed in a day's time.

'So now we can get things straight,' said her mother happily. 'And Ruerd is so splendid—he unloaded a box of the most delicious food for us, and a bottle of champagne. One meets such a person so seldom in life, and when one does it is so often for a brief period. We shall miss him. He sent his kind regards, by the way, love.'

An empty, meaningless phrase, reflected Emmy.

She was to have the children all day as Joke was going to den Haag to the hairdresser's and to do some shopping. It was a bright, cold day, so, with everyone well wrapped-up, she led them down to the sea, tramping along the sand with Tip and Solly gavotting around them. They all threw sticks, racing up and down, shouting and laughing to each other, playing tig, daring each other to run to the water's edge and back.

Emmy shouted with them; there was no one else to hear or see them, and the air was exhilarating. They trooped back presently, tired and hungry, to eat the lunch Cokker had waiting for them and then go to the nursery, where they sat around the table playing cards—the littlest one on Emmy's lap, her head tucked into Emmy's shoulder, half asleep.

They had tea there presently and, since Joke wasn't

back yet, Emmy set about getting them ready for bed. Bathed and clad in dressing gowns they were eating their suppers when their mother returned.

'Emmy, you must be worn out. I never meant to be so long, but I met some friends and had lunch with them and then I had the shopping to do. Have you hated it?'

'I've enjoyed every minute,' said Emmy quite truthfully. 'I had a lovely day; I only hope the children did, too.'

'Well, tomorrow we're all going to den Haag to have lunch with my mother and father. They were away for Christmas—in Denmark with a widowed aunt. They'll be here for New Year, though. You did know that we had parents living?'

'The professor mentioned it.'

'Christmas wasn't quite the same without them, but we'll all be here in a few days.'

'You want me to come with you tomorrow?' asked Emmy. 'I'm quite happy to stay here—I mean, it's family...'

Joke smiled. 'I want you to come if you will, Emmy.' She wondered if she should tell her that her parents had been told all about her by Ruerd, and decided not to. It was his business. They had never been a family to interfere with each other's lives, although she and Alemke very much wished to dissuade him from marrying Anneliese.

There was undoubtedly something Ruerd was keeping to himself, and neither of them had seen any sign of love or even affection in his manner towards Anneliese, although he was attentive to her needs and always concerned for her comfort. Good manners wouldn't allow him to be otherwise. And he had been careful to avoid being alone with Emmy at Christmas. Always polite towards her, his friendliness also aloof. Knowing her brother, Joke knew that he wouldn't break his word to Anneliese, although she strongly suspected that he had more than a casual interest in Emmy.

They drove to den Haag in good spirits in the morning. The children spoke a little English and Emmy taught them some of the old-fashioned nursery rhymes, which they sang for most of the way. Only as they reached a long, stately avenue with large houses on each side of it did Emmy suggest that they should stop. Joke drove up the short drive of one of these houses and stopped before its ponderous door. 'Well, here we are,' she declared. 'Oma and Opa will be waiting.'

The door opened as they reached it and a stout, elderly woman welcomed them.

'This is Nynke,' said Joke, and Emmy shook hands and waited while the children hugged and kissed her. 'The housekeeper. She has been with us since I was a little girl.' It was her turn to be hugged and kissed before they all went into the hall to take off coats and scarves and gloves, and go through the arched double doors Nynke was holding open for them.

The elderly couple waiting for them at the end of the long, narrow room made an imposing pair. The professor's parents were tall—his father with the massive frame he had passed on to his son, and his mother an imposing, rather stout figure. They both had grey hair, and his father was still a handsome man, but his mother, despite her elegant bearing, had a homely face, spared from downright plainness by a pair of very blue eyes.

No wonder he has fallen in love with Anneliese, reflected Emmy, with that lovely face and golden hair.

The children swarmed over their grandparents, although they were careful to mind their manners, and presently stood quietly while Joke greeted her parents.

'And this is Emmy,' she said, and put a hand on Emmy's arm. 'I am so glad to have her with me for a few days—she's been staying with her parents over Christmas at Huis ter Mennolt. Rik's away, and it's lovely to have company.'

Emmy shook hands, warmed by friendly smiles and greetings in almost accentless English. Presently Mevrouw ter Mennolt drew her to one side and, over coffee and tiny almond biscuits, begged her to tell her something of herself.

'Ruerd mentioned that he had guests from England when he phoned us. You know him well?'

The nice, plain face smiled, the blue eyes twinkled. Emmy embarked on a brief résumé of her acquaintance with the professor, happily unaware that her companion had already had a detailed account from her son. It was what he *hadn't* said which had convinced his mother that he was more than a little interested in Emmy.

Watching Emmy's face, almost as plain as her own, she wished heartily for a miracle before Anneliese managed to get her son to the altar. Mevrouw ter Mennolt had tried hard to like her, since her son was to marry the girl, but she had had no success, and Anneliese, confident in her beauty and charm, had never made an effort to gain her future mother-in-law's affection.

Emmy would, however, do very nicely. Joke had told her that she was right for Ruerd, and she found herself agreeing. The children liked her and that, for a doting grandmother, was an important point. She hadn't forgotten Anneliese once flying into a rage during a visit because Joke's youngest had accidentally put a grubby little paw on Anneliese's white skirt. It was a pity that Ruerd hadn't been there, for her lovely face had grown ugly with temper. Besides, this quiet, rather shabbily dressed girl might be the one woman in the world who understood Ruerd, a man who's feelings ran deep and hidden from all but those who loved him.

Emmy was handed over to her host presently, and although she was at first wary of this older edition of the professor he put her at her ease in minutes, talking about gardening, dogs and cats, and presently he bade her fetch her coat.

'We have a garden here,' he told her. 'Not as splendid as that at Huis ter Mennolt, but sufficient for us and Max. Let us take the dogs for a quick run before lunch.'

They went through the house, into a conservatory, out of doors onto a terrace and down some steps to the garden below. Max, the black Labrador, Solly and Tip went with them, going off the path to search for imaginary rabbits, while Emmy and Ruerd's father walked briskly down its considerable length to the shrubbery at the end.

All the while they talked. At least, the old man talked, and a great deal of what he said concerned his son. Emmy learned more about Ruerd in fifteen minutes than she had in all the weeks she had known him. She listened avidly; soon she would never see him again, so every small scrap of information about him was precious, to be stored away, to be mulled over in a future empty of him.

Back at the house she led the children away to have their hands washed and their hair combed before lunch. They went up the stairs and into one of the bathrooms— old-fashioned like the rest of the house, but lacking nothing in comfort. She liked the house. It wasn't like Huis ter Mennolt; it had been built at a later date—mid-nineteenth century, she guessed—and the furniture was solid and beautifully cared for. Beidermeier? she thought, not knowing much about it. Its walls were hung with family portraits and she longed to study them as she urged the children downstairs once again, all talking at once and laughing at her attempts to understand them.

She was offered dry sherry in the drawing room while the children drank something pink and fizzy—a special drink they always had at their grandmother's, they told her, before they all went into the dining room for lunch.

It was a pleasant meal, with the children on their best behaviour and conversation which went well with eating the lamb chops which followed the celery soup—nothing deep which required long pauses while something was debated and explained—and nothing personal. No one, thought Emmy, had mentioned Anneliese once, which, since she was so soon to be a member of the family, seemed strange.

Christmas was discussed, and plans for the New Year. 'We shall all meet again at Huis ter Mennolt,' explained Joke. 'Just for dinner in the evening, and to wish each other a happy New Year. Ruerd will come back just for a day or two; he never misses.'

They sat around after lunch, and presently, when the children became restive, Emmy sat them round a table at the other end of the drawing room and suggested cards. 'Snap', 'beggar your neighbour' and 'beat your neighbour out of doors' she had already taught them, and they settled down to play. Presently she was making as much noise as they were.

It was a large room; the three persons at the other end of it were able to talk without hindrance, and, even if Emmy could have heard them, she couldn't have understood a word. Good manners required them to talk in English while she was with them, but now they embarked on the subject nearest to their hearts—Ruerd.

They would have been much cheered if they had known that he was in his office at St Luke's, sitting at his desk piled with patients' notes, charts and department reports, none of which he was reading. He was thinking about Emmy.

When he returned to Holland in a few days' time, he would ask Anneliese to release him from their engagement. It was a step he was reluctant to take for, although he had no feeling for her any more, he had no wish to humiliate her with her friends. But to marry her when he loved Ermentrude was out of the question. Supposing Ermentrude wouldn't have him? He smiled a little; then he would have to remain a bachelor for the rest of his days.

He would have his lovely home in Holland, his pleasant house in Chelsea, his dogs, his work…but a bleak prospect without her.

Joke, Emmy and the children drove back to Huis ter Mennolt after tea. With the coming of evening it was much colder. 'We shall probably have some snow before much longer,' said Joke. 'Do you skate, Emmy?'

'No, only roller-skating when I was a little girl. We don't get much snow at home.'

'Well, we can teach you while you are here.' Joke added quickly, 'Nanny isn't coming back for another couple of days. Her mother has the flu, and she doesn't want to give it to the children. You won't mind staying for a few days longer?'

Emmy didn't mind. She didn't mind where she was if the professor wasn't going to be there too.

'You've heard from your mother?' asked Joke.

'Yes; everything is going very well at last. The furniture will be gone today and the plumber has almost finished whatever it was he had to do. By the time the term starts they should be well settled in. I ought to have been there to help…'

'Well, Ruerd advised against it, didn't he? And I dare say your mother would have worried over you if you had worked too hard or got wet.'

'Well, yes, I suppose so.'

Emmy eased the smallest child onto her lap so that Solly could lean against her shoulder. Tip was in front with the eldest boy. It was a bit of a squash in the big car, but it was warm and comfortable, smelling of damp dog and the peppermints the children were eating.

The next morning Joke went back to den Haag. 'Cokker will look after you all,' she told Emmy. 'Take the children out if you like. They're getting excited about New Year. Everyone will be coming tomorrow in time for lunch, but Ruerd phoned to say he won't get here until the evening. I hope he'll stay for a few days this time. He'll take you back with him when he does go. If that suits you?' Joke studied Emmy's face. 'You do feel better for the change? I haven't asked you to do too much?'

'I've loved every minute,' said Emmy truthfully. 'I like the children and I love this house and the seashore, and you've all been so kind to me and Mother and Father.'

'You must come and see us again,' said Joke, and looked at Emmy to see how she felt about that.

'I expect I shall have a job, but it's kind of you to invite me.'

'Ruerd could always bring you over when he comes,' persisted Joke.

'Well, I don't suppose we shall see each other. I mean, he's in London and I'll be in Dorset.'

'Will you mind that?' said Joke.

Emmy bent over the French knitting she was fixing for one of the girls.

'Yes. The professor has helped me so often—you know, when things have happened. He—he always seemed to be there, if you see what I mean. I shall always be grateful to him.'

Joke said airily, 'Yes, coincidence is a strange thing, isn't it? Some people call it fate. Well, I'm off. Ask Cokker or Tiele for anything you want. I'll try and be back in time for tea, but if the traffic's heavy I may be a bit late.'

The day was much as other days—going down to the seashore, running races on the sand, with Emmy carrying the youngest, joining in the shouting and laughing and then going back to piping hot soup and *crokettes*, and, since it was almost new year, *poffertjes*—tiny pancakes sprinkled with sugar.

The two smallest children were led upstairs to rest then, and the other two went to the billiard room where they were allowed to play snooker on the small table at one end of the room.

Which left Emmy with an hour or so to herself. She went back to the drawing room and began a slow round of the portraits and then a careful study of the contents of the two great display cabinets on either side of the fireplace. She was admiring a group of figurines—Meissen, she thought—when Cokker came into the room.

'Juffrouw van Moule has called,' he told her. 'I have said that *mevrouw* is out, but she wishes to see you, miss.'

'Me? Whatever for?' asked Emmy. 'I expect I'd better see her, hadn't I, Cokker? I don't expect she'll stay, do you? But if the children want anything, could you please ask Tiele to go to them?'

'Yes, miss, and you will ring if you want me?'

'Thank you, Cokker.'

Anneliese came into the room with the self-assurance of someone who knew that she looked perfection itself. Indeed she was beautiful, wrapped in a soft blue wool coat, with a high-crowned Melusine hat perched on her fair hair. She took the coat off and tossed it onto a chair, sent gloves and handbag after it and sat down in one of the small easy chairs.

'Still here, Ermentrude.' It wasn't a question but a statement. 'Hanging on until the last minute. Not that it will do you any good. Ruerd must be heartily tired of you, but that is what happens when one does a good deed—one is condemned to repeat it unendingly. Still, you have had a splendid holiday, have you not? He intends that you should return to England directly after New Year. He will be staying on here for a time; we have the wedding arrangements to complete. You did know that we are to marry in January?'

She looked at Emmy's face. 'No, I see that you did not know. I expect he knew that I would tell you. So much easier for me to do it, is it not? It is embarrassing for him, knowing that you are in love with him, although heaven knows he has never given you the least encouragement. I suppose someone like you, living such a dull life, has to make do with daydreams.'

Anneliese smiled and sat back in her chair.

'It seems to me,' said Emmy, in a voice she willed to keep steady, 'that you are talking a great deal of nonsense. Is that why you came? And you haven't told me anything new. I know that you and the professor are to be married, and I know that I am going back to England as soon as Nanny is back, and I know that you have been very rude and rather spiteful.'

She watched with satisfaction as Anneliese flushed brightly. 'I believe in being outspoken too. We dislike each other; I have no use for girls like you. Go back to England and find some clerk or shopkeeper to marry you. It is a pity that you ever had a taste of our kind of life.' She eyed Emmy shrewdly. 'You do believe me, don't you, about our marriage?'

And when Emmy didn't answer she said, 'I'll prove it.'

She got up and went to the phone on one of the side-tables. 'Ruerd's house number,' she said over her shoulder. 'If he isn't there I will ring the hospital.' She began to dial. 'And you know what I shall say? I shall tell him that you don't believe me, that you hope in your heart that he loves you and that you will continue to pester him and try and spoil his happiness.'

'You don't need to phone,' said Emmy quietly. 'I didn't believe you, but perhaps there is truth in what you say. I shall go back to England as soon as I can and I shan't see him again.'

Anneliese came back to her chair. 'And you'll say nothing when he comes here tomorrow? A pity you have to be here, but it can't be helped. Luckily there will be a number of people here; he won't have time to talk to you.'

'He never has talked to me,' said Emmy. 'Only as a guest.' Emmy got up. 'I expect you would like to go now. I don't know why you have thought of me as a— well, a rival, I suppose. You're beautiful, and I'm sure you will make the professor a most suitable wife. I hope you will both be happy.'

The words had almost choked her, but she had said them. Anneliese looked surprised, but she got into her coat, picked up her gloves and bag and went out of the room without another word. Cokker appeared a minute later.

'I have prepared a pot of tea, miss; I am sure you would enjoy it.'

Emmy managed a smile. 'Oh, Cokker, thank you. I'd love it.'

He came with the tray and set it down beside her chair. 'The English, I understand, drink tea at any time, but especially at moments of great joy or despair.'

'Yes, Cokker, you are quite right; they do.'

She wasn't going to cry, she told herself, drinking the hot tea, forcing it down over the lump of tears in her throat.

She tried not to think about the things Anneliese had said. They had been spiteful, but they had had the ring of truth. Had she been so transparent in her feelings towards Ruerd? She had thought—and how silly and stupid she had been—that his kiss under the mistletoe had meant something. She didn't know what, but it had been like a spark between them. Perhaps Anneliese was right and she had been allowing herself to daydream.

Emmy went pale at the thought of meeting him, but she had the rest of the day and most of tomorrow in which to pull herself together, and the first chance she got she would go back to England.

The children had their tea and she began on the leisurely task of getting them to bed after a rousing game of ludo. They were in their dressing gowns and eating their suppers when Joke got back, and it wasn't until she and Emmy had dined that Emmy asked her when Nanny would be coming back.

'You are not happy. I have given you too much to do—the children all day long...'

'No, no. I love it here and I like being with the children, only I think that I should go home as soon as Nanny comes back. I don't mean to sound ungrateful—it's been like a lovely holiday—but I must start looking for a job.'

Emmy spoke briskly but her face was sad, and Joke wondered why. She had her answer as Emmy went on in a determinedly cheerful voice, 'Anneliese called this afternoon. I should have told you sooner, but there were so many other things to talk about with the children. She only stayed for a few minutes.'

'Why did she come here? What did she say?'

'Nothing, really; she just sort of popped in. She didn't leave any messages for you. Perhaps she wanted to know something to do with tomorrow. She will be coming, of course.'

'Oh, yes, she will be here. Was she civil? She doesn't like you much, does she?'

'No; I don't know why. She was quite polite.'

I could tell you why, thought Joke—you've stolen Ruerd's heart, something Anneliese knows she can never do.

She said aloud, 'Nanny phoned this evening while you were getting the children into bed. She will be back the day after tomorrow. I hate to see you go, Emmy.'

'I shan't forget any of you, or this house and the people in it,' said Emmy.

She had no time to think about her own plans. The house was in a bustle, getting ready for the guests. Tiele was in the kitchen making piles of *oliebolljes*—a kind of doughnut which everyone ate at New Year—and the maids were hurrying here and there, laying the table for a buffet lunch and getting a guest room ready in case Grandmother ter Mennolt should need to rest.

'She never misses,' said Joke. 'She and Aunt Beatrix live together at Wassenaar—that's a suburb of den Haag. They have a housekeeper and Jon, the chauffeur, who sees to the garden and stokes the boiler and so on. The aunts and uncles and cousins you met at Christmas will come—oh, and Anneliese, of course.'

Almost everyone came for lunch, although guests were still arriving during the afternoon. Anneliese had arrived for lunch, behaving, as Joke said sourly, as though she were already the mistress of the house. Her parents were with her, and a youngish man whom she introduced as an old friend who had recently returned to Holland.

'We lost touch,' she explained. 'We were quite close…' She smiled charmingly and he put an arm round her waist and smiled down at her. She had spoken in Dutch, and Alemke had whispered a translation in Emmy's ear.

'How dare she bring that man here?' she added. 'And Ruerd won't be here until quite late this evening… Oh, how I wish something would happen…'

Sometimes a wish is granted. The professor, by dint of working twice as hard as usual, was ready to leave Chelsea by the late morning. Seen off by Beaker and Charlie, he drove to Dover, crossed over the channel and made good time to his house. It was dark when he arrived, and the windows were ablaze. He let himself in through a side door, pleased to be home, and even more pleased at the thought of seeing Emmy again. He walked along the curved passage behind the hall and then paused at a half-open door of a small sitting room, seldom used. Whoever was there sounded like Anneliese. He opened the door and went in.

Chapter 9

It was indeed Anneliese, in the arms of a man the professor didn't know, being kissed and kissing with unmistakable ardour.

With such ardour that they didn't see him. He stood in the doorway, watching them, until the man caught sight of him, pushed Anneliese away and then caught her hand in his.

The professor strolled into the room. 'I don't think I have had the pleasure of meeting you,' he said pleasantly. 'Anneliese, please introduce me to your friend.'

Anneliese was for once at a loss for words. The man held out a hand. 'Hubold Koppelar, an old friend of Anneliese.'

The professor ignored the hand. He looked down his splendid nose at Koppelar. 'How old?' he asked. 'Before Anneliese became engaged to me?'

Anneliese had found her tongue. 'Of course it was. Hubold went away to Canada; I thought he would never come back…'

The professor took out his spectacles, put them on and looked at her carefully. 'So you made do with me?'

Anneliese tossed her head. 'Well, what else was there to do? I want a home and money, like any other woman.'

'I am now no longer necessary to your plans for the future, though?' asked the professor gently. 'Consider yourself free, Anneliese, if that is what you want.'

Hubold drew her hand through his arm. 'She wants it, all right. Of course, we hadn't meant it to be like this—we would have let you down lightly…'

The professor's eyes were like flint, but he smiled. 'Very good of you. And now the matter is settled there is no need for us to meet again, is there? I regret that I cannot show you the door at this moment, but the New Year is an occasion in this house and I won't have it spoilt. I must ask you both to remain and behave normally until after midnight. Now, let us go together and meet my guests…'

So Emmy, about to go upstairs to get into the despised brown dress, was one of the first to see him come into the hall, with Anneliese on one side of him and the man she had brought with her on the other. It was easy to escape for everyone else surged forward to meet him.

'Ruerd, how lovely,' cried Joke. 'We didn't expect you until much later…'

'An unexpected surprise,' said the professor, and watched Emmy's small person disappear up the staircase. Nothing of his feelings showed on his face.

He made some laughing remark to Anneliese and went to talk to his grandmother and father and mother, then presently to mingle with his guests before everyone went away to change for the evening.

Emmy didn't waste much time on dressing. She took a uninterested look at her person in the looking-glass, put a few extra pins into the coil of hair in the nape of her neck and went along to the nursery to make sure that the children were ready for bed. As a great treat, they were to be roused just before midnight and brought downstairs to greet the New Year, on the understanding that they went to their beds punctually and went to sleep.

It seemed unlikely that they would, thought Emmy, tucking them in while she wondered how best to arrange her departure just as soon as possible.

To travel on New Year's Day would be impossible, but if she could see the professor in the morning and ask him to arrange for her to travel on the following day she would only need to stay one more day. And with so many people in the house it would be easy enough to keep out of the way. Anyway, he would surely be wrapped up in Anneliese. Emmy would get up early and pack, just in case there was some way of leaving sooner.

Fortune smiled on her for once. Sitting in a quiet corner of the drawing room was Oom Domus, middle-aged and a widower. He told her that he was going to the Hook of Holland to catch the ferry to England late on New Year's Day. 'It sails at midnight, as you may know. There will be almost no trains and buses or ferries tomorrow. It is very much a national holiday here.'

'Do you drive there?' asked Emmy.

'Yes; I'm going to stay with friends in Warwickshire.'

Emmy took a quick breath. 'Would you mind very much giving me a lift as far as Dover? I'm going back to England now that Nanny will be back tomorrow.'

If Oom Domus was surprised he didn't show it. 'My dear young lady, I shall be delighted. You live in Dorset, do you not? Far better if I drive you on to London and drop you off at whichever station you want.'

'You're very kind. I—I haven't seen the professor to tell him yet, but I'm sure he won't mind.'

Oom Domus had watched Ruerd not looking at Emmy, just as she was careful not to look at him. He thought it likely that both of them would mind, but he wasn't going to say so. He said easily, 'I shall leave around seven o'clock tomorrow evening, my dear. That will give you plenty of time to enjoy your day.'

As far as Emmy was concerned the day was going to be far too long. She wanted to get away as quickly as she could, away from Ruerd and his lovely home, and away from Anneliese.

Aunt Beatrix joined them then, and Emmy looked around her at the laughing and talking people near her. There was no sign of the professor for the moment, but Anneliese was there, as beautiful as ever, in yards of trailing chiffon. She was laughing a great deal, and looked flushed. Excitement at seeing Ruerd again? Or drinking too much?

Emmy took a second glass of sherry when Cokker offered it; perhaps if she drank everything she was offered during the evening it would be over more quickly. She caught sight of the professor's handsome features as he came across the room; she tossed back the sherry and beat a retreat into a group of cousins, who smilingly welcomed her and switched to English as easily as changing hats.

If the professor had noticed this, he gave no sign, merely passed the time of day with his uncle and went to talk to Joke.

'You look like a cat who's swallowed the cream,' she told him. 'What's going on behind that bland face of yours?'

When he only smiled she said, 'Nanny's back tomorrow. Have you arranged to take Emmy home?'

'No, not yet.'

'For some reason she's keen to go as soon as possible—said she has to find a job.'

'I'll talk to her when there's a quiet moment. Here's Cokker to tell us that dinner is served.'

Twenty persons sat down to the table which had been extended for the occasion, and Emmy found herself between two of the professor's friends—pleasant, middle-aged men who knew England well and kept up a lively conversation throughout the meal.

Emmy, very slightly muzzy from her tossed-back sherry, ate her mushrooms in garlic and cream, drank a glass of white wine with the lobster Thermidor and a glass of red wine with the kidneys in a calvados and cream sauce. And another glass of sweet white wine with the trifle and mince pies…

The meal was leisurely and the talk lively. The professor's father, sitting at the head of the table, listened gravely to Anneliese, who was so animated that Emmy decided that she really had drunk too much. Like me, reflected Emmy uneasily. He had Grandmother ter Mennolt on his other side, who, excepting when good manners demanded, ignored Anneliese. The professor was at the other end of the table, sitting beside his mother with Aunt Beatrix on his other side. Emmy wondered why he and Anneliese weren't sitting together. Perhaps there was a precedent about these occasions...

They had coffee at the table so that it was well after eleven o'clock before everyone went back to the drawing room. Anneliese was with Ruerd now, her friend at the other end of the room talking to Joke's husband. Emmy wondered if the professor would make some sort of announcement about his forthcoming marriage; Anneliese had told her that it was to be within the next few weeks, and presumably everyone there would be invited.

Nothing was said, and just before twelve o'clock she slipped away to rouse the children and bring them down to the drawing room. The older ones were awake—she suspected that they hadn't been to sleep yet—but the smaller ones needed a good deal of rousing. She was joined by Joke and Alemke presently, and they led the children downstairs, where they stood, owl-eyed and excited, each with a small glass of lemonade with which to greet the New Year.

Someone had tuned into the BBC, and Cokker was going round filling glasses with champagne. The maids and the gardener had joined them by now, and there was a ripple of excitement as Big Ben struck the first stroke. There were cries of *Gelukkige Niewe Jaar!* and the children screamed with delight as the first of the fireworks outside the drawing-room windows were set off.

Everyone was darting to and fro, kissing and shaking hands and wishing each other good luck and happiness. Emmy was kissed and greeted too, standing a little to one side with the smallest child—already half-asleep again despite the fireworks—tucked against her shoulder. Even Anneliese paused by her, but not to wish her well. All she said was, 'Tomorrow you will be back in England.'

Hubold Koppelar, circling the group, paused by her, looked her over and went past her without a word. He wasn't sure who she was; one of the maids, he supposed, detailed to look after the children. Anneliese would tell him later. For the moment they were keeping prudently apart, mindful of the professor's words, uttered so quietly but not to be ignored.

Emmy had been edging round the room, avoiding the professor as he went from one group to the other, exchanging greetings, but he finally caught up with her. She held out a hand and said stiffly, looking no higher than his tie, 'A happy New Year, Professor.'

He took the hand and held it fast. 'Don't worry, Ermentrude. I'm not going to kiss you; not here and now.'

He smiled down at her and her heart turned over.

'We shall have a chance to talk tomorrow morning,' he told her. 'Or perhaps presently, when the children are back in bed.'

Emmy gazed at him, quite unable to think of anything to say, looking so sad that he started to ask her what was the matter—to be interrupted by Aunt Beatrix, asking him briskly if he would have a word with his grandmother.

He let Emmy's hand go at last. 'Later,' he said, and smiled with such tenderness that she swallowed tears.

She watched his massive back disappear amongst his guests. He was letting her down lightly, letting her see that he was going to ignore a situation embarrassing to them both. She felt hot all over at the thought.

It was a relief to escape with the children and put

them back into their beds. She wouldn't be missed, and although there was a buffet supper she couldn't have swallowed a morsel. She went to her room, undressed and got into bed, lying awake until long after the house was quiet.

There was no one at breakfast when she went downstairs in the morning. Cokker brought her coffee and toast, which she didn't want. Later, she promised herself, when the professor had a few minutes to spare, she would explain about going back to England with Oom Domus. He would be pleased; it made a neat end to an awkward situation. Anneliese would have got her way, too... She hadn't seen Anneliese after those few words; she supposed that she was spending the night here and would probably stay on now the professor was home.

Emmy got up and went to look out of the window. Ruerd was coming towards the house with Tip and Solly, coming from the direction of the shore. If she had the chance she would go once more just to watch the wintry North Sea and then walk back over the dunes along the path which would afford her a glimpse of the house beyond the garden. It was something she wanted to remember for always.

She went back upstairs before he reached the house; the children must be wakened and urged to dress and clean their teeth. Joke had said that they would be leaving that afternoon at the same time as Alemke and her husband and children.

'Everyone else will go before lunch,' she had told Emmy. 'My mother and father will stay for lunch, of course, but Grandmother and Aunt Beatrix will go at the same time as the others.'

Cousins and aunts and uncles and family and friends began to take their leave soon after breakfast, and, once they had gone, Emmy suggested that she should take the children down for a last scamper on the sands.

'Oh, would you?' asked Joke. 'Just for an hour, so they can let off steam? Nanny will be waiting for us when we get home. They're going to miss you, Emmy.'

The professor was in his study with his father. Emmy bundled the children into their coats, wrapped herself up against the winter weather outside and hurried them away before he should return. She still had to tell him that she was leaving, but perhaps a brisk run out of doors would give her the courage to do so.

At the end of an hour, she marshalled her charges into some sort of order and went back to the house, and, since their boots and shoes were covered in damp sand and frost, they went in through the side door. It wasn't until it was too late to retreat that she saw the professor standing there, holding the door open.

The children milled around him, chattering like magpies, but presently he said something to them and they trooped away, leaving Emmy without a backward glance. She did her best to slide past the professor's bulk.

'I'll just go and help the children,' she began. And then went on ashamed of her cowardice, 'I wanted to see you, Professor. I'd like to go back to England today, if you don't mind. Oom Domus said he would give me a lift this evening.' When he said nothing she added, 'I've had a lovely time here, and you've been so kind. I'm very grateful, but it's time I went back to England.'

He glanced at her and looked away. 'Stay a few more days, Ermentrude. I'll take you back when I go.'

'I'd like to go today—and it's so convenient, isn't it? I mean, Oom Domus is going over to England this evening.'

'You have no wish to stay?' he asked, in what she thought was a very casual voice. 'We must talk…'

'No—no. I'd like to go as soon as possible.'

'By all means go with Oom Domus.' He stood aside. 'Don't let me keep you; I expect that you have things to do. Lunch will be in half an hour or so.'

She slipped past him, and then stopped as he said, without turning round, 'You have avoided me, Ermentrude. You have a reason?'

'Yes, but I don't want to talk about it. It's—personal.' She paused. 'It's something I'd rather not talk about,' she repeated.

When he didn't answer, she went away. It hadn't been at all satisfactory; she had expected him to be relieved, even if he expressed polite regret at her sudden departure. He had sounded withdrawn, as though it didn't matter whether she came or went. Probably it *didn't* matter, she told herself firmly. He must surely be relieved to bring to an end what could only have been an embarrassing episode. As for the kiss, what to her had been a glorious moment in her life had surely been a mere passing incident in his.

She went to her room and sat down to think about it. She could, of course, write to him, but what would be the point? He would think that she was wishful of continuing their friendship—had it been friendship? She no longer knew—and that would be the last thing he would want with his marriage to Anneliese imminent. Best leave things as they were, she decided, and tidied her hair, looked rather despairingly at her pale face and went down to lunch.

She had been dreading that, but there was no need. The professor offered her sherry with easy friendliness and during lunch kept the conversation to light-hearted topics, never once touching on her departure. It seemed to her that he was no longer interested in it.

She made the excuse that she still had some last-minute packing to do after lunch. If she remained in the drawing room it would mean that everyone would have to speak in English, and it was quite likely they wanted to discuss family matters in their own language. It had surprised her that Anneliese hadn't come to lunch—perhaps Ruerd was going to her home later that day. Everyone would be gone by the late afternoon and he would be able to do as he pleased.

Of course, she had no packing to do. She went and sat by the window and stared out at the garden and the dunes and the sea beyond. It would be dark in a few hours, but the sun had struggled through the clouds now, and the pale sunlight warmed the bare trees and turned the dull-grey sea into silver. It wouldn't last long; there were clouds banking up on the horizon, and a bitter wind.

She was turning away from the window when she saw the professor with his dogs, striding down the garden and across the dunes. He was bare-headed, but wearing his sheepskin jacket so that he looked even larger than he was.

She watched him for a moment, and then on an impulse put on her own coat, tied a scarf over her head and went quietly downstairs and out of the side door. The wind took her breath as she started down the long

garden, intent on reaching Ruerd while she still had the
courage. She was going away, but she had given him no
reason and he was entitled to that, and out here in the
bleakness of the seashore it would be easier to tell him.

The wind was coming off the sea and she found
it slow going; the dunes were narrow here, but they
were slippery—full of hollows and unexpected hill-
ocks. By the time she reached the sands the professor
was standing by the water, watching the waves tumbling towards him.

The sun had gone again. She walked towards him,
soundless on the sand, and when she reached him put
out a hand and touched his sleeve.

He turned and looked at her then, and she saw how
grim he looked and how tired. She forgot her speech
for a moment.

'You ought not to be out in this weather without a
hat,' she told him. And then, 'I can't go away without
telling you why I'm going, Ruerd. I wasn't going to—
Anneliese asked me not to say anything—but perhaps
she won't mind if you explain to her... I'm going because I'm in love with you. You know that, don't you?
She told me so. I'm sorry you found out; I didn't think
it showed. It must have been awkward for you.'

She looked away from him. 'You do see that I had
to tell you? But now that I have you can forget all about
it. You've been kind. More than kind.' She gulped. 'I'm
sure you will be very happy with Anneliese...'

If she had intended to say anything more she was
given no opportunity to do so. Wrapped so tightly in
his arms that she could hardly breathe she heard his
voice roaring above the noise of the wind and waves.

'Kind? Kind? My darling girl, I have not been kind.

I have been in love with you since the moment I first saw you, spending hours thinking up ways of seeing more of you and knowing that I had given Anneliese my promise to marry her. It has been something unbearable I never wish to live through again.'

He bent his head and kissed her. It was even better than the kiss under the mistletoe, and highly satisfactory. All the same, Emmy muttered, 'Anneliese…?'

'Anneliese no longer wishes to marry me. Forget her, my darling, and listen to me. We shall marry, you and I, and live happily ever after. You do believe that?'

Emmy peeped up into his face, no longer grim and tired but full of tenderness and love. She nodded. 'Yes, Ruerd. Oh, yes. But what about Anneliese?'

He kissed her soundly. 'We will talk later; I'm going to kiss you again.'

'Very well,' said Emmy. 'I don't mind if you do.'

They stood, the pair of them, just for a while in their own world, oblivious of the wind and the waves and the dogs running to and fro.

Heaven, thought Emmy happily, isn't necessarily sunshine and blue skies—and she reached up to put her arms round her professor's neck.

At the end of the garden, Oom Domus, coming to look for her, adjusted his binoculars, took a good look and hurried back to the house. He would have a lonely trip to England, but what did that matter? He was bursting with good news.

* * * * *

THE VICAR'S DAUGHTER

Chapter 1

It was a crisp, starry October night and Professor van Kessel, driving himself back home after a weekend with friends in Dorset, had chosen to take the country roads rather than the direct route to London. He drove without haste, enjoying the dark quiet, the villages tucked in the hollows between the hills, the long stretches of silent road, the unexpected curves and sudden windings up and down. There was no one about, though from time to time he slowed for a fox or a badger, a hedgehog or a startled rabbit.

The last village had been some miles back and now there were no houses by the roadside. It was farmland, and the farmhouses lay well back from the road; there would be another village presently and he could take his direction from there. In the meantime he was content; the weekend had been very pleasant and this was a delightfully peaceful way of ending it.

The road curved between heavy undergrowth and trees, and he slowed and then braked hard as a figure darted from the side of the road into his headlights, only yards from the Rolls's bonnet. The doctor swore softly and let down his window.

'That was a silly thing to do,' he observed mildly to the anxious face peering at him, and he got out of the car. 'In trouble?'

The girl stared up at him looming over her small person. Her face might be anxious but there was no sign of distress or fear.

'Hope I didn't startle you,' she said, 'and so sorry to bother you, but would you stop at Thinbottom village— it's only a couple of miles down the road—and get someone to phone for a doctor or an ambulance? There's a party of travellers in the woods—' She cocked her neat head sideways over a shoulder. 'One of them is having a baby and I'm not sure what to do next.'

A plain face, the doctor reflected, but lovely eyes and a delightful voice. What she was doing here in the middle of nowhere at eleven o'clock at night was none of his business, and considering the circumstances she was remarkably self-possessed. He said now, 'Perhaps I might help. I'm a doctor.'

'Oh, splendid.' She gave his sleeve an urgent tug. 'Have you got your bag with you? We'll need scissors and some string or something, and a few towels. There's a kettle of hot water…' She was leading the way along a narrow track. 'I told her not to push…'

The darkness hid his smile.

'You are a nurse?'

'Me? Gracious me, no. First aid. Here we are.'

The travellers had set up their camp in a clearing

close to the path, with a tent, a small stove, a few bundles and a hand-cart.

'In the tent,' said the girl, and gave his sleeve another urgent tug. 'He's a doctor,' she said to the two young women, and to the man and young boy standing there. 'Did you lock your car?' she asked the doctor. 'Because if you didn't Willy can go and stand guard over it.'

'I locked it.' What a little busybody the girl was—probably some vicar's daughter. 'I'll have a basin of that water in the tent. With a towel, if there is one.'

He bent his large frame and edged inside, and a moment later the girl crept in with a saucepan of water and a none too clean towel to make herself small on the other side of the woman, waiting to be told what to do.

The doctor had taken off his jacket and rolled up his shirtsleeves. 'Something in which to wrap the infant?' He smiled reassuringly at the woman lying on top of a sleeping bag. 'You're very brave—another few minutes and you'll have your baby to hold.'

The woman let out a squawk. 'It's early,' she mumbled. 'We'd reckoned we'd be in Sturminster Newton.'

The doctor was arranging some plastic sheeting just so, and getting things from his bag set out on it. He glanced over at the girl. 'A blanket? Something warm?'

He whipped a spotless and very large handkerchief from a pocket as she took off the scarf wound round her neck and, urged on by the imminent arrival of the baby, she laid the one on the other just in time to receive a furiously angry infant.

'You'll have to hold her for a moment, then wrap her up tightly and give her to her mum. Right, now do as I say…'

He was quick and unflurried, telling her what to do

in a quiet voice, making little jokes with the mother. Presently he said, 'Go outside and see if anyone has a clean towel or nightie—but they must be clean.'

She crawled out of the tent, and with the other women's help searched the bundles.

She came back with a cotton nightie. 'This one was being saved for when she got to Sturminster Newton.'

'Excellent. Roll it up neatly and give it to me.' In a moment he said, 'Now, put your hand just here and keep it steady while I phone.'

He took a phone from his pocket and dialled 999 and began to speak.

He went outside then, and presently the husband came in to bend awkwardly over his wife and daughter while the girl knelt awkwardly, cold and cramped, her hand stiff.

The father went away and the doctor came back, took her hand away gently and nodded his satisfaction. 'The ambulance will be here very shortly; they'll take you to Blandford Hospital—just for a couple of days so that you can rest a bit and get to know the baby. Have you any transport?'

'Broke down yesterday.'

He went away again to talk to the husband, and came back with two mugs of tea. He handed one to the girl and helped his patient to sit up, and held the mug while she drank. 'If I might suggest it,' he said in his placid voice, 'it would be a good idea if your husband and family stayed for a day or two in Blandford. I think that I may be able to arrange that for you—it will give you time to sort things out. You'll be quite free to go on your way, but you do need a good rest for a couple of days.'

'If Bert don't mind…' The woman closed her eyes

and slept, the baby clasped close to her, its cross little face now smoothed into that of a small cherub.

The doctor glanced across at the girl, still kneeling patiently. She was smiling down at the baby, and when she smiled she wasn't in the least plain. When she looked up he saw how pale she was. 'Are you not out rather late?' he asked.

'Well, it was just after seven o'clock when Bert stopped me. I was on my way home on my bike, you know. There's not much traffic along here after five o'clock. Two cars went by and he tried to stop them, but they took no notice...'

'So you had a go?'

She nodded. 'She'll be quite comfortable at Blandford—but it's a bit late...'

'I'll go in and see whoever's on duty at the hospital.' He sounded so reassuring that she said no more, and they crouched, the pair of them, beside the woman, saying nothing. From time to time the doctor saw to his patient, and once or twice he went to talk to her husband. He was packing up their possessions and stowing them on the hand-cart. When the doctor returned the second time he told the girl that the boy and the young women would stay the night, sleeping in the tent. 'They say they will start walking in the morning.'

'If they stop at Thinbottom I think I could get someone to give them and the cart a lift to Blandford.'

'You live at Thinbottom?'

'Me? I'm the vicar's daughter.'

'I'll give you a lift as soon as the ambulance has gone.'

'No need, thank you all the same,' she said, and, in case that had sounded rude, added, 'What I mean is, you've been awfully kind and it must have been a great nuisance to you. You'll be very late home. Besides, my bike's here.'

'The boy can load it on the cart and drop it off tomorrow when they get to Thinbottom. Won't your family be worried about you?'

'I went over to Frogwell Farm—Granny Coffin. Mother will think that I've stayed the night—she's very old and often ill.'

'Nevertheless, I must insist on seeing you to your home,' he said, and, when she would have protested, added, 'Please, don't argue—' He broke off. 'Ah, here's the ambulance at last.'

He went out of the tent to meet the paramedics, and when they reached the tent she slipped out and stood on one side while they undid their equipment and saw to his patient. Then, satisfied, he stood up and walked back to the ambulance with them, his patient and the baby and the father. As he passed the girl he said, 'Stay where you are,' in a voice that she couldn't ignore. In any case her bike was already roped onto the top of the hand-cart.

He came back presently. 'Shall we introduce ourselves?' he suggested. 'Gijs van Kessel.' He held out a large hand.

She shook it, feeling its firm grip. 'Margo Pearson,' she said, and then, 'That's not an English name—are you Dutch?'

'Yes. If you will wait a moment while I have a word with this boy…'

Once he had done so, he picked up his bag and, with the boy ahead of them with a torch, went back to the road and handed her into the car. Margo, sinking back against the leather softness, said, 'I've never been in a Rolls-Royce. It's very comfortable—and large too. But then you're a very large man, aren't you?' She sounded very matter-of-fact.

'Yes, I am. Miss Pearson, forgive me for mentioning it, but was it not rather foolhardy of you to rush into the road and stop a strange car? There are quite a few undesirable people around after dark.'

'I would have screamed very loudly if you had been one,' she told him sensibly. 'And I dare say Bert or Willy would have come.'

He didn't point out that by the time they could have reached her she might have been whisked away in the car or maltreated in some way.

They soon reached the village and she said, 'It's here on the left, by the church.'

He drew up at an open gateway. The house beyond was large and solid, a relic from the days when the parsonage had housed a cleric's large family, and overshadowed by the church a stone's throw from it. It, like the rest of the village, was in darkness, but as the doctor drew up a light shone through the transom over the front door.

'Thank you very much,' said Margo, and undid her seat belt.

He didn't reply, but got out of the car, opened her door and walked the few yards to the house with her. By the time they had reached the door it had been opened to reveal the vicar in his dressing gown.

'Margo—thank heaven. We had just phoned Frogwell Farm and been told that you left hours ago. You're all right? An accident?' He opened the door wide. 'Come in, both of you…'

'Father, this is Dr van Kessel, who kindly gave me a lift. There's been no accident but he has been of the greatest possible help.' She turned to greet her mother, a middle-aged replica of herself, as he and the vicar shook hands.

'My dear sir, we are in your debt. Come into the sitting room—a cup of coffee? Something to eat?'

'Thank you—but I'm on my way to Blandford to the hospital. Your daughter will explain. I am glad to have been of some help!' He smiled at Mrs Pearson. 'You have a very resourceful daughter, Mrs Pearson. I regret that I cannot stay and tell you of our evening's adventure, but I'm sure Miss Pearson will do so.'

He shook hands all round again, and Margo, having her hand gently crushed, had time to study him in the dim light of the hall. He had seemed enormous back there in the woods and he didn't seem any less so now. Not so very young, she decided. Mid-thirties, with fair hair already silvered, a commanding nose above a thin, firm mouth and startlingly blue eyes. She thought she would never forget him.

That he would forget her the moment he had resumed his journey went without saying; she had been a plain child and had grown into a plain young woman, and no one had ever pretended that she wasn't.

Her father had assured her that one could be beautiful as well as being possessed of mediocre features, and her mother thought of her lovingly as a *jolie laide*, but even George Merridew, who, in village parlance, was courting her cautiously, had told her with a well-meaning lack of tact that she might not have much in the way of good looks but she had plenty of common sense and was almost as good a cook as his mother.

A remark which Margo had found unsatisfactory. Surely if George was in love with her he should think of her as rather more than a cook and a sensible pair of hands? Or was that what he wanted? He was a good farmer and a prosperous man and she liked him—was even a little fond of him—but such remarks did nothing to endear him to her. And now this man had appeared from nowhere and gone again, and had left her feeling uncertain.

She related the night's happenings to her parents over a pot of tea and slices of bread and butter with lashings of jam. Caesar, the family cat, had curled up on her lap, and Plato, the elderly black Labrador, had got into his basket and gone back to sleep. She gobbled the last slice and sighed.

'I'm so sorry you were worried, but I couldn't leave them there, could I?'

'No, love, of course not. You did quite the right thing. They will bring your bicycle in the morning?'

'Oh, yes. I'm going to ask George to lend me the trailer, then they can put their hand-cart on it and go to Blandford.'

'Will George do that?' asked her father mildly.

'Well, he won't be using it until Wednesday, when he hauls the winter feed.'

Margo got up and tucked Caesar into Plato's basket. She put the mugs in the sink and said, 'It's after two o'clock. Don't either of you get up in the morning until I bring your tea. It's your morning off, isn't it, Father? I'll get the breakfast before I go to see George.'

It was still early when she drove over to George's farm in the worn out old Ford her father owned. His laconic, 'Hello, old girl,' was friendly enough, but hardly lover-like. He listened to her request without comment, only saying when she had finished, 'I don't see why not. I'm not needing it for a couple of days. But mind and drive carefully. Will you be at the whist drive this evening? Mother's going.'

Margo, who didn't like George's mother all that much, said that she'd see, and waited while he and one of his farmhands attached the trailer. She drove it carefully back and then parked outside the vicarage in the main street, where the boy and the two young women would see it. She had just finished her breakfast when they came, pushing the hand-cart with her bike on top. They sat, the three of them, in the kitchen, drinking the tea her mother offered and eating bacon sandwiches, saying little.

The road was almost empty as she drove to Blandford Hospital, taking the by-roads she knew so well and getting there without mishap. She hadn't had any idea what was to happen next, but it seemed that the doctor had smoothed their path for them. There was an empty house near the hospital, they were told, and the travellers were to be allowed to stay in it until the mother and baby were fit to travel again.

The man who had come to speak to Margo at the hospital looked at her curiously. He counted himself lucky to have been the casualty officer on duty when Professor van Kessel had arrived and sought his help last night. He was internationally well-known in his profession, and it had been a privilege to meet him. His fame as a paediatrician was widespread, and to have had the honour of meeting him… And he had been very accurate in his description of this Miss Pearson.

He said now, 'Mother and baby are doing well, but they'll have to stay for a couple of days. The professor found the empty house for her family. Don't ask me how at that time of night—the police, I suppose. I'll let you have the address. Oh, and he left some money for them. May I give it to you?'

'Professor?' asked Margo. 'Isn't he a doctor?'

The young doctor smiled down at her. She was rather sweet, even if plain, he thought.

'He's a famous man in the medical world. Specialises in children's illnesses.'

'Oh, I didn't know. I'll take the boy and the women to this house, shall I? They'll be all right there? I ought to get back in case the trailer is needed.'

'That's fine. The social services will have been told, and don't forget it's temporary—they can move on once the mother and baby are fit.'

It was a miserable little cottage, but it was empty and weatherproof. The boy unloaded the cart from the trailer, thanked her in a rather surly voice and, helped by the two young women, took their possessions indoors. Margo gave the money to one of the women. 'It's not from me. The doctor who looked after the baby left it for all of you,' she explained.

The woman gave her a sour look. 'We won't be staying here longer than we must.'

It was the other woman who called across, 'Well, thanks anyway.'

Margo drove back to George's farm and waited while the trailer was unhitched.

'Everything OK?' George wanted to know. 'Not done any damage?'

'No,' said Margo, and thought how delightful it

would be if he would ask her—just once would do—if *she* was OK as well as the trailer. George, she felt sure, was a sound young man, steady and hardworking, but he hadn't much time for what he called all that nonsense. In due time he would marry, since a farmer needed a wife and sons to carry on his work, and she suspected that he had decided that she would do very nicely—little chance of her looks tempting any other suitors, a splendid cook, and capable of turning her hand to anything.

Margo drove the short distance back to the vicarage, childishly wishing for a miracle—glossy fair curls, blue eyes and a face to make men turn to look at her twice and then fall in love with her. 'And not just George,' she said aloud. 'Someone like Dr van Kessel—no, Professor van Kessel. Someone handsome, rich and important. He won't even remember what I look like.'

He remembered—though perhaps not quite as she would have wished. His patient comfortably settled and the help of the police sought, after a friendly chat with the young doctor on call in Casualty he had been free to drive himself back to London.

He'd taken the Salisbury road, and then the rather lonely road through Stockridge until he'd reached the M3. There had been little traffic—even the city streets, when he'd reached them, had been tolerably quiet.

When he was in England he stayed with an old friend and colleague, and since his work took him to various big teaching hospitals he came and went freely, using his borrowed key. He'd stopped silently in a mews behind a terrace of townhouses, garaged his car and walked round to the street, let himself in and had gone silently to his room for the few hours of sleep left to him.

He hadn't been tired; lack of sleep didn't bother him unduly; it was a hazard of his profession. He had lain for a while, remembering with amusement the girl who had brought him to such a sudden halt. A small girl, totally without fear and sensible. Bossy too! He had no doubt at all that she would see her protégés safely housed. He wondered idly how she would get them to Blandford. He had no doubt that she would…

The professor had a busy week. Outpatients' clinics where he had to deal with anxious mothers as well as sick children, small patients for whom his specialised surgery had been required to be visited in the wards and a theatre list which, however hard he worked, never seemed to grow smaller.

An urgent call came from Birmingham during the week, asking him to operate on a child with one leg inches shorter than its fellow. It was something in which he specialised, the straightening and correction of malformed bones in children and babies, and he was much in demand. Totally absorbed, he forgot Margo.

Margo was busy too, although her tasks were of a more mundane nature—flowers for the church, the last of the apples and pears to pick from the old trees behind the vicarage, getting the church hall ready for the monthly whist drive, cutting sandwiches for the Mothers' Union annual party, driving her mother into Sturminster Newton for the weekly shopping… Unlike Professor van Kessel, however, she hadn't forgotten.

Waiting patiently in the village shop while Mrs Drew, the village gossip, chose the cheese she liked and at the same time passed on an embroidered version of the rumpus at Downend Farm when the bull had broken loose, Margo allowed her thoughts to dwell on the man who had come into her life so abruptly and gone again without trace. She was still thinking about him as she left the shop, clutching the breakfast bacon, when she was hailed from a passing motor car.

It stopped within a few feet of her and the elderly driver called her over.

'Margo—the very person I am on my way to see. Get in. We will go back to the house, where we can talk.' He noticed her shopping basket. 'Want to go home first?'

'Well, yes, please, Sir William. Mother expects me back. Can't we talk at home?'

'Yes, yes, of course...'

'I'll not get in, then. You can park in the drive; the gate's open.'

She crossed the narrow street and was waiting for him as he stopped by the door. Sir William Frost greeted Mrs Pearson with pleasant friendliness, accepted the offer of coffee and followed Margo into the sitting room.

'Want to ask a favour of you, Margo. You saw Imogen in church, didn't you?' he asked, referring to his granddaughter. 'Been staying with us for a few days. Intended to take her up to town myself, but got this directors' meeting in Exeter. Can't spare Tomkins; want him to stay at the house with Lady Frost. Wondered if you'd drive her up to her aunt's place in town. Don't care to send her by train.'

Mrs Pearson came in with the coffee and Sir William repeated himself all over again, then sat back and drank his coffee. He was a short, stout man, with a drooping moustache and a weatherbeaten face, liked by everyone despite the fact that he liked his own way with everything. And, even if from time to time he rode roughshod over someone's feelings, his wife, a small, dainty little lady, quickly soothed them over.

He finished his coffee, accepted a second cup and said, 'Well?'

Margo said in her sensible way, 'Yes, of course I'll take her, Sir William. When do you want her to go?'

'Day after tomorrow. Get there in time for lunch. Much obliged to you, Margo.'

It was the vicar who unknowingly upset the plans. His car wouldn't be available—he had been bidden to see his bishop on the very day Imogen was to be driven to her aunt's house.

Sir William huffed and puffed when he was informed. 'Then you will have to go by train. I'll get the local taxi to take you to Sherborne. Get another taxi at Paddington. Not what I wanted, but it can't be helped, I suppose.'

Imogen, fifteen years old, wilful, spoilt and convinced that she was quite grown-up, was delighted. Life, she confided to Margo, was boring. For most of the year she was at boarding-school while her father—something in the diplomatic service—and mother lived in an obscure and unsettled part of Europe, which meant that she was ferried to and fro between members of the family in England.

She made no secret of her boredom while staying with her grandparents—but the aunt in London offered the delights of theatres and shopping. Imogen, recovering from a severe attack of measles, intended to enjoy her sick leave before going back to school.

Of course, she disliked the idea of being taken to her

aunt's as though she were a child, but she got on quite well with Margo and it was nice to have someone to see to the boring things like tickets and taxis.

They made the journey together more or less in harmony, although Margo had to discourage her from using a particularly vivid lipstick and eyeliner the moment the taxi was out of her grandfather's gates.

'Why not wait until you are in London?' suggested Margo, being tactful. 'You will be able to consult one of those young ladies behind a cosmetic counter and get the very best and the latest.'

Imogen reluctantly agreed. 'You could do with some decent make-up yourself,' she observed with youthful candour. 'But I suppose that as you're the vicar's daughter it doesn't matter how you look.'

Margo, trying to think of the right answer to this, gave up and said nothing.

It was quite a lengthy ride from Paddington to Imogen's aunt's house—a substantial town residence in a terrace of well-maintained homes.

Strictly for the wealthy, reflected Margo, getting out of the taxi to pay the cabby. It would be interesting to see inside...

They were admitted by a blank-faced butler who informed them that they were expected and showed them into a small room furnished with little gilt chairs which looked as though they would collapse if anyone sat on them, a hideous marble-topped table and an arrangement of flowers on a tall stand.

'Lady Mellor will be with you presently,' they were told, and were left to perch uneasily on the chairs. But only for a few minutes. Suddenly the door was thrust open and Lady Mellor made a brisk entry.

'Dearest child,' she exclaimed in a penetrating voice, and embraced her niece before adding, 'And your companion. Your grandfather said that you would have suitable company for your journey.'

She smiled briefly at Margo, then turned to Imogen and said, 'Your little cousin is rather poorly. The specialist is with him at the moment, but as soon as he has gone we will have lunch together and a good chat.' She turned back to Margo. 'If you'd care to wait in the hall I'll arrange for some refreshment for you before you return home. I'm sure I am much obliged to you for taking care of Imogen.'

Margo murmured politely that refreshment would be welcome, as breakfast had been at a very early hour. She sat down in the chair indicated by Lady Mellor and watched her walk away with Imogen. She had been thanked and forgotten.

Her stomach rumbled and she hoped for a sandwich at least.

She had been sitting there for five minutes or more when she heard the murmur of voices, and two men, deep in talk, came down the staircase slowly. One was an elderly man who looked tired, and with him was Professor van Kessel. They stood in the hall, murmuring together, with the butler hovering in the background, ready to show them out.

They were on the point of leaving the house when Professor van Kessel, glancing around him, saw Margo. He bade his colleague goodbye and crossed the hall to her.

'Miss Pearson. So we meet again—although rather unexpectedly.'

She didn't try to hide her delight at seeing him again.

'I brought Imogen—Sir William's granddaughter—up to London to stay with her aunt. I'm going back again very shortly, but I'm to have some kind of meal first. I was told to wait here.'

'I have an appointment now, but I shall be free in an hour,' said the professor. 'Wait here; I'll drive you back. I'm going that way,' he added vaguely.

'Well, thank you, but won't they mind? I mean, can I just sit here until you come?'

'I don't see why not. I shall be here again probably before you have had your lunch.' He smiled down at her. 'Whatever you do, don't go away.'

'No, all right, I won't. If you're sure...'

'Quite sure,' he told her placidly. 'I'll see you within the hour.'

She watched him go, and the butler closed the door behind him and went away.

It was all right at first. It was quiet and pleasantly warm and her chair was comfortable; the minutes ticked away and she thought longingly of coffee and sandwiches. At any moment, she told herself, someone would come and lead her to wherever she was to have the refreshments offered to her.

No one came. Fifteen minutes, half an hour went past, and although from time to time she heard a door open or close no one came into the hall. If she hadn't promised Professor van Kessel that she would wait for him she would have left the house. Margo, used to the willing hospitality of the vicarage, felt in an alien world. The magnificent long-case clock across the hall struck half past one, almost drowning the sound of the doorbell, and as though waiting for his cue the butler went to answer it.

Professor van Kessel came into the hall unhurriedly. 'I've not kept you waiting?' he wanted to know cheerfully. 'You've finished your lunch?'

Margo stood up, her insides rumbling again. 'I haven't had lunch,' she said with asperity. 'I have been sitting here...' She gave the butler a nasty look.

His poker face became almost human. 'I am indeed sorry, Miss. We had no orders concerning you. I had assumed that you had left the house.' He gave the doctor a nervous glance. 'If the professor would wait, I can bring coffee and sandwiches...'

Margo, her thoughts diverted from her insides, gave the doctor a thoughtful look. 'Should I call you Professor?'

'It's only another name for Doctor.' He turned to the butler. 'I'll give Miss Pearson lunch. I'm sure it was no fault of yours. Explain to your mistress, will you?'

He whisked Margo out of the house then and into his car. As he drove away he asked, 'When are you expected home?'

'I was going to get the three-thirty from Paddington.'

'Oh, good. We shall have time for a leisurely meal before we start for home.'

She said awkwardly, 'Just coffee and sandwiches would do. It's just that I had breakfast rather early.'

'So did I. And I haven't had time for lunch.' He uttered the fib in a placid voice which reassured her.

'Oh, well—I dare say you're hungry.'

'Indeed I am.' He resolutely forgot the lamb cutlets followed by the substantial apple tart that he had been offered at the hospital. 'I know a very pleasant little restaurant five minutes from here.'

'I expect you know Lady Mellor?' asked Margo, making conversation.

'Never heard of her before this morning. Her doctor asked me for a second opinion on her small son. A pampered brat who needed his bottom smacked. He got at the wine decanter and was first drunk and then sick. No one had thought to ask him what he'd had to eat or drink.' He slowed the car. 'A waste of my time. There's a meter—we're in luck.'

The restaurant was close by and only half-full. Margo gave him an eloquent glance and sped away to the Ladies', and when she got back found him at a table by the window, studying the menu. He got up as she reached him, took her jacket and handed it to the waiter, then said, 'You deserve a drink. Would you like sherry?'

'You can't have one—you're driving—so I won't either. I'd like tonic and lemon, please.'

He waited as she took a menu from the waiter. 'We have plenty of time; choose whatever you would like.'

The menu was mouthwatering and, since there were no prices, probably very expensive. Margo decided on an omelette and salad, thereby endearing herself to the doctor, who chose the same, thankful that when she chose sticky toffee pudding with cream to follow he could settle for biscuits and cheese.

Presently, as she poured their coffee, he was pleased to see that she had a pretty colour in her cheeks now, and a well-fed look. Shabby treatment, he reflected, to leave her sitting there without so much as a glass of water...

He asked idly, 'Do you often run errands for anyone who asks?'

'Well, yes. You see, Father always helps anyone who

needs it, and of course that means Mother and I help out too.'

'You would not wish for a different life?'

'I haven't any training, have I?' she reminded him. 'I'd love to travel…' Just for a moment she looked wistful. 'But life isn't dull. There's always something happening, even in a small village like Thinbottom.'

'You don't hanker for life in London?'

'Goodness me, no. Do you like living here, Professor?'

'Don't, I beg you, call me Professor; it makes me feel elderly. No, I don't like living here—my home is in Holland. I only come here from time to time. I stay with an old friend and, though I'm too busy to go out much, I do have other friends scattered around the country with whom I spend my weekends when I'm free.'

'You're going back to Holland soon?'

Her heart sank when he said, 'Oh, yes, in a few weeks—I have to be back there for Christmas.'

Soon after, they got back into the car, and, encouraged by his questions, she gave him an account of the travellers.

'I went to see them in that house you found for them. The baby's a darling. They plan to move on but they'll be all right; they were given clothes and blankets and they didn't seem to mind that they hadn't a van. I wish I knew someone…'

'They'll probably strike lucky. The weather is good, and that should be a great help to them.' He glanced at his watch. 'Shall we stop for tea, or would you like to get home as quickly as possible?'

'Well, by the time we're home it will be teatime. If you can spare the time I know Mother would love to give you a cup. You don't need to stay if you're going further.'

He hid a smile. 'That does sound delightful.' He began to talk about the country they were passing through, careful to put her at her ease.

'He's Gijs to his friends.' He glanced at Margo and smiled. 'And I hope Margo will allow me to call her Margo...'

'Of course you may, if you want to. Everyone does.'

She gave him a wide smile and skimmed away to fetch her father from his study.

Sitting beside his hostess presently, Gijs reflected that it was a very long time since he had sat down to a substantial tea. At the hospital he drank the cups of tea brought to him and often drank them tepid, since he hadn't the time to stop in his work. If he wasn't at the hospital but at his consulting rooms, his secretary would sneak him a cup between patients—but five o'clock tea, such as this was, was a rarity. Sliced bread and butter arranged on a pretty plate, jam, honey, a covered dish of buttered toast, scones and a large fruit cake. Moreover, the tea was hot and strong, with plenty of milk.

'I don't suppose you have much time for tea,' observed Mrs Pearson chattily. 'Last time I was in London with the Women's Institute we had tea at a hotel—little teapots barely enough for one cup and quite nasty looks from the waitresses when we asked for more hot water. And such mean little sandwiches and cakes. I dare say that's fashionable. Where did you see Margo?'

'At Lady Mellor's house. I'm sure that Margo can tell you about it better than I.'

Margo told. 'I dare say Lady Mellor had a lot to worry about,' she finished, 'and the butler was very nice about it. It wasn't anyone's fault, if you see what I mean.'

From anyone else, thought the professor, that would sound priggish, but somehow not from Margo—she is, after all, the vicar's daughter, brought up to see good in everyone. Let's hope she'll never be disillusioned.

He said lightly then, 'It was just our good luck that we should meet in such an unlikely place. I'm delighted to have had company driving down here.'

'You like England?' asked the vicar.

'Very much.' The two men started a discussion about the English countryside, but the professor volunteered no real information about his own country. Certainly he enlarged upon the social and commercial aspects, and enlarged too upon his homeland, albeit rather vaguely, but Margo reflected that he had told them nothing of his own home or where he lived. Perhaps he was married…

The thought was an unwelcome one which she thrust aside. Why shouldn't he be married with a brood of children? It was none of her business. She did want to know, however.

Margo being Margo, it was no sooner said than done.

'Are you married?' she asked him. Then regretted it the moment she had spoken; the look of amused surprise on his face sent the colour into her cheeks and she mumbled, 'Sorry, that was rude of me…'

'No, I'm not married.' He ignored the mumble. 'I have never found the time.'

Mrs Pearson hastened to fill an awkward pause. 'Of course one always expects doctors to be family men— I'm sure I don't know why. A wife and children must be a hindrance to their work at times.'

He smiled. 'I imagine that doctors' wives quickly learn not to be that—rather, a pleasant distraction after a long day's work. And my married colleagues are doting fathers.'

'Then you should make haste and marry,' observed Mrs Pearson.

The vicar put his dignified oar in. 'I'm sure that

Gijs will marry when he wishes to do so, my dear.' He added thoughtfully, 'I wonder why a patient should expect his or her doctor to be a married man? It's an interesting point.'

So started an interesting discussion in which Margo took no part. She passed the cake, handed cups of tea round and wished herself elsewhere. Which was silly—after all, she hadn't been very rude. She should have laughed it off for the trivial remark it had been, instead of feeling as though she had been nosey. Perhaps, horror of horrors, now he would think that she was intent on attracting him. He wouldn't want any more to do with her. He would go away and she would never see him again. If she had been witty and pretty and charming, it might have been a different matter…

Professor van Kessel was either a man with the kindest heart imaginable or was prone to deafness; he apparently hadn't heard her muttered apology. The conversation flowed smoothly, and presently, when he got up to go, he bade her goodbye with his usual pleasant detachment. He didn't say he hoped to see her again, however.

Watching the Rolls-Royce gliding away towards the village, Margo told herself that he'd gone for good and she could forget him. Whether she wanted to forget him was an entirely different matter, and one she was reluctant to consider.

To her mother's observation that it was a pity that they were unlikely to see him again, she replied airily that it had been pleasant meeting him once more and that she supposed he would be returning to Holland. 'After all, it is his home,' she said.

She collected the tea things and carried them out

to the kitchen. 'I thought I'd go over to see Mrs Merridew tomorrow afternoon. George said she might like some help with the jam. They've a huge plum harvest this year.'

Her mother gave her a thoughtful look. Despite the fact that George's mother had made no secret of the fact that she considered Margo to be a suitable wife for him, the woman had no affection for her. She was, thought Mrs Pearson shrewdly, under the impression that once Margo married she would be able to mould her into the kind of wife she felt her George should have. That Margo wasn't a girl to be moulded had never entered her head. She had too good an opinion of herself to realise that Margo didn't like her overmuch, but bore with her overbearing ways for George's sake.

Mrs Pearson, knowing in her bones that Margo didn't love George, told herself to have patience. Somewhere in the world there was a man for her Margo—preferably the counterpart of Gijs van Kessel…

So Margo took herself off the next day to Merridew's Farm, intent on being nice to everyone, doing her best to keep her thoughts on a future when she would marry George and live there, and failing lamentably because she thought about the professor instead.

However, once she was at the farm, he was banished from her head by Mrs Merridew's loud, hectoring voice bidding her to join her in the kitchen.

'I can do with some help,' she greeted Margo. 'There's an apron behind the door; you can stone the plums… You should have worn a sensible sweater; if you get stains on that blouse they'll never come out.'

I have never known anybody, reflected Margo, rolling up her sleeves, who could put a damper on any occasion, however trivial. She began to stone the plums—a messy business—and paused in her work as the thought that she couldn't possibly marry George suddenly entered her head.

'Why have you stopped?' Mrs Merridew wanted to know. 'There's another bucketful in the pantry. I'm sure I don't know why I should have to do everything myself; you'll have to change your ways when you marry George.'

Margo said nothing—there was no point at the moment. Besides, she was busy composing a suitable speech for George's benefit.

He wouldn't mind, she reflected. He was fond of her, just as she was fond of him, but being fond wasn't the same as being in love. She wasn't sure why she was so certain about that. A future with George had loomed before her for several years now—everyone had taken it for granted that when the time came they would marry, and she had got used to the idea and accepted it; she wanted to marry, she wanted children and a husband to care for her, and at twenty-eight she was sure that romance—the kind of romance she read about in novels—had passed her by.

But romance had touched her with feather-light fingers in the shape of Gijs van Kessel, and life would never be the same again.

She glanced across the table at Mrs Merridew, who was a formidable woman, tall and stout, with her iron-grey hair permanently waved into rock-like formations and a mouth which seldom smiled. She was respected in the village but not liked as her long-dead husband had been liked, and she was always ready to find fault. Only with George was she softer in her manner…

'Fetch me the other preserving pan, Margo.' Mrs Merridew's voice cut into her thoughts. 'I'll get this first batch on the stove. By the time you've finished stoning that lot I can fill a second pan.'

Margo went to the far wall and got down the copper preserving pan and put it on the table.

'Cat got your tongue?' asked Mrs Merridew. 'Never known you so quiet. What's all this nonsense I heard about you and a pack of tramps?'

'Not tramps—travellers. And it wasn't nonsense. One of them had a baby by the side of the road.'

'More fool her,' declared Mrs Merridew. 'These people bring shame to the countryside.'

'Why?' asked Margo, and ate a plum.

'Why? They're dirty and dishonest and live from hand to mouth.'

'Well, they looked clean enough to me,' said Margo. 'And I don't know that they're dishonest—no more so than people who live in houses…'

Her companion snorted. 'Rubbish! If any of them came onto the farm George would soon send them packing.'

'Would he? Would he really? Or would he do it to please you?'

Mrs Merridew went red. 'You don't seem yourself today, Margo. I hope you're not ill—picked up something nasty from those tramps.'

She set the pan of fruit on the old-fashioned stove. 'While that's coming to the boil we'll have a cup of tea, then you'd better go home. I dare say you've a cold coming.'

Margo never wanted to see another plum; she agreed meekly, drank her tea, washed the cups and saucers in the sink, bade Mrs Merridew goodbye and got on her bike. She had wanted to talk to George but she wasn't to be given the chance. She would come up early in the morning; he would be in the cow parlour and there would be time to talk.

'Early back, dear,' commented her mother as she came in through the kitchen door. 'Weren't you asked to stay for tea?'

Margo sat down at the table and watched her mother rolling dough for scones. 'No. Mrs Merridew thinks I may have caught a cold.' Margo popped a piece of dough into her mouth. 'Mother, I don't want to marry George...'

Mrs Pearson was cutting rounds of dough and arranging them on a baking tray. 'Your father and I have always hoped that you wouldn't, although we would never have said anything if you had. You don't love him.'

'No. I like him—I'm fond of him—but that's not the same, is it?'

'No, love, it isn't. When you do fall in love you'll know that. Have you told George?'

'I'll go and see him tomorrow early. Do you think he'll be upset?'

Her mother put the scones in the oven. 'No, dear, I don't. George is a nice young man but I think he wants a wife, not a woman to love. She'll need to be fond of him, of course, and he of her, but that will be sufficient. And that wouldn't be sufficient for you, would it?'

'No. I would like,' said Margo thoughtfully, 'to be cosseted and spoilt and loved very much, and I'd want to be allowed to be me, if you see what I mean. I would be a good wife and have lots of children because we would have enough money to keep us all in comfort.' She laughed a little. 'Aren't I silly? But I'm sure about George, Mother. I'd rather stay single...'

'I know you are doing the right thing, love. See what your father says.'

Margo laid the table for tea and presently, over that meal, the Reverend Mr Pearson voiced his opinion that Margo was indeed doing the right thing. 'And if you feel unsettled for a while, my dear, why not go and stay with one of your aunts? Heaven knows, your mother and I have enough relations to choose from.'

'I'd be running away...'

'No, clearing the decks. And you wouldn't go for a week or two. Give the village a chance to discuss it thoroughly.' They all laughed. 'There's not much happening until the bazaar; it'll liven things up a bit.'

Margo was up early, dressed and on her bike while it still wasn't quite light, and was in plenty of time to see George while the cows were being milked.

She leaned her bike against a pile of logs and, her heart thumping hard despite her resolution to keep calm, went into the cow parlour.

Two of the cowmen were already milking, and George was standing by the door checking some equipment. He looked up when she went in.

'Good Lord, what brings you here at this time of the morning? Mother said you were sickening for a cold. Don't come near me, whatever you do.'

Not a very encouraging beginning, but Margo braced herself.

'I haven't got a cold. Your mother just thought I might have one because I didn't talk much...!'

'Won't do not to get on with Mother,' said George. A rebuke she ignored.

'I wanted to talk to you for a minute or two—this is the only time when we're alone.'

'Well, let's have it, old girl. I've not got all day.'

It was being called 'old girl' which started her off. 'You have never asked me, George, but everyone seems to think that we will marry. Perhaps you don't intend to ask me, but if you do don't bother, because I don't want to marry you. I would make a very bad farmer's wife—and your mother would live with us.'

'Well, of course she would—show you how things are done before she takes her ease and you take over.'

The prospect left Margo short of breath. She persevered, though. 'George, do you love me?'

'What's got into you, girl? We've known each other almost all our lives.'

'Yes, I know that. That's not what I meant. Are you in love with me? Do I excite you? Do you want to give me the moon and the stars?'

'You're crazy, Margo. What's that twaddle got to do with being a good wife?'

'I'm not sure, but I think it must have a great deal to do with it. So you won't mind very much if we don't get married? You're a very nice person, George. There must be dozens of girls who'd give anything to be your wife.'

'Well, as to that, I reckon that's so. Mother always had her doubts, even though she liked the idea of me marrying the vicar's daughter.'

Margo swallowed her rage. 'Well, that leaves everyone quite satisfied, doesn't it?' She turned to go. 'Pass the news around the village, will you? I'm glad your heart isn't broken!'

She got onto her bike and pedalled home as though the Furies were after her. She knew that George hadn't meant to be unkind, but she felt as though he really didn't mind one way or the other—and that was very lowering to a girl who hadn't had much of an opinion of herself in the first place.

To her mother's carefully worded question she gave a matter-of-fact account of her meeting with George. 'So that's that,' she finished briskly. 'And if you don't mind I *would* quite like to go away for a week or two.'

'You need a change,' declared her mother. 'There's so little life here for someone young. I know you're kept busy, but a change of scene… Have you any idea where you'd like to go?'

The vicar looked up from his cornflakes. 'Your aunt Florence, when she last wrote, expressed the view that she would be glad to see any of us who cared to visit her. Sunningfield is a village even smaller than this one, but it is near Windsor and within easy reach of London and I believe she has many friends. Your uncle was a very respected and popular man during his lifetime.'

He passed his cup for more coffee. 'I will telephone her this morning and drive you there myself if you would like that?'

Truth to tell, Margo didn't much mind where she went. All she knew was that she would like to get away for a little while and think. She wasn't sure what it was she needed to think about, but think she must. She wasn't upset about calling off the vague future George had sketched out for her from time to time, but she felt restless and she didn't know why. A week or two with

Aunt Flo would put everything back into its right perspective once more.

It was arranged that she should go in four or five days' time, and in the meantime that gave the village the opportunity to adjust to the idea that she and George weren't to be married after all. She would have been surprised at the number of people who expressed their satisfaction at that.

'There'd have been no life for Miss Margo with that Mrs Merridew,' observed the verger's wife. 'Nice little lady, that Miss Margo is. Good luck to her, I says!' A sentiment which was shared by many.

Margo countered the questions from the well-meaning among her father's congregation in her sensible way, packed a bag with the best of her wardrobe and was presently driven to Sunningfield.

Aunt Florence lived at the end of the village in a cottage which had at one time been the gamekeeper's home on the local estate. Lord Trueman, having fallen on bad times, had prudently let or sold the lodges and estate cottages, being careful to see that the occupants were suitable neighbours. And of course Aunt Florence was eminently suitable. What could be more respectable than an archdeacon's widow?

They arrived in time for tea and, admitted by a beaming young girl, were led across the hall where she threw open a door and said cheerfully, 'Here they are, ma'am. I'll fetch the tea.'

Aunt Flo rose to meet them. A tall, bony lady with short curly hair going white, she had a sharp nose and a sharp tongue too, both of which concealed a warm heart. She embraced them briskly, told them to make themselves comfortable, and when the girl brought in the teatray offered refreshment. At the same time she gave and received family news.

It was when this topic had been exhausted that she asked, 'And you, Margo? You have decided not to marry that young farmer? I must say I never thought much of the idea. You are entirely unsuited to the life of a farmer's wife; I cannot imagine how you came to consider it in the first place.'

'No one had ever asked me to marry them, Aunt Flo. Well, George didn't exactly ask; we just kind of drifted, if you see what I mean. We've known each other for years…'

'That's no reason to marry. One marries for love—or should do. You're not so old that you need despair, although I must say it is a pity that you haven't the Pearson good looks.'

A remark which Margo took in good part, seeing that it was true. They had supper after her father had driven away, and Aunt Florence outlined the various treats she had in store for her niece.

'You have brought a pretty dress with you? Good. We are invited to Lord Trueman's place for drinks after church. You will meet most of my friends and acquaintances there—a good start.'

Aunt Florence lived in some style, even if in somewhat reduced circumstances. Her little house was well furnished and Margo's bedroom was pretty as well as comfortable. Life for Aunt Flo was placid and pleasant. The cheerful girl—Phoebe—came each day and cleaned, and did most of the cooking before she left in the evening, and an old man from the village saw to the heavy work in the garden—although Aunt Flo did the planting and planning. Even at the tail-end of the year, it was a charming little spot, surrounded by shrubs and small trees, tidied up ready for the winter.

Margo felt quite at home within twenty-four hours—joining her aunt in her daily walk and playing cards in the evening, or watching whichever programme her aunt thought suitable, with Moses, the ginger Persian cat, on her knee. On the next Sunday she accompanied her aunt to church and afterwards walked up the drive to the rather ugly early Victorian house built by Lord Trueman's ancestor on the site of the charming Elizabethan mansion he had disliked.

'Hideous,' observed Aunt Florence, and added, 'It's simply frightful inside.'

There were a lot of people gathered in an immense room with panelled walls and a great deal of heavy furniture. Margo was taken to one group after another by Lady Trueman, a middle-aged lady with a sweet face, and introduced to a great many people whose names she instantly forgot.

'Now do come and meet my daughter,' said Lady Trueman. 'She's staying with us for a week or two. I've a small granddaughter too—Peggy. She's a handful—three years old.' She had fetched up in front of a young woman not much older than Margo herself.

'Helen, this is Margo Pearson—come to stay with Mrs Pearson. I've been telling her about Peggy...'

She trotted away and left them to talk. Helen was nice, Margo decided. They talked about clothes and toddlers and babies, and presently slipped upstairs to the nursery to see Peggy, an imp of mischief if ever there was one, who took no notice of her nurse—a young girl, kind enough, no doubt, but lacking authority.

'Such a naughty puss,' said her mother lovingly. 'We never know what she will do next.'

Back in Aunt Flo's house over lunch, that lady expressed the opinion that the child was being spoilt. 'A dear child, but that nurse of hers is no good—far too easygoing.'

The days went by with a pleasant monotony: shopping in the village, visiting her aunt's friends for coffee or tea. And if Margo sometimes wished for a little excitement she squashed the thought at once. Her aunt was kindness itself, and she was sure that the holiday was doing her a lot of good. Taking her mind off things. Well, George for instance. The unbidden thought that she wished that it would take her mind off Professor van Kessel too was another thought to be squashed.

She thought about him far too often, although she tried not to. It wasn't so difficult when she was with her aunt, whose conversation was of a sort to require close attention and sensible answers at intervals, but when she was on her own, doing an errand for her or in the garden, grubbing up the few weeds which had hoped to escape that lady's eye, there was ample time for reflection.

So silly, Margo told herself one day, on her way back from taking a pot of Mrs Pearson's jam to an acquaintance who had expressed a wish to try it. It had been quite a long walk and the afternoon was already sliding briskly into dusk. What was more, it was going to rain at any moment. Margo, taking a short cut across Lord Trueman's park, abandoned her pleasant daydreaming and put her best foot forward.

The park was vast, and this far from the house, which

was just visible in the distance, its planned trees and shrubs had given way to rough ground, a ploughed field or two and sparse woodland through which ran a small stream, swollen now by October rains. The right of way ran beside it for some way and then turned away to join a wider path, leading back to one of the lodges some half a mile away.

Margo walked fast, head down against the rain, which was coming down in earnest now, thankful that she would soon join the path. It was pure chance that she gave a quick glance around her as she stopped to turn up the collar of her jacket. It was a movement in the stream some yards away which had caught her eye—a small, scarlet-clad figure, half in, half out of the water, a small arm trailing gently to and fro, washed by the stream as it raced along.

Margo ran through the rough grass and waded across the water, slipping and sliding, losing a shoe and not noticing, bent on getting to the child as quickly as possible.

It was Peggy, her head, thank heaven, on the bank, but most of her small person in the water. She was unconscious and Margo soon saw why: there was a big bruise on her forehead. She had fallen awkwardly and Margo had a few anxious moments hauling her out of the stream and up the bank. This done, there was the necessity to cross the stream again, for behind her was nothing but wooded country going nowhere.

It's amazing what you can do when you have to, reflected Margo, slipping and sliding across to the other bank with Peggy hoisted awkwardly over a shoulder. Once there, there was the urgent need to get to the house, for as far as she could see there was no other help nearby.

Hoisting the little girl more securely, Margo started off across the field to where, in the distance, she could see the lights of the house.

It was raining in earnest now, hard cold rain which soaked them even more than they already were. Margo squelched along in her one shoe and thought that she would never reach the outer edge of the landscaped park around the house. She paused for a moment to hitch Peggy onto her other shoulder and trudged on. Surely by now they would have missed the child and there would be a search party? It would be a waste of precious breath to shout, she decided, worried now that perhaps she should have tried to revive the child before setting out for the house. Supposing the moppet died? She had felt a faint pulse when she had reached Peggy, but she hadn't tried to do anything else.

She was near the house now, close to its grand entrance. She climbed the broad steps and gave the iron bell-pull by the door a terrific tug. Just to make sure, she tugged again. And again...

The door opened slowly under the indignant hand of Bush, the butler, who was affronted by the misuse of the bell-pull and the excessive noise. He had his mouth open to voice his displeasure, but Margo gave him no chance to utter a word.

'Get a doctor quickly, and get Lady Trueman or her daughter—anyone. Only hurry!'

She pushed past him and made for the stairs, dripping across the hall, short of breath, waterlogged and terrified. There was no time to give way to terror. She drew a breath.

'Will someone come quickly? I've got Peggy...'

She saw the butler hurry to the phone as a door

opened and Lady Trueman, followed by her daughter, came into the hall.

'What is all this noise…?' She goggled at Margo. 'Peggy—she's ill? What has happened? It's Margo Pearson…'

Margo didn't waste time explaining. 'Get her clothes off. She's been in the stream; she's unconscious. She must be rubbed dry and put to bed. I told the butler to get a doctor. Only will someone please hurry…?'

'My baby!' wailed Helen. 'Where's the nurse…?'

We shall be here all day, thought Margo, asking silly questions. She started up the stairs, intent on getting to the nursery, calling over her shoulder, 'Is the doctor coming? It's urgent. And for heaven's sake will someone give me a hand?'

This time her appeal was heard. The housekeeper, made aware of the commotion, had come into the hall and now hurried up the staircase to Margo.

'The nursery's on the next floor. Can you manage? I'll go ahead and turn down the bedclothes and get the place warmed.'

By the time Margo had reached the nursery she was standing ready with towels, the fire poked up and the lights on.

'Let me have her on my lap. Get your wet things off, miss. You'll catch your death. In the stream? You found her and carried her here? Bless you for that, miss. Where's that nurse of hers, I'd like to know—?'

She broke off to speak to Lady Trueman, who had just tottered in.

'Now, my lady, keep calm. Peggy will be all right, thanks to this brave young lady. Get your maid to give you a glass of brandy and give one to Miss Helen—and send Bessy up here, please.'

Helen had joined her mother. 'Peggy—out in all that rain—where's the nurse?'

The housekeeper said briskly, 'That's the doorbell, Miss Helen. Go and fetch the doctor up, will you? No time to waste.'

Margo, dragging off her wet shoe, her jacket a sodden heap on the floor, reflected that this housekeeper and her aunt Flo would make a splendid pair in any emergency.

Bessy came, and then was sent away to fetch a glass of brandy for Margo.

'I never drink it,' said Margo.

'Just this once you will, miss.' The housekeeper was firm. 'It's either that or pneumonia.'

So Margo tossed back the brandy, caught her breath at its fiery strength and felt a pleasant warmth from it. Perhaps she could take off the rest of her clothes… No, not yet. The doctor, ushered in by a weeping Helen, was bending over Peggy, who was now wrapped in a warm blanket on the housekeeper's lap.

She was still unconscious, and there was a large bump under the bruise.

'Will someone tell me what has happened?' The doctor was youngish and cheerful. 'It would help if just one of you could tell me.'

'Ask the young lady here,' said the housekeeper, and waved towards the shivering Margo. 'She found her and carried her here. A proper heroine.'

Margo, a trifle muzzy with the brandy, nonetheless managed a sensible account of what had happened, and then lapsed into silence.

'You undoubtedly saved Peggy's life,' said the doctor. 'She's concussed, but she's warm and her pulse is good. She must be X-rayed, of course, but not for the moment. Just bed and warmth and someone to be with her in case she comes round. How come she was so far from home?'

'I don't know where her nurse has got to. She should have been in the nursery, or playing in the garden with her. I—we—Mother and I were in the drawing room...' said Helen feebly.

'I want a second opinion,' said Lady Trueman. 'Will you get the very best consultant to come as soon as possible?'

The doctor got up. 'Yes, certainly, Lady Trueman. If I might use your phone, I know just the man.' He paused at the doorway. 'I think it might be a good idea if someone were to see to this young lady. A warm bath and a hot drink, and get those wet clothes off—a warm blanket or something.' He looked grim. 'But for her, you might have lost Peggy.'

He went over to Margo and picked up her wrist. 'Dr Wilcox,' he told her. 'I'm in the village—haven't I seen you in church?'

'Yes, Mrs Pearson's my aunt.'

He gave her back her hand. 'Well, your pulse is all right. Get as warm as you can, quickly.'

'Will Peggy be all right?'

'I think so—we'll know for sure when she's been seen by a specialist.'

He went away and Lady Trueman said, 'My dear, you must forgive us—it was such a shock. Bessy shall help you—a hot bath and then a quiet rest by the fire while your clothes dry. I'll phone your aunt.' She added worriedly, 'I do hope this specialist will come soon...'

Bessy came then, and led Margo away to help her out of her wet clothes and to run a hot bath, fragrant with bath essence. Margo sank into it thankfully.

She would have fallen asleep if Bessy hadn't come to rouse her.

'Your clothes are being dried, miss. If you'll get out I'll give you a good rub down and there's a warm blanket to wrap you in.'

'The specialist isn't here yet?'

'Like as not he'll come from London—take him best part of an hour or more, even if he started off the moment he got Dr Wilcox's message. He's here still, waiting for him.'

Swathed in a soft blanket, Margo was led back to the nursery and seated by the fire, and presently Bessy brought her a glass of milk.

'There's a drop of brandy in it, miss, to ward off the chill. Why don't you close your eyes for a few minutes? Lady Trueman's phoned your aunt and you'll be taken home as soon as your clothes are dry. There's only one shoe...'

'I lost the other in the stream. It doesn't matter.' Margo took the glass. 'Thank you for the milk, Bessy, and all your help.'

There must have been more than a drop of brandy, for Margo, nicely warm again, dozed off. She didn't hear the arrival of the specialist, who examined Peggy at some length, conferred with Dr Wilcox and then prepared to take his leave. He was standing having a last word with him when Dr Wilcox said, 'The young lady who found the child and carried her in is still here. She had a soaking and a tiring walk carrying Peggy. I took a quick look at her but...'

'You would like me to cast an eye over her?'

'I believe Lady Trueman would like that—just in case there is further damage.'

'Just so.'

The two men trod into the nursery and Margo opened a sleepy eye.

Professor van Kessel eyed her with a faint smile. 'It seems that we are destined only to meet in emergencies, Margo.'

Chapter 3

Margo blinked, her delight at the sight of him doused by the knowledge that she looked even worse than usual, cocooned in a blanket with her hair still damp. And probably, she thought miserably, the brandy had given her a red nose.

Indeed it had—contrasting strongly with her still pale face. The professor, looking at her, found himself wondering why he was pleased to see her again. He had thought about her from time to time, this plain, rather bossy girl. A typical vicar's daughter, but one, he had to admit to himself, who would keep her head in an emergency and use the common sense she had so obviously been endowed with. Not, he had thought, the kind of girl he would want to spend an evening with. Now he wasn't so sure. There was more to Margo than met the eye...

'Is Peggy going to be all right?' She had wriggled upright in her chair, nothing visible but her face and a great deal of untidy hair.

'I think so; she is regaining consciousness. We'll have her X-rayed in the morning. What about you, Margo?'

'Me? I'm fine; I just got a bit wet.'

He turned easily to Dr Wilcox. 'Margo and I have met before on occasion. I certainly didn't expect to see her here.'

'She's not staying with Lady Trueman; she's visiting her aunt, Mrs Pearson, who lives in the village.' Dr Wilcox smiled at Margo. 'I'll pop in tomorrow and see that you are none the worse for your soaking—'

He broke off as Bessy came in. 'Didn't know anyone was here,' she excused herself. 'I've brought Miss Pearson's clothes. Lady Trueman says as soon as she's ready she'll be driven back to her aunt's place.'

'Ah, well, as to that,' observed the professor mildly, 'by the time Dr Wilcox and I have had a little chat with Peggy's mother, Miss Pearson will be ready to leave. I can give her a lift on my way.'

Dr Wilcox gave him a quick glance. He had known the professor for some years—had met him at seminars, read his learned articles in the medical journals, and got to know him even better at a convention in Leiden. He admired him and knew that he was highly regarded in his profession—knew him to be a reserved man, whose private life was, as far as he was concerned, private. The last man, he would have thought, to show more than a courteous interest in the small pale girl wrapped in that blanket. They already knew each other, though. He must tell his wife when he got home.

Now he said cheerfully, 'Oh, splendid. Miss Pearson will be glad to get back to her aunt.'

He's just being polite, Margo told herself as she got back into her dry but hopelessly crushed clothes. It was no good putting on just one shoe. She was wondering what to do about that when Lady Trueman came in.

'My dear Margo, how shockingly we have treated you. Do forgive us—it has been such a shock. You are sure you are able to go back to your aunt? Bessy tells me that the professor has offered to take you home. So good of him. What a reassuring man he is—Peggy is conscious again and is to be X-rayed in the morning, and he will visit again when he has seen the result. When I think of that child lying there! We can never thank you enough…' Lady Trueman paused for breath.

'Had she run away from her nanny?'

Lady Trueman's pleasant face became quite ferocious.

'That woman. She is to leave immediately. She had left Peggy playing alone in the gardens while she went to chat with one of the gardeners. Do you know, she was still there when you came back? And never once gave a thought to Peggy? I told Helen when she engaged her that she was far too young and flighty…

'Lord Trueman will most certainly wish to thank you when he gets back home…'

Bessy peered round the door. 'The professor's ready to leave, my lady. I was to tell you and Miss Pearson.'

He was in the hall with Dr Wilcox and Helen, and Margo, very conscious of her stockinged feet, padded across the icy, marble-paved floor. It was the professor who came to meet her. He swallowed a desire to laugh at her ramshackle appearance.

'If someone could let Miss Pearson have a pair of shoes—boots—anything...'

It was Bessy who asked what size her feet were and sped away to return in a moment with a pair of wellies. 'Better than nothing,' she muttered.

'Of course we'll replace your shoes, Margo,' said Helen, and took her hand. 'We are so grateful.'

She began to cry again.

A pretty little woman, reflected the professor, but lacking common sense—utterly dependent on everyone else. He wasn't aware that he was comparing her with Margo.

With perfect good manners he got himself and her out of the house, popped her into the car and drove away.

'Will you tell me where your aunt lives? Close by, I gather.'

'The first house on the left when you reach the village in about two minutes. How did you get here? I mean, do you live close by?'

'Fairly near. Tell me, Margo, do you spend your life coping with emergencies? And why are you so far from home?'

He hadn't answered her question; she shouldn't have asked it in the first place. She sneezed. 'I'm visiting my aunt—father's sister-in-law. She's an archdeacon's widow.'

'You spring from an ecclesiastic family—and yet you intend to be a farmer's wife?'

She sneezed again, and he passed her a very large white handkerchief.

'No, I don't. I told George I didn't want to marry

him. He hadn't exactly asked me, but I thought I'd tell him first and save him the trouble.'

He turned a laugh into a cough. 'How very sensible of you. I must admit that I find it hard to imagine you as a farmer's wife.'

'Well, I dare say you do. I expect you think of me as a vicar's daughter.' She spoke without rancour. 'That's my aunt's house on the left. Thank you for the lift; it was most kind…'

All he said was, 'Stay where you are.' And he got out of the car and opened her door, waiting patiently while she sneezed yet again.

'That's going to be a nasty cold. I think I should see your aunt.'

Mrs Pearson opened the door as they reached it.

'Dear child, come inside at once.'

As she ushered them into the sitting room she cast an eye over the professor and he said smoothly, 'Mrs Pearson? I was called in to see Peggy and have brought Margo back to you. Strangely enough, we have met before. Dr Wilcox will call tomorrow and take a look at Margo, but in the meantime perhaps I might advise that she be put to bed at once. Warm drinks and a quiet day in the house tomorrow. I'm afraid she has caught a cold.' He smiled at her. 'Gijs van Kessel.'

Mrs Pearson liked the look of him, and she liked the sound of his quiet, assured voice. She held out a hand. 'Can you spare the time to tell me exactly what has happened? I had a very garbled version over the phone.'

'Certainly, Mrs Pearson. You will want to get Margo to bed at once, will you not?' He looked at Margo. Bed was undoubtedly the best place for her. 'If I might suggest another hot drink and two aspirins? A good night's sleep will put things to rights again.'

Margo peered at him from watery eyes and sniffed from a stuffed-up nose. Nothing, she had discovered at that very moment, could be put to rights again. Life would never be the same again either. How could it be? The peculiar feeling she had been experiencing for the last hour or so wasn't a cold in the head, it was love! And to have fallen in love so completely with a man who looked at her with kind detachment and not a vestige of interest in her as a person was ridiculous, and she must put a stop to it immediately.

She said, as briskly as another sneeze permitted, 'Thank you for bringing me back, Professor. There's really nothing wrong with me; I shall be fine in the morning.' She held out a hand. 'Goodbye.'

He took the hand—small, nicely shaped and capable—and held it fast.

'Not goodbye, Margo. I feel sure that we shall meet again.'

She looked up into his face and saw kindness there. There was something else too—amusement?

She took her hand away smartly. 'Perhaps.'

At the door she said, 'I'm quite all right to put myself to bed, Aunt Flo. I'll get some aspirins and milk as I go.'

Her aunt nodded. 'Very well, child. I'll pop in and see you later on. A little light supper, perhaps?'

She closed the door firmly after her niece. 'Do sit down,' she bade the professor. 'Margo will be all right; she's very healthy and strong.'

'It might be wise to keep her in bed until Dr Wilcox sees her tomorrow. It wasn't only getting so wet; she carried the child for quite a distance, and with only one shoe on—moreover, she was afraid for Peggy's life. She acted with great good sense.'

'Something she has always possessed in abundance. Lady Trueman was full of praise for her conduct!' Aunt Florence settled herself more comfortably in her chair. 'There'll be coffee in a moment, or would you prefer a drink?'

'Coffee would be delightful. Is Margo staying with you for some time?'

'Another week or so. You said you had met her already—at her home?'

'Yes. Actually we first met on a lonely road in the middle of the night...' He told his hostess about it very simply. 'And since then I have been to her home,' he concluded.

Aunt Florence poured the coffee. 'Oh, then you'll know all about George. I must say I was very relieved to hear that she has decided not to marry him. They have known each other for years and it was a gradual thing, you know—his mother liked the idea, thought that Margo could be moulded into the kind of wife she wanted for George. Only Margo isn't a girl one can mould. There was no engagement—indeed, she tells me that he had never actually asked her to marry him and took it all in good part. I shall be sorry for his wife when he does marry—his mother, you know.'

'So now Margo can rearrange her future to suit herself?' The professor spoke idly.

'Well, as to that, she has had no training of any sort. An excellent education, but she has been at home for several years.' She added severely, 'Margo is a good daughter. It is to be hoped that she will get the chance to be a good wife and mother.'

The professor murmured politely, drank his coffee and presently took his leave. He had interrupted a free day—a rare occurrence—in order to confer with Dr Wilcox, and now he wanted to get back to the quiet evening he had planned.

He had been surprised to see Margo again; she tended to pop up in the most unexpected places. She hadn't shown any particular pleasure at seeing him once more—although, he reflected, he had been pleased as well as surprised to see her.

He couldn't think why; she had no looks to speak of, her nose had been red and she had sniffed a good deal! And she had never made the slightest attempt to attract his attention. He remembered briefly the considerable number of women who had done just the opposite. Perhaps that was why he liked her. She obviously didn't mind in the least what his opinion of her was and he was sure that if she thought he should be put in his place then that was exactly what she would do.

He smiled at the idea and decided that when he went back to see Peggy, after the X-rays had been taken, he would call at Mrs Pearson's and see how Margo did.

His decision set at rest a vague feeling of disquiet. He wouldn't like her to be ill. She was young and healthy and clearly not given to making the worst of things. All the same she had put him in mind of a half-drowned kitten he had once rescued...

Margo, much refreshed by a brief nap, ate the splendid supper her aunt brought to her later that evening, swallowed more aspirins and went to sleep again, to wake in the morning feeling quite herself but with a streaming cold.

'You'll stay where you are until Dr Wilcox has been,' ordered Aunt Flo, at her most stern. 'Now just lie back, dear, while I rub your chest with camphorated oil.'

Margo did as she was told—people seldom disobeyed Aunt Flo—and presently, much soothed by the old-fashioned remedy, she lay back on her pillows, reeking of camphor, quite happy to do nothing more energetic than blow her small red nose at intervals.

She was sipping more hot milk when Dr Wilcox called and, escorted by Aunt Flo, entered the bedroom—to recoil at the overpowering atmosphere.

'Camphorated oil,' said Aunt Flo, in a voice which dared him to say anything detrimental about it.

'A splendid old-fashioned remedy—very soothing to the patient,' agreed the doctor.

He took a quick look at Margo and pronounced her none the worse for her wetting, but advised that she spend the rest of the day in bed. 'Paracetamol every four hours and drink all you can. There's no need for me to call again unless you're anxious about anything.'

'Is Peggy better?'

'Yes. No great harm done. Concussion and a nasty bruise. I saw the X-rays. She's to stay in bed for a few days, though.'

He got off the bed. 'Lady Trueman is coming to visit you in a day or two, when your cold is better. She is so very grateful. It could have been much worse but for your prompt action.'

He shook hands and went away and Aunt Flo returned with a bouquet of flowers in cellophane, tied with a great deal of ribbon. 'These have just come. There's a card...'

Margo read the card. They were from the Truemans

and Helen. The thought that they might have been from the professor was absurd, to be dismissed at once. She said brightly, 'Aren't they beautiful? Will you keep them in the sitting room, Aunt? There are so many of them, and I'll be downstairs tomorrow.'

Excepting her thickened speech and a constantly blown nose, Margo was indeed quite herself by the following morning. She was dusting the numerous knick-knacks in her aunt's sitting room when the professor called.

She hadn't expected him, although she had been thinking about him, and the sudden sight of him sent the colour into her cheeks.

'Entertain him while I see about coffee,' commanded Aunt Flo, and went away.

Margo put down the hideous Victorian vase she was holding. 'Hello,' she said. 'Have you been to see Peggy?'

'I've seen her; now I've come to see you.' He smiled gently.

'Oh, yes, well, do sit down.' She picked up a delicate Spode bowl and began to dust it. 'I hope she's better?'

'Going along nicely. And you, Margo?'

'Me? Oh, I'm quite well, thank you.' She very much wanted to blow her nose, but gave a surreptitious sniff instead.

He was sitting very much at his ease, looking at her, making no further attempt to speak. He could at least make an effort, she thought crossly. Her pretty colour had faded, leaving her pale, with puffed eyelids and a pink nose. Aware of this, she said peevishly, 'Haven't you any other patients to see?'

He said placidly, 'Oh, yes, quite a few—but not until this afternoon. A clinic at the hospital...'

'Children?'

'Scores of them—crying and being sick and wetting themselves. They will all be ill, though.'

'So you don't mind if they are tiresome?'

'No. Would you like to come and see them one day?'

'May I? Although I don't go to London very often…'

'Oh, I'd pick you up and bring you back. It would make a good subject next time you have a get-together at the village hall.'

She looked at him to make sure that he wasn't joking. He wasn't.

'Well, yes. There's the Mothers' Union and the WI, and some of the older children from the Sunday School…'

She smiled at him. He wasn't only the man she had fallen in love with, he was a man to admire and trust and be perfectly safe with. Her eyes sparkled and glowed in her face so that he didn't see the red nose and the puffy eyelids any longer, only the gentle curve of her mouth and her sweet smile.

Aunt Florence came in then, and they drank their coffee and talked about the weather and the excellent apple crop and the still distant approach of Christmas.

'November already,' observed Aunt Florence. 'Let us hope that we have a period of good weather… Do you return to your home for Christmas, Professor?'

'Oh, yes. I'm only here for another month or so.'

Just as well, thought Margo; then I can forget him. It took all her common sense to dispel the wave of sadness which engulfed her person.

The same common sense prompted her to empty her head of him once he had bade them goodbye and driven away and plunge into preparations for the church bazaar, the committee of which was chaired by Aunt Flo.

'You couldn't have been here at a better time,' that lady told her, sorting through the piles of contributions for the stalls, housed for the moment in the box-room. 'You will have a stall, of course, dear—good-as-new clothes.'

Margo said dutifully, 'Yes, Aunt. Do people really buy other people's clothes?'

'Good gracious me, yes. Lady Trueman's hats are very popular, and that young woman who works for the BBC and lives at the other end of the village—she has sent some really very nice things. Farmer Deadman's youngest is marrying in the spring; I've no doubt she'll snap up some of the dresses—just right for a wedding— and there's a lovely dressing gown—you know, one of those loose, flowing ones.

'Pass me my pen, dear, and I'll start pricing some of these things. You can fold them up and put them in those boxes ready to take down to the hall in the morning.'

Several days of hard work ensued. Aunt Florence, who Margo decided must have been a regimental sergeant major in some former life, marshalled her helpers, willing and unwilling, and saw to it that no one slacked. To give her her due, by Saturday afternoon, with the stalls stocked, the hall decorated and somebody at the door ready to take the entrance fee, she had achieved everything she had promised the committee she would do.

Margo, arranging the last few clothes, could hear the voices of the small queue already outside the door, which was due to be opened at any moment now. She rearranged the looking glass just so, so that the prospective purchasers could view their chosen articles in comfort, and took a quick look to make sure that her nose, still faintly pink from her cold, wasn't shining.

The door was opened and a great many people surged in, impatient to start looking for bargains but having to wait while Lady Trueman—just arrived in her car—made her usual speech and declared the bazaar open. The rector spoke too, but experience had taught him to make it very brief; his audience were already heading towards the particular stalls they fancied.

Margo did a brisk trade. It was fortunate that some of the things left from several years ago—rejects from bygone bazaars—were, as Aunt Flo observed, quite in style again, fashion being what it was.

The newer clothes went fast too. She had hung them in sizes, which helped a bit but didn't prevent a good deal of impulse-buying which she knew would be regretted later. She was helping an elderly woman choose a hat when she glanced up and saw Professor van Kessel, quite close by, watching her.

She offered the lady a feather toque, and he shook his head slightly and came nearer.

'The brown one with the brim,' he suggested, and smiled at her customer, who, taken by surprise, removed the toque and poised the hat of his choice on her grey hair.

'Well, dearie me, love, the gentleman's quite right. It suits me a treat. How much?'

'Seventy-five pence. A real bargain and just right for you—smart, too.'

'For me grandson's wedding, New Year's Day.' She beamed at the professor. 'Thank you kindly, sir. Got a wife of your own, I dare say, to choose hats for!'

'I'm sure you will look very nice in it.' He smiled his kind smile and she took the hat in the bag Margo had found for it and trotted off.

He said then belatedly, 'Hello, Margo.' He glanced round. 'A pity there is nothing here which I can buy.'

'However did you get here?'

'In my car,' he said, and when she frowned added, 'I had a last visit to pay to Peggy.'

He glanced round him at the women inspecting the clothes on the stall. 'When will you be free?'

'We stay open till half past five and then we clear up.'

He nodded. 'From the look of things, you won't have much to clear up on this stall. Have you seen Lady Trueman?'

'Well, no. She doesn't stay. A lot of people don't come. I mean it's their hats and clothes, if you understand me.'

'Ah, of course. I'm just going to have a word with someone…'

He wandered away, and a moment later she saw him bending his height to speak to Helen and presently joining her to go to the other end of the hall.

How strange it is, mused Margo, that we meet whenever I'm looking a fright or doing something quite unglamorous. She became so lost in thought about this that she sold a size fourteen dress to a size eighteen woman without noticing. Out of the corner of her eye she could see him still with Helen, laughing with her. It didn't seem quite fair. After all, Helen had already got a husband; she had lovely clothes too, and a pretty face.

Margo, ashamed of her thoughts, allowed a pert young woman from the new estate in the next village to buy the last two hats at a very reduced price. The stall was almost empty now. A hard core of dresses, obviously bought by mistake in the first place, hung limply on their hangers; they would be bundled up once again and reappear at the spring jumble sale in aid of church funds.

She was folding the last of them—puce nylon with a pattern of startling green leaves and a draped front guaranteed to disguise the wearer's curves completely— when the professor returned to the stall.

'Finished? Good. How long will you be?'

'Half an hour or so—why?'

'I thought we might have dinner. Your aunt tells me that she is invited out for drinks and will probably be asked to dine with these friends of hers.'

Margo gave him a thoughtful look. 'Thank you, but I've several things to do this evening and I can get my own supper if Aunt Florence isn't there.'

'Ah, you think—mistakenly—that I am obliging her by taking you out for a meal. Nothing of the kind. I consider it high time that we spent an hour or so in each other's company unhampered by emergencies of any sort.'

'Why?'

'I think that if we had time to talk we might find that we have quite a lot in common.'

She had made up her mind not to see him again, to forget him, to pretend that they had never met, and above all to convince herself that she didn't love him... 'All right,' she said, promising herself silently that it was just this once.

'I'll come for you in about an hour,' he told her, and went away to talk to the rector.

Margo totted up her takings, put the discarded dresses back in their box and went in search of her aunt, who, apprised of her plans, nodded her approval.

'Go back to the house as soon as you're ready, child.

I'll be home presently. You had better take a key with
you. Where are you going?'

'I don't know.'

'Wear your blue dress…'

Margo agreed. She had no option; it was the only
suitable garment she had. A pretty colour, and nicely
cut, it was nevertheless hardly a garment to inspire a
man to give it, or her, a second glance. It was all she
had though…

Margo peered at her person in her aunt's pier glass
and decided that she would do. She did her hair with
extra care, applied lipstick and powder and, encouraged by the result, went downstairs to find the professor chatting to her aunt.

He greeted her with easy friendliness, told her in just
the right tone of voice that she looked nice and thought
what a pity it was that her clothes were so dull. A pity,
indeed; she had a pretty figure and nice legs and she deserved better than the uninspired dress she was wearing.

He took her to the Oakley Court Hotel at Windsor—
a country house hotel, with grounds running down to
the river, and inside a pleasant cosiness combined with
charming surroundings and excellent food.

Gijs hadn't bothered to think why he wanted Margo
to have an evening out with him, but when he had seen
her that afternoon, surrounded by cast-off hats and out-
of-date dresses, he had a wish to take her away from it
all, to find out what she was really like, what she wanted
from life, if she was content…

They had a drink at the bar before going to their
candlelit table in the restaurant. Margo glanced round
her as they sat down. The dress was all wrong but there
was nothing she could do about that, and since she was

sitting down no one could see that it was the wrong length too. She dismissed it from her mind and studied the menu.

Spinach tartlets, then roast duck with cherry sauce, game chips and braised celery, followed by a lemon soufflé, accompanied by a bottle of Nuits St Georges, served to put Margo at her ease; never mind the dress, she was with Gijs, eating a delicious meal and drinking wine which tasted quite different from the occasional bottle she'd chosen from the supermarkets for birthdays and Christmas. She began to enjoy herself.

The professor had no difficulty in leading her on to talk about herself. He was aware that normally that was something she wouldn't do, but the wine had loosened her tongue and she answered his gently put questions readily enough.

'You do not wish for a career?' he asked casually.

'Well, I'm too old to start, aren't I?' she observed matter-of-factly. 'I would have liked to have travelled after I left school—just to Europe to have a look round—and I think that I would have enjoyed nursing…'

'You do not regret giving up George?'

'Not a bit.' She chose a chocolate from the dish which had come with the coffee.

'Would you like to marry?'

'Oh, yes, but I don't think too much about that because I don't think it's very likely.'

'Why not?'

She kept her voice light. 'I have no looks. If I had a fortune perhaps it would help—and lovely clothes!' She frowned at him across the table. 'I'm talking far too much. Not that it matters. I mean, you're a doctor and that's almost like talking to a man of the church, isn't it? Besides, we're unlikely to see each other again.'

'When we do meet each other it is on the most unlikely occasions.'

'You're going back to Holland soon. Will you be pleased to go?'

'It is my country. I shall always have one foot in England, though—I have consultancy posts at several hospitals here. I go wherever I'm needed, but Holland is my home.'

She longed to ask him about his life there, but something in his manner stopped her. Besides, she reflected, the less she knew about him, the easier it would be to forget him. She began to talk about the bazaar and the small events in the village, and presently he drove her back to Aunt Florence's house and when she thanked him for her evening told her quietly that he had enjoyed it too. He didn't say that he wanted to see her again before he went back to Holland, nor did he ask her when she was going back home.

'What did you expect?' she asked her reflection in the old-fashioned dressing-table mirror in her bedroom as she got ready for bed. And, although not a girl to cry easily, she cried herself to sleep.

During the next few days she saw something of Helen. Invited to tea, she made friends with Peggy— still in her bed and with a new nanny in charge.

'She's almost well again now,' said Helen. 'Such a relief. I have never been so scared in my whole life. Thank heaven that you found her, Margo, and that Dr Wilcox was able to get hold of that marvellous specialist. Didn't you think he was gorgeous? He's not married.

I asked him, and when he said he wasn't I told him that he ought to get himself a wife. I mean people expect it, don't they?' She waved a hand. 'You know, specialist in children's illness and so on—it would make him even more dependable, if you see what I mean.'

'If he's already well-known I don't suppose it matters much.'

'Wait until you're married and have children; you'll know what I mean.' Helen bit her lip. Margo's chances of marrying seemed to her to be a bit slight.

Margo was to go back home. Her father would drive up in the car and she would go back to the gentle, monotonous routine of her daily life at Thinbottom.

She packed her bag, made her aunt a present of a particular rose bush she had coveted and laid the table for lunch while Phoebe made a casserole.

'You must not travel on empty stomachs,' declared Aunt Flo. 'Put out the coffee-cups, Margo, and go to the kitchen and make sure the coffee's ready, with a plate of Phoebe's biscuits.'

Margo heard the front doorbell while she was warming the milk.

'I'd better take the tray in,' she told Phoebe. 'That must be Father...'

It was the professor, standing before the fire, talking to her aunt.

She put the tray down carefully, her heart in her throat, choking her. Here he was again, and in no time at all she would be gone.

'I'll fetch another cup,' she said, and smiled vaguely in his general direction.

'No need, Margo,' declared Aunt Florence. 'Gijs will

drive you back—I quite forgot to tell you that he phoned yesterday evening to say that he was going your way and wanting to know if you would like a lift. I phoned your father.'

Aunt Florence spoke with her usual certainty that any arrangement she might choose to make was agreeable to everyone else. 'Pour the coffee, dear.'

So Margo poured the coffee and handed out cups and biscuits and answered politely when spoken to. It was hard, she reflected, that, having made up her mind to forget him, he should turn up again. She took care not to look at him, and presently said that she thought she would go to the kitchen and give Phoebe a hand.

'No need,' said her aunt. 'I want you to run down to the rectory with the accounts for the bazaar; I promised the rector I would let him have them today. Gijs can go with you—I dare say he'd like to stretch his legs.'

So Margo got into her jacket, wound a scarf round her small neck and declared herself ready. Going down the garden path, she said awkwardly, 'I'm sorry about this. I dare say you want to leave as quickly as possible, and really there was no need for you to come with me.'

'Why should I wish to hurry away? I have been invited to lunch. Why do you take it for granted that I don't wish to be with you, Margo? You really must cultivate a better opinion of yourself. Are you not pleased to see me?'

'Yes, of course. I was a bit surprised.' She kept her voice steady and looked up into his face. 'I'm always pleased to see you, only each time I do I expect it to be the last.'

He tucked her hand under his arm. 'Next week I'm coming down to Thinbottom to take you to the hospital as I promised. You can spend the day there and I'll bring you back in the evening.'

'You will?' Her eyes sparkled. 'I'll love that. Which day?'

'Tuesday—you will have to be ready quite early in the morning.'

'Oh, I will. Here's the rectory…'

They were both invited in, and while one of the children went to fetch his father his wife led them into the sitting room.

'Do sit down,' she invited. She was a gossipy little woman, wanting to hear the details of Peggy's accident firsthand.

'So romantic,' she cried. 'And you two knowing each other and meeting again at Lord Trueman's. You must both…'

Luckily they were spared the rest because the rector joined them at that moment. A good thing, too, for Margo's cheeks had pinkened and the professor's features had assumed a blandness which she was sure hid amusement.

On the way back she said, 'I'm sorry about that…'

He took her arm. 'Why? It must appear romantic to those who don't know us. After all, how are they to know that neither of us has any interest in romance?'

She had no answer to that.

Chapter 4

It was obvious that Aunt Florence approved of the professor. Over the casserole and the treacle tart which followed it the talk was leisurely and covered any number of subjects. It was only when he glanced at his watch and observed that they should be going that Aunt Florence got up reluctantly from the table.

Bidding them goodbye presently, she said, 'I hope I shall see you—both of you—again soon. Margo knows that she is always welcome—and you, Gijs, if you are so inclined—although I dare say you are a very busy man and have any number of friends.'

She stood in the doorway, watching them get into the Rolls. Margo had been unusually quiet during lunch, she reflected. Probably a little sad at the thought of the mundane life she was returning to. She and the professor seemed to get on well enough—a casual friendliness which Aunt Flo supposed was all that could be expected from two people who lived such different lives. She watched the car until it was out of sight then went back indoors, feeling lonely; Margo had been a pleasant companion, someone nice to have around the house.

Professor van Kessel was thinking much the same thing as he talked casually about nothing in particular. He sensed that Margo was ill at ease and was intent on finding out why.

She sat very still beside him, looking out of the window and making suitable replies in her pretty voice, but she made no effort to start any conversation.

'You're sorry to be going back home?' he asked.

'No, of course not. I've had a lovely holiday, though.'

He remembered the bazaar, and wondered if staying with Aunt Florence had been very much different from being at home. He thought not. Sunday School, Mothers' Union, arranging flowers, visiting parishioners and arranging whist drives, though splendidly worthwhile tasks in themselves, weren't enough to fill a girl's life. Not a girl like Margo, he reflected, who would make a splendid wife and mother. He must contrive to let her meet some of the younger doctors at the hospital on Tuesday.

They arrived back in time for a late tea but he didn't stay for that. He made his excuses with his beautiful manners, giving no reason for his refusal, bade them goodbye, reminded Margo to be ready on Tuesday and drove away.

'I dare say he's on his way to a hospital or a meeting,' observed Mrs Pearson. 'A pity he couldn't stay for tea.' She brightened. 'Perhaps he's having it with friends. Nice of him to give you a lift, love.'

Margo agreed. Well, it had been nice of him, and after all that was all it had been—a lift home because he happened to be going that way too. Not, she told herself firmly, because he enjoyed her company.

There was Tuesday, of course, but she had no doubt that once they were at the hospital she would see nothing of him—probably he regretted his invitation. She should have refused...

It seemed a month of Sundays until Tuesday. In reality it was only a few days away, and those days were fully occupied: driving her father to Blandford, shopping for her mother, sitting in on the committee planning Christmas entertainment for the Sunday School.

It came at last and she stood ready and waiting at half past eight in the morning, sure that he had forgotten.

He arrived exactly when he had said he would, accepted the coffee her mother had ready, then stowed her into the car and began the drive back to London.

'You must have got up very early,' observed Margo. 'I hope you had a good night's sleep.'

He assured her that he had, touched by her concern.

'The colleague I am staying with is an old friend and a most considerate host, but I intend to look around for a small house in London. I come here so frequently nowadays—sometimes for a couple of days, sometimes for weeks at a time.'

'But you have a home in Holland?'

'Oh, yes.'

That was all he would tell her.

'I'm handing you over to one of the housemen at the hospital; he'll take you round and then bring you to my clinic. Alec Jackson—I think you will like him. He has an excellent future ahead of him.' He glanced sideways at her serene profile. 'I'll drive you back some time this evening—I can't be certain when.'

'I'm sure I'm going to enjoy every minute,' she assured him. Even if she didn't see him again at the hospital there was the drive back home to look forward to…

The hospital was in the East End, crammed in amongst narrow streets of small houses and down-at-heel shops. Margo, seeing it for the first time, felt some disappointment at the sight of its elaborate Victorian brickwork and narrow windows, but, once urged inside by the professor, saw that the aspect was quite different: light walls, bright pictures, plenty of lights and potted plants, and as a background to these a steady tide of noise, rising and falling and never ceasing.

The entrance hall was quite small, with corridors leading away from it in all directions. The professor glanced at his watch and Margo saw his faint frown, but his face cleared as a young man came hurrying to meet them.

'Good morning, sir.' He had a cheerful, blunt-featured face, and smiled at her as the professor spoke.

'Good morning, Jackson; this is Margo Pearson. Take her everywhere and take care of her for me. When she's seen all she wishes to see, bring her along to the clinic, will you?'

He smiled down at Margo. 'I hope you enjoy your visit,' he said, and didn't wait for her answer but strode away.

'He's got a busy day ahead of him,' said Alec Jackson. 'Running a bit late already.' He touched her arm. 'We'll have coffee first, if you like, in the canteen, while I explain the lay-out of the place. It's like a rabbit warren.'

The canteen was half-full, but they found a table and sat down facing each other. 'May I call you Margo?' asked Alec. 'Have you known the professor for a long time?'

'No—a month or so. And I don't know him well, only we've met from time to time and he suggested I might like to see the hospital. Do you work for him?'

'I'm on his team—very junior, I must add. He's a splendid man—marvellous with children. There's this op he does to lengthen malformed legs—very complicated. There are a couple of patients here who have had it done; you'll see them presently.' He added, 'If you want to powder your nose the Ladies' is over there. I'll wait for you here.'

You couldn't help but like him, thought Margo as she was whisked from one ward to the next. She would have liked a brother like him, someone she could talk to and laugh with.

True to his promise, he showed her two small boys, each with a leg encased in steel rods and bars with screws at one side.

'They have to be turned once a day,' explained Alec, and at her look hastened to add that it didn't hurt a bit. 'Not feeling squeamish, are you?' he wanted to know anxiously. 'The professor said you never turned a hair under any circumstances.'

'Did he? No, I'm not squeamish, Alec, and it's a marvellous thing to be able to do, isn't it? He must be very clever. Do you operate?'

Alec looked pleased at her question. 'Minor stuff—and I take my turn at scrubbing to assist.'

'So one day you will be like Professor van Kessel?'

'Can't hope to reach his heights, but I'll have a go

at any rate. Come and see the prem ward then we'll go and get something to eat before we go to the clinic.'

They ate beefburgers and chips and jam roly-poly pudding while Alec talked and she listened. They were firm friends by now, enjoying each other's company.

Margo, absorbing information the way a sponge absorbed water, was a pleasant surprise to Alec. He had undertaken to escort Margo when the professor had asked him, resigned to a boring day, but she had turned out to be both intelligent and interested. A great girl, he reflected; never mind her plain face. And when she looked at you her eyes were magnificent...

The clinic was still crowded and very noisy. There was a short corridor at the far end, with doors on either side, and a constant flow of people going to and fro along it.

'The consulting rooms,' explained Alec. 'The professor's got the first one on this side, then there's his registrar and the junior registrar and two more doctors at the end. The professor sees all the new patients and the serious cases, and also any of the children his team refer to him.'

'But there must be hundreds here.'

'Something like that—it seems more with all the screeching and bawling.'

'I wish I could see him working...'

'More than my life's worth. There he is now, going along to see a child in the junior registrar's room.'

Margo craned her neck. He looked different in a long white coat, with a stethoscope slung around his shoulders and a fistful of papers in one hand.

'He looks so clever,' she observed in a whisper.

'Well, he is.' Alec smiled at her. 'He'll come back presently; you'll be able to see him better then.'

When he did return the professor saw them at once, standing to one side. Alec was saying something to Margo, who was smiling at him. They appeared to be on excellent terms. The professor frowned, feeling no pleasure at the sight, quite forgetting that the whole idea of bringing Margo to the hospital was so that she might meet one or two young men...

The pair of them stayed for some time, and then, when there was a mere handful of patients left, went back to the canteen once more to drink strong tea and eat currant buns.

'You should train as a nurse,' suggested Alec. 'A children's nurse.'

'I'm too old,' said Margo matter-of-factly. 'I'm twenty-eight. Besides, I'm quite busy at home. It's only a small village but there's always something...'

'You're not too old. You don't look as though you're twenty-eight either,' observed Alec generously. He added with a burst of candour, 'The professor said you were a sensible girl, with no silly ideas, and I expected a kind of schoolteacher type, if you know what I mean. You're not a bit like that—just the opposite. I dare say he was comparing you with some of his elegant lady-friends.'

Margo laughed with him, inwardly boiling with rage. How dared the professor describe her as a schoolteacher, and a sensible one too? If she didn't love him so much she would hate him. If that's what he thinks of me then I'll be just that, she told herself. Just let him wait until he drives me home.

Alec, unaware of the feelings he had stirred up behind Margo's pleasant little face, was on the point of suggesting that they might meet again when his phone bleeped.

'The professor is waiting for us.'

Margo pondered the idea of having another cup of tea and keeping him waiting, but that might get Alec into trouble. She followed him out, outwardly meek, back through the hospital to the front entrance, and found the professor leaning against a wall reading the porter's evening paper. He handed it back as they reached him, expressed the hope that they had had a satisfactory day, and held the door open for Margo.

'Thanks, Alec,' he said, and listened while he was told that their tour had been most enjoyable. Then he watched as Margo shook hands with Alec and echoed his wish that they might meet again soon. She knew it was not at all likely, but even schoolteacher types had their moments!

She smiled very sweetly at Alec. 'It was lovely,' she reiterated, with a show of warmth especially for the professor's benefit. 'You made it all so interesting...'

She got into the car then, turning to wave as they drove away and then sitting as still as a mouse.

Presently the professor asked, 'So the day was a success? Alec gave you lunch?'

'Yes, thank you.'

He tried again. 'What did you enjoy most?'

She thought before she replied. 'The two boys whose legs were being lengthened. Their little faces and their cheerful acceptance of having their legs in those awful contraptions. And knowing that later on they will be normal, like other boys.'

Her voice was cool but she was still boiling away inside, and he was quick to sense that.

'What is the matter, Margo?'

'Matter? There is nothing the matter, Professor.'

'You would prefer not to talk?'

'Yes.' Such a small word, he thought, and fired like a bullet from a gun. Something had upset her and he wondered what it was. Not Alec, surely? They had parted the best of friends—indeed, with the promise of future meetings. Which was exactly what he had hoped for, wasn't it?

Conversation languished after that, Margo's polite and chilly replies bringing each topic he introduced to a dead end. Only when they reached the vicarage and he stopped before its door did he turn to her.

'I wish to know what has upset you, Margo.'

'Nothing. I'm not upset,' she told him stonily.

'We will sit here until you tell me.'

As she put a hand on the door he reached over and put it gently back into her lap. 'Well?'

She looked at him then. 'You said I was a sensible girl with no silly ideas; Alec thought I sounded like a schoolteacher. If that's what you think of me I don't want to see you again, ever.'

'But you *are* a sensible girl, and to the best of my knowledge refreshingly lacking in silly ideas...'

'There, you see what I mean? It's called damning with faint praise. Now I'm going in. Thank you for letting me visit the hospital.'

She put a hand on the door and this time he didn't stop her, but got out too and walked with her to the front door, where she asked him in a voice straight from the deep freeze if he would care for a cup of coffee.

'In the circumstances, no, Margo.'

He sounded as though he was laughing, and she said fiercely, 'Oh, I hope I never see you again!'

He didn't answer that but got back into the car, and was driving away as her mother opened the door.

'Darling—but Gijs is going? Can't he stop for a cup of coffee or supper?'

Margo stepped into the warmth of the hall and shut the door behind her.

'No, he couldn't stop. He's a very busy man, Mother. Wait while I take off my things and I'll tell you about my day—it was fascinating…'

When she had finished her mother remarked, 'You didn't see much of Gijs, then?'

'Only from a distance. I think he is frightfully important and considered to be very clever because of this special surgery he's so good at.'

'Oh, well, I dare say he'll come and see us one day, when he has the time.'

'Alec said that he has many friends.'

'Well, I dare say—such a handsome man and such beautiful manners. He's a man to trust, too.'

To which Margo said nothing at all. In bed later, she lay bitterly regretting what she had said to Gijs. She hadn't meant a word of it; she had been hurt and angry and had said things she really hadn't meant. She had told him that she never wanted to see him again and her heart would break if that were to happen. Never mind what he thought of her; to see him from time to time was all she asked and expected.

A week went by—a week of unpleasant November weather, cold and damp and dark but tolerated by everyone since it heralded Christmas.

Margo busied herself preparing for the forthcoming festivities—the play for the Sunday School, the making of decorations for the village hall, the wrapping of small presents for the bran tub for the children's party—and never for one moment was Gijs out of her thoughts. She did her best to banish him, to bury him beneath plans for Christmas, but that wasn't easy.

Mrs Pearson paused in her busy life from time to time and wondered what was wrong. Surely Margo wasn't regretting her decision not to marry George? When she had a few quiet moments to spare she would try to find out.

The vicar was free on Mondays and he had planned a day out, leaving Margo to mind the house and deal with any small matter which might crop up while he and her mother went to Exeter for the day. They would buy Christmas presents, treat themselves to a splendid lunch, visit the cathedral, and still have time for Mrs Pearson to indulge in some window-shopping.

Margo saw them off soon after breakfast and went back indoors to feed Caesar and Plato, clear away the dishes and get on with the housework. They would be hungry when they returned, she reflected; she would go down to the butcher and get some steak and make a casserole. It could simmer for hours on the stove and be ready when they got home.

On her return she turned the radio up, filling the house with sound, and busied herself until lunchtime. After her meal Plato needed a walk, and by the time they were home again it was dusk and time for tea. That over, she laid the table, saw to the potatoes, made a custard to go with the plum compote she had made and sat down to wait for the sound of the car.

The six o'clock news came and went and there was no sign of them. She went to look out of the window and saw that it wasn't raining—indeed, there was a glimpse of the moon from time to time—so it wasn't the weather that was delaying them.

She picked up a book and read for a while, but when the clock struck half past seven she gave up her pretence of reading and went to the window again. Her father didn't like driving at night unless it was absolutely necessary, and he had said that they would be home before six o'clock.

'So what's happened?' Margo asked Caesar and Plato, who were sitting beside her. 'They could phone...'

The hands of the clock were creeping towards eight when there was a knock on the door, and when she went to open it Bob Passmore, the village bobby, called through the letter-box, 'It's Bob, miss, if you'll let me in.'

He was a big man with a red face and a flowing moustache, friendly with everyone. He gave the village a feeling of security—admonishing naughty boys, directing what traffic there was, cycling hither and thither on his conscientious rounds.

Now his cheerful face was serious. He came into the hall and shut the door behind him.

'Come and sit down, Miss Margo. I'm afraid I've a bit of bad news for you.'

She led the way into the sitting room. 'Mother and Father? There's been an accident?'

Bob Passmore stood in front of her. 'Yes, Miss Margo.'

'They're hurt?' She saw his face. 'They're killed?'

'I'm afraid so, Miss Margo. A car crashed into the

barrier on the A303 and collided with theirs head-on. They died instantly.'

He had never known anyone so colourless and still alive.

She said quietly, 'Thank you for telling me, Bob.' She was so still that the only living thing about her was her eyes.

'You'll need to phone the family, miss. Shall I do it for you?'

'No—no, thank you, Bob. I'll ring my aunt. I'm sure she'll come here and—and help me. There will be a great deal to attend to, won't there?'

He saw that she was in shock. 'You ring your aunt while I make you a cup of tea. Would you like the wife to come over?'

'How kind of you, Bob, but I'm quite all right, and my aunt will come as soon as she can arrange it.'

'You can't be alone here, Miss Margo…'

'She'll hire a car.' She got up. 'I'll phone her now while you make the tea.'

Aunt Florence had settled down to a pleasant evening with a book from the library when the phone rang, so she lifted the receiver with a touch of impatience and said snappily, 'Hello—who is speaking?'

For a moment she didn't believe it was Margo, telling her in a voice that didn't sound like hers at all that her mother and father had been killed.

'My dear child…this is terrible. I shall come at once, just as soon as I can get a car and pack a bag. Are you all right?'

Margo's voice telling her that she was quite all right

didn't reassure her at all. So quiet and calm and without emotion.

Aunt Florence put down the phone and then picked it up again. A car—that was the first thing—and while she was waiting for it she could phone the rest of the family. She had started to dial when the doorknocker was thumped, and she went to answer it in a rush of impatience.

Someone from the village, she supposed. Well, she had no time for them now. She flung the door wide and met Professor van Kessel's smiling face.

'Oh, Professor—Gijs—how kind. Do come in. You must excuse me while I do some phoning...'

Aunt Florence, never known to lose her cool, had lost it now.

'I've had some bad news. Margo phoned not five minutes ago—her parents have been killed in a car accident. I must go to her. I'm about to arrange... You'd like a cup of coffee?'

He followed her into the sitting room. 'You want to go to Margo? I'll drive you there, Mrs Pearson. While you pack a bag I'll get you a drink; I think you need one...'

'But it's so far—I really can't impose... There's a good garage in Windsor. It can't be true—they make mistakes sometimes, don't they?'

He pushed her gently into a chair and went looking for the brandy.

'Drink this—all of it; you've had a bad shock. Tell me exactly what Margo said on the phone.'

When she had told him he said, 'Go and pack a few things while I see to doors and windows. Do you have a maid? Did I not see someone when I was here before?'

'Phoebe. She's not on the phone.'

'We will stop at her home as we go so that you can give her a key. May I use your phone?'

Aunt Florence, for once unable to cope, thankfully did as she was told. As she sat in the car some ten minutes later, it crossed her mind that he hadn't uttered one word of sympathy—but somehow that didn't matter; while others might have wasted time thinking up comforting words, he had dealt with the situation within minutes.

'Why had you come to see me?' she asked.

'I had visited Lord Trueman and I was calling to thank you for your hospitality; it was a pleasant visit.' He paused. 'Did Margo sound very upset? She was devoted to her parents, was she not?'

'Yes, she was. It didn't sound like her at all—very quiet and composed.'

'In shock. I hope that someone is with her. When she realises what has happened she will need a shoulder to cry on.'

He drove for some miles in silence, then said, 'Presumably she will have to leave the vicarage. There will be a new incumbent and he will need to live there. Has she any family other than yourself?'

'Aunts and uncles and cousins, but all but myself live in the north of England or Scotland. We are in contact—birthdays and Christmas and holidays—but I'm not sure if Margo would be happy living with any of them. Besides, she will need to find work; there won't be much money. She can come to me, of course, until she decides what she wants to do. I'm fond of her and we get on very well.'

He was driving fast, his hands relaxed on the wheel,

his face quiet. Aunt Florence wondered what he was thinking.

The journey seemed endless. 'Are we nearly there?' she asked him.

'Not long now. Try not to think about it, Mrs Pearson. I know that sounds a stupid thing to say, but Margo is going to need your help, and if you can manage to bottle up your own grief for her sake you should. It has been a terrible shock to you, I know, but I believe you to be a stout-hearted woman. Margo is a stout-hearted girl too, but the suddenness of it will have bowled her over.'

There were lights on at the vicarage as he drew up before its door. It was Bob Passmore who answered their knock.

He said in his soft Dorset voice, 'She's in the kitchen, just sitting. You'll stay? Mrs Pearson, isn't it? Her aunt?'

Aunt Florence nodded. 'And Professor van Kessel, a friend of the family—a doctor.'

Bob Passmore looked more cheerful. 'Ah, a doctor. Maybe that'll be a help. I'll be getting along. I'll come any time you want me. There'll be more news in the morning—perhaps tonight...' He gave the professor a good look and nodded, reassured by the size of him.

Aunt Florence took off her coat and went into the kitchen, and after a moment the professor followed her.

Margo was sitting at the kitchen table with Caesar on her lap and Plato beside her. She looked up as they went in and the professor thought that she had never looked so plain; her face was quite white, with no sign of tears, but her eyes were huge.

She got slowly to her feet and Aunt Florence kissed her.

'I've come to stay, my dear, if you'll have me.'

Margo nodded. 'Thank you; that would be nice.' She looked past her to where the professor was standing.

'Gijs,' said Margo. She sounded like a frightened child. 'Oh, Gijs…'

He crossed the room and took her in his arms, holding her gently as though she were indeed a frightened child. He began to talk to her softly and suddenly she was in tears, sobbing into his shoulder, spilling out her sorrow.

He stood solid and reassuring and comforting, and after a moment Aunt Florence went to put the kettle on and gather up cups and saucers and the teapot.

Eventually Margo lifted a sodden face. 'I'm so sorry, I've soaked your jacket. I'm better now.'

He kissed her wet cheek and smiled down at her. 'That's my girl. We're going to have a cup of tea and then I'll see what I can find out for you. Then you will go to bed and sleep. In the morning it will be another day and we shall know more about everything.'

They drank their tea, not saying much, and Aunt Florence was glad to see a little colour creep back into Margo's cheeks. She studied the sad face opposite her and thanked heaven that the professor was here with them.

Presently he went away to Margo's father's study to phone, and she told Margo how it had come about that he was here with them. She talked on at random, and was relieved when he came back.

'Your mother and father are at Yeovil Hospital; it seems it was the nearest to the scene of the accident. They died instantly, Margo. There are certain formalities to be dealt with before they can be brought back here. I'll drive you there in the morning.'

'You'll stay? What about your patients? The hospital?'

'I've arranged to have a day off. I'll stay, if you'll have me.'

'Will you? Will you really?' She turned a sad face to him. 'I can't thank you enough…'

He glanced at Aunt Florence, who nodded briskly. 'An excellent idea. I'll go and make up a bed while you two get some supper. Soup, if there is any, and how about a stiff drink for all of us?'

Aunt Florence, quite restored to her usual brisk tartness, went away. She wept a little as she made up the bed and then laid out towels and soap, but she didn't give way to her grief; there would be time for that later.

Margo, comforted by Gijs's company, the sharp edge of her grief dulled for the moment, set about warming some soup while he found the plates and spoons and knives, keeping up a steady flow of talk as he did so, but making no attempt to avoid talking about her parents. Indeed, he talked about them quite cheerfully, taking no notice when she wept a little, and when she suddenly wailed, 'Oh, why did it have to happen? I don't think I can bear it…' he took her in his arms again.

'Oh, yes, you can. How would your father and mother expect you to behave? Try and think of that and take heart. My poor dear, if I could take your grief onto my shoulders I would. All I can tell you is that as each day passes the load lightens.'

Presently she swallowed her soup, took the pill he offered her and was seen into her bed by Aunt Flo. She had expected to stay awake all night, but she slept at once and only woke as a watery sun shone into her room.

She couldn't lie in bed. She got into her dressing

gown and shuffled downstairs to make tea and found the professor there, standing at the open kitchen door, with Plato at his feet and Caesar tucked under one arm. He was dressed, immaculate as ever, his face calm. His good morning was friendly.

'The kettle's boiling. I was wondering if Mrs Pearson would object to me taking her a cup of tea. Now you can do it for me. Sit down; I'll make the tea. We need to leave here soon after breakfast.' He glanced at her. 'You slept?'

'Yes, thank you. I hope you were comfortable. We don't often have people staying and the bedrooms are a bit unlived-in.'

'It's a nice old house, isn't it? Built for a vicar with a large family who had to keep up appearances.'

'It's too big just for the three of us...' She faltered. 'It *was* too big, I mean.' She drank some tea. 'Of course I shall have to go, won't I?'

'Yes. Although I should imagine they will give you a little time. You will go to your aunt?'

'I expect so, if she doesn't mind. Just while I find some work somewhere.' She finished her tea. 'I'll take her a cup. Will breakfast in about half an hour be all right?'

The formalities, once they reached Yeovil, seemed endless to her. The professor had suggested that he should identify her mother and father for her and she had nodded wordlessly, and afterwards he had said, 'They both look peaceful and there is no sign of injury. Would you like me to arrange their return to Thinbottom?'

He had done that, and attended to all the other arrangements which had to be made, and then driven her back home to find Aunt Florence waiting for them with a substantial tea.

'I have telephoned the rest of the family,' she told Margo, 'and there have been a great many telephone calls for you. I've left a list on your father's desk. You will be kept busy for a while, Margo. Will it be a good idea if I see to the cooking and the house, so that you are free to see people and write the letters and answer the phone?'

The professor took Plato for a walk while they washed up the tea things, and when he returned observed that he would have to return to London that evening.

'I'll come to the funeral if I may,' he said. 'I dare say you'll know more about the future in a few days' time.'

Margo summed up a smile. 'Yes, of course. You've been so kind—I can never repay you.'

She had made a great effort to behave normally in his company. He had been kind and dealt with everything without fuss. Now she wished him goodbye in a determinedly cheerful voice, offering a hand and wishing with all her heart that his large, comforting one would never let it go.

It was Aunt Florence, bustling into the hall, who made it unnecessary for her to say anything more.

'Margo, there's someone—a Reverend Mac-something—on the phone. Would you speak to him?'

When Margo had gone she said, 'Margo will have thanked you; now it's my turn. I don't know how we could have managed without you. Bless you, Gijs.' She put out her hand. 'Do you think that is the new incumbent already? Surely not…' Her severe features crumpled. 'What is to happen to Margo?'

The professor held her hand and bent and kissed her cheek.

'Why, I shall marry her,' he said, in a no-nonsense voice.

He didn't give her time to reply to that but got into his car. It was out of sight when Margo came back into the hall.

Chapter 5

For Margo, the next few days were like a bad dream; she walked and talked, signed forms, answered letters and listened politely to endless sympathy and some good advice, but it seemed to her that it was another person doing these things, a calm, quiet girl, who washed and dressed herself and ate her meals like an automaton. Presently, she told herself repeatedly, she would wake up from the nightmare.

All the while she was scarcely aware of the professor, dealing with the whole unhappy business, sparing her as much as he could with silent efficiency.

It was Aunt Florence who asked him worriedly if he was getting enough rest, for he drove back and forth, fitting in his visits with his hospital work, his ward rounds, his clinics, theatre lists and private patients.

She had to be content with his quiet assurance that he

was perfectly all right, but the tired lines on his weary face disquieted her.

'It is only for a few days more,' he reminded her, smiling.

It was after the funeral, when everyone had left the vicarage and the three of them were standing in the sitting room surrounded by the debris of cups and saucers and plates and left-over food, that he said briskly to Margo, 'We're going for a walk while Mrs Pearson puts her feet up for an hour. Go and get a coat, Margo.'

It was a bright, cold day, the sun already low, but there was still an hour or more of daylight. They set off along the road out of the village, not talking, comfortable in each other's company, with Plato plodding happily beside them. They had walked for half an hour when the professor said, 'This is where we met, Margo,' and stood still and wrapped his arms around her. Great comforting arms, whose warmth after all these days allowed her to give way to her sorrow.

She sobbed and snivelled, mumbling into his shoulder until there were no more tears left. When at last she raised her head, he said cheerfully, 'That's better,' and mopped her face with his handkerchief.

'So sorry,' said Margo on a last hiccup. 'It was all bottled up inside me. I feel better now.'

'You will go on feeling better and better each day. If you want to cry, then do so, Margo. You don't have to be brave with me.'

She couldn't see his face clearly in the gathering dusk. 'You have been very kind. I don't know what I should have done without you...'

'I hope that there will be no need to be without me. Will you marry me, Margo?'

She lifted a tear-stained face to his and peered at him. 'Marry you? You mean us—marry? But we don't—you don't know me; I might not suit you at all. I can't think of any reason…'

'Two very good ones. I need a wife and you need a home. What is more, I believe that we shall get along very well together. In other circumstances I would have suggested that we had the usual engagement and got to know each other, but, as things are, it seems to me that we should marry first and get to know each other afterwards.'

He had turned her round and was walking her back the way they had come.

'You're not hankering after George?'

She answered with some of her usual spirit. 'Good heavens, no. What about you, though?'

'Am I hankering? No. I'm thirty-five, Margo. I've been in and out of love a dozen times. Now I want to settle down, and I should like to do that with you.'

She stopped walking and tugged at his arm. 'It wouldn't work even if I said yes. I have no looks, and it's no use pretending that I have, and I've no idea how the wife of a famous surgeon should behave.' She paused. 'Besides, you're Dutch.'

'So I am,' he said mildly. 'But I'm still Gijs.' He took hold of the hand on his sleeve and held it fast. 'I imagine surgeons' wives behave exactly the same way as any other wife would. And one thing more—you have beautiful eyes, Margo; nothing else matters.'

They walked on in silence until Margo said in a small voice, 'Thank you for asking me, Gijs. I think I'd like to marry you. Not because I need a home, but because I do like you. Only there's a condition. You must promise to tell me if ever you should fall in love…'

'I promise—but you must promise too.'

As a vicar's daughter, she had been brought up not to tell lies. But surely this particular lie wouldn't count as much? 'I promise,' said Margo.

He tucked her hand back into his arm. 'You will be staying here for a few more days, to pack up before the new vicar arrives? Aunt Florence will be with you? Good. I'll come again as soon as I can. Shall we marry as soon as possible? I intend to go over to Holland three days before Christmas. We could marry in the morning and travel on the same day. A quiet wedding?'

'Yes, please. Just us. Well, Aunt Florence will want to be there.' She asked hesitantly, 'Do you have any family, Gijs?'

'My mother died ten years ago; my father died last year. I have three sisters and a brother. Since we shall be going to Holland directly after the wedding you can meet them all then. Would you like to be married here?'

She said, 'Yes, please,' and swallowed sudden tears. 'I expect Sir William would give me away.'

'That's settled, then.' They had reached the vicarage and went in through the kitchen. Aunt Florence came marching through the door as they went in.

'Splendid—just in time to help with the washing-up. Gijs, you'll stay for supper? I'll get it ready now; you'll want to get back.'

'Aunt Flo, Gijs has asked me to marry him and I said I would.'

Her aunt's severe features broke into a smile. 'That is splendid news. When is the wedding to be?'

She embraced Margo and looked at Gijs.

'We intend to marry three days before Christmas and go over to Holland on the same day.' He nodded, took off his overcoat and jacket and rolled up his shirtsleeves. 'I'll wash,' he told Margo, 'and you wipe.'

He went after supper, kissing Aunt Florence's cheek and then Margo's. His kiss was swift, and not in the least lover-like. Margo hadn't expected that anyway.

When he had driven away, Margo asked anxiously, 'I'm doing the right thing, aren't I, Aunt Flo? I'm not marrying him for a home, although I know I need one, and I do like him very much…'

Aunt Flo said something which sounded like 'pish' and 'tosh'. 'My dear child, you're marrying him because you love him, aren't you? So of course you are doing the right thing.'

Margo was horrified. 'How did you know? I never said a word…'

'Don't worry, he hasn't noticed—nor will he unless you want him to.'

She gave Margo a brisk pat on the shoulder. 'Now, we are going to occupy ourselves this evening with plans for your wedding—something your mother and father would have wanted you to do. Get some paper and a pen, child, and let us begin.'

The evening, which Margo had been dreading, went quickly. There wasn't much money but, as Aunt Flo pointed out, there was only need to buy suitable clothes for her wedding and the time she would spend in Holland.

'I imagine Gijs will want to see you suitably dressed. You will be able to fit yourself out when you return after Christmas, but you must have some new clothes before then.'

Margo's list was short, but she insisted that it was adequate. 'If I could find a dress and jacket for the wedding, then I could wear the dress later. My winter coat's still good enough. I'll get a jersey two-piece. And a tweed skirt perhaps? I've several blouses and woollies. Something for the evening?'

'Most certainly.'

'A skirt? Velvet, I think.' Margo wrote busily. 'One of those cream crêpe blouses with a waterfall collar, and another blouse or top…'

'Shoes?' Aunt Florence reminded her. 'And gloves and a decent handbag—very important.'

She glanced at the clock and saw with satisfaction that the evening which they had both secretly dreaded had reached a time when she could reasonably suggest a hot drink and bed.

'Tomorrow,' said Aunt Flo, 'we will go through your clothes and make them ready. I've no doubt there will be buttons to sew on and so forth.'

So presently they went to their beds, each assuring the other that they were very tired and would sleep at once.

Neither of them did, but that was neither here nor there.

A bright, cold morning cheered their spirits. They met for breakfast with determined cheerfulness, discussing the weather at some length, reading the letters of condolence which were still coming and debating what they would have for their lunch. They were weighing the advantages of poached eggs on spinach against toasted cheese when the phone rang.

'Margo?' The professor's voice was reassuringly placid. 'I expect you want to do some shopping? If I come for you both tomorrow morning at about nine o'clock, could you be ready? I'll drive you back around six o'clock. I'll have to work until then.'

'Oh, yes, please. But that makes an awfully long day for you, Gijs. Whatever time will you have to leave London to get to us by nine o'clock? Would you like breakfast?'

'No, no. It's no great distance, you know, and I enjoy driving. Only be ready for me, won't you? I'll see you then.'

He rang off before she could say anything else, and her goodbye fell on silence. She told herself that he was probably busy.

Which he was—going to scrub for a morning's surgery in Theatre, with Margo, for the moment, dismissed from his mind.

With the shopping to look forward to the day went quickly. Margo went down to the village and arranged with Mrs Twigg, who had come to the vicarage for years to do the rough work once a week, to spend the day there and look after Caesar and Plato and at the same time do some cleaning.

'Going out for the day?' she wanted to know. 'Do you good, Miss Margo, what with one thing and another.'

'Yes, my aunt and I are going to London. Professor van Kessel is coming for us…'

'Ah, yes, 'im as is sweet on you, Miss Margo.'

Margo blushed. 'Well, no, not exactly, Mrs Twigg. That is, we're going to be married. Very quietly and soon.'

'Lor' bless you, miss, that's the best bit of news I've

heard for quite a while. You deserve to be happy, and he looks a nice kind of gentleman.'

'Yes, he is!' said Margo. 'We haven't told anyone yet…'

When the paper arrived later, Aunt Florence was quick to point out the announcement of their engagement. Since most of the vicar's friends and the parishioners took that same paper, the phone didn't stop ringing all the morning.

The professor, leaving London very early the next morning, had a good deal to think about. He had dealt with the special licence, arranged his work at the hospital, conferred with his secretary concerning his private patients and discussed his theatre lists with Theatre Sister. There was also the question of finding a house in London, buying it and furnishing it—in the meantime they would have to rent a flat. His secretary, a highly efficient middle-aged lady, had already procured any number of leaflets on suitable houses, and as soon as he could spare the time he would go and look at the best of them. Then there was Holland. He hoped Margo would like his home, since it was going to be her home too.

They were waiting for him, with Mrs Twigg peering from the kitchen, anxious not to miss a moment. He kissed Aunt Florence's cheek, kissed Margo's too, bent to pat Plato, complimented them on their punctuality and ushered them into the car.

Margo, he reflected, looked better. There was colour in her cheeks and her eyes shone—with the expectancy of a day's outing, he supposed. Her hat, he decided, was unbecoming—bought to last, as a mere covering for the head with no pretensions to fashion. It would be interesting to see what the right clothes would do for her when they were married.

To make up for his thoughts, he gave her a warm smile as he started the car.

They didn't talk much as they went. Margo sensed that he needed to get back as quickly as possible, and indeed he drove fast. The road was comparatively empty until they reached the outskirts of London, and even there the early morning rush-hour was over and there were no major hold-ups.

He set them down at Marble Arch. 'Take a taxi to the hospital—be there by six o'clock and wait for me in the reception hall. Have a good day!'

He opened her door and got out to help Aunt Florence.

'Have you enough money?'

'Yes, thank you, Gijs. We'll see you at six o'clock.'

They watched the Rolls slip back into the traffic. 'What a thoughtful man he is,' said Aunt Flo, and took Margo's arm. 'Let's find a place for coffee and then get down to the shopping.'

It wasn't too difficult to find a skirt and woollies, and Margo soon found the evening skirt she wanted. She found the blouse too, and a rather more elaborate top in a delicate apricot. They stopped for a sandwich and then began to hunt for the dress and jacket.

They found it at last in a boutique in Regent Street— just the shade of blue Margo had wished for—and, urged by the sales lady, she bought a hat to go with it. A small velvet affair which perched charmingly on her pale brown hair.

Aunt Flo, not to be outdone, bought her slippers for the evening—black satin with dainty heels. 'You'll both get a wedding present when you get back to London,' she said gruffly. 'And now I could do with a cup of tea.'

After their tea, mindful of the rush-hour, they hailed a taxi to take them to the hospital, where the head porter ushered them to seats against the wall, away from the constant flow of people going in and out.

They sat for some time, surrounded by their parcels and packages, until Margo, incurably inquisitive, got to her feet and wandered off with the whisper that she was only going to look down the various corridors which had aroused her curiosity.

The first one ended in a staircase she didn't quite dare to go up, so she retraced her steps, saw that Aunt Florence was still sitting there alone, and tried the next. This was much more promising, with doors on either side and leading to another even wider corridor. She peered round a corner and looked straight at the professor, standing with two other men only yards from her. He looked quite different in his long white coat, with a pile of papers under one arm: remote and a stranger.

He was looking directly at her; his faint smile was barely perceptible and his slight shake of the head allowed her to release a held breath as she melted back round the corner and sped back to Aunt Flo.

'And what did you find?'

'Well, Gijs is at the end of that corridor, talking to two men. He saw me.' Margo sounded a little doubtful.

'Annoyed, was he?'

'I don't think so. I'm not sure.'

'Well, here he comes, so you'll soon know,' said Aunt Flo briskly.

Beyond apologising for keeping them waiting, he had nothing more to say—only enquired about their day's shopping and ushered them out into the forecourt and into the Rolls.

Presently, sitting beside him as he drove through the city, Margo asked, 'Are you annoyed with me? I wasn't snooping around looking for you; I just wanted to see where the corridor went.'

'I'm disappointed—I'd hoped you *were* looking for me—and of course I'm not annoyed. Don't be a silly goose!'

Reassuring, perhaps, but she wasn't sure if he was joking. She rather thought that he was. She must take care not to encroach on his work and to leave him alone until, hopefully, they settled down together.

Mrs Twigg had not only dusted and polished, she had also cooked supper, and had it waiting for them when they arrived.

'One of my steak and kidney pies,' she told Margo, tucking her wages into a shabby purse, 'and an apple crumble to follow. Had a good day's shopping, have you, Miss Margo?'

'Lovely, Mrs Twigg. I got all I needed to buy.'

She was conscious of Gijs standing at her elbow, and then Mrs Twigg said cheerfully, 'Well, she'll make a pretty little bride, I'm sure, sir.'

'Indeed she will, Mrs Twigg. I'll take you home if you're ready.'

'Lor', sir, that's not necessary. It's but ten minutes' walk…'

'Two minutes in the car.'

He was longer than two minutes. Margo took off her outdoor things, laid the table and cast an eye into the oven while Aunt Florence sat by the sitting-room fire.

With just one table-lamp on and the firelight the room didn't look too bad.

Margo, poking her head round the door, said, 'When Gijs gets back I'll see if there's any sherry left...'

He came in a few minutes later, a bottle under his arm.

'Mrs Twigg's pie smells delicious,' he said, and strolled into the kitchen to look for a corkscrew to open the bottle.

Margo, poking the sprouts to see if they were cooked, turned to look. 'Champagne...'

'We have all had a hard day. Where are the glasses, Margo?'

Supper was a cheerful meal; there was plenty to talk about and it was getting late when Gijs got up to go. Margo, about to worry aloud about the brief night's sleep ahead of him, bit the words back, told him mildly to drive carefully and thanked him for taking them to London. 'It was a really lovely day.' She smiled brightly, but he saw the sadness in her eyes.

'I'm going to be busy for a few days. When do you leave here?'

'In two days' time. I sold the car to the garage, but Jim Potts, who owns it, will drive us and the animals and luggage.'

He nodded. 'Splendid—otherwise I would have arranged a car...'

'Thank you for thinking of it,' she told him gravely, 'but everyone in the village has been so kind. I've had so much help.'

He smiled at her and bent to kiss her cheek. 'Don't be too sad, Margo; we will make a happy life together.' He took her hand. 'Ah—I had almost forgotten.'

He searched around in a pocket and took out a small plush case and opened it. There was a ring inside—a splendid sapphire surrounded by diamonds.

'It is old and has been in the family for many years. I hope it fits—my mother had small hands very like yours.'

She held out her hand and he slipped it onto her finger.

'Oh, it's so beautiful,' said Margo. 'And it fits exactly. I hope your mother would have liked me to have it.' She reached up and kissed his cheek. 'Thank you, Gijs; I'm very proud to wear it.'

He touched her cheek with a gentle finger. 'I'll phone,' he told her, 'and see you again as soon as possible. I have a backlog of work to deal with.'

'I understand. You've already done too much for me. Please forget me until the wedding. I'm quite all right, really I am.' She added matter-of-factly, 'I don't intend to interfere with your work; I know it's important to you. Mother never stood in Father's way when it came to his parish work, and I won't stand in yours.'

He looked down at her earnest face and suddenly smiled. 'I believe I have found a treasure,' he told her, and the next minute he was gone.

Margo, busy with her final packing and goodbyes and then transporting herself, her aunt and the animals and luggage to Sunningfield, none the less wondered from time to time if Gijs would phone. She had told him not to worry about her, but surely, she reflected, it would take only a few minutes to ring up. He couldn't be working all day—and what about the evenings?

The professor was doing just that: working a long day, seeing his private patients in the evenings and catching up on the paperwork before he went to bed. He hadn't forgotten Margo, but he had tidied her away to the back of his mind for the time being—although he *had* found time to arrange to rent a small house in a quiet street close to Wimpole Street, where he had his consulting rooms. It was furnished and had a tiny walled garden; it would serve its purpose until they had a house of their own.

Late one evening he phoned his home in Holland and, well satisfied with the result, took himself off to bed...

As for Margo, she saw to a bewildered Plato and Caesar, unpacked her few clothes and set to with a will to put Aunt Flo's house to rights again. She also opened the various parcels she had been given from well-wishers in the village.

Sir William and Lady Frost had given her a charming painting of flowers, several people in the village had clubbed together and given her a cut-glass fruit bowl, and George and his mother had sent a pair of bookends—bronze pigs, which somehow seemed suitable since George bred them.

Lord and Lady Trueman sent over a splendid porcelain vase, and Helen a charming small silver clock, and by the morning's post there came a shower of gifts from friends and relatives.

Margo begged a large, stout box from the village shop and packed everything away and then sat down to write thank-you letters. It was a pity Gijs wasn't there to see their gifts; she supposed that they would help to furnish wherever they were going to live.

The thought brought her up short; it was something

she hadn't really thought about. Would they live in London or Holland or both? Perhaps they would make their home in Holland and Gijs would travel to and fro, just as he did now? Where would they go to live when they came back after Christmas? Unless he planned to leave her there. The idea was a bit daunting…

It was two days after she had moved to her aunt's when he phoned, quite late in the evening.

'I shall be free tomorrow after midday—may I fetch you to spend the rest of the day with me in town? There are several things to see to… Is everything all right? You've settled in with Aunt Florence?'

'I'm fine; we both are. What time will you come?'

'Some time after twelve o'clock. We'll talk then.'

She heard him speaking to someone, and then he said, 'I have to go, Margo. Tomorrow.'

When she told her aunt, that lady said, 'What will you wear?'

'My winter coat and the jersey dress. I don't suppose we'll go anywhere very fashionable, do you?'

The next morning was clear and cold; Margo got into the jersey dress, found her good gloves and shoes and handbag, and did her hair with more care than usual. Even so her sensible hat didn't look anything other than dowdy, but it was far too cold to go without anything on her head. She hoped that Gijs wouldn't notice…

He did, of course, but it didn't matter. He greeted her with a kiss, spent five minutes asking after Aunt Florence's health, then popped Margo into the car and drove back to London.

'Why do you want me to come with you?' asked Margo, never one to mince her words.

'We have to buy the wedding rings. Let us do that first.'

He took her to Garrard's, where, in the quiet surroundings, she chose a plain gold ring for herself and then, at his smiling nod, one for him. She hoped that they didn't cost too much, for no price was mentioned; presumably Gijs was satisfied, as he got out his chequebook. She wandered away to look at the magnificent jewels on display, and was contemplating a brooch—a true lover's knot in diamonds—when he joined her.

He asked casually if she liked it. 'Well, of course I do—it's magnificent. But I wouldn't want it…'

'Why not?'

'Me and diamonds don't go together,' said Margo ungrammatically. 'They don't, do they? Be honest.'

She felt unreasonably disappointed when he agreed with her.

She was a sensible girl; she had asked for an honest answer and she had got it, and in a way she was glad that he liked her enough not to pretend to something he didn't feel. She smiled up at him. 'Thank you for my ring. What do you want to do next?'

'Coffee while I tell you.'

He turned down a side-street and ushered her into a small café. When the coffee came he told her about the house. 'I hope you will like it,' he finished. 'It is the best that I can do at short notice. We'll go there next, and after we've had lunch we will go and look at houses…'

'Houses?' echoed Margo. 'But haven't we got one? You just said…'

'Well, we have to have a home of sorts until we get one of our own. The agent has several lined up for us to look at.'

'You mean to buy a house?'

'I come over to England several times a year; we shall need a home to come to.' He smiled at her. 'Am I rushing you along too fast? Shall we go? The meter will have almost run out.'

He drove with no sign of impatience through the heavy traffic, and then they were in comparative quiet.

'Wimpole Street,' said Margo, looking out of the window. 'Don't doctors have their rooms here?'

'Yes, and Harley Street. If you look on the right you'll see a green-painted door with a brass plate beside it. I've my rooms there. The house I have rented is down this side-street.'

Margo found it quite perfect. It had a glossy black-painted door, with tubs on either side, and inside there was a narrow hall with a sitting room on one side and a dining room on the other, both furnished comfortably. The kitchen was modern and small, there was a tiny cloakroom under the circular stairs, and a door leading to the garden and another small room, which she supposed Gijs would use as a study.

Two bedrooms faced the street, with a bathroom between them, and a third room overlooked the garden. There was a short passage with a door on one side of it, opening onto a quite large room furnished as a bed-sitting-room, with an alcove holding a shower and a large window.

'The housekeeper's room,' said Gijs, consulting the leaflet in his hand.

'Well, I suppose so—but we don't need one, do we? I'm quite a good cook and it's a very small house.'

'We shall need someone in to do the cleaning. Would

you be happy here for a short time while we find our own home?'

'Oh, yes. It's delightful and very quiet. Can we come straight here when we come back from Holland?'

'Yes. I've the keys already.' He led the way downstairs and out to the car. 'When we have had lunch we will take a look at the houses I thought might suit us. I've arranged to meet the agent.'

He took her to the Ritz, and Margo prudently left her coat and the regrettable hat in the cloakroom. Her clothes were all wrong, but since Gijs didn't seem to mind she decided that she wouldn't either. She looked around her at the magnificent room as they sat down at a table overlooking the gardens.

'It's truly splendid, isn't it?' she observed. 'Just being here without eating would be a treat…'

He laughed. 'I know what you mean, but I for one am hungry.'

So was Margo. She ate Galia melon, Dover sole with Dauphin potatoes and braised chicory and, while Gijs pondered the cheeseboard, she chose orange crême soufflé.

Over coffee, she asked, 'Do you have a lot of friends in England, Gijs?'

'Yes. Most of them people I work with. There are several Dutch friends living over here too. You will meet them all, of course. Gijs van der Eekerk and his wife Beatrice have a flat near Green Park, but, just as I do, he goes back to Holland from time to time.' He put down his coffee-cup. 'Shall we go and see what the estate agent has lined up for us?'

He was waiting for them at the first house, a handsome Georgian residence, one of a row lining a quiet street close to Cavendish Square. 'Opulent' was the only way to describe it, reflected Margo, and it wasn't even furnished. Asked if she liked it, she firmly said no. She said no to the second house too, a three-story Regency house with a semi-basement. The third house she fell in love with instantly. Just as Gijs had hoped she would.

It was at the end of a row of mews cottages, and it was as delightful inside as out. A good deal larger than she'd expected, too, with a long, low room on one side of the door, two smaller rooms on the other side of the hall, and a good-sized kitchen at the back, beside which was a pleasant room with its own shower room.

Upstairs—reached by a graceful little staircase— there were three bedrooms, another shower room and a large bathroom, and through a door at the back of the landing was a short staircase leading to a large attic.

The professor, leaning against a door, watching her, asked, 'Do you like it, Margo?'

'Yes, oh, yes, I do. It's...' She paused to think. 'It's like a home,' she finished lamely. 'Do you like it?'

'Yes, I do.' He smiled and crossed the room to stand in front of her. 'Shall we buy it?'

'Oh, could we? It won't be too expensive? This is rather a splendid part of London, isn't it?'

'It's so convenient for my rooms,' he reminded her. 'About ten minutes' walk. Hyde Park and Green Park are both within easy walking distance; so are Bond Street and Regent Street. I think it will suit us both admirably.'

'There's a tiny garden at the back,' she told him. 'But what about a garage?'

'Being the last in the row, we have a double one at the side.' He took her hand in his. 'You're sure?'

When she nodded, he said, 'Then let us go to the agent's office and settle the matter.'

As they went back downstairs he observed, 'The place has been put in good order. I'll have to have it surveyed, of course, but by the time we come back from Holland it should be ours and you can set about furnishing it.'

'You too—it's your home as well.'

'A pleasant thought,' he said, and smiled at her again.

The agent's office was palatial, in a quiet street somewhere behind Harrods. She had had no idea that buying a house was so easy. She supposed that there would be no mortgage; it seemed to her the kind of place where one handed over a cheque with the minimum of fuss. Which was just what the professor was doing. If she had known the size of the deposit he was paying, let alone the price of the house, strong girl though she was, she would probably have fainted.

As it was, she speculated about Gijs's income. It must be a good one, of course; he drove a Rolls-Royce, didn't he? And his shoes were hand-made, his clothes discreetly elegant. She supposed she would get used to his lifestyle in time, but she had never been a girl to hanker after things she knew she could never have. It would be nice to be able to have some fashionable clothes…

The business dealt with, they went in search of tea. He took her to Brown's Hotel where, she saw at once, he was known, and enjoyed a delicious tea—tiny sandwiches, mouth-watering cakes, and muffins in a covered dish. Drinking Earl Grey tea, she remembered the strong brew offered in a mug which he had drunk with every evidence of enjoyment at the vicarage.

He drove her back to Sunningfield then, but he

didn't stay for long. She hid her disappointment behind a bright smile and thanked him for her day, laughingly agreeing that the next time they saw each other it would be on their wedding day.

Seeing him off from Aunt Flo's door, she speculated as to how he would be spending his evening. He had been in a carefully concealed hurry to go back to London. Perhaps he was dining with friends, or just one friend—a woman, perhaps. A final fling before he married.

Margo allowed her imagination to run riot; only Aunt Flo's voice begging her to come in and shut the door brought her back to good sense again. Gijs, she told herself firmly, was entitled to do what he wanted without her poking her nose into his affairs. She joined her aunt in the sitting room and gave her a detailed account of her day.

She thought about him again, though, once she was in bed.

It was a pity for her peace of mind that she didn't know that the professor had driven straight to the hospital; there was a very ill child there, not yet diagnosed, and he had said that he would return that evening and do more tests. He remained at the hospital for some hours, forgetful of dinner, of the house he had just bought, and even forgetful—just for the time being—of Margo.

Chapter 6

The days until the wedding flashed by in a dream. Sometimes Margo woke in the night convinced that she was making a dreadful mistake, that she must have been out of her mind to agree to marry Gijs. In the small hours the future loomed, fraught with pitfalls: his family, his friends—and he had many, he had told her— the prospect of entertaining them, of buying the right clothes, and that lovely little house which he expected her to furnish. She would fall asleep again eventually, and when she woke it would be morning and all that mattered was that she loved him…

They were to be married at eleven o'clock. Gijs came to fetch them just before nine o'clock.

'This is most unorthodox,' observed Aunt Florence, majestic in a new hat. 'The bridegroom should never see his bride before she comes to him in church.'

'In Holland,' the professor told her placidly, 'the bridegroom goes to fetch his bride with a bouquet and they go to be married together. Where is Margo?'

'I'm here.' She came quietly downstairs, feeling shy, anxious that he should like her outfit.

He crossed the small hall and bent to kiss her. 'What a charming outfit, and I do like the hat.'

She smiled up at him, reflecting sadly that he might have been a brother or a cousin, even an old friend from his manner—certainly not a man in love. Sitting beside him in the Rolls presently, she reminded herself that he wasn't in love with anyone, so why shouldn't he fall in love with her? First she must attract his attention—the right clothes, an elegant house, entertaining his friends, a good hairdresser and the discreet application of the beauty aids recommended in the glossy magazines. All this must be done slowly; first she must get to know his family and something of his life. It would probably take years, she reflected, but it would be worth it.

Gijs kept up a flow of small talk as he drove, with Aunt Florence chipping in from time to time, but presently he said, 'You're very quiet, Margo—cold feet?'

'No.' She turned to smile at him. 'What about you?'

'Certainly not. I have always understood that bridegrooms dread getting married—dozens of guests, satin and wedding veil, bridesmaids, wedding cakes and getting showered with confetti—but since none of these will bother us I'm looking forward to being married.'

'When I married your uncle,' said Aunt Flo from the back seat, 'he shook like a leaf throughout the service and he trod on my train.'

At the church, Gijs parked the car, handed Margo over to Sir William and went with Aunt Flo. Two minutes later they followed them, and as the church door was opened Margo was surprised to hear the organ. It would be old Miss Twittchitt playing: Margo could hear the wrong notes. She had played for years and no one would have dreamt of suggesting a successor. The verger was just inside the door, beaming at her, handing her a small bouquet as Sir William began to march down the aisle, sweeping her along with him.

The church was full; every single person from the village was there, smiling and nodding as they went. She clutched Sir William's sleeve and he patted her hand.

'A surprise, eh? Well, we've all known you for years, my dear.'

She glanced at Gijs when she reached his side and he half smiled at her. She wanted to ask him if he had known about it, but knew it would hardly do with the new vicar standing by waiting to marry them.

He began the service and she gave him her full attention. Only when it was time for the ring to be placed on her finger did she realise that there was a man standing beside Gijs. A big man, about Gijs's age, perhaps older, who handed over the ring without a fuss, smiling a little.

Presently, as they stood at the church door while people took photos, she asked who he was.

'Gijs van der Eekerk. Beatrice is here too; you'll meet her soon.' He took her arm. 'Come along; Sir William and his wife have laid on a reception—the entire village will be there.'

'Oh—did you know?'

'Yes. He rang me a couple of days ago, but I thought it would be best to surprise you.' He smiled. 'It isn't quite the wedding we planned, is it? But they all love you, Margo.'

* * *

Margo, cutting the wedding cake with Gijs's firm, cool hand over hers, said quietly, 'Won't we miss the ferry?'

'We're going on a later one. We shall get home for supper instead of tea.'

She met Beatrice and Gijs van der Eekerk; she liked them both and it was nice to think that she would see more of them in London as well as in Holland—it somehow made the future more solid. She and Gijs went from one group to the next in the Frosts' vast drawing room, bidding people goodbye, exchanging plans to meet again at some time and finally thanking Sir William for their reception.

He beamed at them. 'Well, what I mean to say is, Lady Frost said to me, "William, I insist on having Margo here with her husband. The village is sorry to see her go." She is quite right too. Hope you'll be very happy and all that.'

Aunt Florence, buoyed up by champagne, wished them a safe journey. 'I know you'll be happy,' she told them. 'Come and see me when you get back. I'll look after Caesar and Plato.'

Her sharp nose, slightly pinkened by champagne, quivered. 'I shall miss you both.'

Margo hugged her. 'Of course we'll come and see you when we get back. Have a happy Christmas with Lord Trueman's family.'

Guests surged around them, showering them with confetti and shouting their good wishes as they drove away.

'Comfortable?' asked Gijs. 'I don't want to stop on the way unless we have to. I'm going to Southampton then onto the M3 and up to the ring road at Reigate. Dull driving, but fast. I've booked us on the seven o'clock hovercraft from Dover.'

There wasn't much traffic until they reached the M25; he had kept up his speed and even with the conjested motorway here he slid effortlessly ahead. Margo sat quietly, content to watch his hands, which were relaxed on the wheel, exchanging the odd remark with him from time to time and reminding herself that she was married, that they were on their way to Holland and the future was an unopened book for her.

The wedding had been an unforgettable occasion. She thought wistfully that her mother and father would have enjoyed every minute of it—a happy finish to her old life. The new, she promised herself, would be happy too; she had so much and she loved Gijs—never mind if he felt only a mild affection for her.

It was dark by the time they reached Dover, and they were among the last of the passengers to go on board. Margo, glad to be out of the car for a while, assured Gijs that she saw no reason to feel seasick, accepted the coffee she was offered and looked around her.

There was plenty to see and Gijs, secretly amused at her interest, found himself enjoying her unself-conscious pleasure and laying himself out to entertain her. Once they had landed he took care to point out their route, finding a revived interest in a journey which he made so frequently that he usually scarcely noticed the country through which he drove. They would drive along the coast to Ostend, where he would turn off to Ghent, take the motorway to Antwerp, bypass that city and so go on to Breda.

They had had tea on board and he had told her then

that there was a fairly long journey before them. 'If you want to stop, you must just say so, Margo,' he said now. 'For we have all the time in the world.'

'Just how far is it? Where are we going…?'

'A few miles the other side of Utrecht. Less than an hour's drive once we reach Breda. Breda is roughly a hundred and thirty miles from here.' He glanced at his watch. 'It's half past eight; we should be home in three hours—probably less.'

Probably less, reflected Margo as the Rolls raced along roads which Gijs evidently knew well. He was a splendid driver, and on a road frequently empty of traffic he gave the Rolls her head.

Presently Margo said, 'Don't think I'm criticising—I like going fast—but is there a speed limit in Belgium?'

He laughed. 'Yes, but it's largely ignored. You like driving?'

'Yes, very much.'

'We must get you a car. There's not much point in having one in London, but here we live in the country— close enough to Utrecht and Amsterdam, but I shall be away all day and you'll want to be independent.'

Margo agreed. She had no wish to be independent— she would like to stick to him like a leech—but that was a thought she prudently kept to herself.

She had plenty to think about and she guessed that Gijs would dislike it if she chattered. Besides, she wasn't much good at small talk. She mused over their day and then allowed her thoughts to dwell on her life at Thinbottom. They were sad thoughts; her grief for her parents was still something she hadn't quite come to terms with.

When Gijs said suddenly, 'Are you thinking about Thinbottom and your parents?' she gave a gasp.

'How did you know? Yes, I was.'

'Well, it would be a natural sequence of thought at the end of the day which marks the end of an old life and the beginning of a new one. Do you want to talk about it?'

'Our new life? It will be strange—for me, at least. I shall have to learn Dutch, won't I? Is your home here anything like the house you've bought in London?'

'Er—no. For one thing it is in the country, on the edge of a small village near a lake. It is very convenient for me. I go to Utrecht as well as Leiden, and from time to time Amsterdam.'

'Will we be coming back to Holland in a little while?'

'Yes. I'll be in London and travelling around the country for several weeks, and then we'll be back here for several months—although I quite often go over to England for a few days if something turns up where I'm needed.'

'Do you go to other countries?'

'From time to time. The States and the Middle East—usually to see private patients—and occasionally to Germany and Italy.'

He glanced at her quiet profile. 'It will be nice to have someone to come home to in future,' he told her.

That warmed her heart.

Once they had crossed into Holland, Gijs picked up the carphone. 'I'll let them know we're expecting supper when we arrive home,' he told her. She wondered who 'they' were.

The motorways were good and there were no hills and almost no corners; there was nothing to hinder the car's speed. They skirted Rotterdam and sped on to Utrecht to turn away from that city and go north towards Soest. There was a fitful moon, peering from time to time from billowing clouds, and Margo could see that they had left the flat grassland behind and that the country upon either side of the road was thick with trees and bushes.

'Is this a forest?'

'Not exactly—woods and undergrowth and heath. Hilversum is to the north and Amersfoot to the east— both quite large towns. We turn off here.'

He drove along a narrow country road, the woods on either side broken from time to time by great gateways, and presently slowed to enter a small village, its houses ringed around a church. 'Arntzstein,' said the professor quietly. 'Our home is here.'

He swept through the village, past some elegant houses with lights streaming from their uncurtained windows, and into a narrow lane which ended in an open gateway flanked by stone pillars. The drive was short, curving in a semicircle to the wide sweep before the house at its end.

Margo, blinking at the lighted windows, began to count them and gave up.

'You don't live here?' she asked in a worried voice.

'*We* live here,' he corrected her quietly. 'Yes, this is our home, Margo.'

He got out and opened her door and she stood on the wide sweep, looking at the house.

It was four storeys high, with a gabled roof and a small round tower at each end. Its windows, tall and narrow on the ground floor, decreased in size at each level, the topmost of them being dormer windows set in the gable…

Margo took a deep breath. 'Well—you might have told me, Gijs.'

He took her arm. 'No. No—you would have rejected me instantly as being highly unsuitable. Come and have your supper. You must be tired—it's been a long day.'

Not just a long day, she thought, climbing the double stone stairs to the massive front door, our wedding day.

It was opened as they reached it by a stout elderly man with a jolly face.

'Wim.' The professor spoke to the man in his own language, shaking his hand, and then said in English, 'Margo, this is Wim, who runs this place. His wife is housekeeper; you will meet her presently. Wim speaks English.'

Margo shook hands and smiled at the beaming face.

'Welcome, *mevrouw*. It is with pleasure that we see you.' He stood aside and waved an arm towards the entrance hall, where there were several people standing. 'If it is permitted…'

The professor took her arm and they crossed the black and white tiled floor. Margo was led from one person to the next: Wim's wife, Kieke, Jet, the housemaid, Diny and Mien, the cooks. There was also an elderly man, wizened and wrinkled with the weather, and the professor clapped him on the shoulder and wrung his hand. 'Willem, who has looked after the gardens ever since I can remember.'

She shook each one by the hand and murmured greetings, glad of their friendly faces, and presently she was led away up a carved oak staircase to her room.

'Don't do more than take off your hat and coat,' the professor called after her. 'Supper's waiting.'

She had no time to do more than glance at the room

Kieke ushered her into. It was a lovely room, its tall windows draped in old rose brocade, with the same brocade covering the vast bed with its satinwood headboard. The dressing table was satinwood too, with a triple mirror on it and a padded stool, covered in tapestry, before it. There were two small easy chairs covered in a darker pink, and a chaise longue at the foot of the bed upholstered in ivory velvet.

Margo heaved a sigh of pure pleasure and at the same time thought how impractical the furnishings were; she would be afraid to sit on anything for fear of spoiling it. She poked at her hair, powdered her nose and went downstairs to find Gijs waiting for her in the hall.

'Your room is all right?' he wanted to know. 'Do tell Wim if there is anything you want.' He led the way across the hall into a panelled room hung with portraits. There was an oval table at its centre, ringed by mahogany chairs of the Chippendale period, and against a wall a sideboard of the same period. There was a corner cupboard, its door of marquetry, and a splendid fireplace with a marble surround in which a bright fire burned. Crimson velvet curtains were drawn across the windows and there were fine rugs on the polished wood floor.

Supper was hardly the meal she had expected. One end of the table had been set with lace mats, silver and crystal, gleaming under the light from a chiselled bronze chandelier. She sat down opposite Gijs.

'You have a beautiful home,' she observed. 'I had no idea…it's like being married to a millionaire…' She smiled at him, and then took a quick breath at the look on his face. 'Oh, you're not, are you?'

'Well, yes, I am. But don't let it worry you, Margo.

I have never allowed it to worry me. Perhaps I should have told you…'

'If you had, I don't think I would have married you.'

'In that case I'm glad I kept silent.' He smiled suddenly. 'Am I forgiven?'

'Well, of course—and I dare say I'll get used to it in time.' She spooned her soup. 'I can hear a dog barking…'

'Punch. He was out when we arrived. He knows we are here.'

'Is he allowed in here? What breed is he?'

'He goes all over the house. He's a bloodhound.'

The professor said something to Wim, who went away and presently returned with Punch, who lolloped across the room to greet his master and, when bidden to do so, offered his noble head to be scratched by Margo.

'He's lovely—how you must miss him.'

'Indeed I do.' The professor began to talk about his dog, also mentioning that Kieke had two cats. 'And there are rabbits here, of course, and hares and squirrels…' He talked easily as they ate turbot and winter salad and a Dutch apple tart and cream. 'And since it is an occasion,' said Gijs smoothly, 'we will drink champagne…'

It was late by the time they rose from the table and crossed the hall again to enter the drawing room. This was a splendid apartment, with a massive fireplace in front of which Punch instantly settled himself. There were two chandeliers here, one at each end of the room, but the only lighting came from wall-lights and table-lamps so that the room was dimly lit.

Margo, by now too sleepy to examine her surroundings, drank her coffee and looked across at Gijs with owl-like eyes.

'You're tired,' he said, and got to his feet. 'Stay in bed tomorrow morning if you would like that—Diny will bring your breakfast.'

'I'd rather come down, if you don't mind. It's just that it has been a busy sort of day.'

She waited for him to say something—something about being married and liking it, or what a pleasant wedding it had been. He didn't—only wished her good-night with the hope that she would sleep well.

At the door, which he opened for her, he bent and kissed her cheek. A brotherly peck, reflected Margo peevishly, and was instantly sorry for the thought. What else had she expected?

In her room she prowled around, looking at everything—someone had unpacked and hung her few clothes in the big mirror-lined closet, the bed had been turned down and there was a light on in the bathroom. There was everything here that a girl could wish for: fluffy towels, creams and lotions and bath salts. She opened the door in the far wall and poked a cautious head round. This was Gijs's room, she supposed. Quite small and comfortably furnished. She closed the door again and went to take another look at her own room. There were books by the bed and a tin of biscuits, as well as a handsome carafe of water. Tomorrow, she decided, she would write Aunt Flo a long letter and tell her all about it.

Presently she undressed, had a bath and got into bed, and, despite the thoughts tumbling around in her tired head, slept at once.

* * *

As she went down the staircase the following morning she was delighted to see a Christmas tree in one corner of the hall, and as she reached the last stair Gijs and Punch came in through the front door, bringing a breath of icy air with them.

His good morning was cheerful. 'You slept well? Good. Come and have breakfast. It's cold but fine outside.'

'The tree...' said Margo.

'We will decorate it when we get back this afternoon. The children expect it, you know.'

'Children?'

'My sisters will be coming tomorrow, with their husbands and children. The family always hold Christmas here.'

He had her arm and was urging her into a small room at the back of the hall. A small table was laid there and the fire burned cheerfully. He pulled out a chair for her and Wim came in with the coffeepot.

'I thought we might go into Utrecht this morning,' said the professor placidly. 'Christmas presents—we've left it a bit late, but you will know what to buy.'

Margo was still finding her tongue. She said now, rather coldly, 'I haven't the faintest idea what I am to buy. I—I didn't expect all this...' she waved a hand around the room '...this magnificence. I thought you were just a surgeon.'

'I am just a surgeon. If you can't bear to live here we'll close the place up and go and live in a very small cottage.'

'Don't be absurd,' said Margo, and felt laughter bubbling up inside her. 'How long have you lived here?'

'Just over two hundred years.'

'Well…' She did laugh then. 'I feel as though I've walked into a fairy tale.' She added, serious now, 'But I don't know anything about the presents you want me to buy.'

He said soothingly, 'No, no, of course you don't. But if I tell you for whom each one is you might choose them. I never know what to buy for my sisters.'

'Oh, well, is Utrecht far? Perhaps I *could* help.'

'Five or six miles away. There is a large shopping centre there. We can have lunch out and be back here in the afternoon in time to decorate the tree.' He passed his cup for more coffee. 'Have you phoned Aunt Florence?'

'I got up and dressed and came downstairs and now I'm eating my breakfast. I've not been given the chance to do anything else.'

'Am I rushing you? I don't mean to, but to tell the truth you have accepted everything in such a matter-of-fact manner that I forget that it is all strange to you.' He smiled at her across the table. 'This evening after dinner we will sit quietly together and I will answer all your questions and explain anything you want me to.'

'Yes, I'd like that. Have I time to ring Aunt Flo before we go to Utrecht?'

'Of course.' He glanced at the long-case clock against the wall. 'Twenty minutes.' He got up with her. 'There's a phone in the library; no one will disturb you there.'

He led the way through the hall and opened a door. It was a beautiful room, with a plastered ceiling, shelves of books on its walls and several small tables with comfortable chairs beside them, and at one end of the room was a vast desk. He picked up the phone on it and dialled Aunt Florence's number, handed it to her and went away, leaving her to give her aunt a garbled version of their journey and the house.

'I can't stop to tell you everything,' said Margo. 'We're just off to Utrecht to buy presents. But, Aunt Flo, it's all so magnificent. I'll phone you this evening and tell you all about it.'

'You're happy, Margo?'

'Yes, Aunt Flo...'

'Run along, then, and tell me the rest this evening.'

Margo got into her winter coat, feeling doubtful about wearing it. Her wedding outfit would be too thin, though, and besides, she hadn't time to change from her skirt and sweater and she had no hat. She went downstairs, very conscious that her clothes were not at all right for the wife of a well-known surgeon.

The professor thought the same thing, but nothing of the thought showed on his face. In any case, it was something which could be put right quite easily. They went out to the car with Punch and drove away, with Wim watching them benignly from the porch.

Utrecht looked magnificent, decided Margo presently, staring out of the car window as Gijs drove through a bewildering succession of streets to park. Then, accompanied by Punch on his lead, he led her down a narrow alley and into an enormous shopping precinct.

'Have you brought a list with you?' asked Margo, pausing to look in the window of an elegant jeweller. 'What heavenly shops...'

'Presently.' He took her arm and ushered her into the kind of boutique she had so often looked into and never dared to enter.

'Why—?' began Margo. Surely she wasn't supposed to choose clothes for his sisters?

It seemed that she was to choose clothes for herself. She listened, speechless, while he spoke to the haughty-looking woman who came to meet them. The haughtiness vanished when she saw him. They shook hands, then she patted Punch's noble head and said in excellent English, 'It will be a pleasure to dress you, Mevrouw van Kessel. What did you have in mind?'

Her sharp eyes had taken in the elderly coat and the sensible shoes—fit, in her opinion, for the dustbin.

Margo gave the professor a thoughtful look and he said placidly, 'My Christmas present to you, my dear. Shall we start with something warm—a dress, perhaps?'

It was no sooner said than done. Dresses were produced—fine wool, jersey, cashmere... Margo, still speechless, tried them on and couldn't decide which one she liked best. She showed herself to Gijs in each of them, and when she asked which he preferred he said carelessly, 'The brown jersey and the blue cashmere; have them both.'

'Thank you, Gijs...'

Before she could say more he went on, 'A winter coat and a tweed suit?'

He lifted an eyebrow at the saleslady, who said, 'I have just the thing. Brown cashmere—so warm and light—and there is a suit in greens and blues which will become her very well.'

She disappeared into an enormous closet at the back of the shop and Margo hissed, 'Gijs, you can't—everything's frightfully expensive; you have no idea.'

'Ah, but it is Christmas, Margo. Try them on to please me.'

The coat fitted and so did the suit. '*Mevrouw* has an

exact size ten and a charming figure. If I might suggest a hat…'

The professor nodded. 'Very nice. I'm going to take Punch for a quick walk, and while I am gone you are to choose dresses for the evening. We are very festive at Christmas, so something pretty for the afternoon and a couple of dresses for the evening—we have friends in and I intend you to be the belle of the ball.'

Margo found her tongue. 'I can't think what to say…'

'Then don't.' He smiled at her. 'And don't dare ask the price. Remember this is my Christmas present to you.'

He went away then, and she was led away to the cubicle once again. And, since Gijs wished her to look as elegant as possible, she spent a long time choosing between a dark green velvet dress with a wide sweeping skirt and what she considered to be a very immodest neckline and a wine-red taffeta dress with a tucked bodice and long, tight sleeves.

'I think Professor van Kessel intended you to have two dresses, *mevrouw*,' suggested the saleslady.

Margo remembered that he *had* said 'a couple'. She nodded cheerful agreement and turned her attention to something pretty for the afternoon. Turning this way and that, to examine the excellent fit of a Paisley-patterned silk dress, she observed that she already had the other dresses. Surely they would do?

The saleslady shook her head. 'I have the pleasure of dressing the professor's sisters from time to time— you will wish to look as elegantly dressed as they will be, *mevrouw*. Also, he wished it.'

An irrefutable argument. Margo handed the dress

over to be wrapped up and got back into her skirt and woolly.

'Perhaps *mevrouw* would like to wear the coat?' suggested the saleslady. 'So much easier than packing it— and of course the hat.'

Studying her reflection in the cubicle's enormous mirror, Margo had to admit that clothes did make a difference. She adjusted the hat just so and went back into the shop.

Gijs was there, sitting with Punch like a statue beside him. He got up as she crossed the thick carpet. 'You found what you liked, I hope? Good. We'll have coffee, and when we've done our shopping we'll collect the parcels from here.'

He turned to speak to the saleslady, who smiled and nodded and shook hands again. 'I hope that I shall see you again, *mevrouw.*'

Margo beamed at her. 'I'm most grateful for your help and advice. I like everything, and I know I shall enjoy wearing the dresses.'

They had coffee then, in a bustling café with a giant Christmas tree. It was crowded with customers, several of whom came over to their table to greet the professor—large, self-assured men with their wives and sometimes children whom he introduced to her, uttering names she instantly forgot. They all spoke English and her shyness melted before their kind smiles.

They would meet again, they all assured her, when next Gijs came to Holland. She felt a glow of pleasure at the thought.

They bought the presents next, from a long list. No one was forgotten: Willem had a box of cigars and a corduroy waistcoat; Diny had a vividly patterned sweater.

And when Margo asked doubtfully if she would like it Gijs told her that Kieke had been shopping with Diny and she had admired it. His sisters, he mentioned, wore earrings, so they spent time in the jeweller's spending what Margo secretly feared was a small fortune.

When they finally got to the end of the list, he took her to the Café de Paris where they had roast pheasant and an almond tart with lashings of cream while Punch sat silent beside his master, accepting the odd morsel with quiet dignity.

Somehow, and Margo wasn't sure how it happened, she then found herself in a luxurious shoe shop, trying on soft leather boots, shoes so soft and supple that she hardly knew she had them on her feet and evening shoes, high-heeled and strappy.

She emerged rather pink in the face, and, on the way to the car stopped suddenly to say, 'Thank you very much, Gijs. You have bought me so many lovely things. I have enough clothes for several years.'

He stood looking down at her, smiling a little. 'I had no idea that dressing my wife would be such fun; you must allow me the pleasure of doing it as often as I like. I can hardly wait to get to Harrods when we get back to London.'

The pink deepened, and it struck him that she wasn't a plain girl at all.

'Well,' said Margo, rather at a loss for words, 'I must say it's lovely to have so many clothes all at once.' She put a hand on his arm. 'Gijs, will you change some money for me? I mean, I've got some English pounds with me but I want some *gulden*.'

'Of course. How much would you like?' His matter-of-fact manner made it easy for her.

'About twenty-five pounds.'

He took some notes out of his wallet. 'You can give me twenty-five pounds when we get home. That's the equivalent in *gulden*.'

'Thank you—would you mind waiting here? They'll understand English?'

'Oh, yes. We'll be here.'

She hurried across the complex to a small shop they had stopped to look at. Gijs had admired a folding leather photo frame, remarking how useful it would be for anyone who travelled a good deal. It was a paltry gift compared with those which he had lavished upon her, but at least it was something he might use. She entered the shop, bought it and rejoined him, flushed with success.

The parcels and packages collected and stowed in the boot, they drove back to Arntzstein to tea round the fire and then the pleasurable task of decorating the tree.

Because she felt happy and the house was so beautiful, Margo changed into the velvet skirt and blouse and trod downstairs in Aunt Flo's slippers.

Gijs had changed too, into one of his sober dark grey suits. He was waiting for her in the drawing room with Punch beside him.

Margo said awkwardly, 'I'm saving my new dresses for tomorrow and Christmas Day. Will your sisters be here early tomorrow?'

'Teatime—there will be friends coming in for drinks and we shall dine late, I expect.' He crossed the room and took her hand. 'You are the mistress of our home now, Margo, but it hardly seems fair to expect you to organise everything. Wim and Kieke have been here for years and know the whole set-up. I think that she would be flattered if you went to the kitchen tomorrow morning and have a talk—she will expect you to take over when you're ready. Wim will be there to translate.'

She said gravely, 'Yes, of course. I'd like to get to know her and find out how the house is run. I hope I won't be a disappointment to you, Gijs.'

'I am quite certain that you will never be that, my dear. Now come and have a drink, and after dinner we'll go round the house together.' He bent and kissed her cheek. 'I have thrown you in at the deep end, haven't I?' He laughed a little. 'I know you will cope admirably, though.'

'Because I am the vicar's daughter…?'

'Why, yes.'

If that's a compliment, reflected Margo, I must be thankful for it.

Chapter 7

Feeling self-conscious, Margo went down to breakfast in the new tweed suit, and was instantly reassured by Gijs's look of approval. They breakfasted then, talking about the preparations for the following day.

'I must go down to the village this morning,' he told her, 'but you will be discussing things with Kieke, no doubt, and I'll be back in time for us to take Punch for a walk before lunch.'

She agreed happily. He had told her a great deal about his family on the previous evening, and taken her on a tour of the house, lingering in each room so that she could examine it to her heart's content. She had loved every moment—going through the beautiful old house, looking at the furniture with which Gijs had grown up, examining photos of his parents and family, listening to the snippets of information he'd told her.

She had the feeling now, facing him over the breakfast table, that they had become a little closer to each other. Even the house didn't seem strange—it was as though it had accepted her as its new mistress…!

So, apparently, had Kieke and Wim. In the vast kitchen she was seated at the scrubbed table and the household books were laid before her. It had been the custom, said Wim, for him to make up the household accounts and present them to his master when he returned home, but now, of course, *mevrouw* would attend to the matter and Kieke would be happy to discuss menus and the buying of provisions if *mevrouw* would come each morning to the kitchen.

'Yes, of course I will—if that is what Mevrouw van Kessel always did. But I know nothing about the running of a large house and I hope that you and Kieke will help me. I'll learn to speak Dutch as soon as possible. We shall be back in a month or so.' She smiled at his good-natured face. 'You and Kieke will forgive me if I get things wrong?'

A remark which earned their entire approval. Here was a young lady who would, under their guidance, become a worthy mistress of the ancestral home.

As teatime approached Margo because increasingly nervous. She had got into the cashmere dress and a pair of the new shoes, done her face and hair with the kind of close attention she rarely bestowed upon them, and now she was in the drawing room, sitting uneasily opposite Gijs. She found it annoying that he could sit there, completely at his ease, with Punch lying across his feet, reading *de Haagse Dagblad*, for all the world as though it weren't Christmas Eve with guests arriving at any minute.

'You don't need to be nervous,' he said, without looking up from his reading. 'You must have faced many a Mothers' Union meeting and attended untold village gatherings.' He glanced at her then. 'You look very nice.'

A crumb of comfort, she supposed. If he had been in love with her, she reflected, he would have said that she was lovely or beautiful, because love was blind, wasn't it? Looking nice was better than looking dowdy, however, she comforted herself, and sat up very straight at the sound of cars approaching and then a medley of voices.

The professor put down his newspaper, removed his feet from under Punch and stood up. He plucked Margo gently from her chair, put an arm through hers and walked her into the hall.

It was full of people, all talking at once, with children darting here and there and Wim and Diny taking coats and scarves. There was a rush towards them as they came out of the drawing room and Margo found herself embraced in turn by three young women and then three husbands, and last of all by Gijs's brother, a younger version of him, with his features and blue eyes but not his great height. Margo, with a string of names nicely muddled in her head, bent to greet the children. There were eight of them—four girls and four boys— the youngest a toddler, the eldest rising twelve.

'You poor dear!' exclaimed one of the sisters. 'We are swamping you—it is not good that we should come and stay when you are just married. However, Gijs will not alter the family custom. You do not mind?' She smiled at Margo. 'I'm Lise, the eldest. Franz is my husband,

and Marcus and Jan and Minna are our children. Did Gijs not tell you our names?'

'Well, there hasn't been much time, but it's lovely meeting you all like this, and I'm so relieved that you all speak English. Even the children…'

'We have a Scottish nanny—all the children have a small knowledge. You are exactly as Gijs described you. We will be friends—and my sisters also.'

'I shall like that. Would you like to go to your rooms first or come into the drawing room for tea?'

'You do not mind if the children are with us?'

'Of course not. Christmas isn't Christmas without children, is it?'

'And you will perhaps have added to them by next Christmas,' Franz said as he joined them.

Margo went pink and Lise said comfortably, 'Take no notice of him, Margo; he is a great tease. I think we will go to our rooms, if we may, and then tea.'

Margo led the way upstairs, ushering everyone into their rooms, sorting out the children, making sure that Nanny had all she wanted. Nanny was a quiet little woman who could have been any age between forty and fifty.

'You'll come down for tea,' said Margo. 'I expect you know the house better than I do, so please do exactly as you've always done.'

'Aye, *mevrouw*, I've been with the family since Minna was born—she's the eldest of the children.' She smiled suddenly. 'I'll wish you happy, you and the professor; it's time he was wed.'

Margo went back downstairs and found the men settled by the fire. They all got up as she went in.

'Oh, please don't get up. I'll see about tea.'

She whispered herself out of the room. Gijs had been right; she was on familiar ground. It wasn't the Mothers' Union, but she had had years of meeting people and making them feel at home, listening while they talked, seeing that they had food and drink.

Much later, getting ready for bed, she decided that so far everything had gone well. The house had absorbed their guests into its numerous rooms and she thought the children had behaved beautifully, gathering round the lighted tree before going up to what had once been the nursery to have their supper and go to bed.

There had been a great deal of to-ing and fro-ing, but eventually everyone had gathered in the drawing room for drinks—the men in black tie and the women in long dresses. Margo, in the green velvet and still not sure about the low-cut neck, had nevertheless lost her shyness and apprehension and been the perfect hostess.

Dinner had been leisurely, and it had been late when they'd gone back to the drawing room for coffee.

'There are a few friends coming in later for a drink,' Gijs had said. 'I suggest we put the presents round the tree before they get here.'

There had been a good deal of bustle then, with stealthy creeping upstairs to fetch gaily wrapped gifts and a lot of laughing. She had laid her present for Gijs with the others round the tree and then slipped away to make sure that everyone in the kitchen had had their supper.

Kieke had beamed at her praise for dinner and Wim had assured her that he would be bringing in drinks and canapés in preparation for the visitors who would be calling in presently.

'A very happy Christmas, *mevrouw*,' he had chuckled. 'Everyone is happy.'

The guests had arrived soon after, and she had been so pleased to see Beatrice and her husband. There hadn't been time to talk much but they had arranged to try and meet in Utrecht before Margo went back to England. She had enjoyed herself then, going from one to the other with Gijs, shaking hands, being kissed and congratulated.

A dream, she told herself now, curling up in bed—a dream from which she would have to wake up once Christmas was over and Gijs was back in London, wrapped up in his work. She would make a home for him, she promised herself, and be there when he wanted her and make no fuss when he had to go away…

She slept, for it was one o'clock in the morning and tomorrow was Christmas Day and she wanted to be up early.

It was a day to remember for the rest of her life! The noisy, cheerful breakfast, then church, where she was confident that she looked her best in her new coat and hat and even the carols were sung to familiar tunes, then back to the house for turkey and Christmas pudding.

Just as though we're in England, she reflected, pulling crackers with the children, unaware that Gijs had gone to a good deal of trouble to see that it was. Presently they gathered round the tree and the presents were handed out by Gijs, starting with the smallest child.

There were parcels for her too—not just one or two but a pile of gaily coloured gifts: a silk scarf from a famous fashion house, an evening bag, gloves, a wide leather belt, chocolates, a leather travelling clock. She went round thanking everyone, and when she got to Gijs he put a long jewellers' case into her hand. 'To mark our first Christmas together,' he told her, and bent to kiss her.

There were pearls inside—a very beautiful necklace with a sapphire and diamond clasp. He fastened them round her neck and she leaned up to kiss him. 'But I've had my presents,' she reminded him. 'They are lovely...'

He flung an arm round her shoulder. 'Now you're here, I'll open your present,' he announced. 'Just what I wanted,' he told her moments later. 'We must have your photo taken...'

He kissed her again, the light, cool kiss she had come to expect from him and must learn to accept. For the time being, she reminded herself. She loved him and surely in time he would learn to love her.

Everyone gathered in the drawing room for tea, and when it had been cleared away the furniture was moved to leave a great space in the centre of the room and they played games with the children—Musical Chairs, Grandmother's Footsteps, Blind Man's Bluff. And Margo, caught in Gijs's great arms with everyone shouting at him to guess who it was, forgot herself so far as to murmur, 'Oh, Gijs,' against his vast chest. Heaven knew what she might have added, but, of course, he guessed and released her...

The children, calmed with supper, were put to bed, and everyone else went away to change for the evening. Margo, lying in the bath, decided to wear the taffeta. The pearls would look lovely with it, and it was delightful to dress up...

There was no one else in the drawing room but Gijs when she went down. He was standing in front of the fire, Punch beside him, immaculate in black tie. He and his house suited each other, thought Margo. She said out loud, 'How can you bear to be away from this house, Gijs?'

He smiled. 'Come and sit down. How very nice you look. As for going away, I go because my work is important to me—part of my life, something I must do. Now that I'm married I shall return home each time with even greater pleasure.'

'You like living in England?'

'Certainly I do. When we go back to London we must set about getting the house furnished as quickly as possible. I dare say you already have some ideas?'

'Well, no. There have been so many other things to think about. But I will—can't we do it together?'

She saw the look of faint impatience on his face.

'Whenever I am free, by all means. There are some rather nice pieces in the attic here. We will have a look at them before we return and I'll have whatever we think will fit in sent over.'

The first of their guests joined them then, and there was no more chance to talk together that evening. Nor would there be tomorrow, she remembered: Boxing Day—only they called it the Second Christmas Day in Holland—and they were all going to the village to a party for the children there. Another tradition, she supposed, and a nice one.

The party was fun, with everyone taking part in the games. There was a table laden with soft drinks, cakes and biscuits, oranges and nuts, and in one corner of the village hall a stall serving *potat frits,* hot and crisp with a dollop of pickles in paper pokes. There was a

Christmas tree, of course, and every child there had a present from it.

Margo, helping Gijs hand them out, felt quite at home; she had done the same thing for years at Thinbottom. That evening there were more callers, staying for drinks, so that they dined late.

'You do have a great many friends,' said Margo when she had a moment alone with Gijs.

'They came to see the bride.'

'Well, I dare say they were surprised that you'd got married. I expect I was a bit of a surprise.'

He agreed blandly and she suspected that he was amused, although she wasn't sure why. Probably they had expected an elegant beauty; despite the pretty dresses and the careful hairdo she would never be other than herself. Ordinary.

Everyone went away after breakfast the next morning, and the house seemed very quiet and empty. Margo had a painstaking session in the kitchen with Kieke then went in search of Gijs. A walk would be nice; it was cold and frosty but now and again there was a glimmer of sunshine. They could talk—get to know each other better...

He was in his study when she poked her head round the door, his handsome nose buried in a pile of papers. He looked up as she went in, but she said, 'Don't get up—I can see you're busy.'

'A chance to get some work done without the phone ringing every few minutes. I dare say you can amuse yourself until lunchtime?'

She swallowed disappointment and the beginnings of temper. Surely on holiday he could spare time to be with her? She said, a shade too heartily, 'Oh, yes. Would you like Wim to bring your coffee in here?'

She waited to see if he would suggest that they have it together. His vague, 'Yes, yes, that would be splendid. Off you go and enjoy yourself,' made it obvious that he had no such idea.

She went away quietly, conscious that he was hardly aware of her going.

She went to her room, got into the cashmere coat, tied a scarf over her head, found shoes and gloves, and went downstairs to find Wim.

'I'm going for a walk, Wim. I haven't seen the gardens properly. Don't tell the professor—he's working and mustn't be disturbed. If you'd take his coffee in presently...?'

'And you, *mevrouw*? Your coffee?'

'I'll have it when I get back. It's such a lovely day and I have so much to see.'

She gave his anxious face a reassuring smile and went through the door he held open for her and down the steps.

She explored the garden, which was much larger than she had thought, and then, still feeling put out, went down the drive and out of the gate. She didn't go to the village—she knew where that was and had had a glimpse of it yesterday—but instead took the other direction along the narrow lane bordered by the high walls of Gijs's garden and then by straggling bushes which in turn became open fields.

It was cold. She hadn't realised how cold until she'd started walking in the open country. There were no hills, but flat, orderly meadows bisected by canals, already iced over. There was no one and nothing in sight either, though presently she saw a church steeple and a cluster of cottages. Another village—and she was sure she could see a glimpse of water. Gijs had told her that there were lakes nearby.

She walked on, wishing that she had had coffee before she'd left the house. But away from the house she could think... It was early days, she told herself; she would need a great deal of patience. Gijs was used to being a bachelor. When they got back to London she would set about making a home for them both and at the same time learn to make the best of herself.

A good hairdresser? A visit to a beauty parlour, perhaps? More clothes? And she must find something to keep her occupied so that he need never feel guilty about leaving her alone. A baby crêche, perhaps, or helping at a playschool. At the same time she would learn to be a good hostess and housewife.

Uplifted by these ambitious thoughts, she walked on, and presently, seeing a side-lane and a glint of water beyond, turned down it. There were a few bushes and small trees near the water. There was a small jetty too, and a couple of small boats hauled up on the bank. The water looked cold and grey, and a nasty mean wind was ruffling it.

Margo shivered, and looked around her, suddenly aware that the sky had become dark. She had walked further than she had intended; she glanced at her watch and was surprised to see that in half an hour it would be lunchtime. She started back along the lane as the first soft flakes of snow began to fall. By the time she reached the other lane, it was falling in a thick curtain, turning the surrounding countryside into a formless white blanket.

'A good thing that it's a straight road,' said Margo, her voice sounding loud in the silence. She walked on, her head bent against the blinding snow, unaware that she had gone off the road and that ahead of her were a series of narrow canals, already concealed under the snow...

It was Wim who began to worry as the snow started. He took a large umbrella and went round the gardens calling her, looking in the various out-houses where she might be sheltering. There was no sign of her, and he went back to the kitchen.

'There is no sign of *mevrouw*,' he told Kieke. 'Perhaps she came in without saying anything and is in her room...'

It was Diny who spoke. '*Mevrouw?* I saw her go out of the gate with my own eyes not an hour ago.'

Gijs didn't lift his head from his work as Wim knocked and went in.

'*Mevrouw* has gone out, *mijnheer*, and it is snowing hard.'

The professor was on his feet in an instant. 'Did she say where she was going?' He went to look out of the window then strode into the hall, followed by Punch. 'I'll go after her—she must have gone to the village. Phone the shop there and ask if anyone has seen her, will you, Wim?'

He was getting into his Barbour jacket and taking off his shoes as he spoke. Kieke, who had come into the hall, went without a word and fetched his rubber boots, then thrust a woollen scarf at him. 'Put that in your pocket, *mijnheer*. *Mevrouw* will be cold.'

Wim reported that no one had seen her in the village

although she might be there, visiting, perhaps. It didn't seem likely. It was a small place where everyone knew everyone else's business; if she had been there someone would have known about it.

'If she returns before I'm back,' said the professor, 'get her into a warm bath and bed, Kieke.' He whistled to Punch, nodded to Wim and left his house.

There was only one other way to go, he reasoned, if Margo hadn't gone to the village, and that was along the lane leading to the next village and the lakes.

Once he had passed his own walls and then the few trees he paused to shout before going on again. He had walked for ten minutes or more, pausing to bellow her name, when there was a lull in the storm and the snow thinned, giving him a chance to look around him. He saw her at once, going slowly across the fields. She had stopped to look around her and he began to run, and when he saw her starting to walk again he shouted, 'Stand still, Margo. Don't move.'

She was so surprised, she almost fell over, but she obeyed him and he fetched up beside her, breathing hard, and not altogether because he had been running. All the same his voice was quiet. 'Just in time,' he told her placidly. 'You were rather near a canal.'

He took the scarf off her head and tied the woolly one on instead. She gave a sniff. 'I got a bit lost,' she said in a voice she strove to keep matter-of-fact. 'I didn't expect it to snow quite so hard.'

He took her arm. 'We'll get home before it starts again.' He saw her mouth shaking. 'Punch is so pleased to have found you; he's your slave already.'

He was walking her back to the road, and as they reached it the snow started to fall again. He put an arm around her shoulders and held her close. 'We might get lost again,' said Margo in a small voice.

'Not with Punch leading the way.' She felt his arm tighten. 'This is my fault, Margo. I should never have left you alone. I'm sorry. I have become selfish living on my own—I—'

She interrupted him. 'Of course you're not selfish— what a silly notion. And it wasn't your fault. You weren't to know that I was going out or that it was going to snow. Silly of me not to have told Wim…'

Punch gave a cheerful bark as they turned in at the gate, and ran ahead of them through the door Wim already had open, to shake himself all over the hall floor then lope into the drawing room to flop before the fire. No one reprimanded him; they were too busy getting out of encrusted coats, and kicking off wet shoes and boots while the professor gave quiet and unhurried instructions.

Margo, escorted upstairs by Kieke, had a hot bath prescribed for her, and then, once more warm and dry in a sweater and skirt, went back downstairs.

There was no one in the drawing room, and although the table was laid for lunch in the dining room there was no one there either. She was standing in the hall, wondering if she should go to Gijs's study, when he opened the door of the small sitting room at the back of the hall.

'There you are. Come in and have a drink; it's cosy here. You're none the worse for your adventure?'

He pulled a small easy chair forward and gave her a glass of sherry.

'I have to go to Utrecht in the morning—would you like to come with me? There are some splendid shops and you know your way around there now. I'll meet you for lunch.'

'I'd like that. Perhaps I could find something to take back to Aunt Flo.'

They lunched together, and then went up to the attic where she poked around, delighted at the chairs and tables, sofas and tallboys stored there.

'You could furnish a whole house…'

'You like the idea? Good. Pick out what you want—there must be enough here to furnish several rooms.'

She wanted almost everything. 'This—and this. Oh, and this…'

She stopped to look at an old-fashioned cradle on rockers. On her knees, she examined it carefully. 'It's very old, isn't it? Hasn't it been used for a long time?'

'Good lord, yes. All the van Kessels spend the first month or so in it. 'It's very comfortable, I've been told.' He smiled down at her, amused at her eagerness. 'I can't remember if that is so.'

She stood up and went to look at a little table inlaid with mother-of-pearl, conscious that her face was red and desperately unhappy because it hadn't meant anything to him. Didn't he want children? He had said that he wanted a wife and perhaps that was all he did want—someone to run his house, be a hostess to his friends, be there when he came home…

They went to Utrecht soon after breakfast the next day, with Punch sitting, as usual, on the back seat.

'I'll put you down at the shopping precinct,' Gijs told her. 'You remember the small enclosure in the centre, with the seats round it? I'll meet you there at half past twelve.' He glanced at his watch. 'I'm sorry I haven't time to have coffee with you, but I'm already late.'

'I'll be there,' she told him, and wondered where he was going.

She had coffee and then began her search for a present for Aunt Flo. She had money now; Gijs had put some notes into her purse with the remark that she might see something she wanted to buy and she counted them now. There was enough money to buy the kitchen stove if she'd wanted to.

She strolled round, looking in the shop windows, which were still for the most part filled with Christmas merchandise. She found a silk scarf in misty greys and blues that would be the very thing for Aunt Flo, and then, since she had so much money, bought a gold scarf pin to go with it. Her aunt loved chocolates, she remembered, and so bought a splendid box tied with ribbons and filled with mouthwatering confections, loaded with calories.

Her purchases in an elegant carrier bag, she had another cup of coffee, made sure that her hair and face were as near to perfection as possible, and wandered back to the shops once more. Almost at once her eye was caught by a small, silver-plated calendar—just the thing for Gijs's desk. He had given her so much, and the leather photo frame had been paltry compared with all the magnificent presents she had received. She bought it and had it wrapped in pretty paper then put it with her other purchases. By then it was almost half past twelve.

It was quite warm with the lighted shops all around her and people hurrying to and fro, and she hardly noticed the time passing. Finally, a clock somewhere striking the hour disturbed her thoughts. Gijs was late.

Perhaps she had misunderstood him? But there was only one enclosure…

By half past one she was not only worried, she was cross too. Here I am, she fumed silently, in a foreign country; I don't even know the phone number at Arntz-stein or how to get there. I don't know where he is. I might still be here when the shops close. He's forgotten me. He's forgotten that he's married! Probably drinking with his pals.

She knew that the last assumption was nonsense, but she felt better for thinking it. Just let him come now, and she would tell him how tiresome he was.

'I'm sorry I kept you waiting,' said Gijs from behind her.

She spun round. 'An hour—more than an hour—I've been sitting here. If I'd known where to go I'd have gone.' She took a heaving breath. 'It's not even England…'

His mouth twitched but he answered her gravely. 'I know. Tear me apart if you want to. I hadn't forgotten you, though.'

'Then why didn't you come when you said you would?'

She uttered the words which came so readily to wives the world over. 'Where have you been?'

He came and sat down beside her then. 'I had no idea I would be so long. I went to the hospital to see who they had put on my waiting list and a child was admitted while I was there. She needed surgery—my kind of surgery…'

Her peevishness evaporated. 'Gijs, I'm sorry I was cross. What a mess I'm making of being your wife. Of course doctors' wives expect to get left, don't they? And they don't grumble. I won't do it again, I promise.'

'I must remember to tell you if I'm going to be late home too.' He spoke lightly. 'Although I don't always know.'

'Friends?' asked Margo, holding out a hand.

He shook it. 'Friends for life,' he assured her.

They had their lunch then in perfect harmony, and presently, when she asked him, he told her something of the child on whom he had been operating.

'You'll go and see her again?'

'Yes. Would you like to come to the hospital with me?'

'Oh, yes, please.' She added hastily, 'I won't get in your way.'

'Everyone there wants to meet you...'

After that the days sped by, gradually forming a pattern which Margo could see was to be her life in the future. Pleasant hours with Gijs—walking, sitting by the fire talking and reading, learning to play pool in the billiard room at the back of the house—but also long hours spent on her own while he worked in his study and twice drove to Amsterdam where he spent most of the day.

Certainly he had taken her to the hospital at Utrecht, but as soon as they'd arrived he'd handed her over to an elderly *zuster*, who'd trotted round introducing her to the nurses on the wards. All the same, she'd gone back home with him feeling that she was sharing a very small piece of his working life.

She wasn't lonely, though. She spent time each

morning with Kieke, and Wim helped out with the language—after a few days she began to pick out a word here and there, and even tried a word or two of Dutch herself.

She went down to the village too, and wandered round the church, examining the massive tombstones marking countless van Kessels. She met the *dominee* there, and he took her back to his house to drink coffee with his wife.

On Sundays she and Gijs went to church, and sat in the front pew, its little gate shutting them off from the rest of the congregation. The sermons were long and stern, and to her surprise, Gijs always took her hand in his and held it for the whole of the oration.

Perhaps, she thought hopefully, he's falling in love with me. But nothing in his behaviour suggested that.

Although there were no more trips to Utrecht, their days were filled. Friends called—so many people knew Gijs and were anxious to meet his bride—and they walked a great deal with the delighted Punch, and in the evenings they sat by the fire.

Gijs seemed content, Margo thought, although she suspected that he sometimes longed to go to his study and work or read. She had suggested it tentatively once or twice, but he had assured her that he had no wish to do so.

'I'm on holiday,' he had observed. 'Time enough for that when we're back in London.'

Leaving Arntzstein was a wrench; she had had no idea until the moment they left that she would mind going so much. The sight of Punch mournfully moaning quietly to himself as they got into the car made her tearful. They had driven some miles in silence before she could trust herself to speak.

'Don't you miss Punch?'

'Abominably. We must sneak over for a weekend as soon as I can manage it.'

'Oh, good. I shall miss him too—and your home...'

'Our home,' he corrected her quietly. 'I'm so glad you enjoyed our stay.'

'Oh, I did. I think I'd like to live there always...'

'Well, that is possible. I could go to and fro quite easily.'

She felt shocked. 'But you've bought that lovely little house in London.'

'We need a place there while I still work in England, but once it is furnished and we have settled in there is no reason why you shouldn't stay at Arntzstein for as long as you wish.'

'You'd be in London, though.'

'For some of the time, yes.'

'That wouldn't do at all,' said Margo roundly. 'I'm your wife.'

They talked about other things then, but at the back of her mind was the thought that Gijs would be quite willing to let her do as she wished. If he loved me, she thought miserably, he wouldn't even suggest it.

Once back in London they went straight to the house Gijs had rented. As he stopped the car Margo said suddenly, 'All the lights are on. There's someone there, Gijs.'

He said casually, 'My old nanny has a younger sister. I asked her to come as housekeeper.'

Margo turned to look at him. 'You think of everything, Gijs. You seem to have the gift of making things happen.'

'You think so? Everyone can make mistakes and I am no exception.'

Chapter 8

Margo didn't say anything as she got out of the car. What had Gijs meant? Had he been admitting that he had made a mistake in marrying her? Had it been just a random remark which meant nothing much? She was tempted to ask him, but now hardly seemed the right moment.

The door opened as they reached it and a stout elderly woman stood beaming a welcome.

'Master Gijs, welcome—and you, madam. There's the kettle boiling, for I've no doubt you'll be wanting a good cup of tea…'

The professor bent to kiss her plump cheek. 'Mattie, you've settled in? Did Nanny come to London with you?' He turned to Margo. 'Mattie is a very old friend,' he told her. 'When I was a small boy she used to come and visit Nanny and bring me bull's eyes.'

Mattie chuckled richly. 'Go on with you, Master Gijs. Fancy you remembering that. No, she didn't come with me.

'If you would like to come with me, madam, I'll take you upstairs.' As they went up together she said cheerfully, 'I dare say Mister Gijs forgot to tell you that I'd be here? I hope you won't take it in bad part, madam. He's asked me to housekeep for you, but it's for you to decide.'

They had reached the bedroom, which was softly lit with flowers in a vase and the curtains drawn against the dusk.

'I can't think of anything nicer than to have you for a housekeeper, Mattie. I hope you'll stay with us always. I don't know London at all well and everything's a bit strange.' Margo smiled cheerfully at the elderly face, liking it already. 'Must you call me madam? Isn't there something else…?'

'Well, I could call you ma'am if you'd prefer.'

'Yes, please. This room looks lovely, and so welcoming. You must have worked hard.'

'It's an easy house. Mister Gijs said you had bought a mews cottage…'

'Yes, but it has to be furnished before we can move into it. It's bigger than this one—the rooms are larger. It's in a mews near the professor's consulting rooms. We shall be busy, you and I, Mattie.'

'It'll be a pleasure, ma'am.' Mattie bustled to the door. 'I'll get the tea—you'll be wanting a cup.'

Left to herself, Margo took a look round. Mattie had taken great pains to make the room look welcoming. There were magazines on the bedside table, and the long cupboard along one wall and the drawers in the chest smelled of lavender. She went through the half-open door into the bathroom beyond, and found that it had everything that she could possibly want.

She tidied herself and went downstairs to join Gijs in the sitting room. At the back of her mind was a feeling of resentment that he had installed Mattie without saying a word to her—on the other hand he might have done that to make her sudden plunge into married life easier. He would have overlooked the fact that it was a small house, which Margo could easily have run without any help. She went slowly into the sitting room and found him at a desk under the window, writing.

He pulled a chair forward for her by the fire and sat down opposite her.

'I must be at the hospital by eight o'clock tomorrow morning and I shall be there all day. I'm sorry that I have to leave you alone, but I'll be free on Sunday. I thought we might go and see Aunt Florence, and when we come back we could go to the house and make a few decisions about furnishing it. The pieces you chose at Arntzstein will be sent over as soon as the floors and windows are ready. If we can decide something on Sunday, perhaps you would look around for carpets and curtains? We can collect the rest of the furniture at our leisure—there's a good place at Stow-on-the-Wold and another at Bath. It will be nice to have your own home.'

She had been steeling herself to the idea of being lonely until such time as she had found her way around and made a few friends, but obviously there wasn't going to be much time for loneliness. She said now, 'Well, will you tell me how much I can spend?'

'Of course. As soon as I have time we will go and arrange a bank account for you—for your own personal use. The bills for the house will, of course, be sent to me.'

She thanked him as Mattie came in with the tea, and he talked of something else then.

Later, after they had dined, he suggested that she should phone Aunt Florence.

Aunt Flo sounded brisk. 'Well, so you're back. What did you think of Holland?'

'I liked it very much,' said Margo. 'May we come and see you on Sunday? Gijs will be free. We plan to go and look at the house he's bought and decide about furnishing it, but if we might just call in…?'

'Come for tea—five o'clock. That gives you the whole day at the house. I'm going out to supper, but I dare say you'd like to be back for an evening at home together anyway.'

How cosy that sounds, thought Margo. But it wouldn't be like that—they would dine and have their coffee and presently he would go to his study and she would read until she could go to bed. She frowned at her thoughts. She had no reason to complain; Gijs had his work and she had a lovely little home here and a magnificent one in Holland. She still had to find her feet…

She was secretly delighted when he stayed with her, talking about Arntzstein, discussing the house they would live in once they had furnished it to their liking; they would go over to Holland again in about six weeks' time, he told her. 'For about three weeks,' he said. 'But part of the time I shall be away from home. I'm sure you'll find plenty to do and you will have Beatrice to visit.'

'I'm quite sure that I shall be happy, Gijs. Shall we have the house here ready by then?'

'I don't see why not. Once we have decided what we need it is only a matter of buying exactly what we want.'

Margo, rather overawed at the idea of shopping on such a vast scale, agreed.

Gijs had been gone for an hour by the time she went down to breakfast in the morning. She had assured him that she didn't mind getting up early and having the meal with him, but had realised as she'd said it that he had no wish for her company. She had crept to the window and watched him drive away, hoping that he would look up, but he hadn't.

He was tired when he got home just before dinner that evening.

'I'll be down in ten minutes,' he told her. 'Pour me a drink, will you?'

Presently, settled in his chair, the drink beside him, he asked her if she had had a pleasant day.

'Delightful,' said Margo. 'But what about you? Or don't you want to talk about it? If you do, I'd love to hear.'

He looked faintly surprised. 'Would you? I have always had the impression that people don't like to know what goes on in operating theatres.'

'Well, I'm the exception. I dare say I won't understand half of it, but I'm interested.' When he hesitated she asked, 'Were you in Theatre all day?'

'No, no. I had a clinic this morning—that lasted until almost noon—then I went to the ward and from there to Theatre.'

'Did you have lunch?'

He laughed then. 'You sound just like a wife. I had a sandwich and coffee in Sister's office.'

Margo suppressed an instant stab of jealousy. Probably the sister was young and pretty and very clever. 'Well, Mattie has cooked a marvellous meal. Was your nanny a good cook too?'

'She made excellent chips—we had them for a treat when we had been good—and toffee. We all made toffee on wet afternoons.'

'You were a happy little boy...'

She felt such a surge of love that she couldn't speak for a moment.

'Yes, indeed I was. And you, Margo? Were you a happy child?'

'Yes, I was happy too. You never lose it, do you? The memory of happiness?'

'No—and what a good thing that is.'

Mattie came then to tell them that dinner was on the table—a delicious meal of soup, beef *en croûte* and apple crumble with cream, helped along by Chardonnay. Margo had chosen the meal carefully; Gijs was a very large man, and she thought it very likely that meals, if he ever got to them, might not be eaten at the right times—and even then they might consist of sandwiches.

They talked about nothing much as they ate, comfortable with each other's company, and when Mattie brought them their coffee at the table Gijs observed, 'You haven't lost your touch, Mattie. Dinner was excellent.'

Mattie smiled widely. 'Well, now, Mr Gijs, I've kept my hand in, as it were, but the apple crumble Mrs van Kessel made—as good as ever I could myself!'

'How fortunate I am,' murmured the professor, 'with two good cooks to look after me. I must congratulate you both!'

* * *

The next morning Margo went to their mews cottage armed with a notebook, pen and tape measure. A practical girl, she drew a careful plan of the little place, putting in measurements, inspecting the rooms carefully and imagining them furnished.

The pieces from Arntzstein would fit in beautifully, though the furniture they bought would have to be of the same period. The floors were wooden, so they would have rugs downstairs and fitted carpets in the bedrooms. The kitchen had its original stone floor and would need matting in front of the Aga. The room leading from it would be Mattie's—another fitted carpet, Margo decided, and warm curtains at the window. And, since Mattie was going to live in it, she should be allowed to furnish it as she liked.

Margo went back for lunch then, and spent a delightful but tiring afternoon collecting samples of material for curtains, deciding on the best shop at which to get the carpets and browsing through Harrods' kitchen departments.

Gijs came home soon after she had had tea, but when she got up to get him a fresh pot he declined.

'I had a cup in Sister's office. What have you done with yourself today?'

She told him, showing him her carefully drawn plan and then the samples of material and the colour charts.

'If you aren't too tired would you tell me the kind of curtains you would like and the colours? I won't bother you again unless you want to be.' She hesitated. 'I don't expect you would have the time to come to the shop and choose with me?'

'The day after tomorrow. I'll come home for lunch

and we'll go together. I'll have to go back to the hospital afterwards, and then on to my consulting rooms, but I can be free until four o'clock.'

How easy it was to shop, reflected Margo, sitting beside Gijs trying to decide exactly which shade of mulberry-red was right for the sitting-room curtains, when there was no need to look at the price ticket. What a good thing it was, too, that they had similar tastes when it came to carpets and curtains.

Chintz curtains in the bedrooms and mushroom fitted carpets, and no stair carpet, they agreed, since the small staircase was oak, with the patina of age. As for rugs and carpets downstairs, they would hunt for them in the Cotswolds, taking their time.

He drove her back on his way to the hospital and she spent a delightful half-hour with Mattie discussing Mattie's wishes for her own room before going to her room and changing into one of her pretty dresses. Probably Gijs wouldn't notice it, but she intended to leave no stone unturned.

She need not have bothered. He came home just after ten o'clock that evening, and, since the dinner Mattie had so lovingly prepared was ruined, Margo cooked him bacon and eggs and mushrooms and fried bread, and without asking poured him a glass of Guinness.

He came into the kitchen while she was cooking and sat himself down at the table. 'I didn't expect this,' he told her.

Margo prodded the bacon. 'Well, from now on you can. Don't forget that I was brought up in a household where the master of the house came and went at all hours of the day and night. Father—' she gulped in sudden sorrow '—was at everyone's beck and call. Just as I think you are.'

He said mildly, 'Neither your father nor I would wish for anything different.'

She nodded. 'So it's a good thing that you married me, isn't it?'

She was dishing up and didn't see his look. 'A very good thing,' he observed.

She sat opposite him while he ate and soon after poured coffee for them both, and in a little while he began to tell her of his afternoon's work. There had been complications at the hospital and the patients he had seen at his rooms had taken up more time than he had expected. Small children suffering from unpronounceable illnesses which she couldn't even guess at. She would have to get a medical dictionary, she reflected. She listened intelligently and went to bed presently, glowing with the thought that he had enjoyed talking to her.

On Sunday, when they went to the cottage, she was astonished to see that the bedroom carpets had already been fitted.

'But it's only been days...'

'I did mention that we wanted to move into the place as quickly as possible.' Gijs had wandered out into the tiny garden behind the cottage. 'The pieces from Arntzstein should be here this week. I should be free next Saturday—we might look for carpets. Persian in the sitting room, don't you think?'

They went home presently, and Margo cooked lunch as Mattie had her day off and had gone to visit a niece on the other side of London.

Aunt Florence was pleased to see them, and even more pleased were Caesar and Plato.

'Shall we take them back with us?' asked Margo.

'If you must. But wouldn't it be sensible to wait until you move into your own home?' Aunt Flo said matter-of-factly. 'Another week or two won't make much difference.'

So they went back to London without the animals, and, seeing Margo's downcast face, the professor said, 'We should be able to move in two weeks' time. Once we have the place furnished we can take our time with making it home.'

A very reassuring remark, Margo considered.

An accurate one, too, as it turned out. Standing in the centre of the cottage's kitchen, Margo revolved slowly, admiring the rows of new saucepans, the china on the wooden dresser they had found in a Cotswold town and the solid wooden table with the Windsor chairs at each end of it. There was still a good deal to do, she conceded, but the splendid Persian rug in the sitting room was exactly right with the Dutch marquetry cabinet and sofa table which had been brought over from Holland and the two sofas on each side of the fireplace were lovely.

The bedrooms were almost complete. The four-poster in her room was nicely offset by the applewood dressing table and bedside tables. They had found a chaise longue, too, for the foot of the bed, and two George IV bergères, whose faded tapestry upholstery blended nicely with the curtains. Downstairs in the hall was a long-case clock, walnut and marquetry, which they had come across quite by chance and for which Gijs had paid what Margo considered to be a small fortune.

There *was* still a lot to be done; the third bedroom was by no means complete and she was looking forward to a morning in Harrods choosing towels to match the bathrooms. But Mattie's room was finished, and as comfortable as it was possible to make it. She wandered upstairs and looked in Gijs's room. A picture or two would make it look cosier. She went over to the chest of drawers and picked up his hairbrushes, and then the little leather box where he kept his cuff-links. After a few moments she put them down gently and went out of the room, closing the door behind her.

She mustn't allow herself to get downhearted, even though Gijs seemed no nearer to falling in love with her. They had settled down to an easygoing comradeship, and she was sure that he enjoyed her company. All the same there was an invisible wall between them; she was being held, metaphorically speaking, at arm's length. He had told her that they could get to know each other once they were married and she had been content with that, but in two weeks' time they would go to Holland again, and they were no closer now than they had been when they had married.

'I mustn't worry about it,' said Margo aloud, and went back to the kitchen to see how Caesar and Plato had settled in.

That evening the professor's youngest sister phoned. She was coming over to London to do some shopping and wanted to stay for a day or two.

'Can you manage, Margo?' asked Gijs. 'It's short notice…'

His youngest sister, Corinne, was his favourite. 'Of course,' said Margo happily; it would mean dashing out in the morning and buying one or two things, but

Corinne wasn't coming for a couple of days yet. A small easy chair, thought Margo, and bedspreads for the beds, and that lovely flower painting I saw in that art gallery. 'It will be lovely to have her. Will she be on her own?'

'Yes, Julius is going to Sweden on business for a week.'

They had been married for two years, Margo remembered, and she wondered why Corinne didn't want to go to Sweden with him. A pity she didn't know Gijs well enough to ask him...

The room looked delightful when it was ready, with flowers in a little porcelain vase, a pile of fluffy towels in the bathroom and the bedspreads of pastel patchwork. Margo laid a small pile of magazines on one of the bedside tables, made sure that the water carafe was full and went downstairs to wait for her guest.

Corinne was laughing and talking to Gijs, who had been to fetch her from Heathrow, as they entered the cottage. She was a very pretty young woman and beautifully dressed, and she embraced Margo with warmth.

'What a dear you are to let me come and stay with you so soon after you're married. I promise I will not play gooseberry.' She trilled with laughter. 'I shall go shopping, and I do hope that you will come with me, but I promise I will not be a nuisance.'

'It's lovely to have you,' said Margo, and meant it. 'I love shopping, and Gijs and I are very pleased to see you.'

'I look forward to going to the theatre—it is a play I long to see—and the party will be such fun...'

Margo wiped the astonishment off her face and planted a smile there. Theatre? Party? It was the first she had heard of either. 'Come up to your room,' she invited. 'Tea will be in ten minutes or so.'

She took care not to look at Gijs, and led the way upstairs, made sure that Corinne had everything she needed then went back to the drawing room.

The professor was sitting in an armchair with Plato pressed up against his knees and Caesar perched on its arm.

'Don't get up,' said Margo in a voice to freeze him solid, and bent to give the fire an unnecessary poke.

'It was to be a surprise,' said the professor mildly. 'The theatre. My fault; I should have warned Corinne not to mention it. As for the party, that is something I had hoped to discuss with you this evening, but perhaps I should wait until you have gone off the boil!'

He gave her a friendly smile, having cut the ground neatly from under her.

'I am not—' began Margo, and then added, 'Oh, why are you always right?' She caught his eye and burst out laughing. 'You are sometimes a very tiresome man!' She added swiftly, 'And don't say that I am tiresome too, because I know that already.'

'Never tiresome, Margo. Indeed, since we married—' He broke off as the door opened and Corinne came in, followed by Mattie with the teatray. Margo wondered what he had been going to say as she handed out cups and offered toasted teacakes.

Later that evening, when Corinne had gone to bed, he had the chance to tell her, but he didn't, merely brought up the subject of the party again.

'Dinner?' he wanted to know. 'Eight or ten of us? It's time you met some of my colleagues and their wives, and for Corinne we'll ask a couple of younger, unattached men. Will you agree to that? And, to make things easy, why don't you both come with me to the hospital governers' tea party on Saturday? It's hardly an exciting occasion, but I can introduce you to everyone and break the ice for you.'

Margo agreed; she suspected that if she hadn't he would still have got his own way. 'And the theatre?' she wanted to know.

'Tomorrow evening—can we dine early?'

She agreed readily, with the unhappy thought that he was exerting himself to amuse his sister but had failed to do the same for her. Time for another visit to the hairdresser and a prowl round the cosmetic counters, she decided. Perhaps a new dress? Supposing she dyed her hair? She had long, silky hair, but mouse-brown had never been in fashion. Highlights, perhaps? A hint of gold or even auburn…?

'What are you plotting?' Gijs said suddenly.

'I was deciding what to do about my hair. I think perhaps I'll have it cut very short and then highlighted…'

'No,' said the professor, in such a forceful voice that she looked at him, surprised. 'I like your hair as it is; it suits your face.'

'Well, that's the whole point. If I had something dramatic done to my hair it might improve my looks.'

'Your looks are very nice as they are. I would much prefer you to leave your hair as it is.'

'Very well,' said Margo, reflecting that he probably found that her unassuming appearance didn't distract him from his work. She remembered the rather striking dress she had seen in Harrods' window; it would do nicely for the dinner party, and even if he didn't notice it the guests might…

* * *

Corinne was the ideal guest, knowing just when to disappear for an hour or so, and a delightful companion for Margo. They shopped the very next day, and while Corinne was trying on evening gowns Margo slipped away to look at the dress she had decided to buy herself. When she tried it on she could see that it wasn't for her—the colour was too vivid, the skirt was shorter than short and her sensible mind queried the sense of paying a great deal of money for a few yards of material, however costly that material was. Instead she chose something quite different—pink patterned chiffon over a silk slip, with an ankle-length skirt, long, tight sleeves and a modest neckline. She thought it likely that Gijs wouldn't notice it.

The visit to the theatre was a great success. Gijs had tickets for *Sunset Boulevard* and Margo sat entranced until the final curtain. She had loved every minute of it, and not only the performance but also the theatre, with its bright lights, and the audience, the music and the volume of voices during the interval. She sat like a mouse, noticing nothing else, and the professor, watching her rapt face, smiled to himself. It was rather like taking his nieces to the circus for the first time...

He took them to the Savoy for a late supper after the show, and Corinne's happy chatter made it unnecessary to do more than reply briefly from time to time.

On Saturday afternoon they went to the hospital governors' tea party and Margo was introduced to Gijs's colleagues and their wives, some of whom would be coming to the dinner party. They were friendly people, bent on making her feel at home, and presently Gijs went to speak to one of the governors, leaving her with a group of the wives.

'We were so delighted when we heard that Gijs was to marry,' said one lady, slightly older than the rest of them. 'A consultant, especially a paediatrician, needs a wife.' She beamed kindly at Margo. 'And I am sure that you are exactly right for him—a vicar's daughter, I believe?'

Margo said that yes, she was, and that she hoped she would be a help to Gijs—a remark which earned her the approbation of her listeners.

Gijs was still at the other end of the room, but she could see Corinne talking animatedly to a youngish man with dark good looks. They were getting on very well together—perhaps they had met somewhere else. Margo, mindful of good manners, bent her full attention to a girl with a lisp, married to the hospital secretary, who wanted to know what she had thought of Holland.

The intervening days before the dinner party were taken up with more shopping on Corinne's part. 'I'm going out on my own,' she told Margo gaily. 'You must have heaps of things that you want to do and I know my own way round. I'll stop out for lunch...'

Which suited Margo very well, for she wanted the dinner party to be a success and she needed time to have everything just so. She and Mattie had already put their heads together and thought up a menu, and while Mattie saw to the food she busied herself with the table and the seating arrangements. Everyone who had been asked had accepted.

When she told Gijs he said casually, 'Well, I expected them to—they are all dying of curiosity. They met you at the hospital the other afternoon; now they want to see us in our new home.' He looked up from the papers he was studying. 'The wine will be delivered tomorrow. Leave it in the hall, and I'll take it down to the cellar when I get home.' After a few minutes he put down the papers.

'Where is Corinne?'

'Shopping again. She needs to buy so much, and she wanted to go on her own.'

Gijs smiled. 'She'll make Julius bankrupt.'

A joke, of course. All the same, Corinne *had* been buying a great many things, and once or twice, when Margo had asked her if her purchases were being delivered since she had come home empty-handed, she had told her light-heartedly that she had arranged to have them sent over to Holland.

'Heaven knows, I've enough luggage as it is,' she'd laughed.

It was quite late on the evening before the party when the senior consultant surgeon's wife phoned Margo. Could she possibly bring another guest? she wanted to know. 'This is unpardonable of me, my dear, but he is leaving England in a day or so and I hate to leave him on his own.' She added, 'Actually he is my husband's nephew.'

'Of course he must come,' said Margo, rearranging the table in her mind's eye. 'We shall be delighted to meet him.'

She said goodbye and rang off, and since Corinne was in her room and Gijs had been called back to the hospital to give his opinion on a small child who had fallen from a window in a block of flats she went to the kitchen to tell Mattie.

'I hope the professor won't mind,' she confided uneasily, 'although it will be nice for Corinne to meet a new face. There's plenty of food?'

'More than enough, ma'am. Can I get you anything before I go to bed?'

'No, thank you, Mattie; I dare say the professor will be very late back. There's coffee keeping warm for him, isn't there? I think I'll go to bed in a little while. I'll stay up a bit, just in case he doesn't stay.'

She said goodnight, made sure that Caesar and Plato were comfortable in their baskets, and went back to the drawing room. When the clock struck midnight she put the guard in front of the fire, made sure that the doors and windows were secure and took herself off to bed.

There was no light under Corinne's door. She would be tired after her long day—indeed, she seemed over-tired, reflected Margo, her eyes too bright and always talking non-stop. I shall miss her when she goes home, thought Margo, lying in bed wondering what Gijs was doing.

He was just starting on an operation to try and save the life of the small girl on the operating table, and he wouldn't be home for hours…

He was leaving the house as Margo went down to breakfast the next morning. He wished her good morning and she saw how tired he was.

'Have you had any sleep at all?'

'An hour or so.' He smiled. 'I'll catch up on sleep later. I'll see if I can be home in good time this evening.'

He was already at the door; it wasn't the moment to tell him about the extra guest. She told him to be careful in a motherly voice and watched him drive away.

'He works too hard,' she told Plato, and went to eat

her breakfast. Corinne would be down presently, she supposed.

She appeared five minutes later, bubbling over with chatter, talking about going back home, the clothes she had bought and the people she had met.

'It's been heavenly, so exciting…'

'Exciting? Well, I don't know about that,' observed Margo in her sensible way. 'We haven't done much to entertain you, though I dare say you've enjoyed all that shopping.'

Corinne giggled. 'Oh, the shopping—indeed I have!'

Margo, in the pink dress, was alone in the drawing room when Gijs came home. Their guests were due in half an hour, and after greeting her hurriedly he started for the stairs.

'Gijs.' She hurried to the door. 'There hasn't been a chance to tell you but Lady Colbert phoned late yesterday evening and asked if she might bring her husband's nephew—he's staying with them. It has made it rather awkward at the table, but I couldn't refuse.'

She had expected him to be annoyed; she hadn't expected the anger in his face. 'Jerome Colbert? Since he is to be our guest I can do nothing about it, but I must ask you and Corinne to have nothing more to do with him than common courtesy dictates.'

'Why?'

'I haven't time to explain now. Please accept my advice and do as I ask.'

'Am I to tell Corinne?'

He was going up the stairs. 'Yes—and I must add that Julius is of the same opinion as I am.'

Margo went back to the drawing room, rather shaken

by Gijs's anger, and wondering how to be courteous to someone you had been asked to shun. She looked up as Corinne, a vision in a red silk sheath, came in.

Margo glanced at the clock; there were barely ten minutes left in which to explain. 'Listen,' she said urgently. 'That nephew of Lady Colbert's—Gijs says…'

She relayed his words and was surprised to see Corinne's look of glee.

'Don't tell, but I've been seeing him every day—just for fun, you know. He's so amusing. I told him about this evening and he persuaded his aunt.' She giggled as she sat down.

'But Corinne, Gijs said— What would he say if he knew?'

'Promise you won't tell.' Corinne suddenly looked anxious. 'You must promise, Margo. Gijs'll be so angry with me, and he'll tell Julius or make *me* tell him and Julius will be furious. He's cross with me as it is.' She shrugged. 'You know how it is—we quarrelled and he went off to Sweden on his own. I was only having some fun—nothing serious!' She got up and went to sit by Margo and caught her hand in hers. 'Margo, promise—please? Julius will never forgive me, and I know he's a bit dull, but I do love him.'

'I promise,' said Margo, and turned a serene face to Gijs as he came into the room.

The guests arrived and Margo, standing beside Gijs, welcoming them, did her best to dismiss Corinne's problems from her mind. But she was reminded of them when the Colberts arrived.

Sir Anthony was elderly, within a few years of retirement, and a distinguished and respected surgeon and firm friend of Gijs. His wife was charming but inclined to dominate the wives in her circle. Luckily for Margo, she had taken a liking to her, and greeted her warmly, admiring her dress and the pleasant little house.

'Here is my nephew whom you so kindly invited.' She introduced the man Margo had seen talking to Corinne at the tea party and she shook hands, murmuring a welcome, aware that Gijs, standing beside her, nodded at him but didn't shake hands and his greeting was coolly polite.

With everyone in the drawing room having drinks, Margo circulated, moving from one group to the next, well versed in the hostess's job and trying to keep an eye on Corinne. It was a relief to see that she was at the other end of the room to Jerome.

They were seated at opposite ends of the table too, and as far as she could see they had had no chance to speak to each other apart from a brief greeting. So far so good, thought Margo, counting her chickens before they were hatched.

It was after dinner, while they were drinking their coffee, that Gijs and Sir Anthony excused themselves to go to the study and look at a paper the elder man wished to see. A minute or two later Margo, caught up in a lengthy conversation with several of the ladies, saw Corinne slip away, and a few minutes later Jerome left the room.

Short of getting up and leaving her guests in midsentence there was nothing Margo could do; all she could hope for was that Corinne and Jerome would return before Gijs. They did and she heaved a sigh of relief. It was short-lived, however, for Corinne caught her eye and gave her a look of panic, instantly hidden by a glittering smile as she joined them. As for Jerome, he was careful not to speak to Corinne again for the rest of the evening.

Presently their guests went home and Margo went to the kitchen to see if Mattie and her teenage nephew had coped and to thank them.

'A splendid dinner, Mattie,' she said, 'and thank you both.' She went to a drawer and took out some money and paid the youth. 'We're grateful that you could come and give a hand,' she told him. 'How will you get home?'

'Catch a bus,' he told her. 'And thanks for the money. I'll be off.'

'I'll be off to my bed, too,' said Mattie. 'A first-rate evening, ma'am. How about you having breakfast in bed in the morning?'

'Me? No, thank you, Mattie. I'm not tired and I like to have breakfast with the professor if he's home.'

She went back to the drawing room and Corinne said at once, 'It was a lovely evening, Margo—you were marvellous. Now I'm going to bed.'

She kissed them both and went upstairs.

'A very pleasant evening, Margo. You are a splendid hostess,' said Gijs. 'I was glad to see that both you and Corinne managed to keep away from young Colbert.'

'We did our best. Are you going to tell me about him?'

'Yes…' The phone rang and he picked it up and presently put it down again. 'I have to go. There's been a road accident—a baby and a toddler injured. Go to bed, Margo.'

She saw him out of the house with a quiet goodnight, turned out the lights and went upstairs to her room. She was sitting at her dressing table staring at her reflection when there was a tap on the door and Corinne came in.

Chapter 9

Corinne settled herself on the side of the bed. 'It all started as fun. You see, I was cross with Julius; we quarrelled and he went off to Sweden on his own, and so I came here.

'And when Jerome got friendly I thought I would pay Julius back for being so tiresome. I didn't go shopping, you know; I met Jerome every day. I did tell you that this evening, didn't I? Only now I'm a little frightened.

'Jerome has become quite nasty—he wishes me to have an affair with him, and says if I won't he will tell Gijs, who I think will kill him if Julius doesn't kill him first. He insists that I meet him tomorrow afternoon but I do not dare. I will go back home on the first flight I can get in the morning.'

She turned a tearful gaze on Margo. 'Dear Margo, will you meet him for me and explain that I wasn't serious? Make him understand—you are always so serious; he will listen to you.'

'Supposing we go together?'

'That will not do at all, for now he frightens me. I want to go home to my Julius and in a little while I will tell him. He loves me very much so he will forgive me.' She added eagerly, 'No one needs to know that you have seen Jerome, and you have promised not to tell anyone. It can be our little secret.'

'Gijs asked me to have nothing to do with Jerome.'

'Darling Margo, he won't know, and besides, you're not meeting him because you want to, only to help me.' Corinne began to weep in earnest. 'Whatever shall I do if he tells Julius? We love each other very much, you know. You must understand how I feel—supposing you were me and Gijs was Julius?'

She got up and flung her arms around Margo. 'You will help me, dear, kind Margo? Just this once?'

'Very well,' said Margo. 'Tell me where he will be and at what time.'

'At three o'clock. On the steps of the National Gallery. Now I will phone Heathrow and book a seat on a morning plane.'

'What will you tell Gijs?'

'I will tell him nothing. I will go when he has gone to the hospital and you can explain that Julius phoned and asked if I would go home—said that he was no longer angry.'

'That's not true.'

'It will be. When I am home I am certain that is what he will say. You do not like to tell a fib, I know, but this is such a little one and it hurts no one, Margo.'

Her next remark clinched the matter.

'I think that I am going to have a baby...'

Long after Corinne had booked her morning flight and gone to bed, Margo sat up in bed worrying, until her common sense told her that that would do no good at all. She had promised to help Corinne and that was that, however much she disliked the idea. Getting to sleep was a different matter, though. It was after two o'clock in the morning when she heard Gijs's quiet tread pass her door, and only then did she sleep.

When she went down to breakfast it was to find him gone. Which was a good thing, she reflected, for he was the one person she would have gone to for advice. 'Something I can't do,' she told Plato, who was gobbling the toast she couldn't eat. 'So it's a good thing he isn't here.'

She wanted him there, though—his vast, calm, reassuring person sitting opposite her, telling her what to do...

Corinne joined her presently, quite recovered from her frightened outburst about Jerome. She kissed Margo, informed her cheerfully that her bags were packed and asked if she could phone for a taxi to take her to Heathrow.

Margo saw her off during the morning. 'You will go and see Jerome?' asked Corinne anxiously. 'And you won't tell anyone?'

'No, I won't tell. I only hope I can make him understand. He's bound to be angry.'

'Oh, dear—but only for a little while,' said Corinne airily, and smiled brilliantly. 'You have no idea how happy I am to have the whole silly business settled.'

To which Margo said nothing, choking back what her father would have described as her baser feelings.

It was a relief when, after a half-eaten lunch, she could get ready for her rendezvous. It was a cold day, and she buttoned herself into her cashmere coat, chose a felt hat which she hoped added dignity to her appearance, told Mattie that she would be back for tea and set out.

She prudently stopped the taxi on the far side of Trafalgar Square and walked unhurriedly to the National Gallery, aware that if Jerome was already there he would be able to see her.

He was there, all right, halfway up the steps and looking in the opposite direction, so that he turned with surprise when she said quietly, 'Good afternoon, Jerome.'

'Mrs van Kessel—Margo. This is unexpected—I mean, I hardly expected to see you here...' He was flustered, and that gave her heart.

'Well, no, you expected Corinne, didn't you? I've come instead...'

'She's ill?'

'No, she has gone back to Holland. She asked me to come here and explain to you...'

When he would have spoken she said, 'No, let me finish. She asked me to tell you that she is sorry to have misled you—it was light-hearted fun on her part, a game until she returned home to her husband.'

'I don't believe you,' he blustered. 'She said—I was led to believe...'

'Never mind that now, and anyway you should have known better than to flirt with her.'

'Flirt!' His sneer was ugly. 'What do you know about

flirting? I don't suppose any man has bothered to look at you more than once.'

'Probably not,' agreed Margo calmly. 'But rudeness won't help you, will it? Corinne intends to tell her husband how foolish she has been.' She added severely, 'It was very wrong of you to encourage her.'

He gobbled with rage. 'Really? And who are you to tell me what I may and may not do? Corinne egged me on.'

'Don't make matters worse with excuses. You should mend your ways.' She nodded a brisk goodbye. 'I don't expect to meet you again.'

She went back down the steps and hailed a taxi, feeling pleased with herself.

Fortunately for her peace of mind she was unaware that Gijs, caught up in a traffic jam in Trafalgar Square, was a surprised and angry witness to her meeting with Jerome. Glancing idly round, he had seen her at once. What was more, he could see that she and Jerome were apparently deep in an interesting talk, and when Jerome put his hands on Margo's shoulders he had difficulty in preventing himself from jumping out of his car and throttling the man. It was a pity he wasn't near enough to hear Margo's icy, 'Take your hands off me!'

The traffic untangled itself then, and he was forced to drive on. He was already late for his clinic for Down's Syndrome babies and toddlers, and somehow he managed to erase Margo from his mind so that by the time he reached the clinic he appeared his usual kindly self, listening patiently to anxious parents, examining the little ones gently, giving advice and offering hope.

When the last small patient had been borne away he had tea with Sister, giving no sign of haste, before getting into his car and driving back to his rooms to go over his appointments book with his secretary. Finally, he drove himself home.

Margo was in the drawing room with Caesar and Plato, and, despite the fact that she had told herself over and over again that she had no need to feel guilty for she had done nothing wrong, she heard Gijs's steps in the hall with a nasty sinking feeling.

He came quietly into the room, greeted her in his usual quiet voice and went over to the table by the window to pour their drinks.

Margo got to her feet, spilling an indignant Caesar onto the floor. 'Have you had a good day?' she asked, and then, unable to put it off, began, 'Corinne...'

He turned to look at her. 'Yes?'

'She's gone home,' said Margo in a rush. 'Julius is back and—and wanted her to return as soon as possible. And as there was a seat on the late morning flight she took it. It was all a bit of a rush.' She stopped talking, aware that she was beginning to babble.

Gijs sat down. 'All rather sudden, wasn't it?'

'Well, yes, but I expect she wanted to see Julius again. She said she would phone you this evening and she was sorry not to see you to say goodbye.'

There was a silence then, fortunately broken by Mattie coming to tell them that dinner was ready, and Margo, feeling that she had crossed her bridge safely, allowed herself a certain amount of complacency.

A mistake. Drinking coffee in the drawing room

after dinner, Gijs asked casually, 'And you, Margo—what have you done with yourself today?'

She spoke too quickly. 'Me? Oh, nothing much. I phoned Aunt Flo and did the flowers...'

'You didn't go out?'

He watched the colour creep into her face.

'Well, yes, I did. Just out, you know—nowhere special.'

Gijs reflected with bitter amusement that Margo, a vicar's daughter, was hopeless at being devious. He asked in a quiet voice which chilled her to the bone, 'And are the steps of the National Gallery not special?'

'The steps...?' She faltered, staring across at his impassive face, seeing the controlled anger in it.

'You were there, were you not?' His voice was silky. 'I was in a traffic jam and I saw you and Jerome together. Not a chance encounter, I imagine? There was a certain familiarity...you were absorbed in each other...'

When Margo said nothing, staring at him with eyes suddenly enormous in a white face, he added, 'I asked you to have nothing to do with him, Margo. Had you forgotten that? Or was the attraction so great? Will you tell me about it?'

She shook her head. 'I'd rather not.'

'I realise that perhaps you are bored with your life here, that it holds little excitement, and Jerome is young and good-looking and adept at charming women. I thought that you—' He stopped, and then continued levelly, 'Perhaps we can discuss the whole thing at our leisure some time. Unfortunately, I have a great deal of work for the next week and shall be seldom at home. Why not spend it with Aunt Florence?'

Margo swallowed tears. He was angry, but he didn't

seem to care enough to ask her why she had gone to see Jerome; he had just taken it for granted that she had been bored. Not that she could have told him the truth, but he might have asked. He didn't care tuppence about her; she might just as well be with Aunt Flo.

'Very well, I'll go tomorrow.'

'Just tell me this, Margo. Did you go to see Jerome of your own free will? Had you arranged to meet him?'

She could only nod, looking no higher than his tie—which was a good thing; his face might have frightened her.

'I'll go to bed,' said Margo.

She didn't sleep, of course, but when she went down to breakfast the next morning she found Gijs already there. He wished her good morning exactly as usual, only as she sat down he asked her when she planned to go to Aunt Flo's.

'After lunch, I thought. There's a train...'

'I'll ring for a car and a man to drive you down. Will half past two suit you?'

She thanked him. He was making sure that she went, she thought miserably.

'Enjoy your visit,' he told her. 'I dare say that you have some plans. I hope you will behave with discretion. Aunt Florence is too nice to be upset.'

'Behave? Behave? Whatever do you mean?' Margo's normally mild nature flared into temper. 'How dare you talk to me like that? What in heaven's name have I got to be discreet about?'

She got up, quelling an urge to throw her coffee-cup at him. 'If that's the way you are going to talk, then I'm glad I don't have to see you for a week.' She added, quite reckless now, 'Perhaps it had better be for a month, or a year—or for ever...'

Gijs remained unmoved. 'That is entirely up to you, Margo.' He even smiled a little, although it wasn't a very nice smile. 'Sit down and finish your breakfast.'

'No, I won't,' said Margo, and flew out of the room and upstairs to her bedroom, where she had a thoroughly comforting weep before washing her face and going downstairs again—reluctantly, but there was nothing else to be done...

He had gone. Mattie, clearing the table, remarked cheerfully that the master was a one for work and no mistake. 'And you'll be off after lunch, ma'am? If you'd tell me what to cook for the professor... He said he'd be out all day but he will want a good meal in the evening. A week, he said. You'll miss each other, I'll be bound.'

She glanced at Margo's pale face and added sympathetically, 'It's hard when you can't be together when you're first wed.'

Margo remembered then that she hadn't phoned Aunt Flo. Supposing she was away or didn't want a guest? But when she rang it was to hear that Gijs had already phoned. He thinks of everything, thought Margo peevishly.

She didn't like leaving Caesar and Plato.

'Don't you worry, ma'am,' said Mattie. 'The master will take Plato out before he goes in the morning and when he gets home in the evening, and Caesar is happy enough in the garden. I'll take good care of them.'

Aunt Florence was pleased to see her. 'Need a change from London, do you?' she wanted to know. 'Gijs told me he was very busy—don't suppose you see much of each other.' She took a look at Margo's face. 'You look down in the dumps, child.' She sounded brisk. 'A good long walk in the fresh air will do you good. The Truemans have asked us to dinner tonight and the rector and his wife are coming to dinner tomorrow evening. Not exciting, but I dare say you will enjoy a change of scene.'

The week seemed never-ending, and although Margo dreaded seeing Gijs again she longed for him. Obedient to her aunt, she took long walks each morning, ate the nourishing food Phoebe cooked, and made conversation with various of Aunt Flo's friends who called. She described Arntzstein in minute detail to her, behaved just as she should at the Truemans', and made a reluctant fourth at Aunt Flo's bridge evening.

On her last evening she received a phone call from the driver who had brought her to Sunningfield. He would come for her at two o'clock on the following day, if that suited her— 'But Professor van Kessel says you are to do as you wish, madam.'

'I'll be ready at two o'clock,' said Margo. Gijs wanted her back; they would be sensible and talk quietly and she would explain that she didn't care a row of pins for Jerome, although how she was going to do that without giving away Corinne's part in the miserable business was a problem she had yet to solve.

Since it was a Saturday she was sure that he would be at home, but only Mattie was there, ready with tea and a warm welcome. Margo, with Plato and Caesar for company, nibbled sandwiches and pondered what she would say and presently went to her room and changed into a patterned silk dress in a pleasing shade of forest-green.

She took pains with her hair and her make-up too, and went down again to sit in the drawing room and wait.

Gijs came home a scant half-hour before dinner. He came into the room unhurriedly, his hello pleasant, so that she took heart.

'It's nice to be home,' she told him. 'Have you been at the hospital?'

He sat down opposite her. 'No, I spent the afternoon with friends and stayed for drinks.' He pulled Plato's ears gently. 'You enjoyed your stay with Aunt Florence?'

She began to tell him about her week, only to realise halfway through that he wasn't listening. She stopped talking then, and presently they sat down to dinner. It was better then, for good manners forced him to make some sort of a reply to her efforts at conversation, and she felt more cheerful as they went back to the drawing room.

She had poured their coffee and was searching for something to talk about when he said casually, 'I am going over to Holland tomorrow. If you remember, I did intend going within the next week or so, but I find that I can leave here for the time being and there are several urgent cases in Utrecht I want to deal with.'

'Not me?' asked Margo, regardless of grammar.

'I think not. You must feel free to do as you wish, Margo.' He gave her a steady look. 'You still feel that you are unable to talk to me? Believe me, I will listen sympathetically. I am not so middle-aged that I cannot appreciate that one can fall in love whether one wishes to or not. We have been good friends—can you not confide in me?'

She shook her head, not looking at him; if she did she might forget her promise.

'I leave early in the morning. Draw on our account at the bank for any money you need. I have left our solicitor's phone number in case you need advice of any kind.'

She asked in a wispy voice, 'How long will you be away?'

'Difficult to say, but you can count on two weeks at least—possibly longer.'

There seemed to be nothing more to say, so she drank her coffee and said that she hoped he would have a safe journey. 'Please give my love to Punch. I—I rather think I'll go to bed; I'm tired.'

He opened the door for her, and as she passed him he kissed her hard. It was almost her undoing. Another moment and she would have told him everything, promise or no promise. Instead she flew upstairs to her room.

Sitting on the bed, she told herself that the kiss had been his goodbye—not just for a few weeks but for ever.

She slept badly and got up early, hoping that she might see him before he left the house, but when she went downstairs Mattie was clearing away his breakfast things, pausing only to wish her good morning and suggest scrambled eggs.

'Feel a bit down, I dare say, ma'am, but he'll be back just as soon as he can. A good cup of coffee will make you feel more cheerful.'

Margo thanked the good soul, reflecting that it would take more than a cup of coffee to cheer her up; she would have to plan her days so that they were filled. Long walks in the park with Plato, visits to the picture galleries and the museums. The British Museum was in itself large enough to absorb at least two weeks, and perhaps by then Gijs would be home again.

She kept resolutely to her plans for the whole of that week—walking herself tired each morning, stuffing her head with useful information from a number of museums and picture galleries in the afternoon and working away at a tapestry cushion in the evening. There was no news of Gijs, and in the middle of the second week she allowed panic to take over.

He had left her; he was never going to see her again—never even write or telephone. Presently she pulled herself together; he wouldn't do any of those things. He might be angry and unforgiving but he was fair. Perhaps, she thought, he was waiting for her to make the first move. Perhaps he expected her to ask for a divorce—no, she corrected herself, an annulment.

She thought about this for some time, and then made up her mind as to what she should do.

Mattie wasn't at all surprised when she told her that she was going over to Holland.

'The professor wants you there, I dare say, ma'am. Can't get away, most likely.'

'I'll try and get a flight tomorrow, Mattie, and let you know how long I'm staying when I get there. Will you be all right with Caesar and Plato—would your nephew take Plato out each day if I leave some money for him?'

'He'll be glad to do that, ma'am. Saving up for one of those nasty motorbikes, he is.'

'Oh, good. I'll leave you plenty of money—did the professor say anything about your wages? I forgot to ask him.'

'Paid me before he went, ma'am.' She smiled cosily. 'Just you go to Holland. I'll keep an eye on things here until you're back.'

She had been lucky, thought Margo, looking down at the coastline of England as the plane gained height. There had been a seat available on a flight in the early afternoon. She had packed a small case, dressed herself in the blue cashmere dress and wrapped herself into her topcoat, and, mindful of first impressions, had perched a brown velvet hat with an upturned brim on her carefully arranged hair.

With the same object in view she had spent a long time before the looking glass doing things to her face, but somehow she hadn't looked right when she had finished, so she had taken all the make-up off again. Her face looked its best with cream, powder and lipstick and nothing else.

Schiphol was vast and busy. It took time to reach the street at last—or rather several streets, choked with buses and cars. She stood for a moment, getting her bearings, and presently saw an empty taxi.

At least she didn't have the worry of wondering whether she had enough money, she thought, getting in. She had plenty; Gijs had seen to that.

'I hope you speak English?' she said to the driver, and was relieved when he nodded.

'Enough, *mevrouw*.'

'Would you take me to a village called Arntzstein? It's a few miles from Utrecht?'

She had had time to look at a map before she left home; it was fifty or so kilometres from Schiphol.

Once they were clear of the airport and on the motorway, the driver drove fast. Margo was still rehearsing what she would say to Gijs when he turned off the highway and presently reached Arntzstein.

'It's through the village—you can see the gates at the end of that lane after the church.'

There were lights shining from the house. She got out, paid the driver, tipped him lavishly and climbed the steps to the door. She tried the handle but it was locked, so she pulled the old-fashioned bell. Funny to ring your own front doorbell, she reflected, and smiled at Wim when he opened the door.

It was nice to be welcomed so warmly. 'You have come to stay, *mevrouw*—what a pleasure for us all! Please to wait. I will fetch Kieke and she will take you to your room. We had it prepared; we had expected you…'

Kieke came, with Diny and Mien, to shake her hand and exclaim with delight at the sight of her.

'Such a surprise for the professor when he returns home,' said Kieke, going upstairs with Margo to make sure that everything was as it should be.

Margo agreed, quelling sudden panic.

When she went downstairs again, Wim was in the hall.

'Wim,' said Margo, 'please don't say a word to the professor when he comes in—I want to surprise him. When do you expect him?'

Wim beamed. 'How delighted he will be, *mevrouw*. He is expected sometime after six o'clock. If I bring tea now…'

'Yes, please. I'll have it in the small sitting room. I expect the professor will go straight to his study.'

'Always, *mevrouw*.' He was delighted at the idea of a conspiracy. 'You will remain there, *mevrouw*?'

'Yes, Wim. Where is Punch?'

'With the professor. He will also be delighted that you are here, *mevrouw*.'

She had her tea sitting by the cheerful fire in the cosy room and then, feeling nervous, got up and wandered around, looking at the photos in their silver frames and the family portraits hung on the walls.

The house was quiet so she heard Gijs and Punch come into the hall. She turned off the table-lamp, although the room was out of sight of the hall, and stood with a thumping heart, listening to distant voices. Not visitors, surely? She went to the door and opened it a crack and heard Gijs call to Punch as he crossed the hall and went into his study, shutting the door with a firm click.

Margo counted to ten to give him time to sit in his chair and to allow her heart to quieten down a bit. She wished now that she had never come, but this was something which couldn't be avoided. Moral courage, her father had once told her, was as important as the physical kind. She opened the door, crossed the hall and opened the study door.

Gijs looked up and got slowly to his feet, and Punch padded over to her, lifting his head to have his ears rubbed in Margo's special way.

'This is unexpected,' said the professor. 'Won't you sit down?'

When she had, he sat down again himself, watching her without speaking so that she made haste to break the silence.

'I thought we had better have a talk,' she began, and looked at him across the desk. He was tired, and there were lines she hadn't noticed before etched on his face, but he was impassive, waiting for her to go on.

'I don't know much about it,' said Margo, 'but I think we can be annulled. I mean, that's better than being divorced, isn't it? I expect you could arrange that? I've been thinking about it a great deal and I expect you have too...'

His brief grave nod did nothing to encourage her to have any hope. She went on doggedly, 'You see, you don't trust me, do you? And things will never be right between us, will they?'

He said evenly, 'If you wish for an annulment, Margo, it can be arranged.'

'That's what you want too. I've been a disappointment to you, haven't I?'

She paused, wishing with her whole heart that he would tell her that it didn't matter about Jerome, that they could start again, that everything would be all right...

'I want you to be happy, Margo,' was all that he said.

She could think of nothing more to say then; she had said what she had come to say and it had broken her heart. She stood up.

'You will stay here as long as you wish,' said the professor, going to open the door for her. 'I hope Kieke has made you comfortable. If there is anything you need you have only to ask.'

His cold courtesy chilled her to the bone.

'Yes—yes, thank you. I'll go back to London tomorrow.'

'In that case let us say goodbye. I am going out immediately and shall not be returning until late tomorrow evening.'

She stared up into his face. 'Gijs…'

'No, let us say nothing more, my dear. You are unhappy and I love you too much to allow that.'

'You love me? Oh, Gijs, what am I to do?' She was suddenly distraught.

He smiled. 'Why, surely that is obvious. I'm sure that young Colbert is waiting for you.'

He might be smiling, but he was in a cold rage, his eyes hard and stony. Unless she broke her promise to Corinne there was nothing more to be said, but a promise was a promise.

She went back to the little sitting room and sat there, icy cold despite the fire. Somehow she must put a brave face on things, make some excuse to Wim, get a seat on a plane and be well away before Gijs came back. He had made it clear that he didn't want to see her again.

She had no idea how long she had been sitting there when Wim came to tell her that dinner had been served. She went to the dining room and ate her solitary meal, agreeing with Wim that it was a great pity that the professor had been called away. 'I have to go back to London tomorrow,' she told him. 'Will you see if you can get me a seat on an afternoon plane, Wim?'

Presently, in the kitchen, presiding over supper, Wim declared himself concerned. 'Something's not right,' he told Kieke. '*Mevrouw's* going back to London tomorrow almost as soon as she's got here and the professor went out of the house on his own. It's disturbing…'

There was no hurry in the morning—after all, Gijs wasn't coming back until the late evening. Margo went round the gardens exchanging talk with the gardener; neither of them could understand what the other was saying but that hardly mattered. She wanted to see everything before she left—the neat kitchen garden, the greenhouse, the swimming pool tucked away behind the shrubbery, the rose garden, bare now but surely a lovely sight in the summer. She went back indoors to be met with the news that her flight had been booked.

'I've got you a seat in the late afternoon, *mevrouw,*' said Wim. 'Five o'clock—if we leave here at three o'clock that should be time enough. No need for you to wait too long at Schiphol.'

She had lunch and then wandered round the house, going in and out of the rooms, looking at everything, picking up ornaments and putting them down again. Then she made her way to the attic. It was cold there, and a bit dusty, and quite a lot of the furniture had gone to the London house, but there was plenty left for her to look at: stacks of pictures against one wall, a love-seat upholstered in faded velvet, a magnificent doll's house and in one corner the cradle she had admired. All the van Kessels had been rocked in it, Gijs had said.

She sat down beside it, running a finger along its delicate woodwork, and started to cry.

The professor, with Punch beside him, had got into his car and driven himself to Friesland—a journey of just over a hundred miles.

He'd had time to think as he'd driven to the small farm he owned there, to be greeted with unsurprised pleasure by the old farmer and his wife who looked after it for him. They were accustomed to his erratic visits, if and when he could spare the time, and found it quite normal to prepare his room and give him supper. They had been equally unsurprised when he'd told them that he would leave early in the morning, since he had appointments at the hospital.

He'd eaten the simple meal they'd offered him and gone to his room with Punch at his heels, and presently he'd gone to bed to lie awake thinking of a future without Margo.

He was too old, he'd thought wearily, and Jerome Colbert was a past master at charming women. Margo wasn't his usual type of woman, though—perhaps he really had reformed and loved her...

He'd driven back to Utrecht in the early morning, glad of Punch's warm body beside him. When he had finished at the hospital he would go home and talk to Margo again...

He had dealt with his small patients and was having his coffee in Sister's office when he was requested to go to his own office, where he had a visitor.

It wasn't Margo; it was Corinne. He schooled his features into a welcoming smile and asked her what he could do for her. 'You look worried,' he added. 'Have you come out without your purse?'

She shook her head. 'Gijs, Julius said that I must come and tell you. You'll be angry with me.' She gave him a beseeching look. 'It was all just for fun, you see. Only then he got nasty...'

Gijs sat down at his desk. 'Go on.'

'Jerome—you know, Jerome Colbert—you told Margo we weren't to have anything to do with him. Well, he seemed such fun...'

It all came tumbling out then, until she said finally, 'So, you see, it wasn't anything to do with Margo, but I made her promise not to tell, and Julius says that it was wrong of me to ask her because she might want to tell you. So I thought that when you got back to London you could tell her first. She doesn't like him, you know, but she went to see him instead of me because she knew that Julius loved me and that he might be very angry. She knows that I love Julius too, and I'm going to have a baby.' She burst into tears and Gijs got up and took her in his arms.

'What splendid news, my dear, and don't worry about Margo; she's at Arntzstein.' He smiled thinly. 'But don't, I beg of you, *liefje*, ask her to make any more promises. Remember that she was brought up to keep them. At all costs.'

Corinne mopped her eyes, declared him to be the best brother any girl could wish for and went away, her spirits quite restored. As for the professor, he sat down at his desk and picked up the phone, rearranging his day so that he could go home at once. It was still early afternoon and Margo might still be there...

The house was quiet as he went in, but Wim came to him in the hall.

'*Mevrouw* is still here?' asked Gijs.

Wim nodded. 'I shall be driving her to Schiphol at four o'clock, Professor.'

'No, you won't,' said Gijs. 'Where is she, Wim?'

'I am not sure, *mijnheer*. She went upstairs some time ago—perhaps she is in her room?'

The professor, with Punch at his heels, went up the staircase and knocked on Margo's door. When there was no answer he went in. There was no one there, only her overnight bag standing ready packed.

He looked in the other rooms on that landing, and was standing at the head of the staircase deciding where to look next when he heard a faint sound. Somewhere on the floor above? He went up a second flight of stairs, found no one in any of the rooms, and then opened a door in the landing wall. The sound was louder now, and he went up the narrow, steep stairs two at a time and opened the attic door.

Margo was still by the cradle; the first few tears had turned into a torrent. She sniffed and sobbed and snuffled, oblivious of time or place, hopelessly unhappy.

The professor stood in the doorway, looking at her sitting there, clinging to the cradle, and when he made a slight movement and she looked up he thought she had never looked so beautiful, her white face streaked by grubby tears, her eyelids puffy, her hair in a fine tangle.

He was across the floor and she was in his arms before she had time to do more than gasp.

'Don't say a word, my darling. Corinne came to see me. Dear heart, could you not have told me? A promise is a promise, but surely there should be no secrets between man and wife?'

Margo gulped. 'Oh, Gijs, I wish I'd thought of that.' Her voice was thick with tears. 'I nearly did tell you when you said you loved me…'

'Forgive me, Margo. I have loved you for so long, have waited patiently for you to love me, and I thought that I had lost you.'

'Lost me? But I love you, Gijs. I didn't know until we were getting married.' She peered up into his face and smiled at what she saw there. 'Oh, Gijs, don't leave me ever again.'

He kissed her then, which was actually a much more satisfactory answer than any words.

Punch's polite yawn caused them to look round. He

was sitting by the cradle, patiently waiting, so they walked to the door, turning to have a last look.

'The cradle will need a good polish...' said Margo, standing on tip-toe to reach her husband's cheek.

* * * * *

SPECIAL EXCERPT FROM

⒣ HARLEQUIN®

ROMANTIC suspense

*State Trooper Kelly Roberts joins Special Agent
Tony Lazzaro's task force, determined to bring down
a cybercriminal preying on young victims. Solving
this case is a chance for redemption. If Kelly catches
the killer, she'll be one step closer to solving her best
friend's abduction. She never expects to fall for Tony...*

*Read on for a sneak preview of
Dana Nussio's next book in the True Blue miniseries,*
Her Dark Web Defender.

"Ready to try this again?"

"Absolutely."

Kelly met his gaze with a confidence he didn't expect.
Was she trying to prove something to him? Trying to
convince him he'd made a mistake by shielding her
before?

"Okay, let's chat."

The conversation appeared to have slowed during the
time he'd gone for coffee, but the moment Tony typed
his first line, his admirers were back. Didn't any of these
guys have a day job?

It didn't take long before one of them sent a private
message at the bottom of the screen. GOOD TIME GUY
wasn't all that shy about escalating the conversation
quickly, either. Kelly took over the keyboard, and when

the guy suggested a voice chat, she didn't even look Tony's way before she accepted.

"Hey, your voice is rougher than I expected," she said into the microphone.

Only then did she glance sidelong at Tony. He nodded his approval. He'd been right to give her a second chance. Dawson and the others didn't need to know about the other day, the part at the office or anything that happened later. Kelly would be great at this.

When the conversation with GOOD TIME GUY didn't seem to be going anywhere, they ended that interaction and accepted another offer for a personal chat. She navigated that one with BOY AT HEART and even a repeat one with BIG DADDY with the skill of someone who'd been on the task force a year rather than days.

Her breathing might have been a little halting, and she might have tightened her grip on the microphone, but she was powering through, determined to tease details from each of the possible suspects that they might be able to use to track them.

Tony found he had to admit something else. He'd been wrong about Kelly Roberts. She was stronger than he'd expected her to be. Maybe even fearless. And he was dying to know what had made her that way.

Don't miss
Her Dark Web Defender *by Dana Nussio,*
available November 2019 wherever
Harlequin® Romantic Suspense
books and ebooks are sold.

Harlequin.com

Looking for more satisfying love stories
with community and family at their core?

Check out **Harlequin® Special Edition**
and **Love Inspired®** books!

New books available every month!

***

CONNECT WITH US AT:

Facebook.com/groups/HarlequinConnection

 Facebook.com/HarlequinBooks

 Twitter.com/HarlequinBooks

 Instagram.com/HarlequinBooks

 Pinterest.com/HarlequinBooks

ReaderService.com

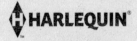

**ROMANCE WHEN
YOU NEED IT**

HFGENRE2018

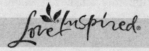
Christmastime brings a single mom and her baby back home, but reconnecting with her high school sweetheart, now a wounded veteran, puts her darkest secret at risk.

Read on for a sneak preview of
The Secret Christmas Child *by Lee Tobin McClain, the first book in her new Rescue Haven miniseries.*

He reached out a hand, meaning to shake hers, but she grasped his and held it. Looked into his eyes. "Reese, I'm sorry about what happened before."

He narrowed his eyes and frowned at her. "You mean…after I went into the service?"

She nodded and swallowed hard. "Something happened, and I couldn't…I couldn't keep the promise I made."

That something being another guy, Izzy's father. He drew in a breath. Was he going to hold on to his grudge, or his hurt feelings, about what had happened?

Looking into her eyes, he breathed out the last of his anger. Like Corbin had said, everyone was a sinner. "It's understood."

"Thank you," she said simply. She held his gaze for another moment and then looked down and away.

She was still holding on to his hand, and slowly, he twisted and opened his hand until their palms were flat together. Pressed between them as close as he'd like to be pressed to Gabby.

The only light in the room came from the kitchen and

the dying fire. Outside the windows, snow had started to fall, blanketing the little house in solitude.

This night with her family had been one of the best he'd had in a long time. Made him realize how much he missed having a family.

Gabby's hand against his felt small and delicate, but he knew better. He slipped his own hand to the side and captured hers, tracing his thumb along the calluses.

He heard her breath hitch and looked quickly at her face.

Her eyes were wide, her lips parted and moist.

Without looking away, acting on impulse, he slowly lifted her hand to his lips and kissed each fingertip.

Her breath hitched and came faster, and his sense of himself as a man, a man who could have an effect on a woman, swelled, almost making him giddy.

This was Gabby, and the truth burst inside him: he'd never gotten over her, never stopped wishing they could be together, that they could make that family they'd dreamed of as kids. That was why he'd gotten so angry when she'd strayed: because the dream she'd shattered had been so big, so bright and shining.

In the back of his mind, a voice of caution scolded and warned. She'd gone out with his cousin. She'd had a child with another man. What had been so major in his emotional life hadn't been so big in hers.

He shouldn't trust her. And he definitely shouldn't kiss her.

But when had he ever done what he should?

Don't miss
The Secret Christmas Child *by Lee Tobin McClain,*
available December 2019 wherever
Love Inspired® books and ebooks are sold.